Meredith Webber lives on the sunny Gold Coast in Queensland, Australia, but takes regular trips west into the Outback, fossicking for gold or opal. These breaks in the beautiful and sometimes cruel red earth country provide her with an escape from the writing desk and a chance for her mind to roam free—not to mention getting some much needed exercise. They also supply the kernels of so many stories that it's hard for her to stop writing!

With two beautiful daughters, **Lucy Ryder** has had to curb her adventurous spirit and settle down. But, because she's easily bored by routine, she's turned to writing as a creative outlet, and to romances because—'What else is there other than chocolate?' Characterised by friends and family as a romantic cynic, Lucy can't write serious stuff to save her life. She loves creating characters who are funny, romantic and just a little cynical.

D1419011

ONE NIGHT TO FOREVER FAMILY

MEREDITH WEBBER

TEMPTED BY THE HEART SURGEON

LUCY RYDER

MILLS & BOON

First Published in Great Britain 2020
by Mills & Boon, an imprint of HarperCollins*Publishers*
1 London Bridge Street, London, SE1 9GF

One Night to Forever Family © 2020 by Meredith Webber

Tempted by the Heart Surgeon © 2020 by Bev Riley

ISBN: 978-0-263-27985-6

MIX
Paper from
responsible sources
FSC C007454

This book is produced from independently certified FSC™ paper
to ensure responsible forest management.
For more information visit www.harpercollins.co.uk/green.

Printed and bound in Spain
by CPI, Barcelona

ONE NIGHT TO FOREVER FAMILY

MEREDITH WEBBER

MILLS & BOON

CHAPTER ONE

SAM REILLY KNEW she shouldn't be walking into a large hospital with a well-travelled and probably germ-laden backpack towering over her, the soft roll of the sleeping bag on the top pushing her head forward so she probably resembled a bedraggled turtle as she made her way towards the reception desk.

She leant against the counter, easing the weight on her back slightly.

'I know I don't look much,' she said to the polite woman on the other side of the desk, 'but the road out from where I was working was washed away in a typhoon and it's taken me a month to get here. I need a shower, some scrubs, and if possible a white coat so that I can present myself as a reasonably competent doctor up in the PICU. My name's Sam Reilly—well, Samantha, really, but people call me Sam.'

'*You're* the new PICU doctor? I was told to expect you but, oh, my dear, you can't possibly go up there looking like that! Think of the germs you're probably carrying.'

'Exactly!' Sam said, 'Which is why I need that shower and something clean to wear. Can you help me out?'

The woman eyed her doubtfully.

'I guess you'd be okay in the ED staffroom. There are

always plenty of clean sets of scrubs in there—showers, too, of course. Just continue down this passage and you'll find it on the left.' The woman hesitated. 'It's often a bit messy,' she added, as if a scrawny, redheaded backpacker might not have understood messy...

'And I'm not?' Sam queried with a smile.

Apart from a youngish man, sleeping like the dead on a most uncomfortable-looking couch, the staffroom was empty—but it *was* only six in the morning and he'd probably been on duty all night.

The showers were easy to find, but the cubicles were small, so Sam set her backpack down in the adjoining changing room, removed the sleeping bag—why on earth had she not thrown it away?—and dug into her pack for the meagre selection of new clothes she'd bought at Bangkok airport.

Four bras, four pairs of knickers, three pairs of socks and a new pair of sneakers, which had cost more than double all her other purchases put together. She found her toiletries, too, deodorant, toothpaste and brush, a wide-toothed comb that could handle her unruly locks, and a couple of strong hair clips she hoped could hold those locks in place.

Next, she removed a plastic-wrapped bundle and took out her stethoscope, watch and tiny torch.

A cupboard on one side of the changing room yielded sets of scrubs stacked under small, medium and large labels. Sam selected a large, which would swim on her small frame but experience told her she needed them for her height, though she'd also need something to use as a belt to hold up the trousers.

And finally, leaving everything she wanted to wear on the small bench in the cubicle, she stripped off and stepped under the water, cold at first but then so deliciously warm she could have stayed there for hours.

Unfortunately, the time she'd spent with her mother in the small hospital near the Thai-Cambodian border—three weeks that had become seven when the typhoon had taken out the access road—had taught her the importance of clean water. She used soap from the dispenser on the wall to wash her hair and then the rest of her body, sluicing away the stiffness of thirty hours', mostly uncomfortable, travel, and whatever foreign microbes she might have been carrying.

Once clean she roughly towelled her hair as dry as she could get it, used another towel on her body, then dressed in new underwear and the scrub suit—way too big but still better than a medium that would have her ankles and wrists sticking out.

She dragged the comb through her hair, taming it sufficiently to pull it up onto the top of her head and secure it with a couple of clips. Somewhere there'd be a supply of bandanas—one to cover her hair and another she could possibly use as a belt—but in the meantime, with a white coat purloined from the cupboard—she felt presentable enough to find a café or canteen and have breakfast before fronting up for work.

In the outer passage, she found a row of lockers and spotted an empty one with a key in the door. She dumped her gear into it, locked it and pocketed the key. Now to find the canteen and some much-needed food.

Excitement at being back at work and back at home—back where she belonged, even if *was* a new hospital in a new city—made her want to skip along the corridor, but hunger was gnawing at her stomach. She'd been travelling for hours and she knew she had to eat before starting work as a senior PICU physician.

Andy looked up from the meal he was eating, unsure whether it was dinner or breakfast—just that he'd needed it after a more than hectic night on call for the PICU. The little boy with the burns to the soles of his feet had reacted badly to the pain relief they'd given him in the Emergency Department and had had to be stabilised before they could turn their attention to his injuries.

Redheaded little boy...

Andy smiled to himself. He'd once heard a statistic about children with self-inflicted burns that suggested nearly all of them were redheaded boys, and since he'd heard it he'd been surprised by how often it had turned out to be true.

Just then, he noticed another redhead who entered the canteen. She was anything but a boy, and he felt an all-too-familiar jolt in his chest.

He'd known she was coming, of course—how could he not? As head of the PICU he'd read her résumé and been present at her interview. But the interview itself had been by a very static-filled radio link-up to some obscure place on the Thai border with Cambodia, and he hadn't seen her.

Not physically at least.

But in his mind's eye, she'd been as clear as day—a tall, redheaded woman who strode through life towards whatever it could throw at her, prepared to meet and beat any challenge.

Except that the last time he'd seen her she'd been in a hospital bed, the scattering of freckles across her nose and cheeks standing out against sheet-white skin, fury flashing in her pale green eyes as she'd told him to get out and never come back...

'Now!' she'd added in a strangled voice, and he'd left—walked away, his heart heavy with the loss of his best friend and aching for the woman on the bed who had looked so lost and vulnerable. Sorrow, anger and grief had churned inside him—fear for her, too—and words he should never have said had come out of his mouth. But now his head had told him just how stupid he had been, virtually accusing her of Nick's death, adding to her pain, while his heart?

Who knew where his heart had been back then...?

Life had thrown plenty at her since then, yet here she was—shoulders back, head held high, walking into the place as if she owned it.

Hiding the butterflies in her stomach—surely she'd worked in enough places to no longer have that uneasy feeling when she entered somewhere new—Sam crossed the canteen towards the self-serve shelves. She slotted onto the end of a small queue of people either coming off duty and needing food because they'd been too busy to eat all night or going on duty but needing sustenance before they tackled a new day.

She grabbed a packet of sandwiches and a bottle of some greeny-yellow juice and headed for the checkout, suddenly aware of a prickly feeling on her skin, as though someone was watching her.

She glanced around at what appeared to be a typical crowd in any hospital canteen at change of shifts, with subdued conversation and exhaustion leaking into the air. Sam paid her bill and headed for an empty table she'd spotted on the far side of the room. She had an hour before she was due to report to the head of department, but she'd eat then go on up to the ward, explain who she was and familiarise herself with the place—once she'd found a belt.

'You've gone all out to impress your new colleagues in that outfit,' a voice said above her head, and as her heart registered just who the voice belonged to, Andy Wilkie lowered his tall, solid frame into the chair opposite her.

'Andy?'

Damn her voice! The word came out as a pathetic squeak!

'What are you doing here?'

Much better—practically a demand...

'Did you not do *any* research on the place before you applied for a job?'

Andy's expressive eyebrows lifted above blue, blue eyes.

Sardonically?

Damn the man!

'I saw the ad online in an internet café in Bangkok. I'd just got off a flight from London and knew my stay with Mum would only be a few weeks, so I shot off an application and résumé while I was there. But I didn't have time to look into either the hospital or the staffing side of things.'

She hoped she sounded more composed than she felt, because the realisation that she'd be working with Andy had caused panic and despair to swell inside her.

The same Andy who'd blamed her for his best friend's death...

Which she probably had been...

But that was her guilt to cope with, her memories to haunt her, and right now she had to make some rational explanation about why this had come as a total shock.

This was the start of a whole new life for her—she had to put the past behind her and start afresh.

She slammed the door closed on those painful memories, and remembered instead the good times when she, Nick and Andy had been friends—good friends who had laughed together. Although she'd seen less of Andy after she'd married Nick...

But right now she had to explain. Preferably without sounding as if she was making excuses.

'I was spending a few weeks working in a small hospital—more a clinic, really—near the Thai border with Cambodia when the phone interview was set up. Actually, the interview on my side was mostly static. Were you one of the voices on the phone?'

'Of course!' he replied, no glimmer of expression on his face. 'I am, after all, the department head.'

Her boss!

Andy had employed her in spite of what had happened between them in the past?

'But *you* must have known it was me. After all, you had my application and résumé,' she said, trying to ease the tension in her body, praying it wasn't revealed in her voice. 'You gave me the job.'

He half smiled, and while her heart skipped a beat at the sign of this softening on his part, his voice was still cool and unemotional as he said, 'You were by far the best applicant. Anyone who's done eighteen months in the PICU in the biggest children's hospital in London has had more experience than all the other applicants put together.'

Sam closed her eyes, just briefly, stilling the confusion inside her.

She could do this.

She could work with Andy.

Actually, she doubted there were many better than Andy to work with. He'd headed east to America after Nick's death, while she'd fled west, first to Perth on the other side of the country and then London—the other side of the world—before spending three weeks that had grown to nearly seven with her mother in the tiny medical outpost on the Thai-Cambodian border.

Of course she could do it!

Play it cool!

'I'm sorry about the scrubs, but we had a typhoon a month ago just when I was due to leave, and the road to the nearest town was washed away. I finally got out, and onto a flight from Bangkok last night, changed flights in Sydney, and came straight from the local airport.'

'With no clothes?'

He sounded so disbelieving she had to smile.

'I could hardly take my winter clothes to Thailand, but I did buy some new undies at the airport in Bangkok,' she assured him, 'and as today was to be an orientation day, I'm hoping I'll have some time later to get out and buy something new. I'll need to book into a hotel, too, until I find somewhere to stay.'

He shook his head—disbelief at her story clear in his eyes.

'I'd have been here a month ago if it hadn't been for the typhoon. Plenty of time to have found things to wear and a place to live!' she said, cross with herself for the defensive justification.

'Well, eat up and we'll do the business side of things, and then I'll show you around the hospital. Just get some clothes, but don't bother with a hotel. I can give you a bed at my apartment for a night or two.'

He flung the words at her so casually—coolly—she didn't have a clue how to take them.

Simple politeness?

Or exasperation that she was so disorganised?

'You don't have to do that. I'll be fine in a hotel,' she told him, not adding that she'd also be far more comfortable away from him.

Staying with Andy? The very thought had tension tightening her nerves...

He studied her, eyes revealing nothing, although the words, when they came, were cold—their meaning clear.

'You *are* the widow of my best friend, of course you should stay with me, Sam.'

The best friend you think I killed, Sam thought as she drained the rest of her juice to help swallow the dry piece of sandwich.

But given that, could she really stay with him, even for a few days while she found somewhere else to live?

Although the offer might just be a peace offering. And it wasn't going to be for ever, she might have found somewhere else to stay by tomorrow...

And they *had* been friends.

And just what were you thinking? Andy asked himself. Inviting her to stay like that?

Especially as just seeing her again had stirred up so much consternation in his gut.

Even in baggy scrubs and her wet hair bunched somehow on the top of her head, she was still one of the most attractive women he'd ever met.

But she'd ended up with Nick—and, as far as Nick was concerned, she'd belonged to him. But could a woman as strong-willed and determined as Sam ever *belong* to any-

one? Nick had certainly thought so, and somehow she'd
made their marriage work. Though, knowing Nick, that
wouldn't have been easy...

Why was he thinking of the past when it was the immediate future he needed to solve?

It could be weeks before she found a place, months
even, because the summer holiday season was approaching fast and accommodation owners made more money
with short-term holiday rentals at this time of the year.

So why the hell had he suggested she stay with him,
even for a couple of nights?

Exhaustion was the answer. He'd been operating the
department without a first-class number two for nearly
six months, the previous incumbent having left in a huff
for not getting the top job. Others had filled in, of course,
but none of them had wanted to take on too much respon-
sibility for a job they'd never get.

But he'd asked her now and he had to live with her
answer. Maybe she'd feel just as uncomfortable about
the arrangement as he did and would find somewhere
else really quickly.

But there was no time for conjecture, Sam was already on her feet, pushing back her chair, the far too big
scrubs sliding down her legs to reveal a startling pair of
lacy purple panties.

Scarlet with embarrassment, she grabbed the trousers and pulled them up, glaring at him as she muttered,
'There was very little choice of underwear at Bangkok
airport!'

'Great colour!' he said, mainly to see her blush deepen.
'Pity you can't wear them on the outside like a superhero.'

She looked seriously at him and he guessed she was

wondering how things would be between them, working together in the PICU.

'I'm no super-hero,' she said quietly. 'But I've learned a lot and can do my job.'

And having put him right back in his place, she offered a small smile before adding, 'But right now I need a bit of string or something to hold up these trousers.'

She marched ahead of him out of the canteen, one hand holding the errant scrub trousers tightly to her waist.

He followed close behind her, his head still asking why the hell he'd done this—chosen her for the job when he'd known it would mean the pair of them working closely together.

Yes, she'd been the best candidate and he had no doubt she'd be superb, but that strong niggle of attraction—he'd always hesitated to call it more—he'd felt from the first moment he and Nick had laid eyes on her, in the staff's favourite bar across the road from their old hospital, had never really gone away.

He flinched with embarrassment as he remembered that night. He and Nick had done Rock, Paper, Scissors to see who'd ask her out and the rest, as the saying went, was history. Sam and Nick had been married within three months, and he'd managed to distance himself from the happy couple as much as possible. Nick had been his friend from childhood—no way could he be lusting after Nick's wife...

'Something to keep my trousers up,' that same woman reminded him, bringing him out of the past and back to the present—and to the decision that as Nick's widow Sam was even more unattainable.

'There'll be a bungy cord in the janitors' room—everyone needs bungy cords.'

He ducked in front of her to lead the way, but as he passed, he couldn't help wondering how *she* was feeling about this. She'd certainly been startled to see him, so obviously hadn't had time to learn much about the new hospital or its PICU staffing.

He opened a door on the right and rummaged around through miscellaneous junk, finally finding not a bungy cord but a ball of twine.

'Put your hands out from your sides while I measure how much we'll need,' he said, stepping behind her and unrolling the twine, wrapping it around her waist—not easy when one hand still held tightly to the trousers— until his fingers met at the front.

'Leave enough to tie a bow,' she said, grabbing at the other side of the trousers before they slid down again. 'I don't want to be cutting myself out of it later.'

He didn't answer—couldn't. This was Sam, right here in front of him, more or less in his arms...

He'd denied this attraction, even to himself, for the three long years she and Nick had been married. He'd avoided her—avoided seeing her with Nick—and now she was here, and her closeness filled his senses. The smell of her seemed to invade his whole body.

It was hard to deny his attraction now, when she was so close.

So why the hell had he asked her to stay with him?

And why had she agreed? Especially given how much he must have hurt her with his accusation as she had lain in hospital...

Or had she agreed?

Not in as many words.

She just hadn't outright refused.

There'd surely be a hotel available—could he find her one?

Or would that look churlish?

Yep!

And it wasn't as if he'd asked her to live with him, He'd just offered her a bed until she found something else.

Soon, he hoped...

He pulled back, away from her, the twine ball clutched in his hands. He had to get a life, find a diversion, take out a woman, any woman—anything to keep Sam out of his system.

He found a knife and cut the length, then handed it to her to tie it around her own waist, easing further away from her, his mind churning with the knowledge that she still had such an effect on him.

Sam tied the twine around her waist then turned the top of the trousers over it so the tunic hung neatly over them—more or less. Fiddling, fiddling, giving herself time to get over the startling discovery that Andy's arms around her—innocent as the movement had been—had brought heat to her cheeks and sent shivers down her spine.

Prolonged abstinence—that's all it was! In the three years since Nick's death she'd had only one relationship and although occasional sex had been involved in it, it had been more comfort than physical fulfilment that she'd wanted.

But Andy?

She'd met him and Nick together, and although it had been Nick who'd asked her out then courted her into a whirlwind marriage, she'd always liked Andy, had felt a kind of kinship with him. There'd always been something steady and reliable about Andy, though she'd seen less of him after her marriage.

Now he marched away after handing her the twine, and she had to hurry to catch up with him, falling in almost beside him, just a half-step back.

Deference to the boss, or fear that being closer might disturb her in some way?

Nonsense. It was simply because of the past that she was feeling uneasy...

He used a card to access what was obviously a staff elevator and punched the number for the fourth floor.

'You'll get one of these with your information pack,' he told her, 'and sometime today you'll need to have a photo taken to put on your ID—it only takes a few minutes.'

End of conversation, the elevator doors opened and they stepped into a corridor, Andy turning left and pushing through pneumatic doors.

They'd barely entered when a nurse appeared.

'Andy, they need someone down in the ED, eighteen-month-old with a temp of thirty-nine C, listless, flushed, unresponsive.'

'Come with me,' Andy said to Sam as he turned on his heel and headed back to the elevator.

'These two elevators are staff only. Well, they're used for moving patients as well, but the hospital is fairly new and the design is really brilliant, which makes working here a dream.'

He paused, then added, 'How often have you stood in an elevator and known there are at least three people in it who'd like to ask you a question about a patient?'

'And often did,' she added as she nodded her agreement. This was good, this was work. She could not only handle working with Andy but she would enjoy it, aware that he was extremely good at what he did.

If she locked the past away where it belonged, treated Andy like any other colleague, and just concentrated on work...

He led the way into the ED, which was strangely quiet early in the morning, and a nurse hailed him as he walked in.

'We've put her in an isolation room—she's pink but that could just be the fever,' she explained.

'Or measles,' Andy ground out savagely.

He walked into the room and leant over the child, Sam slipping around to the other side of the bed, the small girl on it staring blankly at the ceiling. Her eyes were red, her nose oozing mucus, and flat red spots covered her forehead and were appearing as they watched, down her face and neck and onto her torso.

Speaking quietly to the child, Andy eased her mouth open and peered inside, finding tell-tale signs of measles in there as well.

'We need to check with her parents if she's been vaccinated, although somehow I doubt it as the measles vaccine provides almost one hundred percent protection.

'What checks have you done so far?' he asked the nurse.

'We've removed her clothes and sponged her down, given her twenty milligrams of paracetamol, tried to get some water into her but she's so unresponsive I was afraid she'd choke.'

Andy nodded.

'We'll admit her, take her up to PICU and isolate her up there. We can use IV fluids and add ibuprofen six hourly via her drip.' He paused, drew a deep breath, then said, 'I'd better talk to the parents. Who brought her in?'

'The father, but he had to leave. Both parents are lawyers apparently, but I have a phone number for him.'

Sam followed, trying to thrust images of the sick child from her mind, wondering just how this had happened in this day and age of preventative measures. But as Andy used the card for the elevator, another thought struck her.

'You've just come off duty, haven't you? Why are you following up on this infant?'

'You've never worked a few hours after your shift ended?' he asked, and she shrugged because, of course, she, and probably thousands of other doctors, had.

'Thought not,' he said. 'But I've not just come off night shift—it's one of the few perks of the job that I don't do night shifts. I came in earlier and then again at about four to see a child on the ward who was having breathing problems.'

He smiled, and although it was a tired smile, it affected her, deep inside, in a way she certainly didn't want to think about.

Andy had been Nick's friend, and for all the irritations she might have felt in her marriage, the difficulties and disappointments, she still felt loyalty to Nick's memory, and somehow being attracted to his best friend was surely the ultimate disloyalty...

And, anyway, it was just a smile!

Andy had always had a nice smile.

They left the elevator, and Andy led her to the main monitoring desk, pointing out the way all the rooms could be monitored at once and introducing her to Karen, who was the head nurse on duty that morning.

She watched as his eyes scanned the monitors, and

knew he'd been taking a mental note of every patient, even leaning over the desk and picking up a paper file to check on something he'd seen.

He explained the new admission to Karen, adding, 'Keep trying the number they have for the father in case the ED didn't get hold of him. Let him know where we are at and how to find us.'

A short discussion on their other patients, then Andy turned away, leading Sam along a corridor and returning to the conversation they'd been having.

'Actually, it was my last shift on call, and I'd worked my schedule so I could be here for your orientation before heading off this afternoon for a rest and to try to get my biorhythms back into sync.'

'I thought biorhythms had been totally debunked,' she said as the elevator doors slid open.

'Not totally and anyway it always seems to me that it's a better word to use because it's more than the physical side of yourself—well, myself anyway—that has to sort itself out after being on call, but the emotional and intellectual sides as well. I don't know about you, but I don't think well after a change of shifts—not until the sleep thing is sorted.'

'And the emotional side?' Sam asked as she followed him along the corridor.

'Oh, that's been totally stuffed for years,' he said. 'Unless you're involved with someone else who works ridiculous hours and often has to dash off at two in the morning for an emergency, a normal relationship is impossible.'

'Is there such a thing as a normal relationship?' she couldn't resist asking, thinking of the trials and anxiety she'd often felt in her marriage to Nick. But they'd reached the room where the little girl was already up from the ED and was being intubated by a nurse in full sterile covering, while Andy was looking intently at the chart he'd collected from the door.

With ninety-nine percent of his attention on the child in front of him, that tiny one percent had been caught by something in Sam's voice as she'd asked that question. The one about relationships...

Had her and Nick's marriage not been the one of connubial bliss he and everyone else had always thought it?

Nick had certainly painted it that way.

'We'll need to find out about her family,' he said, dragging that errant one percent back into place. 'Siblings, parents and grandparents, children she might mix with in day care or kindy.'

'I know most kindergartens won't accept unimmunised children. I'm not certain whether family day care is covered by it,' Sam told him, although he'd been speaking to the nurse.

'Her family—or at least one of them—should be with her,' the nurse muttered, but Andy ignored them both.

'There's a phone number for the father. When you speak to him just check out all you can about anyone she's been in contact with. If she has siblings who haven't been vaccinated, we need to get them in—or get them to their local doctor—for vaccination now. If she's been with other children at risk, we need to find them and get them vaccinated too.'

'Within seventy-two hours,' Sam finished for him. 'I could do that.'

He frowned at her.

'You're here for orientation,' he reminded her, a little too sharply because what he could only put down to lack of sleep was making him overly aware of Sam by his side. Reminding him he'd been foolish enough to ask her to stay with him at his apartment.

He stepped aside and wrote up the protocols for the day, handed the chart to the nurse, saying, 'I'd have liked to speak to a family member before admitting her, but I couldn't leave her in the ED. We'll have to explain that to someone later.'

He left the room, Sam on his heels.

'Why Intensive Care not the children's ward?' she asked, and he seized on the question to shake off the weirdness going on with this woman's reappearance in his life. Dear God, he'd known she was coming—had been looking forward to working with her again, given the experience she'd gained—and stupidest of all, he'd thought that long-ago attraction would surely have burnt out…

He banished the distracting thoughts, put them down to tiredness. This was work, a child's life was at stake.

'We can isolate her better here, watch for any signs of complication.'

'Pneumonia, encephalitis?'

'Ear infections,' he added, shaking his own head as if that might dislodge the softness of her voice.

Forcing his mind back to work, he led her towards the nurses' station, situated in the centre of the ward where a team of five nurses monitored the live feeds from all the PICU beds while two clerical staff handled phones and paperwork.

'This is Dr Sam Reilly,' he said as several of them looked up. 'She starts here tomorrow and I'm showing her around.'

He waved Sam forward before adding, 'No point in introducing you all now, she'll meet you in time.'

He turned to one of the clerical workers.

'I've just admitted a three-year-old girl with measles and put her in Isolation Room Two. Could you chase up the electronic file from the ED and make sure the room's online for monitoring?'

'We use paper files that stay with the patient, as well as electronic,' he said to Sam as he whisked away, aware she was just a step behind him—aware, too, that he should slow, they should walk together, as colleagues did.

But although he'd been prepared for her arrival, even looked forward to seeing her again, having her on his team, the fact that her physical presence still perturbed him had thrown his mind into chaos.

It was only temporary, this reaction. They hadn't parted on the best of terms—no, they'd parted on the worst of terms, he'd hurt her badly—so this would pass.

Soon, he hoped...

He thought back to that day in shame, but he'd seen her there in the hospital bed, so pale she'd have disappeared against the white pillow case if the scattering of freckles across her nose and the tangled red hair hadn't stood out so clearly.

She'd been injured, but just the sight of her—the pain he'd read on her face—had knotted something in his gut, something that he'd tried to burn away with anger.

And now?

Now she was a colleague, and he had to think of her that way, because that was surely the only way she thought of him, She'd certainly never given the slightest indication that she was interested in him—in anyone but Nick, in fact...

'Abby has encephalitis,' he said, forcing his mind back to work as he led Sam into another room.

The young girl in the bed opened her eyes and smiled wanly at them.

'We've no idea what brought it on, have we, Abs?' he added, coming closer to take Abby's hand, 'but we do know she's on the mend.'

He motioned Sam forward.

'This is Sam, Abby, a new doctor and a very good one. We'll let her have a go at your records and see what she can sniff out, eh?'

Abby smiled again, then her eyes closed and she drifted back to sleep.

Andy handed the file he'd picked up from the back of the door to Sam, but kept his eyes on the sleeping girl.

Abby was thirteen, the same age Sarah had been when she'd died—Sarah, his beautiful, loving, always happy sister...

Sam flipped through the pages, noting the myriad tests that had been carried out on the sick child, realising that nothing had shown up as a possible trigger.

'Had she had a sore throat—could it have been as simple as a cold virus that triggered the swelling in her brain?' she asked as she slotted the file back in its place on the door, knowing she could read up on it on the computer later.

'Or some autoimmune thing, we've been thinking,' Andy replied, obviously still puzzled over the case. 'In fact, we did the regular tests, then stopped worrying what might have caused it and simply treated her. She's a little more alert every day, so I'm hopeful, given time and rest, she'll make a full recovery.'

'So much of what we do in PICU is rest and monitoring, isn't it?' Sam said, hoping she sounded rational and professional, although this being with Andy, trying to pretend he was nothing more than a colleague, was tying her stomach in knots.

And then he grinned at her.

'Ah, but the monitoring needs to be constant,' he said, while her head whirled. But Andy had always had that teasing grin so why…?

She dragged her mind back into gear and caught up with the conversation.

'Which is why the children are here and not down in the normal kids' wards. Come and meet Ryan—he's one of our frequent flyers.'

Sam laughed at the familiar phrase, reminding herself that this was work.

'Premmie?' she asked, and Andy nodded.

'He's two years old now, but still susceptible to any damn virus floating past in the air.'

'Usually RSV?' Sam asked, aware that respiratory syncytial virus, with its respiratory and breathing difficulties, was common in premature children.

Andy nodded.

'It's bronchiolitis this time. All the small passages in his lungs are inflamed, but six months ago it was pneumonia.'

'Poor kid,' Sam said, entering the room and peering down at the small form in the small cot. The little boy was probably only two thirds the size of a normal two-year-old, though what was really 'normal' with any child?

But she was intrigued by the small mask taped to the little boy's face and the tube from it leading back to a tiny CPAP machine.

'Non-invasive positive air pressure?' she said, intrigued why the usual nasal prongs weren't delivering oxygen to the little body.

'We're finding, particularly with smaller children, that it's easier to get them off the oxygen when we use the continuous pressure air pump. There've been various small trials on it, and no definitive data as yet, but it works for young Ryan here, so we stick to it.'

Aware there was no treatment apart from oxygen to help their battling lungs, fluid to keep them hydrated, and paracetamol to keep the child's temperature down, Sam followed Andy out the door. Studying him, thinking…

He would have had the final decision on her employment, yet he'd employed her anyway—even though he obviously blamed her for Nick's death.

She shut the box in her mind that held memories of that day. This was now a new life, and Andy would be, inevitably, a big part of it so sometime soon that box had to be opened and some of the contents discussed. Their last encounter especially needed some explanations and she knew they couldn't go forward with it in both their minds, blocking out any proper conversation or even, possibly, friendship.

But in the meantime, Andy was right here—her boss—and she had to prove herself to him.

He was tall—taller than Nick had been—and he carried himself well, except for stooping slightly to hide his height as he was wont to do. He was good looking, too, with his dark hair and blue eyes.

But not married—well, apparently not—there was no ring on his finger.

And why would you be checking that out? she asked herself. He doesn't even like you.

'We talked about monitoring earlier.'

The words brought her mind back to the job. It was probably a bit of jet lag that had it wandering so far and so fast.

'And though it seems such a simple thing, it's paramount. It means we can see when they're about to crash and need resuscitation, or stop breathing and need urgent intubation, or have a seizure and need protective care and medication to ease it.'

He frowned slightly, turning to look directly at her, before adding, 'Though why I'm justifying our work to someone who is as experienced as you I don't know!'

Blue eyes looked steadily into her wishy-washy green ones, and about a million synapses in her brain fired to chaotic life.

Breathe!

'You forget I've just come from a hospital that's barely more than a shed with some beds, and the most sophisticated medical machinery was an X-ray machine that we couldn't work because of a lack of electricity.'

Andy stared at her. 'Seriously?' he said, and she smiled, relaxing as she talked about the place she'd grown to love. A place where her mother, a nurse, had worked for so many years it had become her home.

'Well, we did have a generator and when we had fuel for it, and it actually decided to work for a while, we could get the occasional X-ray. Whoever had donated the X-ray machine to the clinic had included plenty of film, so from time to time it was very handy. Mind you, I wasn't there for long enough to get totally frustrated by the lack of technology, but it was very educational in its own way!'

Andy shook his head, and she followed him into the

next room, where a very pale girl of about twelve, was lying listlessly on a bed. Her eyes were open but whether she was seeing them, Sam didn't know.

'Kayla has recently been diagnosed with Type One diabetes, but it took a while for her GP to get to the root of her problem.'

'Or for her to agree to even see a doctor,' Sam suggested, and saw the girl give a wan smile. 'A lot of girls going into the teenage years complain of being tired, of having headaches, or they're irritable. So it isn't always picked up on at home and they don't always get to a doctor until something drastic happens.'

'You're right, of course,' Andy agreed, and Sam was just deciding that this would be okay—this working with Andy—but then he smiled, and it was such an open, warm, typical Andy smile that something inside her began to crack.

Could it be the film of the ice she'd sheathed around her heart when Nick had died?

CHAPTER TWO

IT TOOK ANOTHER hour to visit the other patients in the ICU, including the little girl with measles who'd now been installed in an isolation room.

'Has someone been in touch with the family?' Andy asked the nurse who was checking the drip stand.

'The ED phoned the number the father left, but couldn't get him, but we'll keep trying. He could already have realised the implications and be taking his other children for vaccination.'

Sam nodded, hoping this was true, but Andy wasn't appeased.

'Come on,' he said brusquely. 'We're done here. I'll make sure one of the nurses gets on to someone in that family and tells them they need vaccinations urgently. It's probably best I don't talk to them when I'm tired and—'

'Angry?' Sam offered, and he shrugged.

'More frustrated,' he said slowly. 'You see a child so sick from a preventable disease and wonder what people are thinking of. Anyway, it's time I left. I'll take you back to my place, and you can do some shopping.'

Very frustrated, Sam realised, so she kept her mouth shut until he'd led her out of the hospital and into the car park, opening the door of a dark saloon.

The flashback hit her without warning—Nick's voice, loud and insistent, the car swerving. Then nothing...

She knew she couldn't get into the car; couldn't get in with an angry—or frustrated—driver.

Not again.

Not after the last time.

'I have to go back and get my things,' she said. 'My backpack. But you go. I think I'll stick to my initial plan and get a hotel for a couple of weeks until I find somewhere more permanent.'

The tightness she'd read on his face vanished like mist burnt off by the sun, and now anxiety drew its lines in his skin.

'Hey, it's okay,' he said. 'I just get a bit upset when I butt up against parents like that.'

'Like what?' she retorted. 'A couple where both parents choose to work? Where neither wants to set aside the expensive training they've had, largely through public funds, to be with their children twenty-four seven? You don't know those people, Andy. For all you know, he could be representing a young girl in a rape case and can't afford *not* to be in court this morning, and the mother could be helping refugees in an offshore detention centre.'

He stared at her.

'You're saying they could both have legitimate reasons *not* to be with their child?'

'I am,' she said. 'I know there are parents who aren't totally involved in their children's lives, but we can't judge *all* working parents. Half the doctors at this hospital are working parents. Is a surgeon going to cancel a possibly life-saving op to sit with his sick child?'

Andy said nothing but she could see the idea taking root in his mind.

'So he'd focus on what had to be done—put his personal anxiety aside for as long as it took to get the best result for his patient—and then go back to the child.'

'Of course he would. Ninety percent of parents would.'

Andy studied her for what seemed like for ever.

'You've given this a lot of thought,' he finally said, and saw a deep sadness cloud her pale eyes.

But all she said was, 'Indeed I have,' before she turned and walked back towards the hospital.

He went after her, catching up in a few strides.

'Hey!'

He turned her so she faced towards him and used one finger to tilt her head so he could look into those tantalising eyes.

'Why don't you forget about a hotel for a while? Come and stay with me while you find somewhere permanent,' he said, hoping it didn't sound like a plea. 'It'll be fun—like the old days, although we probably won't see that much of each other because our shifts won't coincide, but...'

He paused and tried a smile.

'But when we *are* together, you can teach me not to judge, and remind me that every picture could be telling many different stories.'

She stood there, lips pursed—kissable, but he definitely wasn't going there—and he remembered she'd always done that when she was thinking.

When they'd all been friends.

'Okay!' she said, 'but I still need to get my backpack.'

He followed her back to the building, surprised when she led him into the ED staff lounge.

'I needed a shower before I ventured anywhere further into the hospital,' she explained, digging a key out of the pocket of her scrubs and leading him to a locker.

He watched as she unlocked the locker and reached in to haul out what seemed like an enormous backpack.

Sliding it out of her hands, he slung it over his shoulder, bending at the knees in faked collapse.

'It's not *that* heavy!' she told him, although he did win a smile.

Silly really, but the smile made the weight lighter, and he led the way back towards his car, feeling alive and alert, despite the early start. And if a tiny whisper suggested they should have parted when she'd suggested it earlier, he could easily ignore it.

It would be good to have Sam back in his life.

It *would*!

'It's not far from the hospital—my place,' Andy said, as Sam settled herself into the comfortable passenger seat in his car, 'but at night I like to use the car, the streets are dark and you never know who's hanging around.'

It was such an ordinary conversation Sam should have felt relaxed, but instead she was wondering why she hadn't insisted on going to a hotel. It wasn't that she didn't enjoy Andy's company—she always had, although she'd seen a lot less of him after she'd married Nick. He and Andy would meet up for a drink when she was on a late shift, or Andy would be busy when she and Nick were having friends over.

Then, so upset by what had been just his unthinking reaction to the accident, she'd refused to see him again while she'd been in hospital. But she'd been hurt by his angry words—hurt, if she was honest, because they had been too close to the truth.

But working with him meant they'd be colleagues, and colleagues were often friends, and she and Andy—

For heaven's sake, stop analysing everything. Whatever happened to your philosophy of taking each day as it came. That's what got you through the accident, and that's what you have to do here.

She glanced towards him, pleased he was concentrating on the road so she could study him for a moment. And wonder if perhaps she'd always felt a slight attraction towards him?

She shook her head.

'Bad thoughts?' he asked. He'd obviously seen her frown and head shake.

'No, just wondering where we are and how long it will take me to find my way around a new place.'

'You'd never been here before? Never had a holiday on the coast?'

She shook her head again.

'Mum worked full time—and I mean full time—two jobs usually, just to keep us fed and watered. Any extra money was put aside for the university education she insisted I had to have. Holidays never entered the picture.'

'Well, I'll just have to educate you. Port Fortesque was first settled way back, much of the original building done by convicts,' he explained. 'It was a stopping-off place for boats going north from Sydney to the new penal colony in Moreton Bay, which is now in Queensland but back then was part of New South Wales. There are still some lovely old buildings here, especially the lighthouse. We should go there for dinner tonight to welcome you back to Oz. They've turned the lighthouse-keeper's cottage into a fine restaurant.'

She'd let him talk, let his voice wash over her, although—

'I don't need fine dining,' she told him, 'and I definitely don't want you running around after me. You'll want a relaxing, early night after your four a.m. start, and I've got shopping to do and clothes to sort and wash.'

She paused, aware that what she was about to say was for her own protection. Andy was too darned attractive for his own good, and the less she saw of him outside working hours the better.

'I also need to get onto a real-estate website. There might even be a self-contained B&B I can use as a base until I get to know the area. In London, there were dozens of them set up close to hospitals.'

He glanced her way.

'Whatever suits you best,' he said, his voice noticeably cooler. Surely he hadn't been *looking forward* to her staying with him. Wouldn't that put a crimp in his social life, for a start?

Although what did *she* know about his social life? Except that he'd be sure to have one. The Andy who'd been half of Nick and Andy had always had a beautiful woman in his life.

An image of Andy walking into his flat with a beautiful woman, chatting politely for a while before disappearing into his bedroom, had Sam feeling distinctly uncomfortable. Which was a totally ridiculous reaction as Andy's social life was none of her business, whether she was sharing his apartment or not.

Nothing to do with her.

At all!

He'd been—probably still would have been—her husband's best friend. She'd known him as long as she'd known Nick—which, much as she'd loved him, had, at times, seemed a very long three years—but Andy had always been there whenever he'd been needed, with a smile on his face and a ready laugh on his lips.

Except after the accident…

He'd been pointing out landmarks as they passed, the river with its old wharf now only used to tie up visiting pleasure yachts, the surf beaches between rocky headlands to the south of the river mouth.

The sun sparkled on the ocean, making magic in the air, so when Andy turned into the drive that led to the basement of newish block of apartments, pressed a fob for the metal doors to rise, she began to regret accepting his offer.

It might be hard to leave the views this place must have, the rocky headlands curling protectively around the surf beach, a stretch of golden sand, the broken waves rushing up the beach as the tide came in.

'I thought you said it wasn't far from the hospital,' she said, as Andy expertly parked his car and came round to open her door.

She beat him to it, but only just, so she stood to find him so close they could have kissed.

If they hadn't been separated by the car door.

If this had been that kind of relationship.

And just where had *those* thoughts come from?

She might have felt a sudden awareness of Andy as a man, but she was probably the last woman in the world *he'd* consider getting involved with!

'I brought you the long way around to see some of the sights, but the hospital is only ten minutes directly west, twenty minutes on foot. Though I must warn you...' he added with a smile that raised goose-bumps on her skin.

What was wrong with her?

She tuned back into Andy's conversation.

'There are some steep hills to tackle if you're walking to work. This was once a rocky peninsula that reached out into the sea. There's actually good diving on it further out, colourful soft corals and tiny, brilliant fish darting in and out of it. Do you dive?'

'Dive?'

She invested the word with such disbelief Andy had to smile.

'You might not remember, but I come from a land-locked village in the top western corner of the state. We're lucky when we have a good enough wet season to have a swim in the local dam,' she told him. 'Plus, as you may have noticed, I have the kind of skin that turns beetroot red after about five minutes in the sun. The English climate really suited me!'

He did remember now—remembered more and more about her. She had two laughs, an infectious giggle and a full-blown laugh that was a sound of sheer delight.

And he'd asked her to stay with him?

He must have been out of his mind, especially when he loved to come home to the peace and quiet of his apartment after a busy day.

And now he was leaning on the top of the car door, talking about diving, of all things, and thinking about laughter from a time that seemed so far in the past it was practically ancient history.

Except that she was, and always would be, to him, quite lovely, with her vivid hair and pale skin, her easy smile and laughter.

Did he not want this light-hearted moment to end?

Or was he afraid that once she'd imprinted herself on his living space, he'd find it hard to reclaim it as his own?

His attraction to her had led him to distance himself from her and Nick after the wedding—not far, just far enough. Protection really, but she'd stayed in his head, usually laughing at some silly—

'Do you not want me to see your apartment, or have you sent an urgent message to some woman to vacate the place for a while?'

Her teasing smile plucked at his nerves, so it took him a moment to recover.

'Tribes of women having to vacate it,' he managed to say lightly, fully opening the car door for her and heading to the trunk to retrieve her backpack.

But the tension he felt as the elevator rose to the eleventh floor strengthened the feeling that maybe this hadn't been one of his better ideas.

Perhaps even his worst since the rock, paper, scissors fiasco all those years ago.

His mind did a quick mental scan of the state of his place. He liked it neat and tidy, but he'd left in a rush this morning. Although, while his bedroom might be a bit chaotic, she'd hardly be inspecting that. And this thought caused nearly as many strange reactions in his body as her pursed and kissable lips had earlier.

Enough!

This was Sam, his best friend's widow, remember, invited to stay while she sorted herself out.

A few days—a week—she was already talking about real-estate sites...

The problem was he'd known she was coming, but he'd been unprepared for actually seeing her again. *And* he'd been unprepared for the memories her presence had evoked.

He'd been attracted to her as far back as the day he and Nick had first met her, and he'd hoped she'd say no when Nick asked her out...

He'd telephone Susie later today, get his social life organised.

'Oh, but it's beautiful!'

Sam's words made him turn to see her gazing, wide-eyed, at his view.

'It takes in so much—the rocky headland, the sea, and then the sky. How lucky are you?'

He could hear the genuine delight in her voice, and for a moment wanted to tell her she could always stay on here, pay a little rent if it made her feel better. There was plenty of room...

Are you mad?

He hid more than a few qualms as he led her deeper into the apartment. This was not a good idea, given that he still felt a lingering attraction to her. Especially when, in his heart, he still blamed her for Nick's death, only too aware that never driving over the speed limit was a part of Nick's mild OCD.

In fact, the whole situation was a bloody mess.

'I like this room that looks back towards the mountains,' Sam was saying while he stood in the passage, clutching her backpack, random thoughts jostling in his head.

'Here, give me that.'

Her words broke the spell.

'I'll find something clean and relatively suitable to go shopping in and leave you to catch up on your sleep.'

He set her backpack down on the bedroom floor,

aware of some new tension in the air. Had she guessed what he'd been thinking? Not that she needed to guess his thoughts about the accident—he'd more or less accused her of causing it.

'The bed's made up—friends and family are always turning up, so I leave it with clean sheets on,' he said awkwardly as he backed out of the room. 'I'll find some spare keys you can use.'

This was *not* a good idea, Sam decided when Andy had disappeared. They'd barely met again, and yet she felt unsettled when she was with him. It was an awareness, really—even an attraction—yet this was the man who'd blamed her for Nick's death, probably still did...

Not that she had time to be worrying about a little awkwardness, let alone attraction. She'd lost a month of preparation back in Cambodia and she had a lot of organising to do. Clothes first—sensible clothes for work, that's all she'd need for a while. A new swimming costume, there'd be days when she'd be able to fit in a swim before work, before the sun got too hot...

She opened her bag and rummaged through it, finding some long loose trousers and a tunic top—the kind of thing she'd been wearing all the time at the little clinic. The clothes might look a little odd in the shopping mall at Port Fortesque but they were clean and decent.

Once showered and dressed, she found Andy in the kitchen.

'We passed a shopping mall on the way here. If I just go out the front door and turn left, I'll find it, won't I?'

He smiled at her outfit—making her think again of awkwardness and attraction, and definitely finding a real-estate office online...

'They're clean and respectable,' she told him, defending her choice of clothing. 'The shopping mall?'

'Left and left again at the second street, you can't miss it,' he said, the smile still teasing at his lips. 'Phone me if you buy so much you need a lift home.'

He crossed to the bar on one side of the kitchen, undoubtedly used for most meals, and picked up a card and a set of keys.

'The fob opens the garage doors, the flat one you swipe for the elevator, the big key is for the front entrance and this lovely purple one is for my front door. Eleventh floor, Apartment Two. My number's on the card. Okay?'

She took them from him, their fingers tangling around the flat elevator key, sending such a weird sensation through Sam she involuntarily looked up to see if Andy had also felt it.

But although that teasing smile still hovered on his lips, he showed no sign of any sudden reaction.

Which was hardly surprising...

Sam departed, tucking the keys into her small backpack, reminding herself that was something else she should buy—a handbag.

She shook her head. Her small backpack had served her well for the past three years. It had originally been Nick's, but he'd replaced it with a much smarter leather briefcase once he'd been promoted. She'd found it when she'd been cleaning out their flat and realised how handy it would be for her travels.

Besides, it was so long since she'd used a handbag she'd feel foolish with one, and she certainly wasn't going down the briefcase road. But she *did* have a small, pretty, handwoven bag with a long strap that would hold her wallet and a few tissues. She could always take that if she ever *did* go out at night.

The mall loomed in front of her, and she wondered just what it would offer in the way of clothes-buying options.

She needn't have worried, because all the old familiar stores were there, and within half an hour she had a selection of slacks, long shorts, skirts, T-shirts and shirts, and two swimming costumes. She'd stuck with basics—black and white with a few floral and striped tops to brighten things up—but as she walked out—newly bought shopping weighing down her arms—she passed a small boutique offering a fifty percent off sale.

The clothes were beautiful, mainly linen and silk, and simple in style but shrieking elegance. She tried to persuade herself that she'd never wear such clothes, but a pale green linen shift drew her like a magnet, while a black silk dress with a low scooped neckline and flaring skirt refused to be left behind. Sandals, shoes and a pair of comfy slides for the beach soon followed and she spent the walk home telling herself there'd surely be a Christmas party at the hospital so, depending on how formal it might be, either the shift or the black dress would do.

Back when she'd been growing up, buying her own clothes for the first time, her mother had always assured her that a little black dress could go anywhere. And her mother's LBD had gone many places—the single mother of a growing daughter not having had the money to spend on a range of 'going out' dresses!

'You didn't strike me a shopper,' Andy greeted her when she walked back in.

'I'm not,' she said. 'But having discarded all my London clothes before I left, and with the few Cambodian outfits not really suitable here, I had to start again. Basic shopping from the skin out, plus toiletries and odds and ends. I decided that being second in charge meant I had to at least look respectable.'

He smiled, eyes gleaming so she knew a tease was coming.

'Going to give me a fashion parade? You could start with the purple undies!'

She shook her head, but she was smiling too. This was the old Andy—often teasing her to see her blush, Nick laughing with him at the result.

Enough memories.

Be practical.

'You must be ready for an early night after your four a.m. start. As you've been good enough to take me in, would you like me to send out for a takeaway? Although I did grab a few groceries on the way home. I'd be happy to do a Cambodian stir-fry.'

'You cook?'

He sounded astounded.

In fact, so astounded Sam felt a little stab of pain. She'd always cooked and enjoyed it, but Nick had liked to give their friends the impression that she was a pampered princess, and he had always cooked the meals when they'd had guests.

She'd grown to hate it, but had kept quiet about it, at first putting it down to Nick showing off and only later realising it was part of his problem; his need to be the best in other people's eyes, both as a husband and a cook—even a doctor...

And she'd put up with it because she'd loved Nick, and she'd been determined to make their marriage work. Right up until the end—that last fateful day...

Focus!

'Well?' she demanded of Andy, possibly a little too abruptly.

He'd been frowning off into the distance, and turned, startled, back towards her.

'Well, what?'

'Would you like me to cook dinner?'

'Well, yes, of course,' he managed to say. 'If you really want to.'

'I do.' she said firmly, although she'd had to close her eyes for an instant to control a rising heat of anger.

So not only had Nick done his best to make *her* feel useless, but Andy's reaction had made her realise he'd convinced his friends of that as well.

The kitchen was neat and functional. No wok, but she could cook in a frying pan.

'Do you eat chicken?' she called to Andy, last seen standing on the balcony looking out to sea.

'Love it,' he said, sounding so close she started and spun around to find him on the other side of the breakfast bar.

'And you,' he asked, 'would you like a beer as you slave away over a hot stove?'

'Love one,' she said. 'You might not know it, but Cambodia has some very good beers, and one always goes down well while I'm cooking.'

He put the small stubby of beer in a foam holder beside the chopping board she was using to finely slice spring onions, bok choy, capsicum, carrots, snow peas and cabbage.

'Thanks,' she said, setting down her knife and lifting the beer. 'Cheers!' she said, and clinked it with Andy's.

'Welcome home!' he replied, smiling at her as if he

meant it, and she had to turn away to hide the silly tears that had, for no good reason, filled her eyes.

Andy watched as Sam sliced and diced, taking a sip from her beer occasionally.

He'd thought he'd known this woman who'd been married to his best friend for three years, yet small things were causing him to question all he'd known.

Not that it mattered. They'd be working and living—temporarily at least—together, plenty of time to get to know her. And if he was right about glimpsing a sheen of tears in her eyes when he'd said welcome home, then there was a lot about her to get to know.

He'd always admired her for the way she'd handled Nick, who hadn't always been the easiest of friends to have.

Nick had always wanted to win, to be the best.

Andy closed his eyes on memories and concentrated on the woman in his kitchen. Tall and lean in the loose-fitting, distinctly Asian outfit, she'd bunched her hair up on top of her head to keep it out of the way, and was humming to herself as she worked.

'You seem to enjoy cooking,' he said, watching as she opened a bottle of sesame oil she'd obviously bought earlier and poured a fine stream into the pan.

'Love it,' she said, echoing the words he'd said earlier, but turning to smile at him at the same time.

Tears—if they had been tears—now gone.

The pan sizzled as she slid the sliced chicken in and tossed it around so it would cook quickly. The vegetables followed, more sizzling, more tossing and turning.

She pulled her shopping bag towards her with her free hand, and half turned to him.

'I've cheated with the rice. Can you cut the top off the packet and microwave it for two minutes for me, please?'

He put down his beer and lifted the packet.

'Chilli and coconut, my favourite,' he said, as he did his part in the dinner preparation. 'I've come to regard microwave rice as one to the world's great inventions.'

She grinned at him, then added a variety of sauces to the stir-fry—small amounts but the aroma made the dish come alive.

'Right, rice into bowls, some eating utensils, and we're done,' she said, turning off the gas beneath the pan and raising her beer to her lips again.

Her eyes were shining, with pleasure now, he was sure, and as he watched the pale skin on her throat move as she swallowed the beer, a feeling in his gut told him this cohabitation might not be such a good idea.

But as they ate, sitting at the small table on the balcony, the moon silvering the sea, and the soft shushing of the waves the only noise, Andy found himself enjoying the company, the laughter Sam brought with the stories of her travels, and the allure of his beautiful companion, fine skin pale in the moonlight, stray strands of red-gold hair tumbling in long curls to her shoulders.

They talked of many things beyond her travels—the hospital, Andy's time in the US—but never Nick, for all he'd been an important part of both their lives. She thought Andy's conversation had swerved that way from time to time, but she'd turned the question or remark away, not yet ready to discuss this part of their past.

And aware she might never be able to...

Except she should—had to really—or it would fester and ruin any chance of a friendship between them.

She took a deep breath and launched right into it.

'That night at the hospital, Andy. I was upset when you said Nick would never have spee—'

'I should never have said it,' he interrupted. 'Never said anything so hurtful to you. Since we offered you the job, I've had this last month to think about how to apologise, trying to work out what—'

She reached out and touched his lips with one finger to stop his words.

'Me first,' she said, looking directly into his eyes, desperate to see understanding there, though at the moment there was only concern.

'I loved Nick to distraction,' she said quietly, 'but later I grew to hate our marriage. Not Nick—the love was still there always—but I hated what I'd let myself become, hated that I'd given so much of myself away to be what he wanted me to be, to fit into *his* life the way he wanted me to—the way *he* felt a wife should.'

She paused and looked down into her lap where her hands were tightly clasped, fingers twined into each other as she struggled with the emotion of those days.

'But that day—in the car—it suddenly got too much and the temper I was sure I'd conquered just erupted again, and I threw all the unkind and hurtful things I could find at him, at the man I loved...'

Another silence and she looked into Andy's face again.

It told her nothing, and a cold certainty that she'd ruined any friendship they'd had and the one they might have had in the future spread through her.

But she had to finish.

'You were right,' she said, almost gabbling the words to get them said. 'I probably did cause the accident. I was as angry as I've ever been, yelling at him—him yelling back at me, both unwilling to give an inch. Then, suddenly it was over, a loud bang, and I was in hospital, Nick dead...'

She bowed her head, so he didn't see the tears—tears of pain for what else she'd lost that day.

'So you were spot on,' she finished, battling to keep her voice steady. 'Nick wouldn't have broken the speed limit, but he was as angry as I was, hurt and hurtful.'

She waited, praying silently that Andy would understand, wondering why life had to be so complicated.

But all he did was reach one hand across the table and squeeze her fingers.

Then he smiled, a weary, tired smile but one that still lit up his eyes.

'Oh, Sam, you shouldn't still be blaming yourself. I know I made things so much worse for you with my cruel, thoughtless words. And I've been wondering for a month how I could apologise to you. I had no right to say that to you—to hurt you further. Of course it wasn't your fault—you weren't driving, Nick was, and no matter the provocation *he* was the one speeding.'

He took both her hands in his now, and added, 'Can you forgive me? Can we be friends?'

She squeezed his fingers.

'Friends,' she said.

They sat a little longer, their hands still clasped, until Sam began to feel uncomfortable.

'You should be in bed,' she told him, needing to get away, to think about what had just happened between them, but first and foremost to remove her fingers, which seemed to be quite happy sitting there in his light clasp.

* * *

Andy had been trying to ignore their tangled fingers—ignore the tension rising in his body.

He stood up, probably a little too abruptly.

'I should, and so should you,' he said, clamping his lips together as beer and a single glass of wine had weakened his resistance, and the suggestion they could share a bed threatened to escape his lips.

As if, given how she'd just said she still loved Nick... Or *had* still loved him?

He brought reality back with talk of work—safe talk.

'I did tell you, didn't I, that we'll be working together? Same shifts for the first few days, just until you settle in and get to know our routines and procedure protocols. Basic stuff, but I always found it difficult moving hospitals, so it seemed like a good idea.'

'That's great!' Sam said, a bright smile underlining the words. 'So, what time do we need to leave?'

Her enthusiasm *and* the smile made him wonder if it had been all *that* great an idea, but he battled on.

'We'll leave about seven-thirty,' he said, forcing the distraction of this beautiful woman away with practical words. 'See you then?'

CHAPTER THREE

'SEE YOU THEN?'

The words echoed in Sam's head as she made her way to her bedroom.

Did he not eat breakfast before he left for work?

And what was she supposed to do?

She remembered how she'd hated staying with a friend for the first time, never sure when to get out of bed—would everyone be up, or would she wake them?

And she'd certainly need breakfast but could she just open and shut cupboards in Andy's kitchen until she found breakfast-type food?

Not that she regretted him leaving so suddenly. Something had shifted between them after they'd talked about Nick. It was as if the breeze had strengthened in some way and caused vibrations in her body, a sense so fine she knew it had to be imagined.

Or hoped it had to be imagined...

Yet Andy's abrupt departure had eased that tension at least, although he'd left her wondering just what it was she felt.

Andy was just Andy—a friend from years back—and his having her to stay was nothing more than a sign of that.

But, practically, could they get back to the easy friend-ship they'd had when she'd first met him? From the way he'd spoken, he'd obviously regretted the harsh words he'd said to her after the accident, so she could put that behind her and go forward.

In friendship... Something, she realised now, she wouldn't like to lose.

She closed her bedroom door and was pulling off her T-shirt when there was a light tap from outside.

'I should have said there's plenty of food in the pan-try and refrigerator, or there's a café on ground level that opens early to do breakfasts.'

She moved closer to the door, awareness of him just outside prickling her skin.

'Thanks,' she said. 'The café sounds good!'

She was close enough now to press her hand against the wood, aware he was just as close on the other side.

Was his hand also against the door?

Did she want it to be?

Did *he* want it to be?

She waited, wondering if he'd suggest they eat break-fast in the café together.

Should *she* suggest it?

But all she heard was a shuffle of feet on carpet and a quiet, 'Goodnight!'

She stayed where she was, hand on the door, trying to disentangle the various emotions this nothing of a con-versation had just stirred up in her.

Had she *wanted* him to come in?

She shook her head to that one, although she wasn't totally convinced.

Had *he* wanted her to ask him in?

Well, on that point she had no idea at all, but would

guess not. Andy was far too…proper, really for something so crass…

They were going to work together—be colleagues—and relationships with colleagues grew muddled. She and Nick had discovered that.

Nick.

She'd thought three years would have made it easier to think about him—even talk about him—but the resentment and anger she'd begun to feel towards the end of their marriage had surfaced again when she'd started talking earlier. Perhaps it was best to leave things as they were…

She moved away from the door, stripped off her clothes and stepped under the shower in the little en suite bathroom.

But once in bed, a book propped on her knees, she wondered again about her agreement to stay with Andy—if only for a short time…

She did have breakfast in the café but ate alone—fruit toast and strong tea. No sign of Nick, no sound of him in the apartment before she'd left it.

But that was explained when she returned, and he was in the kitchen, mixing up some type of green sludge—presumably a healthy smoothie—a beach towel wrapped around his waist and his bare chest still damp in patches from an early morning swim.

She'd walk to work in future, she decided then and there. That way she wouldn't have to work out why that bare chest, tanned and sculpted by the swimming and whatever other exercise he did, had caused a hitch in her breathing, and a warmth to fill her body.

'I can walk to the hospital today,' she said, the words shooting out of her mouth. 'It'll do me good.'

He swallowed a mouthful of his green sludge and shook his head.

'I'll be five minutes,' he told her, 'I've had my shower, and—'

Dear Heaven, he was naked under that towel!

The warmth became heat, which she knew would be showing in her cheeks.

'No, I need the exercise, and it will be good to get a feel for the place.'

She grabbed the little backpack, checked the keys were in it, and with a casual wave of her hand escaped out the door.

What she really needed was a real-estate office or to start searching online for somewhere else to live.

No way could she continue to live with Andy now he'd started to affect her the way he did. Neither could she really find another man—just a friend with benefits—to ease her frustration, not while she was living with Andy. *That* would be far too awkward!

She needed to move out, find somewhere of her own. Somewhere she could think about the future, put Nick behind her for ever, and, in the classic phrase, move on!

How had she got herself into this?

But as she walked up onto the top of the next hill and looked north this time, to the river's mouth and beyond it to the sweeping, golden beach and brilliant, dark blue ocean, a sense of peace stole over her.

Coming here *had been* a good decision.

And having a friend—for that was all Andy was—to show her around was also a good thing.

She walked on, breathing in the sea air, her feet beating out a rhythm that echoed in her head—Andy is a friend, Andy is a friend...

Rosa, the three-year-old with measles, was their first stop, after being alerted by a nurse that her condition hadn't improved.

'In fact, it's worsened,' Sam said as she read through the chart, while Andy bent over the cot.

'Yes,' he said. 'The night duty doctor phoned, and we discussed using the cooling pads.'

Sam had been looking at the small pads on Rosa's wrists, neck and temples, white against the raw redness of the rash that now covered her body.

'We're just getting new ones for the inside of her elbows,' the nurse explained, 'and her father's been here all night.'

She pointed to the big adjustable chair that could be tipped back to allow someone in it to at least doze.

'He's gone home to see his other children and take them to their local GP for vaccinations, then he'll be back.' She paused. 'He's devastated,' she said. 'Blames himself.'

Sam took one glance at Andy's face and stepped into the conversation.

'Some people genuinely believe the vaccination could harm their child. They fear it, no matter how much education we do.'

Andy shook his head. 'Were you always Little Miss Sunshine, refusing to see any bad in people?' he said, but it was more a tease than a sarcastic remark.

She grinned at him. 'I try,' she said.

They moved on to the boy with the burnt feet, Jonah.

He was sleeping, and as Andy studied his chart, Sam looked at the bandages and shook her head.

'How on earth can you burn the bottom of your feet?' she asked, and it was Andy's turn to smile.

'He lives near the beach and, apparently, he was clever enough to know he'd probably end up in serious trouble if he started a fire in the scrub on the headland. So he decided to experiment with a small one on a sandy patch hidden in amongst the rocks at the point. Had a great time, then his mother called him for dinner, and he covered it over with sand.'

'And walked on it?' Sam guessed.

'Worse,' Andy said. 'He stamped the sand down to make sure the fire was out.'

Sam shook her head. 'His poor parents,' she said. 'They must wonder what on earth he'll get up to next.'

They discussed his treatment—the worst of the wounds had been debrided, and both feet were now bound in bandages to prevent infection. Given his improvement, he could go into a general children's ward later that day.

Together they checked the most seriously ill children, three of them in isolation rooms following chemotherapy. Then Andy excused himself to attend a department heads' meeting, and Sam was left to visit the other children—twenty-three in all, quite a number for a provincial city's ICU.

'They come in from all the outlying areas,' the nurse with her explained. 'The district hospitals don't have the specialists or Intensive Care.'

'Certainly not as up to date as this place,' Sam said, constantly surprised by the facilities in the unit.

A loud beep took both of them to the small alcove

where the child with RSV lay limply in his cot. One glance at the bedside monitor told Sam what was happening. His struggle to breathe, even with the ventilation, had caused his overworked heart to stop beating.

As the nurse pressed the button for a crash cart, Sam started chest compressions, the heel of her hand on the little breast bone, pressing hard and counting.

'Remove his mask for a minute and suction his trachea, in case the oxygen isn't getting through' she said to the nurse, as Andy, no doubt alerted to the crisis, appeared.

'His chest is rising and falling so the ventilator is keeping him oxygenated.'

Andy felt for a pulse, shook his head.

'Epinephrine?' Sam asked, and he shook his head again.

'There are so many questions about the use of it in the long term these days,' he said. 'It will probably restart his heart but could also cause brain damage. We'll shock him. You've got his weight?'

The nurse read it out from the chart and Sam watched as Andy translated it to voltage, using four joules per kilogram. The nurse was already attaching miniature pads to the small chest while Andy set the machine.

They stood clear and the little body jerked, Sam bending over him ready to begin chest compressions again, although the steady heart-rate lines were already running across the monitor.

It had been a heart-stopping moment—literally for the child—and the tension had somehow thickened the air in the room, while all eyes remained on the monitor, dreading they'd see that line waver.

Sam turned to practical matters, beginning compressions again, aware that continuing compressions for a couple of minutes helped the failing heart regain its normal momentum.

The nurses were cleaning up and wheeling the crash cart away, but Andy continued to study the boy.

'We need to go back in his history to see if there was any suggestion of an abnormality in his heart from birth.' He shook his head before answering his own question. 'Surely not. Premmies are always tested every which way, scanned and checked on an almost daily basis.'

Sam smiled to herself. Back when she'd first met Nick and Andy, and had worked with Andy when she'd been on a month's student placement and he a junior registrar, she'd often heard him debating his thoughts aloud.

'What about an atrial septum defect?' she suggested. 'They can sometimes be so small they're not picked up until adulthood, although they do affect the lungs as well as the heart.'

Andy smiled at her, which, given the situation, shouldn't have had the slightest effect on her, but when he added, 'I knew I'd got you here for a reason,' she felt a flush of pride.

'We'll let the little fellow rest for an hour,' he continued, while she told herself it really *was* pride, not something else that had caused the heat, 'then see what an ultrasound can find.'

'They're often picked up in adults with a murmur,' Sam said, concentrating on their small patient and sticking the buds of her stethoscope in her ears. 'If it was audible it would have been picked up before now, but I'll just have a listen in case the stoppage made it clearer.'

She blew on the pad to warm it, then pressed it gently to the little chest, hearing the beat of his heart, steady and regular now, and perhaps just a whisper of something else.

Andy listened too, but shook his head. 'We'll leave it for the ultrasound.'

He paused, thoughtful again. 'Although if it does show something up, we then have a decision to make—or the heart specialists will.'

'Operate to close it, or just leave it and watch?'

He nodded, frowning now at the child who'd had such a bad start to his life.

They checked the rest of their patients, including a large lad of twelve who looked out of place in the PICU.

'He took a knock on the football field, lost consciousness, then had a grand mal seizure,' Andy explained. 'The neurologist who admitted him wanted him monitored for forty-eight hours before he does an EEG to see if there's a likelihood of recurrent seizures.'

He watched Sam flicking through the lad's chart, pleased he had such good support from his number two, even though working with Sam felt disorientating in some way. For so long she'd just been Nick's girl and that's the way he'd forced himself to think of her from the time they'd started going out together—Nick's girlfriend, Nick's partner, Nick's wife.

But Nick had been lost to both of them and now she was just Sam—a woman he'd been attracted to, and, he rather thought, still was...

And he'd been stupid enough to ask her to stay!

'His CT scan showed no visible damage,' she said, glancing up at him with a flash of pale green eyes. 'No bleeds or clots, no abnormalities that could have caused it, so it was likely the result of the concussion.'

He nodded, aware some response was needed, but—

You've got a patient! an inner voice said sternly, and he turned his full attention on the boy, asking him simple questions, noticing his patient's growing exasperation.

'And before you ask, I don't know who the prime minister is, and I didn't know it before either. It's a stupid question,' the lad said.

'So, tell me about your mates instead,' Andy suggested, and listened while the boy rattled off the names of his friends and gave them brief descriptions of each of them.

Andy smiled at him. 'I don't think there's much wrong with your brain, and the EEG—that's just short for electroencephalogram, which you must admit is a bit of a mouthful—will show if there's likely to be a recurrence, and you'll need to be on medication to stop it happening again.'

'But that would mean no more football,' the lad complained.

'No football for four weeks anyway,' he told the lad.

'Try tennis—it's much better for your head,' Sam suggested, but a little frown between her eyebrows made Andy wonder what was bothering her.

'Let's get a coffee,' he suggested as they left the boy to his video game. 'We'll talk about the children we've seen and you can tell me what you think.'

He led her into the small, comfortable staffroom and turned on the coffee machine.

'You okay?' he asked, carefully not looking at her but aware of her presence.

Aware of *her*...

Wondering if he'd made a mistake in appointing her

when there was a close connection between them and he'd always been attracted to her.

Then reminding himself he couldn't have not employed her. She had been far and away the best candidate.

Wondering, also, why she hadn't answered.

It had been the kind of question that usually got a reply immediately.

So he had to turn, *had* to look at her, had to put up with the disturbances her presence was causing him, because she *was* the best and his patients deserved that.

'*Are* you okay?' he asked this time.

She smiled at him, but it was such a pathetic effort he forgot about the coffee, and his personal concerns, and sat down beside her on the couch.

'What is it?' he said, trying to sound gently persuasive but missing it by a mile.

Even to him the question sounded abrupt to the point of rudeness, but it had been the best he could do when every fibre in his being was telling him to put his arm around her—tell her that whatever it was they'd work it out.

Hold her...

Comfort her...

That might be what she needed right now, but was it what *he* wanted?

Forget that, think about her. It's what a friend would do—any friend.

But *were* they friends?

They'd certainly made peace between them...

She smiled again, a better effort, and added a half-laugh.

'Stupid, really,' she said. 'But I was looking at young Nathan and wondering if I could let my child play football.'

She studied him for a moment before adding, 'When you've got children—a family of your own—how do you make those decisions? Do they worry constantly, every parent, or is it worse for us because we see what *can* happen?'

He thought of the children he'd probably never have— the women who hadn't wanted to risk having a child with him—the scars that had made him stop thinking about a family, about any permanent relationship...

'I'm not sure,' he said, 'about other parents but I think it's probably easier not to have them, then you don't have to worry at all. That's where I've got to in my thinking.'

He knew it was a flippant answer but he didn't want to go into all of that with Sam when she was obviously upset.

Thrusting the confusion of thoughts out of his head, Andy returned to his coffee-making. But he *had* to think about Sam's questions because there'd been genuine concern in her voice, as if having a family was important to her and she'd need to know how to handle things.

Had she and Nick been arguing about that?

Nick certainly wouldn't have wanted a family—it would have diverted the attention from him. He chose instead to just answer her original question.

'About sport, that lad could just as easily have fallen out of a tree and hit his head or tripped at home. I guess most parents just do what they think is best at the time and hope their children survive childhood.'

She made a sound that could have been agreement but continued to look pensive—even worried.

He carried over a coffee, realising as he placed it down in front of her that he hadn't even asked how she took it, and wondering why he'd remembered her coffee preferences from the past.

'You remembered?' she said, looking up at him, her eyes wide with surprise.

'It wasn't a hard choice to remember,' he said. 'Black no sugar.'

He carried his own coffee over, along with a tin of assorted biscuits.

'Like white, skimmed milk and half a teaspoon of sugar?'

She spoke lightly, but he heard a hint of tension beneath the words and wondered, not for the first time, how she'd ever managed to live with Nick's little peculiarities.

She'd loved him to distraction, she'd said, but had come to hate who she'd become in fitting into his mould of her.

He understood that. He'd known Nick nearly all his life and had accepted his pedantic ways—for the most part—as simply Nick being Nick.

But he'd been able to walk away; to find someone else to play with, someone else to discuss their studies with, when Nick had become too controlling.

Sam had not only loved the man, she'd been married to him. Hard to walk away from that.

Impossible, Andy guessed, to find someone else...

He watched as she dunked a biscuit in her coffee and sucked on the soggy end, drank some coffee, *then* looked across the table at him.

'You've probably read the latest studies on OCD, linking it to serotonin issues,' she said quietly. 'I tried to persuade Nick to try some anti-anxiety medication, which works for some people, but, as you know, he really couldn't see he had a problem.'

Which made Andy remember the accident, and his own personal conviction, at the time, that Nick would never have driven above the legal limit, could never speed—it was part of his make-up.

Perfectionism was how Nick had termed it.

So, now the fact they'd had an argument had been revealed, rather than solving things, it had made Andy more curious. It must have been about something really really important, drastic even, for Nick to have reacted the way he had.

Had it been about them having a family?

Sam had finished her coffee. 'Back to work?' she asked.

'There's no rush. The staff know where we are. And we *did* come here to discuss the patients.'

He hesitated, wanting to ask how she was finding things but knowing it was far too early for such a question.

And, anyway, what he really wanted to know was more about her—about her life over the last three years—and how she felt about Nick now. Was she still mourning him?

Well, he wanted to know everything really.

Which was so unsettling a thought he stood up, collected her cup and the biscuits and made a business of washing the dishes, aware of her standing, moving towards the door—every nerve ending in his skin alive to her movement...

Weirdest coffee break she could remember, Sam thought, leaving her cup on the table because carrying it over to the taps would have meant getting close to Andy again.

She escaped from the comfortable room to the routine

movement on the ward but couldn't escape her thoughts. Thoughts that must have been written clearly on her face earlier because Andy had been so concerned—so caring—when he'd sat her down and asked if she was okay.

Which she really wasn't, considering it was so close to the anniversary...

But she'd welcomed the coffee break, sure they'd be discussing patients or talking about the hospital in general—even gossiping, which was the most common pursuit in staffroom coffee breaks. All of which would have got her mind off her own bleak thoughts.

But, no, somehow, without really speaking, they'd ended up discussing Nick.

And children—that had been the other topic, and a revealing one. Andy had spoken lightly but it sounded as if he'd, for some reason, already decided not to have children.

For a moment she wondered why, then realised all this was just another way to keep her mind off the upcoming date.

Work! That was a far better answer.

Her first stop was at the nurses' station to check that families of children who might have been in contact with young Rosa had been alerted by the hospital staff.

'Yes, we've got on to the private day care place she went to twice a week. Only five kids in all, and the woman who runs the place said she's spoken to all the parents, but we got names and telephone numbers and spoke to them again ourselves.'

The nurse—Damian, his name tag read—frowned. 'It's not the children I've been worried about but the old people,' he said.

'Old people?' Sam echoed, as she felt Andy materialise by her side.

'Yes. Rosa also went to a playgroup. The nanny took her one day each week. It was run in a nursing home. Apparently, the residents loved having the little ones running around.'

Sam closed her eyes, considering how quickly something like measles might spread through such a place.

'It might not be too bad,' Andy said, coming to stand beside her. 'A lot of older people have the measles vaccine when they're expecting their first grandchild. It's actually recommended by most GPs.'

'But would they all remember whether they've had it or not? And can we really vaccinate everyone in the place, given that many of them would have complex health problems?'

Sam had turned towards Andy as she spoke so read her own concern in his face.

'I'll get on to the people at Infections Diseases Control—talk to them,' he said. 'But I think it's going to be safer to vaccinate them all.'

'Is this really our problem?' another nurse asked, and Andy and Sam both turned back towards her.

'Who else's would it be?' Sam demanded. 'It's not as if we have to do the actual work, but we need to get authorities alerted to what's going on. And they, in turn, can make the decisions, even publicise the risk if they feel it's necessary.'

The nurse nodded, though she still seemed unconvinced.

'It's a very real risk,' Sam told her. 'A measles outbreak—even with a limited number of patients—almost inevitably results in some deaths.'

She turned away, disturbed by her own words, wanting to go back and check on Rosa.

And, if she was honest, wanting to put some space between herself and Andy, who'd been standing beside her for far too long. This awareness thing she was feeling would disrupt her work if she didn't get it under control. It wasn't as if Andy would ever be interested in her, given how he'd seen her role in the accident.

And hadn't he said that the reason he'd asked her to stay had been because she was the widow of his best friend?

Hardly a romantic invitation.

Rosa was still febrile. The drugs and cooling packs would be keeping her temperature below a really dangerous level, but she was still a very sick little girl.

Sam watched the monitors. Her heart rate was a little elevated but it would be, blood oxygen level fine, but it was being helped by the nasal cannula providing supplemental oxygen. A tube dripped fluid and drugs into her little body, but what else could they do?

She knew this was the problem with choosing to work with seriously ill children—some of them could not be saved. But deep inside she felt that wasn't good enough. They *all* deserved a chance at life—something her child had never had...

A nurse distracted her with a message about one of the chemo patients, and she was pleased to turn her attention from such dismal thoughts. She met the oncology consultant in the child's room, and from then on it seemed as if the world had conspired to keep her mind fully focussed on work.

Sometime in the early afternoon she grabbed a cup of

tea and an apple in the staffroom and was looking forward to the end of the day when she could finally relax.

But Rosa's condition had worsened and neither she nor Andy felt happy about leaving the child. Andy made the excuse of paperwork while she stayed with the father in the room, bathing the little girl's body with a cool, damp cloth.

'She's not going to make it, is she?' the father asked at one stage, and Sam couldn't answer. He sat back in his chair and bent forward, elbows on knees, face bowed into his upturned hands, his despair seeping into the room.

Rosa died at four minutes past midnight in her father's arms, Sam standing with a protective arm around the man's shoulders, tears glistening in her eyes.

After a few minutes the duty doctor and nurses moved in quietly, taking care of both the father and the formalities.

Andy slipped his arm around Sam's shoulders and led her firmly out to his car, aware of a terrible tension in her body.

But as he walked around to the driver's door, he looked up at the star-bright sky and wondered what the hell was going on. He'd understood Sam's desire to stay and care for Rosa, but when he'd forced her to leave the child for long enough to eat earlier in the evening he'd seen the tension in her body, and he'd had the sense of someone holding themselves together with only the greatest difficulty.

Now she sat, rigid in the seat beside him, her hands knotted in her lap, and instinct told him to get her home—unfamiliar though that home might be. She needed to be somewhere away from the hospital, somewhere he could put his arm around her shoulders when he asked her what was wrong.

But they only made it to the elevator of his apartment block before he saw the tears on her cheeks, so he held her as they rose, steered her gently into the apartment, and enfolded her against his body as soon as they were inside.

'Tell me,' he said quietly, sliding his fingers into her hair to tug her head back gently so he could see her face, flushed and tear-stained.

She looked at him, so much pain in her eyes—pain he couldn't understand—but still he felt it. He tried to ask, to get her to talk explain, but found he couldn't speak, words weren't enough.

He brushed his lips across hers, murmuring her name, aware this might be a very wrong response yet feeling her take something from it—feeling passion, heat, and some unable-to-be-spoken agony as she kissed him back.

Somewhere in his head a voice was yelling warnings, but his body felt her urgency and responded to it.

The kiss deepened, her hands now on his back, tugging at his shirt so she was touching his skin—cold hands, cold fingers digging into his skin, dragging him closer and closer. His hands exploring now, feeling the dip of her waist, the curve of her hips, moving lower to press her into him.

Then clothes were shed in an undignified scramble, Sam pushing his hands away and quickly peeling garments off herself.

They kissed again, and that magic moment of skin touching skin swept over Andy as he guided them both towards his bedroom, to the rumpled, unmade bed he'd had no time to straighten that morning.

* * *

In some dim recess of her brain Sam was aware this was madness—they had to go on living together—but right now, on the anniversary of her own baby's death, she needed the release—the oblivion—of sex.

So, as Andy's lips moved down her neck, as his hand grasped her breast, fingers teasing at the nipple, she groaned with the sheer, mindless pleasure of it, bit into his shoulder, and pressed her body hard against his.

They fell together onto the bed, mindlessly engrossed in pleasure—in pleasing each other and being pleased, teasing and being teased—until Sam could take no more and guided him into her body, revelling at how natural it was, moving in an age-old rhythm that eventually brought with it total release.

A long time later, it seemed, Sam woke to find Andy propped on his elbow, looking down at her, and as she watched, he reached out and wiped a tear from her cheek, holding it up for her inspection.

She rubbed her hands across her face, hoping to obliterate any more tell-tale signs there might be, then slid carefully out of his bed, wanting to take a rumpled sheet to wrap around her naked body but feeling that would make her look as if she was ashamed.

Which she probably was, but right now leaving was the best thing she could do, before he started asking questions.

Andy was far too astute for his own good!

But at the door she did turn to say thank you, adding honestly, as heat flooded her cheeks, 'I really needed that.'

He gave her a mocking smile that didn't quite hide the hurt she saw in his eyes.

'Any time. Only too happy to oblige.'

She fled, not wanting to make things more complicated than they already were. What they'd shared had been surprisingly intense and fulfilling for first time lovers, but that was all it could be. For all she knew, he had a woman in his life already.

And having a relationship with a colleague wasn't a good idea.

She showered, dressed for work, and came out to find him already gone. No doubt to the beach for his morning swim.

Images of his naked body danced before her eyes and she knew she didn't want to be around when he returned, even though he'd not be entirely naked. She grabbed her things and headed for the café. Avocado and smoked salmon on toast sounded good, and if she kept her mind on food, and then on work, she wouldn't be thinking about how good it had felt to be held in Andy's arms—*or* what today's date meant to her and how hard she was going to find it…

CHAPTER FOUR

THEY WORKED THROUGH the day, carefully polite with each other but equally careful not to get too close. Fortunately, it was busy, some children transferred back to children's wards while new patients came in.

Two were high priority, one an oncology patient who'd received a stem-cell transplant from a non-family member and needed a total isolation room, which meant anyone entering the room, staff included, needed mask, gloves, booties and a long gown.

It was the mask Sam was having trouble with, in the small airlock area outside the isolation room. The strings had somehow become entangled with her hair and as someone else came in, she closed her lips tightly to capture the swear words that wanted to escape.

'Here, let me!'

His voice, right there behind her, stopped her breath, and the touch of his strong hands releasing her fingers and the tape from her hair stole her ability to breathe.

'It didn't mean anything, you know that, don't you?' The words tumbled out with a desperation she couldn't control. 'Can we forget it happened? I was upset, overwrought. The clock ticked past midnight and it just brought it all back. It's the anniversary, you see.'

He must have finished untangling her mask for now both hands rested on her shoulders, drew her back against his body.

'What happened?' he said gravely, and all the pent-up anxiety left her body in a long sigh.

'I can't talk about it today. But thank you, Andy,' she said quietly, then she stepped away because, contrary to what she had said, being held against him was extremely comforting.

Even enticing?

Definitely exciting to many parts of her body.

But she had to focus on work.

The small boy was Jake Andrews, and as Sam entered the room, he was sleeping. To one side sat the dedicated nurse, while on the other side his mother slept, not in a comfortable chair but on a narrow hospital bed, as sterile as the room itself.

While Andy examined their patient, Sam read through the notes, sighing again to herself when she realised what this child and his family had already been through. Superstitiously, she crossed her gloved fingers, hoping this time the treatment would succeed.

'I don't know that crossing gloved fingers works as well as un-gloved ones,' Andy murmured to her a little later as they stripped off their protective gear and threw it into the various bins.

She smiled and although her own body was asking what harm there'd be in a purely sexual relationship with him for a while, her brain was yelling to forget such folly. Andy hadn't the slightest interest in her. In fact, given how he'd felt about Nick's accident she was surprised that he seemed to tolerate her at all, let alone offer her a bed.

Although, as he'd said to her that first afternoon, she *was* the widow of his best friend...

And if that reminder filled her with a deep sadness, well, that was her problem.

She left the changing room, but Andy was close behind her.

'Our next arrival, Grant Williams, was riding his bicycle home from a mate's last night and was knocked over by a hit-and-run driver. It took a while to stabilise him, both at the scene and in the ED.'

'After which,' Sam guessed, 'he spent a good deal of time in Theatre getting put back together again.'

He'd also been put into an induced coma, Sam discovered when they reached his room, where his two anxious parents sat.

'Did someone speak to you about his condition?' she asked quietly, although both parents looked too shell-shocked to have taken much in.

'Broken pelvis, broken leg, fractured shoulder, cracked head,' the father recited, and was about to continue when Sam intervened.

'Did they tell you he's been put into an induced coma so he's deeply asleep, unconscious really, which will give his body, and particularly his brain, a little time to recover.'

'Someone said something,' the mother said quietly, and Sam smiled at her.

'What it means is that he won't regain consciousness until the specialists think he's well enough to cope with it all. That won't be for a few days, so although I know you want to be near him, you're better off going home and getting some rest. One of you might like to come back a little later just to sit and talk quietly to him, smooth his skin. But when the specialists decide to bring him out of the coma, we'll contact you so you can both be here, and you'll be the first people he sees.'

'What if we don't want to go home? If we both want to stay with our boy?'

The aggression in the man's voice suggested he was already exhausted so Sam knew she'd have to tread very carefully.

She was assembling her most persuasive arguments when she heard someone come into the room behind her and knew it was Andy.

'Of course you may stay if you wish,' he said, speaking directly to the father. 'But it's likely to be three or four days—perhaps longer—before the specialists decide to reverse the drug that's helping his body and mind deal with what happened. When that decision is made, we'll let you know so you can be here to reassure him he's safe.'

The father nodded and put his arm around his wife.

'Maybe the doctor's right, love,' he said. 'We'll be no good to him if we're exhausted, now, will we?'

She gave a wan smile but stood up at his urging, and after the lightest of kisses on her son's pale cheek left the room.

Sam was wondering why it still was—in a world where women often outnumbered men as doctors—that a man's explanation of a situation still held more weight. With other men, at least.

Musing on this, she missed the first bit of Andy's conversation.

'So I've a three-day conference in Sydney from tomorrow, but the welcome stuff starts this evening.'

She caught up as they followed the couple out the

door. 'I wouldn't go if I felt you still needed me here, but you'll be fine.'

He walked away, paused, then turned to look at her, hesitating, before adding, 'I'll leave the car keys on the kitchen table—use it if you like.'

Another glance her way. 'And definitely use it if you're called out at night. I'll get a cab to the airport.'

Although, when she considered them again, those two looks towards her had told her everything, as well as his abrupt departure to a conference in Sydney.

He was ruling a line under what had happened between them the previous night, just as she had done earlier.

But would three days be enough for her body to get with the programme?

To stop fizzing with excitement at the sound of his voice and flaring with heat if he accidentally brushed up against her?

It had been bad enough discovering she was physically attracted to Andy when they'd met again, but it was far worse now, when every square inch of her skin knew the feel of his skin against it and seemed determined *not* to forget that night.

And yet...

Andy walked out through the front entrance to his apartment building, confident he'd find a cab cruising past. Confident, also, that he was doing the right thing—getting right away from the beguiling woman who was his best friend's widow,

He'd never been good with calendar dates so he hadn't had a clue that it had been the torturous pain of loss that had driven Sam into his arms the previous night. She'd been so willing, so hot really, responding with a ferocity he'd been foolish enough to believe was because she felt as much attraction to him as he did to her.

The intensity of the experience had stunned him, to the extent that his body felt as if she'd imprinted herself on his skin.

Cursing quietly under his breath, he threw his overnight bag into the taxi, pleased he had the diversion of a trip to Sydney, although Antarctica might have been a better option. But a couple of days away from the distraction that was Sam would help him get his life back on track—get things into perspective again...

Possibly!

He shook his head, so lost in his memories of the passion they'd shared he barely heard the cabbie's conversation.

Something about football, perhaps?

Left to her own devices, Sam visited the rest of her patients, discussing each of them with the dedicated nurse on duty with the child.

Whoever had trained these nurses in the fairly new hospital had done an excellent job because all the ones she saw today—and had seen earlier—were really invested in their patients, showing empathy as well as caring.

It was a special job, nursing in a PICU, and although the majority of nurses who chose to work there were empathetic, she'd known a few who just did their job—and did it well—but stayed detached from the child and his or her family.

And she was thinking about this, why? she wondered when she sat down at her desk to write up some notes and check the medication orders.

She knew the answer.

Thinking about anything was better than thinking about the previous night—and the way she'd behaved.

Like a wanton hussy, her old secondary school teacher would have said. Throwing yourself into that man's arms...

But that man was Andy, and although she'd seen less of him after her marriage she'd always been impressed by his dedication to his work—impressed by him as a genuinely nice person.

In fact, it had been his decision to leave the hurly-burly of the Emergency Department that Nick had loved so much to work in Intensive Care and then Paediatric ICU that had influenced her own decision.

Though just why she was thinking of Andy on the anniversary of Nick's death, she wasn't sure. She pressed her hand against her flat stomach and forced her mind back to work.

A call from the nurse with the oncology patient killed any wayward thoughts and she went back to his room, gloved and gowned, and managed the mask herself this time before quietly opening the door.

Jake lay pale and wan on the bed, but a nasty rash was appearing on his torso.

'Have you called his oncologist? Sam asked, and the nurse nodded.

'It's most likely a reaction to one of the drugs he's on to suppress his immune system so his body doesn't reject the new stem cells, but I'll take some blood to test for infection.'

Sam was watching the monitor as she spoke, seeking any variation in the patterns of his heart rate or his blood oxygen level, listening to his chest, feeling the slightly raised nature of the rash.

She used a port in his left arm to extract some blood and labelled the three phials she'd taken while the nurse organised for someone to collect them from the changing room to get them to the laboratory as quickly as possible.

'Fluid overload,' Sam muttered to herself, and checked the drip to see how much fluid had gone into him since the last check, then his catheter bag to ensure he was getting rid of fluid.

Graft versus host disease was the most common complication and the rash could be a symptom of that. It was mostly seen within the first three months after a transplant but could occur up to three years afterwards.

She'd written up the information of all she'd done, including the tests she'd ordered, when the oncologist appeared and took the chart from her.

He was a silver-haired man with a tanned skin and a charming smile, and he spoke to young Jake like a family friend, reassuring the boy that they'd sort things out.

'What did you request with the bloods?' he asked Sam, turning away from the chart.

'Infection, low platelets, and any sign of organ failure,' she said, and he nodded.

'The results will be copied to me, and I'll be right back if they show anything. In the meantime, we might use a little more supplemental oxygen, and I'd suggest a simple mix of bicarbonate of soda and water on the rash to help ease the irritation.'

Sam smiled at him. 'It was my mother's panacea for all ills and certainly helped me survive chicken pox.'

The oncologist gave a theatrical shiver. 'Don't even

think of things like that. The poor lad has enough possible complications without introducing childhood diseases. I'm thinking he might need another blood transfusion, but we'll wait for the test results. Then, of course, there's a possibility the stem cells didn't take, and he'll need more of them.'

Sam looked at the frail figure lying on the bed and prayed that the rash was nothing more than a reaction to one of the drugs coursing through his body in the drip fluid.

The nurse was already speaking to someone to arrange the soothing liquid and Sam would have left to see other patients, but she caught sight of Jake's mother gowning up in the anteroom, and waited to speak to her, to update her on what was going on.

For parents of children who were up to the stage of trialling bone-marrow transplants to save their child's life, the hospital processes were well known. They'd had to cope with the highs and lows of the previous treatments and procedures and the hope and despair that came with each one.

For Jake's mother, this was just one more bridge to cross, her faith in finding a cure for him never wavering.

Could she have handled that as well as most of the parents she saw did? Sam wondered.

If her child had lived...

She shut the memory down, but not before tears had pricked her eyes.

Three years today. It was stupid to even think about it!

But at least Andy hadn't been around to see her momentary weakness...

Andy boarded the plane for the short flight to Sydney with a strange sense of relief. Sam had drawn a line under what had happened the previous evening, which was, he was almost certainly sure, a good thing.

So why was he feeling a nagging sense of...

What?

Regret?

Not exactly...

No, he wouldn't think about it—particularly not how she'd felt in his arms, or the heat of her body as he'd slid into her—her cries of passion as she'd clung to him in that final release.

Get your head straight, Andy.

This was Sam! She'd needed comfort, and he'd been there to give it to her.

A tightening of his stomach muscles suggested that he was damned glad he *had* been there. Heaven forbid, she might have gone off with anyone!

Not, he told himself sternly, that it would have been any of his business if she had. He'd known she was grieving for Rosa, the child who'd died. That was only natural, all of them felt an unnecessary loss like that very deeply, but on top of the date of her own loss...

No, he couldn't begin to imagine what her feelings had been, and furthermore it was time to stop this pointless speculation and concentrate on the reason he was on the plane.

Not to escape Sam but to hear one of the US's top PICU physicians speak about making the experience for families more comfortable.

He prided himself on how well they did it at his hospital. He'd been consulted about it as it was being built, and, having spent so much time in hospital with his patient, smiling sister, he knew just how uncomfortable places they could be, and he'd had a raft of ideas to offer the designers. And you could always learn something from other hospitals, even if it was what not to do.

But his focus was obviously shot to pieces for surely one of the first among any '*not* to do' lists of his own was take your best friend's widow to bed!

Even if she'd been so willing, so excited, in turn both tender and torturous and loving, so totally irresistible he'd lost himself in her, lost all inhibitions, and had responded with a passion he knew he'd never experienced before.

He was jolted out of his heated memories as the plane landed in Sydney, and he shut the memories away.

He was here to learn, to pick up ideas to take back to his hospital that hopefully would produce better outcomes for his patients and their families.

His and Sam's patients—and *that* was definitely the last time he would think about her.

Today...

It was weird returning to Andy's apartment without him being there.

Weird and definitely unsettling!

There'd been a small, discreet 'Manager' sign on the door on the ground-floor apartment, opposite the café, and she'd thought it wouldn't hurt to ask about an apartment—maybe there'd be a one-bedroomed, which was all she'd need.

She knocked on the door, which was opened almost immediately by a youngish man with a slightly unkempt look about him who was clutching a puffy black garbage bag in one hand.

'Sorry, just on my way to the bins. I can't put this down without spilling the lot, so would you like to wait, or maybe walk with me?'

'I'm happy to do either, but all I really wanted to ask was whether you had an apartment for rent. Just for me.'

She found she'd fallen in beside him as she spoke, so kept walking.

'One bedroom?' he asked.

'Well, that's all I'd really need.'

She'd sleep on the couch if her mother came, but, given her mother's life, it wasn't all that probable.

'Yeah, there's one available,' he said, leading her down a concrete stairwell into the basement garage. 'But we're coming up to the Christmas holidays when all the empty apartments double in price. I'm only the manager for about forty different owners—most of them absentee owners—and some of them only rent out over Christmas, because that pays the bills on the place and they can use it themselves any time over the rest of the year.'

'So I'd be paying double normal price?'

'From next weekend when the season starts, yes,' he said, rather gloomily.

Intrigued, Sam asked, 'You don't like the holiday season?'

He shook his head. 'I don't dislike it,' he said, 'but it's just so much extra work, and the young people I employ for the season as cleaners also want to have fun so they're not exactly reliable.'

They'd reached the bins, corralled behind a high wooden fence, and he lifted the lid of one to dump the bag, before turning to a nearby tap to wash his hands.

'I do have a couple of rooms in my place I let out as B and Bs, only the second B is a chit for the café across the hall. They each have an en suite bathroom and a small open kitchen-cum-sitting area with a hotplate and a microwave and TV and such. If that'd suit you?'

'I think that would be more than enough for me,' Sam told him, and was about to shake his hand on the deal when she thought of Andy. Would he think her ungrateful? Even rude?

'Can I let you know later?' she asked the manager as they emerged into the foyer once again.

'Sure, I'm Rod, by the way.'

Sam took his hand and shook it.

'Sam,' she said, and smiled at him.

'But you'd be living with a stranger—a man you don't even know,' Andy protested when she put the idea to him on his return on Saturday afternoon.

'I'm renting a room,' Sam corrected him. 'That's not exactly living with someone!'

'You could do that here,' he argued. 'Heaven knows, I don't need it, but you could pay rent if it would make you feel better.' He paused. 'It's because of what happened, isn't it?' he said, as grumpy as she'd ever heard the usually upbeat Andy.

'Not entirely,' she said. 'You know very well I've always intended to get my own place, and I like what I've seen of this area.' She hesitated. 'And, given you're the only person I know in this city, I thought it would be nice to be near you.'

'Just not in my apartment—in some other man's!'

Sam looked at him in disbelief. 'Andy, you're being ridiculous! The fact is, as Rod pointed out, summer holidays are a week away and rents on regular accommodation double for two months. He can't charge double for his rooms, so it works out well for me because it gives me a chance to settle in, get to know my way around, meet other people, make friends, then maybe, when the holidays end, find something permanent.'

She watched as he bit back the words she was sure he wanted to say, before muttering something about taking a shower and disappearing in the direction of his bedroom.

But did he *really* want her to stay?

Or was it simply a kindness to an old friend, something he was doing for Nick as much as her?

The question made her stomach hurt, as if, deep down, she'd wanted him to want her to stay for herself...

She shook her head, aware such thoughts were madness...

He *was* being ridiculous, and he knew it, but as Andy stalked off to his bedroom, it was all he could do to keep from grinding his teeth.

And his reason for this sudden, and quite irrational, anger?

He shook his head, not wanting to think about it, but still it gnawed away inside him, to the extent that he turned back towards the living room, where Sam stood at the window, silhouetted by the moon rising over the waters in front of her.

And, suddenly, he didn't want to argue with her— didn't want discord between them.

He walked closer, his footsteps on the timber floor causing her to half turn towards him.

'I thought it would be for the best,' she said, in such a small voice he knew he'd upset her with his tirade. 'I mean, it can't be helping your love life any, having me living with you. And maybe if I ever decide to chance such a thing again, it would be awkward for me as well.'

'What love life?' he snorted. 'That's not high on my

list of priorities! Anyway, how many intensivists do you know who can manage a relationship successfully?'

'Plenty!' she snapped, any hurt she may have felt burned off by sudden anger. 'And this entire conversation is stupid. You took me in when I had nowhere to stay and for that I'm grateful, but it was never meant to be for ever and, providing I don't see any evidence of rats when I look at Rod's rooms tomorrow, I'm moving on. I've only delayed because I thought it would be polite to discuss it with you first. Not that this conversation has had any resemblance to a discussion.'

And this time it was Sam who stalked off, leaving him standing by the tall windows, gazing out to sea.

He'd heard—even understood—her final, angry words, but it was something she'd said earlier that had snagged in his mind.

Something about 'should she ever decide to *chance* such a thing again'...

'Chance' was a strange word for her to have used.

It implied risk. Had her marriage to Nick not been the nuptial bliss Nick had always made it out to be?

Had she found it harder than he had realised to live with Nick's mild OCD?

Though had it really been mild?

He shook his head.

Questions to which, he was reasonably sure, he'd never find answers, yet for some unfathomable reason he'd have liked to know...

CHAPTER FIVE

THE ROOM ROD offered Sam had a view out over the ocean and she was immediately entranced.

The bedroom was small, divided, she realised, in some clever way to make room for the small sitting room, a few cupboards, refrigerator, sink and microwave tucked into a corner, and to Sam's delight, a small barbecue out on the balcony, along with a couple of easy outdoor chairs and a table.

'It's perfect,' she told Rod, beaming with delight. 'I'll take it.'

'You're supposed to ask how much the rent is,' Rod reminded her, and Sam shook her head.

'I'm sure it's not over my budget. Not that I have a budget.'

But they did discuss the rent, and a good deal besides, out on the balcony, with the fresh north-easterly sea breeze cooling the air around them.

'So, you work with Andy,' Ron said, and Sam nodded.

'He's an old friend of my dead husband,' she explained. 'And he took me in when I arrived to save me going to a hotel while I got my bearings.'

'Nice,' Rod said. 'He's a good man.'

Something about the conversation was making

Sam feel uncomfortable—talking about Andy with a stranger?—so she made the excuse that she'd need to pack her few things, took the keys Rod gave her and, after learning which key did what, she departed.

Andy, who'd been in a meeting when she'd left the hospital, was back when she walked in, new keys in her hand.

'Does your room have a lock?' he asked, looking at them dangling from her fingers.

She frowned at him, disturbed by the inference that she'd need a lock. To keep Rod out?

Surely not!

'You should change it,' Andy said, and Sam shook her head in disbelief.

'You think he'll come creeping into my room in the dead of night and ravish me?' she snapped, the anger she'd thought she'd learned to control sparking suddenly. 'I should be so lucky!'

Really shouldn't have said that, she muttered in her head as she strode towards her bedroom. It was just that Andy was being so darned unreasonable about this. He should be glad to be getting rid of her, not acting like her moral guardian!

She shut the bedroom door and leaned back against it, taking deep breaths to sweep away the anger he'd aroused, especially as the real reason she was moving out was because of him.

Well, not him as such, but the way she was beginning to feel about him—and seeing him at home as well as at work—well, it was just too much...

She had to pack.

She opened the door, intending to go out, find Andy, apologise for losing her temper then ask politely if she could borrow a suitcase for a few hours to stop her new clothes getting crumpled and wrinkly in her old backpack. But Andy was right there, outside the door, and her immediate reaction was not suspicion about his presence but a flood of attraction.

'I'm sorry!'

Their voices formed a chorus, but Andy recovered first.

'I don't know why I was upset,' he said. 'I guess I was kind of enjoying you being around. It's been a while since I've had company at home.'

Sam grinned at him.

'It's only been five days and you were away for two of them,' she pointed out, 'and, anyway, I'll still be around at work.'

He nodded but remained where he was—rooted in the passage.

Her turn to talk, obviously.

'I was wondering if I could borrow a suitcase just for this evening, to take my clothes down to Rod's.' She paused, before adding, 'And to say I'm sorry I lost my temper earlier.'

She tried a smile, but knew it was probably fairly pathetic. 'Every time I think I've conquered my wretched temper, something happens and I'm blowing up again.'

Another pause.

'Although you did provoke it, you must admit, talking about changing the locks!'

He laughed now, a joyous sound that made her toes curl inside her sneakers. She *so* had to get away from him, if only after work hours.

'So you're apologising but blaming me at the same time,' he teased, his eyes twinkling in such a way she had to forcibly clamp her hand to her side to stop herself reaching out and touching his face.

She *had* to move! Had to get away from this man who could have her hormones rioting with the twinkle in his eyes.

'I'll get you a case,' he was saying as he moved away from her, and she ran her hands through her unruly hair and clutched her head, trying to restore some balance to her mind in the hope it would do the same for her body.

He'd asked her to stay because she was Nick's widow and though he'd proved an exciting and satisfying lover when she'd thrown herself into his arms, that was no indication that he was in any way attracted to her.

In fact, the way he'd been so quick to agree with her about drawing a line under the incident proved that she was no more than an acquaintance—or friend at best...

And if that thought caused a tiny ache in her chest, then that was her problem, not his.

Andy dug into the back of his small storeroom, dislodging a broom and mop he rarely used because he was blessed with a cleaning man who came once a week, and left his often untidy apartment spotless.

Was it because they'd had sex that he'd been behaving irrationally about Sam moving out?

Great sex, admittedly, but that's all it had been...

He'd answered a need in her, for which she was grateful, but she'd made it very clear that that was that. Which was just as well as he was having a lot of trouble working out just how he felt about Sam.

He was definitely attracted to her, now more than ever, it appeared. But attraction usually—well, often—

led to love, and in his mind there was a huge blockage that would stop such a process.

Actually, there were two problems—the discomfort about her being his friend's widow, and the big one— what if she was still in love with Nick?

Would the latter explain her desperate need on the anniversary of his death?

She'd said she'd hated what she'd become as his wife, but she'd also said she'd loved him to distraction.

And the way she'd said it suggested the love part had been paramount, so probably she still loved him.

Enough to stop her loving someone else?

Hell's teeth, get the suitcase and take it to her. Stop trying to fathom what's going on in someone else's head when you can't work out what's going on in your own. And given the mess you've made of the love business in the past, it certainly shouldn't be entering the equation.

You've given up on it, remember? Twice burnt by it. Surely that was enough for any man to realise he was better off single—free to enjoy brief encounters with willing women who might come his way.

He grabbed the suitcase and backed out of the small room, then pushed the case down the corridor, but his mind was right back on Sam, only this time he was telling himself he was done thinking about her—done guessing about her marriage and Nick and whether she still loved him.

Telling himself the easiest way to find out was to ask.

Right!

March up to Sam and say, 'Are you still in love with Nick?'

Honestly, man, for a supposedly intelligent human being you haven't got a clue!

He knocked on her door.

'I'll just leave the case here,' he said, but before he had time to turn away she'd flung open the door.

'Don't rush off,' she said, clearing a space on the bed between small piles of clothing. 'I won't be long, and I thought I could take you to dinner at the café as a thank you for having me.'

'You don't have to do that,' he said, but he did go into the room, sitting down where she'd made a space for him on the bed, watching her as she efficiently cleared the bed of clothing and packed it into the suitcase.

Watching her and wondering...

'I was only too happy to give you a bed.'

She looked up at him from where she knelt, a question in her eyes.

'Because I was your best friend's widow,' she said. A statement not a question after all.

'More than that, Sam,' he said. 'We'd been friends, you and I, back when we all met.' Even to him that sounded weak—mawkish—so he quickly added, 'Besides which you were a new member of the team, and had nowhere booked to stay. I'd have offered the bed to whoever it was.'

'Okay,' she said, as if his explanation had sorted out something in her mind, which was good because it had only made him feel even more confused...

She turned her attention back to the packing, filling the edges around the neatly folded skirts and shirts with toiletries and, yes, the purple underwear!

He smiled to himself then realised she'd caught him for the rosy colour was rising in her cheeks.

'It's best I move,' she said quietly, then zipped the case

shut and pulled it upright onto its rollers. 'But I'd still like to take you to dinner.'

He stood up and took the case, rolling it towards the door, turning to say, 'Ah, but I felt it was my turn to cook. I bought steaks and some stuff for a salad.'

'In a packet, no doubt?' she teased, and he felt a sense of relief—a sense that everything was all right between them again.

On the surface, at least.

Well, he'd just have to live with that.

Though in his heart he hoped that before too long they'd be able to talk—talk properly—about the past.

About their feelings?

And the future?

He shook his head. He and Sam may have enjoyed one glorious night of sex, but as far as she was concerned that was that. There'd been no suggestion—at any time really—that she might be feeling the same attraction towards him as he did towards her.

He'd grill the steak.

With her clothing installed in her new home, Sam returned to join Andy on his balcony, and now sat, sipping at a glass of white wine he'd produced, and watching him at the barbecue.

Out to her right, a low rising moon had silvered the ocean, whose soft murmur, this calm evening, filled her with a sense of peace.

A rare sense of peace, given she was with Andy.

But the muddle of emotions she usually felt with him—the attraction, the sense that it was wrong, the awareness that it probably wasn't reciprocated, especially now he *knew* she had been instrumental in his best friend's death—all those worries seemed to have slipped from her shoulders. Tonight she was just going to enjoy the sheer pleasure of being in a beautiful place with a friend.

'I feel good,' she said, and he turned to look at her, eyebrows raised.

Surprised?

'Well, you have to admit it's been a frenetic week,' she said. 'Getting here was bad enough, I kept worrying I wouldn't make it in time to start on Monday, then finding out you're my boss—which is good, don't get me wrong—then all the stuff with Rosa and the anniversary—my mind and body have been in turmoil.'

'And now?' he prompted, turning back to prod the meat—or just not wanting to look at her when she answered?

'Now I feel at peace,' she said. 'As if I can go forward into a whole new life stretching out in front of me. New hospital to work in, new staff to meet and get to know, and this beautiful town to explore. The beach, the sea, the sand—rock pools out on the headland, I'm sure—a whole new world.'

She paused, and as he carefully lifted the steaks onto two waiting plates, she added, 'I ran away, you see, after the accident. Couldn't face any of it, especially the thought of a life without Nick. But a couple of months ago, when I was offered a better post in London, I thought about it for, oh, all of two seconds, because I suddenly knew it was time to go home.'

'And now you're here?' he asked as he set the plates down on the table.

'I know it was the right decision, so really, why wouldn't I be feeling good?'

He nodded, as if satisfied with her answer and disappeared inside, reappearing with the salad bowl and cutlery and sitting down opposite her. 'Eat!' he said, smiling.

Which she did—they both did—so for a while there was no more talk and when it did resume it was work talk mixed with travel talk—his work in Boston, hers in London, comparisons of hospital systems, staffing arrangements. It was all nice, safe, work-related talk that skated fairly easily over the muddle of emotions she'd landed in when she'd met Andy again, and the mess she'd made of things the night Rosa had died.

They'd have to talk about that, too, sometime, she knew, but now to just sit in the soft moonlight with Andy, relaxed by the sound of the sea, was enough.

Might have to be enough always.

She pushed *that* thought away.

Jake's father was with him when they did their rounds on Monday morning, and looked as anxious as Andy felt. They didn't yet have the results of all the blood tests, but those they did have offered no clue as to what might have caused the rash.

Sam was explaining this to the father when Andy was paged to an emergency in the ED.

He excused himself and left Sam to get on with the round. She'd contact him if she needed any help. With the shift change on Thursday, they'd be working together less often, which, he decided as he made his way downstairs, would be a good thing. The urge to touch Sam, just lightly on the shoulder, as he'd left Jake's room had been almost overwhelming.

That, he reminded himself as he went down to the

ED, was why relationships between colleagues could be difficult.

Even now, when he *wasn't* in a relationship with her, she was far too often in his thoughts and far, far too often those thoughts could be distracting.

And distraction was one thing a PICU physician just could not afford.

He was relieved when the elevator disgorged him outside the ED, and his focus returned immediately to work.

He heard, first, that it was a child saved from drowning, then, as he walked into the resus room, he realised the pale, anxious father was an old acquaintance—a fellow medical student he'd last seen in the Sydney hospital where Sam had been admitted after the accident.

Ned Radcliffe—the name came back to him as he held out his hand in greeting—but he could have been Santa Claus for all the notice Ned took of him. One hundred percent of his attention was focussed on the boy of about three who lay, unmoving, on the examination couch.

'Edward Radcliffe, two years four months, nonresponsive when the ambos reached him,' a nurse said quietly to Andy. 'Father had been giving CPR, ambos took over and heart restarted. He's on oxygen, but he's remained deeply unconscious.'

'Any sign of a head injury?' Andy asked, almost automatically, his mind on the child and how they might achieve the best possible outcomes for the small boy and his family.

'No, the ambos checked and the duty doctor here checked. Apparently, he went straight in.'

'How long would he have been in there, Ned?' Andy asked, and the father frowned as he heard the question, his eyes still on his son.

'I would say less than five minutes. I opened the pool fence gate to get a toy the dog had left in the garden, and turned to throw it back to the dog. But Chippy ignored it and raced back into the pool enclosure, barking like crazy, and that's when I realised Eddie must have followed me in.'

He looked at Andy now and frowned, then said, 'Andy?' in a bewildered voice.

'That's right, Ned. I'm head of the PICU here. We'll be admitting Eddie. He'll get the best of care.'

He turned back to the child, considerably pleased by the knowledge of such a short immersion.

'Hello, Eddie,' he said, in a loud voice, but there was no response, not even when he clapped his hands beside the little head. Neither did Eddie retract his foot when Andy stuck a pin into the sole of it, testing for physical response.

'We'll take him to Radiography on the way up to the PICU. I'll order an EEG and MRI,' he said to the nurse as he wrote up the requests. 'Do you want to stay with him, Ned?'

Ned nodded. 'I'll phone my wife on the way, let her know what's going on.'

He looked at Andy, a plea for reassurance in his eyes. 'Do you think...?'

Andy patted him on the shoulder.

'You were right there on the spot and did the best possible thing in giving CPR immediately. His heartbeat returned quickly, and he wasn't in the pool for long. They're all good indicators, Ned.'

An orderly arrived to transfer the boy, via Radiography, to the PICU, so Andy returned to the ward, aware the radiography he'd ordered probably wouldn't show much at this stage but still wanting a baseline from which to work.

He found Sam at the desk, and told her what was happening, asking if she'd known Ned.

She shook her head, but obviously hadn't taken much notice of the question because she asked, 'Would you consider continuous EEG monitoring?'

He shrugged. 'I'd been thinking of it, why?'

She grinned at him. 'I often wonder if it does much good and I think it must freak most parents out, seeing all those electrodes attached to their child's head. It's almost yelling "brain injury" at them.'

He shook his head. 'I must admit I've never thought of that aspect to it, but I'm really hoping he'll be responsive by the time he gets up to us.'

'And his father—this Ned—was he at university with you?' Sam asked, aware she'd usually have put an 'and Nick' at the end of that question.

But the peaceful, pleasant evening she'd enjoyed with Andy the previous night had left her more aware of Andy than when she'd been living with him.

And *that* had been bad enough!

Then she'd been able to put it down to proximity, especially after the night together, but now she was beginning to wonder if the awareness was more than physical attraction—not that she was even going to think about the L word.

Love had been too hard, like a prison she couldn't escape.

The arrival of young Eddie blocked all extraneous thoughts from her mind, especially as his father was beaming with joy.

'He reacted to the noise of the MRI in spite of the earmuffs,' he told them, although the little boy lay still, eyes closed again.

'He opened his eyes and moved his legs.'

'That's great, Ned, but we'll still keep him here and do further tests. The bloods should be back soon, and they'll tell us more, but everything is looking positive for the moment.'

'I'll phone my wife,' Ned said, and disappeared out of the room.

'He didn't want us to see him crying,' Sam said softly.

'And you,' Andy asked, looking intently into her eyes. 'Are you worrying again about the myriad things that can endanger a child and how a parent can protect them from everything?'

She shot him a quick smile. 'No, I was thinking how lucky they were to have such an intelligent dog!'

And with that she walked away, because of course she'd been worrying about how parents managed to survive their children's childhoods, Though the likelihood of her ever having to go through such agony was diminishing fast.

She'd known when she'd chosen to go into intensive care that it would be six hard years before she became qualified, then another six months before she qualified for paediatric intensive care. She'd done those final six months in London and had stayed another six months because the hospital had offered so many learning opportunities.

So now, at thirty-five, it wasn't that she was running out of time to have a child, but running out of time to have children—a family, something she'd dreamed about since she'd been a child herself, brought up by a single mother who'd been banished from her own family as a disgrace.

CHAPTER SIX

SAM WAS STANDING at the monitor desk, checking through some lab results, when she saw Ned again, returning to the hospital, this time with a woman she guessed must be his wife.

He stopped to introduce her to Sam, who was slightly startled when the woman said, 'Oh, I know who you are.'

'Oh, yes?' Sam said politely.

'Yes, of course. You were the new doctor at the hospital where Nick and Andy worked and they both fancied you. You must remember, Ned—they tossed a coin to see which one would ask her out and Nick won. How is Nick, by the way?'

'Nick was killed in an accident three years ago,' Sam said, but her mind was whirling.

He and Andy had actually *tossed up* to see who asked her out?

For some reason, the idea disturbed her. Made her feel like a cheap prize at a funfair.

The woman, whose name she'd forgotten almost as soon as she'd heard it—was it Ann?—and Ned were now arguing about whether or not he'd been in the pub that night, making Sam feel even worse.

Although, she decided, maybe it was keeping their minds off their concerns for Eddie.

'Eddie's doing well,' she said, glad to have found a way to interrupt things she didn't want to hear. 'You must both be pleased.'

But it didn't help much as Ann was now berating her husband for his carelessness in letting little Eddie fall in the pool.

'We *are* pleased,' Ned said, ignoring his wife's accusations with an ease that suggested they argued often. 'How long do you want to keep him in?'

'Overnight at least,' Sam told him, then watched as he steered his wife, still talking, to Eddie's room.

She moved on to see Jake, who was brighter today, his test results showing positive signs that the stem-cell transplant had taken. His father was with him today, explaining to Sam that he'd taken some personal time off work so his wife could have a proper rest at home.

'With two other children, it's hectic, but both our sets of parents help out all they can. My mum's staying with us at the moment, and the other kids love it as she spoils them rotten, doesn't she, Jake?'

Jake smiled, and touched his father's gloved hand.

'Me too,' Jake said, and pointed to a stuffed alligator that looked ready to eat the child.

Andy came into the changing cubicle as she was pulling off her gown, and although her body felt the usual rush of attraction that was becoming part of her normal life, it was Ann's earlier words that came back to her.

'Did you and Nick actually toss a coin to decide which of you would ask me out?' she demanded as pique at such behaviour overcame the silly attraction thing.

'Not at all,' Andy said, in an offended tone. 'We did rock, paper, scissors!'

Sam frowned at him, aware he thought the whole thing a joke, but feeling...slighted by it?

'And after you lost, that was it?' she muttered at him, as she hauled off the rest of her protective gear. 'You must have been really keen!'

And without waiting for a reply, she stalked out of the tiny room.

But once away from Andy, she tried to understand why hearing the silly nonsense had upset her so much.

It had been years ago, she'd married Nick, so how or why he'd asked her out shouldn't matter a jot.

A call from the ED made her push the past away, although she was aware it would niggle away deep inside her no matter how much she ignored it.

'We've isolated another girl, and the red spots in her mouth with their tiny pinpricks of white in the centre confirm it's measles,' Phil, the young intern on duty, told her as she came into the emergency department.

He led the way to one of the two isolation rooms in the ED and introduced the patient, Ruby, and her parents, Alice and Bob.

Not knowing the local area, Sam asked the intern to stay so they could try to work out if the two cases were connected in any way.

While she examined the little girl, a year older than Rosa had been, she listened to Phil's questions, and from the way he shook his head she realised there wasn't an obvious overlap in the two children's activities or friends.

'I'll admit her to our Paediatric Intensive Care unit,' Sam told the parents, 'but that's just because we can isolate her better than on the normal children's ward, where the contagion could spread.'

She left instructions on the chart and returned to the PICU, her mind puzzling over this second admission. She knew immunisation rates in the country as a whole were above ninety percent—she'd looked it up when Rosa had been admitted—yet two children in a regional city, two children out of the—at the most—ten percent not immunised had contracted the disease.

'Who does what?' she asked Andy, when she caught him in the staffroom and explained her concern. 'Do the Infectious Diseases people have staff who follow the trail of the two children, or do the police do it, or do we do it?'

Andy frowned at the question, and as she looked at him the question of whether she'd have gone out with him if he'd won their stupid game popped into her head.

Forget it!

But she knew she probably wouldn't have. Knew it was the kind of question that could bob into her head as she fell asleep at night or walked on the beach, thinking of nothing in particular.

'I think the infectious diseases staff use the police if they need them,' Andy was saying, while her mind wandered. 'We'll inform them of this second case, and they can publicise it, warning parents of the dangers, suggesting unimmunised children should be done before it becomes more widespread.'

'Has there been anything special here recently?' Sam asked. 'A local agricultural show, surfing contest people might have watched, a circus, or funfair of some kind?'

'Somewhere people from all walks of life could have met,' Andy said, more or less to himself. 'You're right, that's something they'll look into, I'm sure. And there *was* the annual show about a week before you came, and it had a big sideshow alley and all the fun of the fair.'

'I think I'd rather you said there'd been nothing like that, because if it came from a travelling fair anyone could be the carrier, and who knows where they went next.'

He grinned at her, which made her think she *would* have gone out with him—way back when…

'Which makes me doubly glad it's someone else's job to locate him or her,' he was saying. 'Have you admitted the new case?'

'She should be on her way up. Her name's Ruby, and she's not as feverish as Rosa was, but I thought it best to keep her away from other children so she'll go into another of our isolation rooms.'

'I'll see her before I go,' Andy said, and Sam realised with a slight shock that this was the first day of a new shift. She'd known about it, had it noted in her diary, knew exactly when she would and wouldn't be at work, but suddenly Andy was departing and, for all she'd have a registrar or a young resident on duty with her at all times, she'd be in charge.

Andy must have read what she was thinking in her face, for he reached out and touched her shoulder.

'You handled it all extremely well when I was in Sydney, remember, and I'll only be a phone call away,' he told her. 'It's the paperwork more than the patients that'll get you down!'

'I'll be fine,' she said, as forcefully as she could, but again guessed he'd read her doubts.

'Of course, you will,' he assured her. 'And you're off on Sunday—well, on call—so bring your phone and I'll take you for a drive around the place if you like, show you some of the sights of the great Port Fortesque!'

'That sounds good,' Sam said, although she had more doubts about that plan than she did about running the department in his absence.

Andy walked away, not at all concerned over Sam's ability to keep the place running, more concerned that she'd been upset over his and Nick's silly bet.

But she *had* agreed to go out with him on Sunday, although as he was the only person she knew in the area, that didn't mean much.

He went back to his office and tidied his desk, then decided to call in on young Eddie before he left.

His mother was sitting with him, reading a story to the bright, alert child.

'He could really come home now, couldn't he?' she said, smiling sweetly at Andy.

'Tomorrow,' he said firmly. 'We want some follow-up bloods and another EEG, but Dr Reilly will discharge him tomorrow, probably by eleven-thirty.'

'Oh, pooh!' the woman said. 'I was hoping Sam would be off duty tomorrow. I was going to ask the two of you to dinner at the weekend. Ned was so pleased to meet up with you again, especially as we're new in town. He's just joined a practice on the north side. I didn't want to leave Sydney, but he thought it would be better to bring Eddie up in the country.'

She gave a theatrical shudder and added, 'This was a compromise, and look what just happened.'

Andy closed his eyes and thanked the merciful fates that Sam was not around because he was pretty sure she wouldn't want this gossipy woman—it had to be she

who'd told Sam about the rock, paper, scissors fiasco—
linking their names like that.

He checked Eddie's file, spoke briefly to the bright
little boy, and escaped before Ann could think of another plan.

'Would you have asked me out if you'd won the bet?'

It was the first question Sam asked when she climbed
into his car on Sunday morning, dressed in pristine white
slacks and a black and white striped shirt, her usually
unruly hair somehow knotted rather severely on the top
of her head.

Her question had come just in time to stop him saying
she looked terrific and Andy had to concentrate on getting out of the underground garage far more intently than
he needed to. But once on the road, taking the one that
led to the lighthouse first, he knew he'd have to answer.

'Of course,' he said.

He didn't need to glance her way to know she was
frowning—he could actually feel her tension in the air.

'But couldn't you have asked at another time?'

The question made him frown.

'Once you were going out with Nick? Of course not!'

'Because I was somehow marked as his?' she demanded, as he pulled into the parking area near the track
that led to the top of the headland.

He turned to face her, puzzled by the question—trying to think back to that fateful time.

'Not marked as his—I don't think I thought that way.
It's just, well, you were going out with him—why would
I assume you'd say yes to me? And how would he have
felt if I'd done such a thing? And what would he have

thought of you—well, of us both—if you'd said yes? Life just doesn't work that way.'

She'd been staring out the window at the sea, but as she turned back towards him he wanted to ask her if she would have said yes, but it was all so pointless.

'What happened, happened,' he said, reaching out to touch her cheek with one finger. 'There aren't any set rules or guidelines for life, you know. We just have to stumble along as best we can, doing what we feel is right at the time, and hopefully not having too many regrets when we look back at the past.'

She smiled and touched her hand to his.

'We tend to remember the regrets—the bad things, more than the good, don't we?' she said, giving his hand a squeeze before opening the car door, signalling, without a doubt, that that particular conversation was over.

They climbed the hill to the top of the rocky outcrop, coming out on the grassy knoll with the wide Pacific Ocean stretching out on both sides of them.

Sam threw her arms wide and turned to him in sheer delight.

'This is what I dreamt about—all the time I was in London, and while I was with Mum in the wilds of South-East Asia. I dreamt of living near the ocean. Working in Perth gave me a taste for it, for being close to the sea and beaches—although with my skin I really should have stayed in London or gone even further north to Scotland. But I think Aussies need the ocean—well, I do,' she said, her face aglow with the wonder of it.

So it seemed natural to take advantage of those outflung arms and wrap his around her body, holding her close—a friendly hug—for all his body screamed for more.

They drew apart but somehow were holding hands,

and walked across the grass to the brilliant white light-house and the squat building that had been the keeper's cottage nestled beside it.

They climbed to the top and from there looked back over the countryside that surrounded the sprawling coastal city.

'It's mainly dairy farms, some cattle properties and plenty of hobby farms, where people keep everything from goats to llamas,' he told her. 'There are local markets on the second and fourth Sunday of the month. You'd be surprised what you can buy there. Everything from local wines and beers, to hats, and mats, and guinea pigs.'

'Well, that's next Sunday accounted for,' she said. 'And next Saturday or maybe on one of my early finish days next week, I want to have a look for a car, just something small to get me to the hospital at night when I'm on call.'

She turned to him and put her finger against his lips.

'Don't bother telling me I can always take yours,' she said, 'because I wouldn't dream of it. And, anyway, you might be using it.'

She frowned, as if about to say more, but other people arrived at the top and the moment passed.

Could this count as courting? he wondered as they made their way back to the car, her hand still captive in his.

Such an old-fashioned word, but he couldn't remember ever being so uncertain with a woman—uncertain how to proceed, wondering whether, if he rushed things, he might spoil what they already had—which *had* to be friendship.

But if he were to court her, start with occasional dates maybe...

Dear God, it all seemed so infantile when they were both mature people and had already slept together!

But he couldn't help but be aware of the distance she usually kept between them; her avoidance of an accidental touch, let alone a real one. And instinct told him it was to do with her marriage, her previous experience that had either been so great she'd never stopped loving Nick, or so tricky she didn't want to repeat it.

Could he ask?

Get her to talk about it?

Not really, when either love or loyalty to Nick would colour her reply. And given the failure of love in *his* life, he doubted he'd be able to judge which it was.

And, to be honest, he'd been wary of proximity himself—of getting too close, of touching her by accident.

Yet, still hand in hand, they reached the car, and the mood was broken.

'Nick would have asked me out if you'd won,' Sam said quietly, and Andy felt his gut clench as the words told him with a stark certainty that Nick was never far from her thoughts.

Sam used the excuse of needing to shop for food and sort out her new living quarters to turn down Andy's invitation to spend the afternoon at the local gallery before an early dinner—even just fish and chips by the shore.

The morning had been confusing enough.

Spending non-work time with Andy had been wonderful and having seen more of this beautiful place where she'd ended up had made her delighted with her decision.

But Andy's hug, the hand-holding had stirred up memories of their night together, and her body ached for more intimacy—for kisses and touches, for being held, and whispered words...

But to get more involved with Andy was really impossible. In Andy's mind this might appear to be a prelude to marriage and even after three years the M word brought up an image of a black hole into which she'd disappear.

Andy was as different from Nick as it was possible for a man to be, and he'd be a loving, supportive husband and wonderful father to the children she really wanted to have.

But would *she* change, as she had with Nick?

She didn't blame Nick for the person she'd become within the marriage because it had been something she hadn't liked in herself. She'd felt as if she was always trying to prove something, and somehow always failing...

Growing up with only a mother and with no extended family around by which to judge people's marriages, she'd had no idea she'd find it as overwhelming as she had.

But Andy was different, and having found her way back to being herself again, surely she wouldn't lose that with Andy.

Would it be a risk?

She'd been lying on her bed while these thoughts had worked their way through her head, coming back now to the fact that it would be wrong to have an affair with Andy because he'd be hurt when she ended it. And, what's more, she'd have to find another job, as working with him afterwards would be just too hard.

Actually, working with him during an affair would also be hard—the discretion part of it almost impossible, and that, too, would damage Andy more than her.

And wasn't all this futile? Hand-holding hardly counted as a declaration of love!

She climbed resolutely off the bed, changed into one of her new swimming costumes, slathered fifty-plus sun block all over her skin, pulled on a light shift as a cover-up, and headed for the beach.

An hour battling the waves would chase all these gloomy thoughts away. And, besides, Andy might just have been holding her hand because they were friends.

She slipped on her sandals, slapped on her hat and, with a towel slung over her shoulder, she set off.

Perhaps if she talked to Andy about these things it would help.

Or would she be making a complete fool of herself, if he wasn't the slightest bit interested in her—even attracted to her?

Just because he had been once, it didn't mean much six years later...

Hoping an hour out on the waves would clear his head and tangled thoughts, Andy changed into board shorts and a light wetsuit, went back to the garage to get his board from the lock-up section in front of his car, and headed for the beach.

He was sitting on his board out beyond the breakers, hoping for one last good wave to carry him all the way back to the beach. If it didn't come, he'd paddle into shore, but it was so peaceful and serene out here, he didn't mind a wait.

The wave, when it did come, was a beauty, and he caught the top of it before it curved into a barrel, crouching on the board to get his body into this green curl of the ocean, exultant as he rode out the other end.

A loud cheer from the beach told him he wasn't alone, and as he rode the wash of the now-broken wave through to the sand, he realised it was Sam.

'I didn't know you could surf,' she said, then frowned. 'In fact,' she added in a puzzled voice, 'I really know nothing about you—the now you, not the six-years-ago you. I've been rude, babbling on about me and my travels, but what of you?'

She'd stretched her towel on the beach and was sitting on it, spreading sunscreen on her arms and legs—long, long, and quite lovely, legs.

'Who are you, Andy Wilkie?' she said, smiling up at him as he stripped off the top half of his wetsuit, letting it dangle from his waist, and picked up his towel. 'And what have *you* been doing? I know we talked briefly about Boston and our travels. In fact, I read a paper you wrote from there—the dangers of hyperthermia in children, I seem to remember. But the real Andy Wilkie. You're not married, unless you have a wife tucked away in a cupboard somewhere, so what's been happening in your life?'

She patted the sand beside her, and when he'd dried off his face and torso he sat down next to her. She'd obviously been swimming, for her hair hung in wet tendrils down her back, and clustered ringlets curled around her face.

'Did you ever marry?' she asked, bringing his attention back to what was obviously going to be an inquisition.

'Got close to it twice,' he said, and immediately felt guilty that he'd said it so casually—with such a lack of feeling.

But wasn't it the truth?

'Wrong women?' Sam persisted, and this time, looking

at her as he answered, he could say truthfully, 'Maybe I was the wrong man.'

'I doubt that,' she said. 'You're one of the good guys, but I assume that took up quite a bit of the six years, wooing and winning not one but two wrong women. But there has to be more—a grand passion?'

That he definitely wasn't going to answer!

'Several not so grand passions,' he did say, because he didn't want her persisting. 'But fun relationships with no expectations at the end of them. Really, Sam, you must know yourself how hard it is to keep a relationship alive when one, or in my case often both, the parties are involved in either emergency medicine or PICU.'

'We should have been skin specialists—they hardly ever get called out at night,' she said, but she was smiling, and he knew her passion for the job they did was as strong as his.

It was time to change the conversation, but he'd missed his chance. Sam was already asking, 'Were there reasons?'

He looked blankly at her. 'Reasons for what?'

She gave an exasperated sigh. 'For neither of the relationships going on to marriage? And don't talk to me about work pressures. The majority of specialists in all fields manage to make marriage work and the ones who don't probably wouldn't have stayed married if they were bank managers or garbage collectors.'

'Garbage collectors?' he echoed, and she had to smile.

'You know perfectly well what I mean! What happened?'

Tell her, or not tell her?

He thought how peaceful this was—or had been—just being with Sam, enjoying her company and the beautiful setting. Medical matters had been the last things on their minds.

So he told another truth…

'I just wasn't right for them,' he said, 'or perhaps they weren't right for me. It was a long time ago, Sam, and I've settled into a life I'm comfortable with—comfortable in. I like my life just as it is. Work does have pressures, as you know, and to be able to come home and just relax and renew myself is exactly what I need.'

Liar, a voice was yelling in his head, although it was only a partial lie. He really *did* like his nice, uncomplicated lifestyle.

'Nonsense,' Sam told him. 'You've got to get out and about. You're far too good a man to be frittering your life away on brief romances. You'd make a wonderful father—anyone who sees you with a patient would realise that in an instant!'

He could tell she was winding up towards more marital advice, so it really *was* time to change the conversation.

'So now you've obviously done all you needed to do in your enormous new living space,' he said to her, 'you've got no excuse—so how about fish and chips on the beach? I know the best fish and chip shop in Port F.'

And to his surprise she smiled, and said, 'You're on! But I like calamari and chips if that's okay, and I do need to shower and do something to control my hair before we can leave. Will we walk?'

'It's not too far,' he said, his mind racing ahead to the possibility of holding hands—if not on the way there, at least on the way back.

You are nuts, he told himself, but his mind had already

moved on to a dark spot at the end of the esplanade that would be perfect for a very chaste kiss...

But right now she was standing up so he picked up her towel, took it a little further downwind on the beach and shook the sand from it before handing it back to her.

She seemed surprised by the gesture but simply thanked him, then wrapped the towel around her body, covering her swimsuit but leaving the lovely length of leg for him to enjoy.

Which he probably shouldn't be enjoying as much as he was.

'Are you checking out my legs?'

Sam's sudden question brought him out of this consideration.

'Yes, I was,' he told her, 'and very lovely legs they are too. And you must remember it's allowable on Aussie beaches for men to admire women's legs. It's one of the reasons we have beaches!'

She laughed and told him he was talking nonsense, but the colour in her cheeks suggested she hadn't minded it, nonsense or not!

They *did* hold hands, and although Sam suspected Andy had used the excuse of helping her up the first steep hill to take hers, she found it was comfortable, her fingers wrapped securely in his, and did nothing to stop the small pleasure.

They ate their paper-wrapped meals sitting on a bench that overlooked the river, dog walkers strolling by, seagulls clamouring around their feet for the occasional dropped scrap.

And they talked of work—Sam bringing Andy up to date on the progress of their current patients, explaining that Ryan had picked up quite a lot and could possibly go home the following day.

'Although you know him better than I do. So I decided to leave that decision to you.'

She fed her last chip to the clamouring seagulls and crumpled up the paper.

'Have you enjoyed it?' Andy asked, and she smiled at him.

'The fish and chips by the river? Enormously!' she said.

He grinned at her, sending tendrils of delight threading through her body.

'You know very well we were talking about work!' he scolded. 'Have you enjoyed your first two weeks?'

She turned to him.

'Loved it,' she said. 'And that's mainly thanks to you for making it so easy for me to fit in.'

He looked at her for a moment, then said, 'I think you'd fit in anywhere.'

They walked back, Andy leading her to a track that would take them up through the scrub to the top of the hill near the apartment block. But when he stopped beneath a dramatic pandanus palm, and drew her into his arms, she looked into his dimly lit eyes and had to ask, 'Are you courting me?'

His answer was a light kiss on her lips.

'Would you like me to?'

She shook her head, unable to really answer that, but she nestled closer to his body, finally pulling away enough to say, 'I'm not sure I'm good courting material, Andy.'

'Because?' he asked, kissing her cheek, then the hollow beneath her ear.

'I wasn't good at marriage,' she blurted out, because Andy's kisses were tantalising, and her body, as well as her brain, was going haywire. 'I loved Nick, but it wasn't enough somehow. And I lost myself somewhere in it. Mum was away, in South America most of the time, but I doubt she'd have been much help, because she'd never been in a long-term relationship. And how could I ask a friend how their marriage worked?'

He kissed her lips again, and before she dissolved into the bliss of being kissed by Andy—which she had done all too recently—she eased away again.

'Nick wouldn't have been easy to live with,' Andy pointed out, still holding her loosely in his arms.

'That's no excuse for my failure,' Sam told him, her voice thick with remembered unhappiness. 'I just don't know, Andy.'

He turned, but kept one arm around her waist as he steered them both back onto the path.

'I doubt you lost of all of yourself,' he said gently, 'because to me you're every bit the Sam I used to know, only wiser, but just as fierce in protection of something you believe is right, and passionate about your patients.'

'Doesn't mean I'm good marriage material, though,' she said gloomily.

'Well,' he said, 'as I've already told you, I didn't even make it to a wedding, so I can't judge anyone else. But do we have to look that far ahead? What about now?'

Sam was tempted, so tempted, yet still something held her back.

'We're colleagues,' she reminded him.

'And surely professional enough to keep our work lives

separate?' he countered. 'So forget about the future and let's try just for now?'

She wished she could see his face, but the track was narrow and dark so he led her by the hand, about half a step ahead.

Just for now. The words echoed in her head, sounding far too tempting, while somewhere deep inside her body some traitorous little impulse was dancing up and down with joy at the thought of an affair with Andy.

But whether either of them could do 'just for now' without someone getting hurt was a totally different question.

They came out on the top of the hill, meeting up with the reality of streetlights, apartment blocks and occasional traffic.

'You don't have to decide this right now,' Andy told her, wrapping his arm around her waist again now they could walk side by side. 'Just think about it for—oh, a few minutes, maybe an hour?'

He was smiling, sure they'd reached the place he wanted to be, but still caution held her back.

'Tomorrow,' she said, 'and, because I'm not nearly as sure as you are about the "professional at work" side of things, I'll tell you when you knock off tomorrow.'

'What about when your shift ends, then?' he said with a smile, and she shook her head.

'I'm on early, as you well know, and I'm going out to look at cars when I finish work, so we'll leave it till your shift ends, thank you very much. I'll even cook us dinner if I can use your kitchen, and perhaps your balcony to eat on.'

She could see his face now, and guessed he was holding back an urge to say he'd look at cars with her, or maybe they wouldn't need two cars, but he did hold back, and she squeezed his hand.

Maybe it *would* work out—if only just for now…

CHAPTER SEVEN

SAM LOVED EARLY-MORNING SHIFTS. The wards were quiet, lacking the buzz and bustle that seemed to build up during the day, and many of the children were still asleep.

Those who were awake were usually chatty. Kayla, her diabetes now stabilised with the knowledge and drugs she'd need to keep it that way, was due to go to the wards, where she'd spend a day with one of her parents and a specialised nurse to run through the pin-prick blood test she'd need to do several times a day with her special device, and practise using the syringe with which she'd be injecting her insulin.

Sam sat with her for a few minutes, talking to her about what lay ahead, reassuring her that she'd soon be able to manage it all without stress, telling stories of six-year-olds she'd seen who had been doing their own injections for a year.

Then on to Grant, who was due to be brought out of his coma today. So much rested on this, although evidence of mild brain damage might not be noticeable for some time.

But the shock for the child, waking to find so much plaster on his body, one leg suspended above the bed by a sling around his ankle, his other leg held together with an external frame, would be the most immediate problem.

'How do I explain it all to him?' his mother, who was sitting by the bed, asked.

Sam smiled at her. 'With any luck he'll find it exciting—something to tell all the kids at school. But he'll be woozy for a day or two, so don't get alarmed. As far as all our tests show, there was no substantial damage to his brain, just some slight swelling, which has gone down now.'

She waved her hand towards the sling.

'Boredom's going to be the main thing—he's not going to be able to move around much for a while. Does he have some kind of device with games on that he can use while lying in bed?'

His mother gave a huff of rueful laughter.

'He has some hand-held thing he plays with all the time. In fact, I feel so guilty because that's why he was out on his bike. I told him if he didn't put the silly device away and get out in the fresh air, I'd confiscate it for good.'

'You can't blame yourself,' Sam told her, knowing it would do no good at all. How often had she told herself she wasn't to blame for Nick's death when she knew full well it was the argument that had caused it.

It wasn't rational, she knew that, but it lingered anyway, as this would with Grant's mother...

Abby was sufficiently recovered to be transferred to a ward, and Sam was writing up the protocols for it when a shiver down her spine told Andy had just walked into the room.

'You're early,' she said, not turning to look at him in case her too-ready blush gave her away.

'Wanted to see Abby before she left us,' he said, going to stand by the bed and taking Abby's hand.

'Happy to be getting out of here, Abs?' he said, and the girl smiled radiantly at him.

'But I'll miss you all,' she said, the words belying the smile. 'You've all been so kind, especially you, Dr Wilkie!'

Now *she* was blushing, and Sam bumped Andy's arm as they left the room.

'Do all the teenage girls fall for you, Dr Wilkie?'

'Behave yourself,' Andy said sternly, but the twinkle in his eyes told her how hard this 'just colleagues thing' could prove to be.

'Why *are* you here early?' Sam asked, as they stood outside the door, the file in Sam's hands between them so it *could* look like a normal colleague conversation.

'Paperwork,' he said briefly, but she knew it was more than that.

He'd wanted to see her just as much as she'd wanted to see him, and how they were both going to get through their shifts when the air between them was so charged it was a wonder the lights weren't flickering.

'Go do your paperwork!' Sam said, needing to get away from him so she could sort out what was going on in her head *and* her body.

He left, but it didn't help much.

How hadn't she felt this charge last night, when they'd been so serious and adult about not committing too much? How stupid had that been? Surely if they'd gone to bed last night, she'd have been satisfied enough not to want to rip his clothes off in the hospital corridor this morning.

Focus!

She forced Andy from her mind and concentrated on the patients, possibly a little too hard because one mother asked her if everything was all right in the panicky voice parents got when a doctor was looking worried.

'She's fine,' Sam said. 'I was just wondering if she was ready to go to a children's ward today or to leave it until tomorrow.'

'It would suit me better tomorrow,' the mother told her, 'so I can bring in some everyday clothes for her. I noticed when someone showed me the ward she'll be going to that the children were in day clothes, not pyjamas.'

'Then tomorrow it is,' Sam said. 'And you're right, she'll feel more at ease if she's wearing day clothes like the others.'

It was a nothing conversation, but it brought Sam's mind back into balance. This was work, and her mind was now firmly fixed on it, and would remain there for the rest of the shift.

Which, as it turned out, was a nightmare.

A call from the ED with a third measles case, this time a boy of eleven. Sam went straight down and although the boy wasn't particularly sick, she knew he could deteriorate. Plus the fact that they could isolate him best in the PICU meant she had a new patient.

Peter Collins—a nice-looking kid—was obviously unhappy about being in hospital.

'But I'm not that sick!' he complained to Sam, when she visited him on his arrival in the PICU.

'We don't want you spreading the disease any further,' Sam told him, as she read through the information the ED had collected on him.

'It says here he has had all his immunisations,' she said, turning to Mrs Collins who was telling Peter to behave himself. 'Did they include measles?'

Mrs Collins nodded. 'I'm sure they did—we had to show the papers to his kindy—but I don't know what happened to them after that. It was years ago.'

'Well, it might explain why he's not as badly affected

as the other two,' Sam said. 'But we're trying to track the source. Did Peter go to the show that was on here not long ago?'

Mrs Collins nodded. 'We all went. It was just after Peter's birthday and some of the family had given him money to go on all the rides.'

'Can you remember what rides you went on?' Sam asked her patient, then had to listen to how rad the dodgem cars were and why he hadn't gone on the Ferris Wheel—far too high and he'd have been sick—but had loved the ghost train, and the hall of mirrors, but mostly he'd been on the dodgems.

Sam shook her head.

The other two children were surely too young to have been on dodgem cars but at least the authorities now had someone they could track through the fair.

She left Peter and his mother and sat down at the main desk to get on to the details of the contact they now had at infectious diseases control.

'We'll send someone to talk to Peter and his mother,' the voice promised. 'It will give us two visits to compare—we haven't liked to disturb Rosa's family at this time. And we'll have to publicise this now. Be ready for a few journalists, TV cameras, et cetera.'

'My boss can do that,' Sam said firmly, and the woman laughed.

'If you can get Andy Wilkie to front the cameras, you're a better woman than I am,' she said.

'No way—no, never!' Andy told Sam very firmly when she came to his office at the end of her shift to tell him journalists would be on their way.

'But why not?' Sam asked, frowning at him, the spark

that had flared between them earlier tamped down now under the pressure of work.

'I just don't do it!' he said bluntly. 'This is a small regional hospital, and once the press latch onto someone they can use as an "expert" or "hospital spokesperson—"' he put the words in inverted commas with his fingers '—they never let him or her go.'

He paused then spread out his hands.

'Have you ever done it? They put powder all over your face and shine bright lights into your eyes so you look like a startled rabbit. Only in my case I look like a very tall, gangly, startled rabbit. Never! The Administrator can do it. He can get all the info he needs off the computer, and he'll handle the press far better than I would.'

But still Sam frowned, apparently not at all placated by his flood of words.

'What?' he asked, and now she smiled.

'You must have done it at some time,' she pointed out, 'to know you look like a very tall, startled rabbit.'

'I did it when Nick died,' he said, voice flat and cold, obviously still distressed by the memory. 'I was there at the hospital that day. Some people knew I was his friend and sicced a reporter onto me.'

Holy cow! What had he done, blurting that out?

He didn't need to see Sam's stricken face to realise that, just like that, he'd spread all the horror of the past on his desk in front of her—in front of them both—because she'd know immediately why he'd been at the hospital that day. He'd been there to yell at her!

'Shit!' he said, and buried his face in his hands. 'I'm sorry, Sam, so sorry.'

But sorry was too late. She'd been transported as rapidly as he had back to that dreadful day, and now the ten-

tative attraction that had flared between them, piping hot
only a few hours earlier, had vanished beneath the weight
of old, and very cold, memories.

'I understand,' she finally said, in a voice devoid of
feeling. 'I'm sure they'll find someone else to do it.' And
with that she was gone.

This relationship was never going to work.

No matter how he felt about Sam, the past would always be there, hovering in the background, ready to leap
out and bite them at the most unexpected moments.

Sam left work feeling unsettled and anxious. She'd thrust
Andy back into those memories with her teasing him
about being on TV, but did that mean...

You are over Nick, she told herself firmly. You won't
ever forget him, the great times with Nick and the love
she'd had for him, but it was time to move on.

And given the effect Andy was having on her, surely
he was the man to move on with?

For now, at least.

Although those last two words made her stomach ache.
If she wanted even just for now, she somehow had to
show Andy that everything was all right between them.

Somehow...

Tom Carey was the first man she'd seen in a suit since
her arrival—very smooth and efficient, rattling off numbers she really didn't understand, or want to learn about.

But she'd already spotted the car she wanted, a vivid
yellow, compact four-wheel drive tucked into a back corner of the showroom.

'But will you need a four-wheel drive? Wouldn't a nice
sedan—a small one—suit you better?'

'Not if I'm going to explore the places around Port on my days off,' she told him, pleased the name the locals used had come easily to her lips. 'I saw from up on the lighthouse hill that the country begins quickly on the outskirts of town, and while I don't intend to do any dangerous off-road driving, I'll be more comfortable in something that doesn't hate country roads.'

Tom took her across to look at the interior of the car, though she assured him she didn't need to see the engine as she had no idea what it was supposed to look like.

'Want to take it for a spin?' Tom asked, and she smiled and nodded.

It was a glorious car to drive, not too high off the ground but high enough to see over many of the cars around her.

'I love it,' she told Tom, then realised that probably wasn't a good bargaining point, but it already had its price written on the back window, and with new cars she wouldn't have a lot of bargaining power, but she tried anyway.

'Can I get the window tinting included in the price?' she asked, and Tom agreed without any argument so she guessed the company allowed for that in its profit margin.

Fifteen minutes of paperwork later, the car insured and registered, she drove out of the dealership filled with the joy and pride of ownership.

Remembering the uneasiness between her and Andy before she'd left the hospital, she drove to the shopping centre and picked up all she'd need to cook a decent meal for the two of them, deciding on roast lamb because she knew people living alone rarely bothered with a roast dinner.

The residual chill she'd felt in Andy's office remained

with her, but it hadn't completely doused the heat that had flared between them earlier, and if she wanted to retrieve that—wanted to be with Andy, even just for now—she had to make things right between them again.

Rod had given her a remote to access the garage and she drove in proudly, finding the double space for Unit One and parking her car beside what was presumably Rod's.

Would Andy guess it was hers when he drove in past it?

She smiled at the thought then bundled her groceries out of the car and up in the elevator to Andy's floor, pleased she still had his keys.

But even as she marinated the roast in rosemary and lemon, and prepared the vegetables so everything was ready to go into the oven when he returned home, misgivings swirled in her stomach and she was tempted to open the bottle of quality shiraz she'd bought and have a drink to settle her nerves.

Better to go downstairs for a shower and change of clothes, she decided, but as she reached the elevator, it stopped and Andy stepped out.

He took her in his arms and held her close.

'I was so sure I'd ruined everything, bringing up the past like that. I just didn't realise what I was saying. I was so adamant about not appearing on television again I wasn't thinking.'

He nuzzled his lips against her neck, then kissed her lips, the kiss deepening as the charge she'd felt this morning returned.

'I was just going down for a shower,' she murmured weakly.

'I need one too,' he told her, so somehow it was inevitable they both ended up in his shower, exploring each other with touch and kisses, less frantic this time, prolonging their pleasure until satisfaction could wait no longer, and they joined beneath the running water, gloriously slick, and cool, intensifying the experience.

'Well, that's going to make dinner a little late,' she said, smiling at him as she towelled her hair dry, marvelling at the sight of him naked, his body lithe yet muscular from his swimming and surfing. 'And I need to get clean clothes from my room but don't want to go down there wrapped in a towel.'

He slipped out of the bathroom, returning with a T-shirt with a large dog on the front of it and a pair of his boxers.

'They've an elastic waist so should stay up on you, although maybe not for long,' he teased, his blue eyes glinting with mischief.

But Sam had a dinner to prepare, so she put on the offered clothes and headed for the kitchen, turned on the oven, and when it had heated put the meat and vegetables into it.

'And wine, too?' Andy said, when he returned, similarly attired in a baggy shirt and boxers, explaining when she raised her eyebrows, 'I thought it'd be nice to match.'

He opened the wine and poured two glasses, kissing her lightly on the lips as he handed one to her.

'Let's sit outside,' she said, and headed for the balcony, quite sure where kisses would lead if they stayed in the kitchen.

'I didn't think you'd come,' he said, as they raised their glasses in a toast. 'But you'll be pleased to know I did the interview. I decided I'd let Nick's death colour my life for far too long. I knew I'd hurt you when I brought the whole darned thing up again this morning, so I did my powdered, startled rabbit thing not long after you left. If you want to see it, we'll probably catch it on the late local news.'

She smiled at him.

'If we happen to be around to catch the late local news!'

Sam felt herself blush as she said it. That was surely flirting, and she'd never flirted much—certainly not with Nick, who could so easily take something the wrong way. But Andy winked at her, and she knew everything was going to be all right.

Andy looked out over the ocean, dark now as the moon hadn't yet shown itself. He felt at peace, and knew it was to do with the woman sitting beside him.

Fate had brought this woman back into his life, and now she was here, with him—and even if it *was* just for now, he could be content with it—just for now, anyway...

He understood some of her reservations about relationships, he'd known Nick well enough to know he wouldn't have wanted to work with him. With Nick, everything had to be a contest, with him as the winner, and throughout their friendship, from childhood on, Andy had been content with that.

Winning had never seemed important to him.

Being the best he could—that was something else— but coming second, or even thirty-first, had never bothered him.

And then there were the disasters of his own relationships, failures that had led him to wonder if they were worth the investment he'd put into them; that had led him to step back from too much commitment to anyone.

'Want to share?' Sam asked, and he was startled out of his thoughts.

'Share what?' he said, aware he certainly didn't want to share those particular thoughts, especially not with Sam.

'The myriad thoughts that were chasing across your face—and not all of them good, I suspect.'

He shrugged the words away. 'Just random things floating past, nothing deep and meaningful,' he said. 'I suppose just sitting here with you is enough for me at the moment.'

He smiled at her, sitting with her feet up on the railing of his balcony, her long legs sending a frisson of excitement through him.

'Do you want me to do anything about the dinner—turn something over in the oven, get the cutlery?'

'Just sit and relax,' she said, sipping at her drink. 'And after dinner, if you like, I'll take you for a drive in my new car.'

'You bought a car? Why didn't you say? We could have gone straight down and looked at it.'

'Yes?' she teased, and he had to laugh, but her lack of excitement over such a purchase bemused him. Buying a new car, for him, was right up there with surfing big waves as far as excitement went.

But Sam?

He studied her for a moment, saw her in profile as she watched the moon put in its appearance over the ocean. She was different, this woman. He sensed she had an inner calmness of spirit that meant she could cope with whatever life threw at her. Someone at ease with herself.

Yes, she'd been upset about Rosa, but in no way had it affected her work, or her capacity to empathise with all the other patients and their families, all of whom he knew, even after a week or two, liked and trusted her implicitly.

If he'd been the peevish type, he might have resented her easy popularity—the way nurses would turn to her, parents seek her out—but instead he was proud, not only because he'd appointed her but because she was Sam, and he was happy for her.

Sam sipped her drink, delighting in the peace and quiet of the early evening, happy she could sit like this with Andy, not having to talk, or plan, or, in fact, do anything much.

Shortly she'd have to get up and check on their dinner, but right now all she had to do was sit, comfortable in his presence, relishing his closeness—the feeling of a bond between them that worked without words.

'Sure I can't do anything for you in the kitchen?' he asked and she turned to smile at him, shaking her head.

'Starving, are you?' she teased. 'You can't hurry a roast dinner. I'll take care of it, but we can sit a while longer.'

She paused, remembering the bad moments they'd had earlier in the day, *and* the outcome when he'd arrived home.

This could work, but being with Andy, enjoying the physical side of things, could she let it go when the 'just for now' ended?

She rather doubted it, so with a less content feeling she lowered her legs and headed for the kitchen to pull the lamb out of the oven and wrap it in foil to let it rest, then called Andy, asking him to set the table while she served up.

Which involved coming into the kitchen to get the cutlery and, it appeared, seizing her by the waist and waltzing her around the kitchen island, before releasing her to get on with her job.

But that carefree impulse had left her smiling and wondering again if 'just for now' *would* be enough.

The drive was forgotten as the meal became an erotic feast, feeding titbits to each other, feet tangling beneath the table, hands touching, stroking, the meal in the end only three-quarters eaten as the need grew too great and they moved to the bedroom to pursue the by now red-hot attraction.

Sam woke at three and slid out of the bed, careful not to wake Andy. She pulled on yesterday's clothes to make her way down to her own small living space, showered and slipped into bed. She'd get a couple of hours' good sleep before her alarm told her the new day was waiting for her.

Andy wasn't surprised to find Sam gone when he awoke the next morning. Her work shift began at seven and he'd slept until close to eight. But as he touched the cold sheets beside him, he wished she was still there.

Not for sex, although that would have been nice—but just for company. And with nearly two hours before *he* had to be at work, he could afford to lie here for a while and think about her.

He felt comfortable with Sam—talking to her, being with her, even knowing she was close by when they were on the ward.

And somehow, to him, he decided, that was nearly as good as the sex—though it was great sex—something you couldn't really say about most new relationships—well, in his case anyway.

To get his mind off that particular subject, he ran

through the patients on the ward, mentally checking where they all were in their treatment. Grant was a worry. X-rays and scans of his head had revealed little damage to his brain—no swelling, no obvious injuries at all, and although the anaesthetist had reversed the anaesthetic he'd been given to keep him calm for a few days, he'd remained unresponsive.

A neurosurgeon was due to visit him today, and Andy closed his eyes briefly, praying there was nothing the other specialists had missed.

And Jake's rash—still no answer to that.

He drifted back to sleep...

Colin Forbes had appeared as Sam was finishing her first round, checking on any changes to patients' statuses during the night, noting down any problems or anomalies that would require more attention later.

But right now there was a visiting neurologist standing at the monitor desk, going through Grant's file.

'He was alert immediately after the accident?' he asked, when Sam had introduced herself.

'Alert and responding to questions the ambos put to him,' Sam confirmed. 'It was because of the extent of his physical injuries that the surgeons who patched him up decided to put him into an induced coma for a few days, to allow the healing process to begin.'

'And they reversed it, when?'

'Yesterday, late afternoon.'

'And no change?'

'None!' Sam told him, drawing a vacant monitor towards her and pulling up Grant's scans and X-rays.

'Did they do an MRI?' Colin asked, and Sam shook her head.

'Get one done now and ask Radiography to copy to me. Now let's see the boy.'

Sam spoke to the nurse about organising someone to take Grant down to Radiography, then led the specialist to Grant's room, where his mother was reading to the unresponsive boy.

'Good stuff!' Colin told her, then introduced himself. 'The more stimulation a coma patient has the better,' he said, before adding, 'although plenty dispute that. But you keep it up, touch him, talk to him, let him smell things and feel things. It can't do any harm, and who knows what will help.'

Grant's mother happily agreed, saying to Sam as Colin left the room, 'What a lovely man!'

And indeed he was. Sam totally agreed with his notions about providing stimulation for coma patients.

But little Jake was her main problem, his rash far worse. She'd wondered if it could be measles, however unlikely that would be given the child's isolation, but she did return to his bedside to open his mouth, trying to find tell-tale spots among the ulcers the chemo had caused, which was impossible.

Aware he'd been home before the bone-marrow transplant, she wondered if he might have been taken to the fair for a treat.

'Oh, no—no way!' Mrs Wilson responded. 'We kept him well away from any other children and definitely away from crowds. We wanted him as well as possible for the transplant.'

Sam examined him gently, aware he was in a world of misery right now.

The rash was confined to his torso, which really ruled

out the wild supposition of measles, the rash usually starting from the face down.

'Could the donor have had some infection?' Mrs Collins asked, but Sam shook her head.

'The donor cells are tested, and then treated to ensure
they're totally clear of any infection. But for some reason
he's just reacted badly to the transfusion.'

'But on the upside,' a voice behind her said, and this
time Andy had come into the room without shivers running up or down her spine, 'it might just be a rash and it
will clear up in a couple of days.'

Mrs Collins smiled at him, and Sam wondered at the
ease with which Andy could reassure both patients and
their families.

They left Jake's room together, Sam explaining the
neurologist's visit and his wanting an MRI for Grant.

Andy frowned, and shook his head.

'Surely they'd have picked up anything when they
did that in the ED before he was operated on,' he said.

'Unless there was a small bleed, and it's just continued
to bleed. He's not on anti-coagulants—I checked what
the surgeons had ordered, but—'

'You're right—a small bleed could have been missed,'
Andy finished for her.

And, as if summoned by their thoughts, two uniformed police officers appeared.

'Grant Williams. We were told he'd be conscious again
today,' one of them said.

'Might have been but even if he was, he wouldn't be
in any fit state to answer questions,' Sam told the two
men. 'He's badly injured, and he's still in a coma, but
you must realise that even when he comes out of it, he'll
be sleepy and confused.'

'That right?' one of them asked, turning to Andy as if he needed a male viewpoint on the situation.

'Dr Reilly is in charge of the patient, so she should know,' he said, and Sam felt her pique at the policeman's question subside.

The two men left, and she turned to thank Andy for his support, but he just grinned at her.

'Actually, I did it to save that poor fellow from one of your pithy set-downs. I could see the colour rising in your face.'

'Wretch!' she muttered at him, then added, 'But I *am* worried about Grant—worried we've missed something important.'

'Let's wait for the MRI and the neurologist's report before we start worrying. The kid's had a rough few days—he needs time as much as anything else.'

A nurse appeared at that moment with a request from the ED, for someone to see a child with status epilepticus.

'I'll go down,' Andy said, but Sam was already on her way.

'You're not on duty for another two hours,' she reminded him, although inside she was rather hoping he'd come in early because he wanted to see her, maybe even brush against her—as she'd wanted to do with him.

Mind on job, she scolded herself as she arrived on the ground floor, though the thoughts she'd just dismissed did make her wonder again whether relationships between close colleagues were a good idea.

The child, Ahmed, was four years old, Sam read from his paper file as the ED doctor explained.

'Suffers from epilepsy but usually controlled by drugs. Mother gave oral dose of a benzodiazepine, and the ambos established an IV line and gave a second dose.

We have a breathing tube in place, blood sugar is low, so we gave a bolus of glucose IV but he's still—well, you can see...'

The little boy was stiff, but his limbs were twitching and his little body twisting.

'We'll admit him,' Sam said, aware they might have to begin second-level drugs, and do further blood and neurological tests. She was pleased to see the neurologist who'd been visiting Grant was listed as the child's regular specialist. Perhaps he was still in the hospital or had rooms nearby.

Colin Forbes was not only in the hospital, but was in the PICU, at the monitor desk, reading a report on Grant from Radiography.

'Look at this,' he said to Sam, turning a monitor so she could see the screen. 'Here!' he said, using a pen to point to a darker mass of matter towards the back of the skull. 'Poor lad was hit so hard by that damn vehicle he had a contra coup injury to the left side at the back of his brain—just a small contusion but it has bled. From his injuries, we know the car hit him on the right side, and his brain must have jolted forward then back against his skull. It wouldn't have been picked up earlier because it wasn't bleeding directly after the accident, then he went up to surgery and it was missed.'

'Would it be causing his lack of response to the reversal of the coma?' Sam asked, but Dr Forbes shrugged.

'Possibly. A case of delayed concussion maybe—that's always possible. But let's just wait and see. It could resolve itself in a day or two.'

Not something Sam wanted to say to the parents, but she knew the specialist was right.

She told him about Ahmed, who should have arrived

in the unit by now, and led the way to the room that had been allotted to him. Sam explained the treatment he'd received from the onset of the seizure, and to her surprise he asked, 'And what would you use next?'

'I suggested downstairs they use a second-line antiepileptic drug like phenytoin, and if that doesn't work by the time they get him transferred, paraldehyde diluted with point nine percent saline.'

He smiled at her. 'You really don't need me, but as Ahmed is one of my patients, I'll definitely see him. I'd like to speak to his mother about the circumstances around the seizure—whether it was brought on by anything, or if the severity of his seizures has been increasing.'

Ahmed was settled in a bed, an ECG connected to his frail chest, the nurse checking the IV line hadn't kinked during the transfer.

Sam checked the file and saw that phenytoin had been administered in the ED more than five minutes ago, and although Ahmed's body seemed less rigid, the twitching continued.

'Go ahead with paraldehyde,' Colin told her, and keep me posted on his progress.'

CHAPTER EIGHT

AND SO THE days progressed, some patients leaving, new ones arriving, but the small core of seriously ill children remaining with them. Grant had regained consciousness but remained in the PICU because of the severity of his injuries and Colin Forbes's desire to keep an eye on his head injury.

But Jake was causing the most concern, the source of his rash still unidentified, although as yet he was showing no sign of rejecting the transfusion of stem cells he'd received. However, far from improving, he remained limp and listless.

Sam had gone from a week of early shifts to six days of night shifts so she'd seen far less of Andy, grabbing a meal together occasionally if he was home from work before she left for her shift.

She'd finished her final night shift and was looking forward to a full day's sleep, possibly two or three, and sat in her office, writing up some notes. She'd visit Jake before she left, his condition still the main source of concern in the unit.

But as she came out into the airlock room to disrobe, there was Andy, looking so great even robed in white paper that her heart flipped.

'How's our boy?' he asked, although his eyes said other things. Things that made her blush.

She pulled off her mask to smile properly at him, and was untying her gown when she started to feel sick. She ripped off her gown and raced out of the room, still wearing her booties and gloves, heading post haste for the staff lounge and its bathrooms.

Flushed with heat, she knelt by the lavatory, throwing up everything she'd snacked on during the night.

Then, clammy, and still feeling distinctly wonky, she sat back on the floor. She was aware she had to get up, wash out her mouth, wash her face and hands, and generally sort herself out, but she was unable, for the moment, to move.

Snacking on night shift was normal, mainly because the time seemed all wrong for eating a large meal, but what had she eaten that could do this to her? A couple of cups of tea with biscuits, coffee at some stage, and a sandwich from the machine in the corridor. She couldn't even remember what had been in it, but that seemed the most likely culprit.

Hauling herself to her feet, she made her way out to the washroom to clean herself up and remove her gloves and booties, dumping them in the disposal bin.

Andy was waiting outside when she opened the door.

'Are you all right?' he asked, concern clouding his features.

'Fine now,' she said, 'but I must have eaten something that disagreed with me.'

'Or you've a virus of some kind. Maybe even something you brought back from South-East Asia. You'll have to go home, Sam,' he said. 'I can't risk you being here, maybe passing on something contagious to the children.'

'I *am* going home,' she reminded him. 'End of night shift, four days off, remember, but I doubt it's some bug I picked up before I came—just too long ago. It's something I ate. I'll be fine once I've had a sleep.'

He stepped towards her and she knew he wanted to hold her as much as she wanted to be held—not a done thing in a staff common room.

'I'll call in and see you when I get off,' he said, reaching out and touching her lightly on the shoulder. 'For now, go home and rest—we'll talk later,' he said quietly, then turned away, leaving Sam feeling weak and sick and badly in need of a hug that just hadn't come.

Sorry she hadn't driven her new car to work, Sam trudged home, feeling quite well now but upset that she hadn't finished the handover and had let the team down— let Andy down!

She'd get her car and go to a pathology lab in town, ask for all the tests they could think of for possible overseas viral or bacterial complaints. But not today—today she'd sleep...

By the following morning, she felt so well she knew it couldn't possibly be anything other than something she'd eaten that had disagreed with her. She phoned Andy to explain how well she was, but only midway through the conversation the sick feeling returned, bile rising in her throat, so she said a hasty goodbye and headed for her own small bathroom.

Where, fifteen minutes later, sitting on a different cool, tiled floor, her brain began to work again, and she had to close her mind against the answer it had reached.

Surely not?

It couldn't be!

But it had been over two weeks since Rosa's death, and she knew from the last time that a pregnancy was dated from the date of the last period, and that morning sickness could begin within three to four weeks of that date.

Which, to her, last time, had seemed totally unreasonable!

But this time?

It was impossible!

How could she possibly be pregnant after one night of grief-driven lust?

True, there'd been more nights together since, but she'd gone onto the Pill, and Andy had been scrupulous in using protection until it was well into her system.

So, what the hell was Andy going to think?

She went cold all over, dreading a repeat of the storm her previous pregnancy had caused—remembering the tragedy that it had led to. Not that she had long to find out what Andy thought...

Deciding the best thing to do would be to cook him dinner that evening, and as they relaxed over fine food she'd—well, probably blurt it out!

She'd leave a note on her door that she was up in his apartment, and—

Stop!

First and foremost was the decision *she* had to make.

How did *she* feel?

What did *she* want?

The first was easy—she was delighted at the thought— and the answer lay in the second question—a baby.

She'd already lost one baby and although it had been barely the size of a fist, her arms had ached for it.

This baby she would keep.

And, yes, it would be difficult as she still wanted to

work—would *have* to work in order to provide a decent life for herself and her child.

And, really, apart from wanting to keep working, she owed it to Andy, who'd employed her, to stay on. But working women had options these days, and a hospital as new as Port's would almost certainly have a crèche and day-care centre tucked away somewhere in its building.

So, that was *her* decisions made.

In, what, in all of three minutes?

You really gave this a lot of thought, Sam!

But chiding herself didn't stop the secret glee she clutched inside her, ignoring all she knew about the uncertainties tied to the first months of any pregnancy.

It would be the start of her family, her mum's longed-for grandchild. She hugged herself in sheer delight...

Her happy secret kept her going all day as she shopped and prepared a meal for herself and Andy, but about the time he was due to arrive home it occurred to her that Andy would be entitled to some say in this matter. After all, it would be his baby too...

Although if he didn't want a baby, wasn't ready, or thought they should be married but didn't fancy that idea, she'd be quite happy to raise the baby on her own.

All Andy had to decide was whether he'd like to take an interest in it—or even accept a fatherhood role—be part of its life for ever.

The glow was fading slightly, especially now she'd *really* considered Andy and his reaction. He might be horrified.

Probably would be horrified...

She had to stop thinking about it, and definitely stop projecting all the possible reactions Andy might have to hear the news before she became too worried about it that telling him would be impossible.

She *did* blurt it out in the end, but at least not until they'd eaten, and she'd stacked their dirty plates and cutlery in the dishwasher and left the kitchen sparkling clean. Eventually she'd joined him on the balcony, a glass of sparkling mineral water in her hand.

He'd taken her hand to draw her closer but she'd resisted, thinking it best not to be too close, actually edging her chair a little further away.

All the things she'd been going to say, all the ways of telling him she'd practised, vanished in a split second as she clutched her water more tightly in her hand and came out with an abrupt, 'I'm pregnant!'

And apart from seeing his face freeze in reaction, she took no further notice of him as everything else she wanted to say came rushing after those two words.

'I didn't have a virus and this happened last time, the early morning sickness thing, and I'm happy to bring the baby up on my own, or if you want involvement then that's okay too, and I know it will interfere with my work but I'll make sure it interferes as little as possible because I want to keep working and—'

He held up his hand like a policeman, signalling her to stop, and as her flow of words did stop he said, 'What last time? And how come you get to say if my involvement is okay or not? And, anyway, we need to talk about this, Sam!' He paused, then added, 'Seriously talk, Sam.'

Feeling completely deflated, Sam waited, and when he said nothing else, anxiety began to grow where the joy had once been. And well aware of how quickly anxiety could lead to anger, she had to prod.

'So talk,' she said, pleased her voice didn't shake too much as she spoke.

He squeezed the fingers of the hand she was surprised to find he still held.

'This is hard,' he began, 'but, seriously, Sam, you shouldn't have this baby.'

Sam stared at him in total shock. She'd been prepared for him not wanting involvement, even for him to be angry at the place they'd landed in, but for his first reaction to be a termination, without any discussion or reasoning, that blew her mind.

And took her right back to three years ago when Nick had made a similar pronouncement, only his had been a blunt, 'Get rid of it!'

And ten minutes later he'd been dead.

Red mist gathered in her head and she knew she had to leave, snatching back her hand and rushing off the balcony, through the living room and out the front door, only vaguely aware of Andy saying something to her, getting up to follow her and knocking over his chair on the way.

But she was gone, racing down the fire stairs rather than waiting for the lift, needing to get back into the small space that was her own, where she could hold herself and breathe and remember the excitement she'd been feeling all day long.

Andy let her go.

She had another three days off then a late shift. Hopefully she'd feel well enough to keep working.

Oh, for heaven's sake, why the hell are you thinking about Sam's work hours and shifts? You have to see her, tell her, explain, sort things out.

This wasn't the end of the world.

Then something she'd said—something else—echoed in his bemused brain.

'This happened last time!'

When had she been pregnant before?

Not by Nick, surely, given Nick's steely determination that they both finish their specialty courses before they even thought about a family.

And, slowly, a glimmer of light appeared. She'd said she probably *had* caused the accident—that they'd been arguing—and knowing Nick, nothing would have made him angrier than an announcement by Sam that she was pregnant...

He sighed, remembering the harsh words he'd flung at her at a time when her whole world must have been crashing down around her—when the pain of loss would have been crushing her usually indomitable spirit.

But that was the past, and right now he had problems of his own to solve.

Sam had been happy, her face aglow as she'd announced her pregnancy, and he'd said exactly the worst possible thing.

But how to explain?

How to tell her that genetic testing only identified eighty-five to ninety percent of carriers, which was great, of course, but oh hell and damnation, he'd already been through all this before, the first time after his engagement, but the second time he'd explained first.

And neither of those women, who had professed to loving him deeply and wholly, had wanted to go ahead with a marriage to him.

Could he watch Sam walk away if he told her—*when* he told her?

Especially now, when he'd known this 'just for now' talk was nonsense and he wanted her—loved her—more than anything else in his life. Probably had done for years.

He closed his eyes to the beauty around him and tried to think, but his mind refused to work, blocked by fear of losing Sam.

He had to see her, talk to her, explain…

Sam lay on her bed and stared at the ceiling, her hands cradling her stomach, although it had yet to produce the slightest of bumps.

Stupid, that's what she'd been, reacting like that—like a spoilt child told she couldn't have what she wanted.

She should go back.

Andy must have had a reason for saying what he had. Surely he did!

But memories of that other time cut too deep—the bitterness, the implacability of Nick's attitude, the anger then the crash—made her dread the conversation that she knew, only too well, she'd have to have with Andy sometime.

But not tonight. Tonight she was far too irrational; the two rejections somehow melding into one.

She had another three days off. She'd sleep and read, and maybe go to the beach or drive around the town, and tomorrow night—surely by tomorrow night—she'd be able to talk sensibly and calmly to Andy, explain how she felt, assure him she could do it on her own, that he needn't be involved.

She shook her head.

Andy *not* be involved?

She'd seen enough of him around the ward to know he'd make a fantastic father. So maybe it was her? Maybe she was okay 'just for now' but not for long term, as a mother of his children.

Dear heaven, she had to stop thinking like this, stop her mind going round and round in circles. She should pick up a book and lose herself in it until she fell asleep. She'd been on night duty, she was tired…

She had a shower, thinking it would soothe her—help her sleep—but Andy's words were a constant echo in her head—*Really, Sam, you shouldn't have this baby…*

Rod woke her with a soft tapping at the door, calling her name. Face crumpled from sleep, hair like a haystack from her tossing and turning all night, she went to it, opening it a crack.

'Andy is here. He wants to see you, just for a minute, before he goes to work.'

Rod was looking anxiously at her and a sideways glance at her mirrored wardrobe doors told her just how bad she *did* look.

Then the nausea came—she'd slept late and not eaten—and she had to flee, managing a garbled, 'Sorry,' to Rod as she shut the door in his face and rushed to the bathroom.

And as she sat on a cool, tiled floor yet again, her stomach empty and the muscles around it complaining, she wondered if Andy was right.

Maybe she *shouldn't* have this baby?

But the mere word 'baby' made her smile, and she hugged her body and told herself she'd manage, get through this, and make a life for herself and her child.

* * *

The text was there when she awoke the second time.

I've booked a table for dinner at the Lighthouse Restaurant for tonight at eight. Bring a warm wrap so we can sit outside and talk. I'll knock on Rod's door about seven forty-five. Please let me know.

They *did* need to talk, but there was something very remote about the text—something detached—one colleague to another, rather than a text between lovers.

Not that love had ever been mentioned, although now Sam thought about *that* she felt distinctly unhappy. As if somewhere in the just-for-now scenario, love had entered the picture.

On her side, anyway.

So a cool, unemotional, colleague-type text made her heart ache.

But love wasn't the issue right now, she reminded herself. This was about the baby—someone she could love unreservedly!

She'd bought fresh bread the previous day and was trialling dry toast and a cup of tea for breakfast, hoping it would quell the nausea so her work days wouldn't be disrupted.

And if it worked, she'd head for the beach this morning, slathering on sunscreen and not staying long—just time for a swim and a short sunbake to dry off.

Andy stared at his phone. Sam had replied to his text, but somehow the single word—Okay—made him feel worse than no reply.

No, he couldn't feel worse, but what the hell did Okay tell him? Abso-bloody-lutely nothing, that was what!

Somehow he made it through the day, pleased to see improvement in most of his patients, although some of the new admissions were causing problems, including a fourth measles case.

Given the high percentage of children who *did* receive all their immunisations, he hated to think how many there would have been if more parents had opted out.

But at least the people at Infectious Diseases had isolated the carrier now, an older man who'd fallen ill in Port, but unfortunately he hadn't been ill enough to take to his bed and keep away from the general population.

'It was just a cold and a sore throat,' he'd told his interviewer. 'Yes, maybe a bit of a rash, but I didn't connect the two. You can brush against something, get a rash anywhere!'

It was the only real diversion in a long work day, which finally ended with a Heads of Department meeting that dragged on and on.

He'd finally stood up, apologising but saying he had to leave for another appointment, surprising not a few of the other department heads, who all assumed he had no life outside the hospital.

Not that they'd been wrong about that—not until recently, anyway...

Now, as he drove home—having driven to work to avoid being late—his gut was clenching and his nausea was probably rivalling Sam's morning sickness. Just thinking those two words filled him with so much confusion he had to shut down his wretched imagination and concentrate on practical matters, like what shirt to wear.

Did it matter?

Not one jot, he suspected, but he had to think about something.

Sam had been waiting by the door and opened it when Andy knocked.

Her mind had played out so many scenarios of this moment, most of them as formal as his text, so she was totally undone when he opened his arms and drew her close, murmuring, 'Oh, my love, I'm so sorry!'

Hugging her to him, rocking her in his arms, just holding her.

'This *is* the main entry foyer and a public space,' a voice behind Andy said, and they broke apart, Sam glaring at Rod's huge smile and furious with herself for blushing.

Grabbing hold of Andy's hand, she said, 'Come on, let's go!' and all but dragged him out the front door.

Andy's car was sitting in one of the drop-off, pickup bays.

'I thought we'd walk,' she said, embarrassed now by her reaction to Rod's tease.

'Driving, we can talk,' Andy said, turning so he could take both her hands in his. 'And we *do* need to talk.'

She looked up into his anxious blue eyes.

'It's not the baby, Sam. There's nothing I'd like more,' he said quietly, then he opened the car door for her, and she slid into the seat.

'But there's something I need to tell you,' he added, as he joined her in the car.

Sam waited, her anxiety, which had vanished in Andy's warm hug, slowly squirming its way inside her once again.

They drove up to the lighthouse, the moon sparkling

on the ocean below, the night picture perfect. As was the restaurant, with elegant starched white tablecloths and gleaming silver and glassware, while the outside deck looked north along the coastline and the ocean, occasional clusters of lights suggesting small beachside hamlets.

But it wasn't until they each had glasses of sparkling mineral water in their hands, and the waiter had departed with their orders, that Andy broke the tension that had been gathering between them.

'It's a genetic thing,' he said, and she knew she'd frowned because he held up his hand to stop her questions. 'I'm a carrier for cystic fibrosis. I had a younger sister who had it, so I was tested as well. It means you will need to be tested because most carriers have no idea they are carrying it, unless they've been impacted by a relative with the disease.'

'And you were?' she asked, thinking of very sick children with CF that she'd cared for in the past. 'You *had* a sister? She died?'

She saw the sadness in his eyes, but he waved her questions away, needing, she guessed, to get said what he wanted to tell her.

'Unfortunately testing only reveals eighty-five to ninety percent of carriers. There are rare mutations that aren't revealed.'

He sounded so stressed she reached out and took his hand, aware that this was very difficult for him, while her own mind whirled through possible consequences. Survival rates for cystic fibrosis were much better these days, and if a sufferer could get a heart-lung transplant they had a good chance of leading a good life.

But it was a condition that limited a child's life enormously, and not something she would ever want to see a child of hers go through.

'So, I get tested to see if I'm a carrier,' she said, 'and hope I'm not one, for a start. I guess there's nothing we can do about the chances of my being one of the five to ten percent who might have it but don't get picked up?'

She could hear the hesitation in her voice and knew how hard it was for him to tell her this.

Andy nodded. 'Yes, but in case you are in that group, we should test the foetus too,' he said. 'CVS testing at ten to twelve weeks or amniocentesis at sixteen to twenty weeks, although even if we are both carriers there's only a one in four chance the baby would have it.'

Sam could only stare at him, aware he'd lived with this for most of his life so the facts and figures rolled off his tongue.

CVS—chorionic villus sampling—was where a small number of cells were taken from the placenta close to where it attached to the uterus. Her hand went automatically to her belly, as if she could hold the baby safe from this intrusion.

'Did your parents know?' she asked, wondering if she'd be willing to take the chance of having children if something like this could occur.

Andy shook his head. 'As far back as either of their parents or grandparents were concerned, no one remembered a child who was seriously ill from birth.'

He paused, then added, 'Not that that mattered. They had Sarah and she was a blessing to our family. She was so funny and smart, Sam, and so unconcerned about the difficulties she faced every day.'

He paused.

'We loved her,' he said simply, but his voice was tight,

and Sam reached out to hold his hand. Some other time they'd talk more about Sarah, but for now she had to concentrate on her child—their child...

She'd get tested for CF, and if she wasn't found to be a carrier, there was only a minimal chance of her being one of the rare ones, and even if she was... She shuddered at the thought then pushed it away—all the odds were in her favour, although she knew nothing of her father's family, nothing of her father, for that matter.

'If I'm not a carrier then there's no problem,' she said.

'We'd still have to test the baby,' Andy told her. 'Remember the small percentage of people with the rare mutation that testing doesn't reveal.'

Sam sighed and shook her head, unable to take it all in, staring down at the table and fiddling with her cutlery, twirling her knife on the stiffly starched tablecloth.

'Let's wait and see,' she said. 'At the moment it's just all ifs and buts and maybes—all hypothetical. Whatever my test reveals, I'll get the foetus tested and go from there. Okay?'

Andy had to smile at Sam, refusing to get carried away with possibilities, or be concerned over things that might never eventuate. He might mull over it all, and run through dozens of scenarios in his head, but she just got on with things—meeting problems head on. Practical, loving Sam.

Their meals arrived, and as they ate they talked about the food, how good it was, how special to be eating with the ocean right there below them, yet he knew Sam's brain would be working through consequences, and that this was only a temporary lull in the main conversation.

And as the waiter took their plates and left them with a dessert menu, the topic did resume again.

'There's a huge amount of research being done about CF at the moment,' she said, 'and treatments are improving all the time. Imagine if a heart-lung transplant had been available for your sister, Sarah.'

She was smiling at the thought, and Andy could only shake his head. He'd hit Sam with what must have been quite frightening news and here she was thinking of the positives.

Although… Andy knew she was speaking calmly and rationally, but his mind had snagged back at the testing part of her conversation. Sam's use of the little words 'I' and 'I'll' had rattled him. Surely it should have been 'we' and 'us'…

Did she not want it to be a shared venture—not want to marry him and make a family with this baby and maybe others?

Because she didn't love him?

Or because of the CF thing?

His heart ached, and he longed to ask, but his fear of her answer was greater than his need to know. So he changed the subject.

'You said, when you told me you were pregnant, "that last time" your morning sickness had begun early. When was "that last time", Sam? Surely I'd have known of it?'

CHAPTER NINE

To TELL OR not to tell?

Did it really matter after all this time?

Sam studied the dessert menu as she pondered the questions, not seeing any of the options, just trying to think. Then, aware of the tension growing between them, she lifted her head to meet Andy's eyes.

'That was the cause of the argument,' she said, the words blunt and hard as stones. 'Between Nick and me—when we crashed.'

Another pause, the words that had been held in by locked-away memories caused such pain and guilt she could barely speak. Then, slowly, it came out.

'Nick said a baby would interrupt my career trajectory—and to me it was such a stupid thing to say, especially as I so wanted a family. I blew up.'

She studied Andy's face, seeking understanding—compassion even—but in her emotional state saw nothing.

'I hadn't had a family—not a real one. Just me and Mum. I thought Nick knew how much I wanted children, I'd talked about it often enough.'

Andy nodded, but it was an uncomfortable nod. He'd

always known a family hadn't been part of Nick's agenda, although, apparently, Sam, his wife, had not!

But she had a story to tell—a confession to finish.

She took a deep breath, twiddled her dessert spoon, then met Andy's eyes again.

'He said, get rid of it. Those were his first words, then he went on and on about how it would wreck my career and his career, and I lost it, Andy. Said he didn't know me at all—didn't know how much I ached for a family. I was furious with him—I said things I should never have said, things about him having controlled my life for too long. I was so angry—real redhead rage—I was yelling like a madwoman. It was no wonder Nick was speeding.'

'Sam!'

The single word made her blink, and now she *did* see concern and understanding on his face, and as he took her hands in both of his, the hot memories of her anger melted away and she clung to his fingers—a lifeline back to the present...

'You can't keep blaming yourself,' he said, his voice scratchy with emotion. 'I know I was in shock and somehow took that out on you and I'll never forgive myself for that, but you weren't to blame. Yes, the things you said might have upset Nick, but he was a grown man, thirty-five, and reacting by speeding was a stupid thing to do—*his stupid reaction* caused that crash, not your words.'

'But I lost the baby,' Sam said, still trapped in her memories. 'I could have walked away from Nick—divorced him, kept the baby and followed a new career, even though I'd never considered my work as a "career"—never even thought about a bloody career trajectory!'

Andy smiled at her. 'I know that, love,' he said gently, and that one little word, tacked onto a simple reassurance, made her heart leap.

'Dessert?'

She shook her head, hugging the word to her, although she knew it was probably just a casual endearment.

He'd made it very clear he'd taken her in because she was his best friend's widow—love between them had never been mentioned, although she hadn't realised how she'd felt about Andy until...

Well, that had been her reason to move out.

'So, whatever happens, you want to keep this baby?' he said.

Brought back to earth with a thud, she could only shake her head.

'I'll get genetic testing first and let's go from there. CSV sampling will tell us the baby's okay, and after that— Oh, Andy!'

She knew she was probably looking piteously into his eyes, and could hear the plea in her voice, but how the hell did you make that kind of decision? Surely, as a medical practitioner it would be an ethical one, but for her as a person such a very personal one.

'Let's pay the bill and walk,' he said, as she saw the shadows on his face—shadows of the past, reflections of the shadows she'd have had on hers earlier.

'*Two* near marriages?' she probed, as they walked towards the cliff-top in front of the lighthouse, desperately needing to get away from her own problems.

He nodded.

'So tell me,' she said gently.

'The CF thing did raise issues,' he said, sliding his hand out of hers and clasping both hands behind his back, a clear signal to her that this was not a subject he wished

to pursue. Because he still felt deeply about the women—
or about one of them in particular?

She'd loved Nick, but would have left him in a heartbeat to have the child she'd so longed for. Which kind
of answered the question about this baby. Providing she
wasn't a carrier, and the baby tested negative for CF,
then she'd...

Damn and blast, why did life have to be so difficult?

'Hey, you'll be over the cliff if you don't slow down!'

She should be thinking about Andy, not her own problems, she reminded herself, stopping by the protective
railing and looking down.

Andy's voice brought her out of her useless speculation, and she turned back towards him, aware she'd been
getting carried away—aware of him.

'There's too much to think about,' she said, walking
back and taking his hands in hers as she faced him. 'And
I *have* to think about it, Andy.'

'I know, love,' he said, so gently and quietly she
thought her heart might break.

She moved closer and put her arms around him, held
him—waiting, hoping.

For what?

Words of love?

'Just get the testing done and we'll go from there,' he
said, easing her back a little so he could look into her
face. But with the moon behind him, his remained in
shadow and told her nothing.

They walked back to the car in silence, the magic all
around them unnoticed or maybe it had gone completely.

'Just get the testing done, and we'll go from there.'

His words echoed in her head.

Go where? she wanted to ask, but if she proved to be a carrier...

They could have this baby if it tested negative, but other babies—the family she wanted? She could go the IVF route so the fertilised eggs were tested, and only the ones without CF implanted, but...

You are getting far too carried away with yourself You want a family, but Andy has said nothing about it—might not even want to be part of this one.

Just get the test and go from there!

They drove home in silence, both, she imagined, lost in their own thoughts. And as he pulled the car into the underground car park she knew the silence needed to be broken. It had already grown to something far too big between them.

And any bigger?

Well, there'd be no them.

If there *was* a them to begin with.

Her heart ached at the thought. 'Just for now' hadn't really started, and it was over—or all but over—before it had begun.

'Do you know of a good medical practice nearby? I'll need a referral for the test.'

It wasn't the perfect way to break the silence, but at least it was practical. And Andy grasped at it.

'There's one in the main shopping centre in town, the one behind the hospital.'

The silence resumed, but only for an instant.

'I'll come with you,' he said, and she had to smile.

'Andy, it's only a blood test, or maybe a swab from inside my cheek. I could do it myself and send it to a private testing agency but let's not get too carried away.'

He'd stopped the car and opened his door so they had

a little light, and she saw the concern on his face—concern that seemed to be easing towards dread.

She took his hand.

'I'll be fine,' she told him. 'It's a lot to think about, but it's pointless getting too far ahead of ourselves with all the what-ifs. Let's just get this first test done and take it from there.'

'If you're sure you don't want me there...'

The hesitant words made her smile.

'Andy, it's a *blood test*!'

He didn't answer, getting out of the car and coming around to open her door, which she would normally have done herself, only she was puzzling over why he was so concerned.

Had the last woman he'd asked to take a test broken his heart?

Refused, and walked away?

Did he still love her?

She slammed the door on the thoughts sprouting in her brain, and took Andy's offered hand so he helped her out of the car, and then he took her in his arms and held her close.

'Kind of put a dampener on the evening,' he said softly into her ear, and the warmth of his breath against her skin had her body stirring. But she knew she had too much thinking to do to be getting more involved with Andy.

Although as his lips moved to the little hollow beneath her chin she wondered just what harm there'd be in going ahead with 'just for now'.

Heaps, you idiot, her head yelled at her. Your heart's already far too involved, don't make it worse,

'We'd better go before Rod appears and tells us it's a public car park,' she said, easing away from him. She fled, aware she'd been rude, hadn't even thanked him for dinner, but right now she needed solitude, and a space she could call her own in which to think.

Andy watched her disappear through the heavy fire door, and realised he had absolutely no idea where he stood with this woman he was pretty sure he loved.

Had loved, certainly, when he and Nick had first met her.

She'd been an intern, rostered onto the ED for a term, and she'd been so bright, so alive, even on days when she'd worked through the night and stayed on because she was needed.

And he'd stupidly, as it turned out, had his one and only experience of love at first sight. It had been ridiculous, really, as he'd kept telling himself all through Nick's courtship of her and her starry-eyed wedding to his best mate.

But that was a long time ago, and what he felt now—well, this was certainly different, this was like a deep ache in his gut.

As if he was right back in the past again, in the agony of wanting a woman he couldn't have. Loving her?

He shook his head, aware he didn't want to answer that question even to himself.

He'd loved Annabel, but she'd obviously not loved him enough that she could back away at the first mention of CF, refusing even to consider a genetic test because she'd wanted children and wouldn't risk him as a father.

Which left him where?

Forget it, he told himself. He might not need to think about any of this or make any decisions. The next decision would surely be Sam's.

* * *

The medical centre had an appointment for her. Port being a holiday centre, they usually employed extra locums at these times. The pathology office was next door, so by midday she was done.

The genetic testing of the foetus would need a specialist, who had offices in the private hospital, where she could also have the sample taken under ultrasound.

While on a roll, she made an appointment to see an obstetrician in a couple of weeks, then, because she'd driven into town, took a detour home so she could get a feel for the place and check out the private hospital.

Aware she was getting far too far ahead of herself but unable to stop herself hoping, she began to think about options.

If she stayed with the obstetrician through her pregnancy, she'd probably have her baby here, although if she stuck with the public system she'd probably have a group of other mothers with her all the way and a midwife she could contact at any time.

And, if anything went wrong—like a premature birth—her baby would end up in the public system anyway, as they had the best neonatal facilities.

But she was impressed by the cottagey look of the private hospital—she'd check it out when she had her specialist appointment.

Following no particular route, she drove through suburb after suburb, most of them fairly new, as if the town's expansion into a city had been recent, but she loved the tree-lined streets—the trees still small but promising shade and privacy in the future.

Her phone rang as she climbed out of her car.

Andy!

'How did it go?'

'The blood test was fine, as easy and straightforward as you imagine. No instant results so we just have to wait. But I've made an appointment for an obstetrician to do the CVS, and I drove past the private hospital where he has his offices and through some new and not quite so new suburbs. It seemed from the amount of building that the town developed rapidly.'

'A new hospital, a university, even a big government science establishment, which could, from all the rumours, be developing robots small enough to be inserted into humans to control bad impulses. Or hamburgers made from insects—that's another school of thought. In truth, no one knows but they've a big establishment on the edge of town and every kind of animal imaginable in paddocks around it, leading to a fair few unlikely rumours about interbreeding between species, so who knows?'

'Don't you know anyone working there that you could ask?' Sam said, intrigued by the ideas.

'I do, and they just smile at me so my imagination has even more lurid fantasies.'

Sam laughed. 'More lurid than mind-controlling bots?' she teased.

'Far more lurid.' He laughed, and asked if they could meet up when he finished work.

'I guess so,' Sam said, but she did wonder if she needed a bit of distance between herself and Andy so she could get her head straightened out.

But meeting after work didn't eventuate, Andy being kept late by the admission of a two-year-old who had found small button batteries in a jar and swallowed them, thinking they were candy.

An X-ray showed eight still in the stomach but fortunately revealed none in the oesophagus or windpipe.

'We'll do a small procedure called an endoscopy,' he explained to the parents, aware he wouldn't want to leave the hospital until he knew the child was all right.

But this was how life would be for him and Sam, should they ever manage to get together.

He swore inwardly and continued his explanation to the parents.

'He'll be given light anaesthesia and the surgeon will pass a tube down his throat into his stomach to retrieve the batteries, and also check that there's no damage to the lining of his stomach. He'll be very sleepy after it, but it's not a major procedure for him.'

After settling the parents in the waiting room, with tea and biscuits and magazines in an attempt to take their minds from what was happening, he accompanied the surgeon to Theatre. He'd do the anaesthesia, and that way see what was going on inside his patient.

'I can see eight on the X-ray,' the surgeon said. 'Do we know how many he swallowed?'

'The mother didn't have a clue, but the father thought maybe there could have been ten in the bottle.'

'What on earth were they used for?' the assisting nurse asked, and Andy shook his head as he considered how easily such things happened.

'Apparently, one of the parents' elderly grandfathers lives with them, and he wears hearing aids, but he's always taking the batteries out and leaving them all over the place, so they're gathered up as soon as they're seen and put into the bottle, to be used when he loses another pair.'

'Well, I've got eight,' the surgeon said, and peering

at the screen Andy could see eight of the tiny batteries now encased in a tiny bag.

'I'll bring them out, but some could have gone further into his digestive tract, so the parents should watch for more appearing in his stools.'

He paused before adding, 'I'd be happier if we'd known the exact number.'

'None appeared in the digestive tract in the X-ray,' Andy reminded him, although they both knew with the folds within the small intestine something so small would appear as little more than a tiny blip.

'We'll just have to hope for the best,' he added, wondering if hoping for the best was all you could do with your own children in many situations.

He was beginning to think like Sam, worrying about possible accidents and illnesses to possible children.

Because now there was a child?

The thought excited him to the extent he smiled, although he knew there was still a long way to go before he and Sam could explore their options further as far as the current possibility went.

He and Sam?

Would there ever be an Andy and Sam?

'All done,' the surgeon said. 'You should keep him up in the PICU for twenty-four hours, but I couldn't see any obvious damage to the lining of his stomach so he should be fine.'

Andy stayed with the boy in Recovery, wanting to assure himself he really *was* all right. And possibly as an excuse not to go home just yet.

He had to talk to Sam—to talk about things other than CF—but he was fairly sure that, at the moment, it was in the forefront of her mind, and the admissions of love he'd like to make to her would go unheard—or, worse, unheeded.

Sam was sitting on the couch in his living room with bits of paper strewn around her.

'I had to get the CF thing straight in my head and you know what? Even if we're both carriers there's only a one in four chance of our child having CF. Those are pretty good odds, don't you think?'

'Weren't you the one who was saying we wouldn't bother with it until we got the test results?' he teased, although his heart had leapt at Sam's use of the word 'our'.

So he moved closer, stepping cautiously through the mess of paper, to take her hands and haul her to her feet, where he wrapped his arms around her and held her until he felt her body relax against his—slumping in tiredness from her emotional research.

'Come to bed,' he said, and when she began to object, he kissed the words away.

'We don't know anything yet,' he reminded her as he slid kisses down her neck. 'So, just for now...' he added, as his kisses reached the top of her breast, his lips seeking a way in beneath the loose tank top she was wearing.

Now his tongue had reached her nipple, lapped at it, and he felt her quiver, her body pressing closer to his, her lips now against his neck, her fingers tugging at the buttons on his shirt. Now she hauled his head, lips found lips, while their hands took over stripping their clothes off, and as his tongue met hers, felt it slide against his, desire ramped up a notch, and together they fell to the couch, his feet still entangled in his trousers, but nothing mattered but the sensation—the slide of skin on skin, fingers and lips teasing each other, the pressure for release building and building.

His fingers felt her heat and moistness, and her cry of, 'Please, Andy,' broke any restraint he'd managed to hold onto and he slid into her, moving with her, holding her arching body close, until with another cry she went limp in his arms and his own release surged through him, a groan of utter abandonment escaping him.

They lay, bodies slick with sweat, held together by the force of the passion they'd shared, neither moving, neither speaking, their breathing somehow synchronised. Until, after what seemed like for ever, Andy slid his body beneath hers, kicking off his trousers in the process, and looked up into her face.

'Repeat after me: I will forget about everything genetic until I get the test results.'

Sam smiled down at him, hair beautifully tousled around her flushed face, eyes shining with the aftermath of sex.

'Consider it said,' she answered huskily. 'I'm far too pooped to think of anything tonight and should be back to my normal sensible self by morning.'

'Stay the night with me?' he asked, not wanting to let her go.

Ever!

But that was a way off yet.

He saw her smile and a sleepy nod, which was more than enough encouragement to slide off the couch and lift her in his arms, carrying her through to the bedroom, where he dropped her on the bed.

Sam looked up at him. She was so tired—pleasantly tired, ready to sleep tired—and yet she wanted more—something more—and as she turned onto her side, already half-asleep, she was aware of Andy pulling a sheet over her naked body, and knew what she'd wanted from him.

Love.

CHAPTER TEN

SAM WOKE TO find Andy gone—sometime in the night, she rather thought, vaguely recalling a phone ringing and Andy's hushed voice.

She stretched luxuriously in the big bed, aware of the musky smell of sex on her body, and pleasantly surprised to find memories of Andy's touch still alive on her nerve endings.

But noises outside the bedroom suggested he was back, his voice calling to her, 'Up, lazybones, breakfast in fifteen minutes!'

She leapt out of bed, heading for the shower, sorry she hadn't kept some clothes—undies at least—in Andy's bedroom. But once showered and clean, she pulled on the previous day's tank top and skirt.

Breakfast was a plate of bacon and eggs with hot rolls and butter, served on the balcony. What could be a better follow-up to a night of passion? The honey pot was on the table, already attracting the interest of flying insects, and a couple of small jars of jam the insects seemed equally interested in.

She sat, at peace with the world for the moment, until the smell of the bacon had her stomach roiling, and she fled to the bathroom.

'Dry toast?' Andy suggested sympathetically, as she came out.

She nodded.

'Well, go back out onto the balcony—I've removed the other breakfast but left the honey in case you needed something sweet.'

The brisk breeze from the ocean and, Sam suspected, a little air freshener had removed the smell of bacon and she was able to relax into a chair—but only for as long as it took to remember she had to make an appointment with a doctor to get her CF test results later today.

'We haven't talked about what happens if the test is positive,' Sam said, as the thought of finding out was already churning her delicate stomach.

'Because there's no point,' Andy said firmly. 'We could talk—discuss—for hours all the what-ifs, but why waste our breath on that? We'll wait and see then talk about what next, okay, love?'

There was the word again, the word that let hope creep into her heart.

He came and stood behind her, his hand resting on her shoulder, kneading gently, his fingers straying into her hair, lifting tendrils of it and letting them drop, running strands through his fingers...

He sighed and his fingers tugged gently at her hair so she lifted her face to look at him, look into eyes that didn't hide the confusion—despair?—he was feeling.

'I'd already decided—after Annabel—that it was best I didn't marry, didn't father children. Now here we are, and everything is different, Sam. And, anyway, I have to get back to work.'

He bent and kissed her on the lips—making her glad

she'd put a bit of toothpaste on her finger and given herself a bit of a tooth clean so at least her breath was sweet.

But what use was that?

And why the kiss?

Hadn't he just told her he didn't want to marry?

But if he loved her...

There it was again—love.

Her mind was going round in circles, so she cleaned up the few dishes she'd used, stacked them in the dishwasher, and headed downstairs. What she needed was a swim to clear her head, keep busy so she didn't have to think about Andy, and the decision he'd made well before she'd happened along—his decision not to marry...

Andy couldn't remember a day at work when his mind hadn't been fully focussed on the job. Over the years he'd learned that even a slight distraction might mean he'd miss a minor change in a patient's status or, worse, forget a test he could have performed to get a better result.

So, to have his mind wandering to Sam, to the feel of her in his arms last night, the sweet musky smell of her, and most frequently of all to the test results she'd get today, was a new distraction.

He'd had enough distractions in the past to know how to retrieve his focus, but keeping it there?

Would she know by now?

His gut twisted at the thought, although he knew the percentages of her *not* being a carrier were far higher than a positive test.

Work—think about work!

But he'd held her in his arms as they'd slept, learned the way her body fitted best into his, and felt her heartbeat against his chest. And had known he loved her...

* * *

'Are you sure?' Sam demanded of the doctor, although such a question would have irritated her no end if she'd been working.

The doctor smiled and passed her the second sheet of paper.

'See, they've even sent us pictures!'

He pointed to two strings of figures printed on the page.

'This is the little bugger we want to look at.'

It was typed in red so it was totally obvious.

'See, no mutation in it whatsoever—check for yourself.'

She looked at the two sets of numbers and letters, which were both identical.

Her relief must have shown in her face for the doctor raised an eyebrow.

'Especially good news?' he said, and Sam smiled and nodded at him.

'Very, especially good,' she said, taking the papers from his hand and collecting her little backpack from the floor beside her chair.

'I'm glad,' the doctor told her. 'All the best to you.'

Sam departed, aware she should have been asking questions about the possibility of being one of the rare genetic carriers who didn't show up on tests, or discussing possible referrals to an obstetrician for the foetal test, but she'd sort all that out later. Right now she needed to send a text to Andy.

But that thought stopped her dead on the pavement outside the medical centre. She had absolutely no idea how Andy felt about her pregnancy.

She clutched her hand to her belly, protective of the

new life there. There was still the foetal testing to be done but she felt reasonably certain that would be okay.

No! This baby was here to stay, with or without Andy.

With or without Andy?

The joyous bounce in her step slowed—stopped.

Just because *she* was desperate for a family it didn't mean Andy was.

And even if he did want one, did he want one with her?

There'd been no word of love between them—oh, he'd called her 'love'—but in the same way he might have called her 'sweetheart'.

But neither had she mentioned how she felt about him.

Too wary of rejection to lay her feelings bare?

Although early on she really hadn't been sure of love herself, hadn't been sure it wasn't just an overwhelming relief to have someone she knew and liked working with her.

Then slowly he'd crept into her thoughts—worse, into her blood, and bones, and sinews—until a casual touch could send her heart racing, a smile make her whole body sing.

Damn it all, life wasn't meant to be so complicated— she was sure of this. For the past three years she'd lived, if not at first but much more lately, quite happily single, never thinking about a long-term relationship, still living with a doubt that marriage to Nick had been *her* failure rather than his.

And *never* thinking about love…

'So, when should we get married?' Andy asked, walking into his flat where she'd been preparing a meal and handing her a large bunch of blue cornflowers. 'Must have had mainly girls arrive today to have had only blue ones at the hospital florist,' he added with a smile, then he kissed her cheek, and said, 'Well?'

Disturbed in ways she couldn't put in words, Sam thrust the flowers back at him.

'It's your flat—you'll know where you keep vases, if you have such things, and when did marriage come into the equation?'

'But of course, we'll get married. I want to be part of this child's life and isn't marriage the easiest way to achieve that? This is just the start—we can have a family!'

Sam closed the oven door on the chicken and lentil casserole she was making and turned to face him.

'There's more to marriage than having kids,' she said quietly.

'Of course, there is,' Andy said, the bunch of flowers still clutched in his hand. 'There's sharing lives, and hopes, and dreams, and ups and downs, I guess, and being there for each other through good times and bad, and just, well, having each other to lean on.'

Sam sighed. Should she prompt him? Tell him how she felt?

But if he didn't love her back, they'd both be embarrassed...

Embarrassed? She'd be downright devastated!

Damn it all, surely, she was old enough now to talk honestly about emotions and not get herself twisted up in knots like a fifteen-year-old.

Well, here goes nothing!

She took a deep breath, looked directly at him, aware there'd be challenge in her eyes.

'And love, Andy? Where does love come into it?'

He stared at her for a moment, then crossed the

kitchen, rooting around in a cupboard and finally coming up with a large jar that had presumably held preserved fruit at some time.

He rinsed it then filled it with water, plonking the stems of the flowers into it.

Sam curbed the urge to say he should have trimmed the stalks and cut the string around them, she was far too tense.

Hands free now, he came towards her, put his hands on her shoulders and studied her face, his own concerned—a little wary.

'Sam,' he eventually said, 'I have loved you from the moment I first saw you in that bar. You married Nick, and I was happy for you both, but it didn't stop how I felt, so I kept away. And now you're here, lovelier than ever, carrying my child, and I've still been too…cowardly, I suppose, to tell you how I feel.'

He drew her closer, still speaking.

'You asked the question, Sam—the love question—the one I haven't dared ask you in case you weren't ready to love again, might never want to love again. But *my* love, if you'll accept it, is big enough for both of us.'

Now she was held against his chest, his arms tight around her, her face buried in the curve of his neck.

'You never said,' she muttered against his shirt.

'Cowardly, I know, but to have spoken of it, and been rejected, would have been almost more than I could bear.'

She moved so she could hold him, tightened her arms, and still talking into his shirt muttered, 'Rejected? Never! Of course I love you! How could I not?'

She leaned back so she could see his face, the smile quirking up one side of his lips.

'You are the kindest, most unselfish man I've ever met.

You'd do anything you could to help others—everyone can see that from your doctoring. But you're warm, and protective, and, well, you're Andy, and I love you with all my heart!'

It was some time later that Sam found the words she needed, to ask one final, vital question.

One that she hardly dared to ask…

'Would you have walked away from a relationship if I'd been a carrier?'

He looked at her and shook his head.

'I doubt very much that I could have, Sam, not loving you as much as I do. But we'd have had to have had a serious conversation about children and, knowing you want them so much, that might have made things different.'

There was a pause that made her heart stand still.

'*You* might have walked away!' he added.

She moved back into his arms, holding him tightly.

'I couldn't walk away from you, Andy. I love you more than life itself, so you're stuck with me.'

She eased back so she could lay a palm against his cheek.

'And given that I could still be one of the five percent who don't show up as carriers, we'll have this baby, and any other baby, tested, okay?'

And, again, he drew her close.

'I like the sound of other babies,' he murmured, then kissed her on the lips, a kiss that said so much that could never be put into words. A kiss that was a promise and a pledge and a deep declaration of love…love that would last for ever.

EPILOGUE

THEY WERE MARRIED three weeks later, high on the cliff, beneath the lighthouse. With the sparkling sea as a backdrop, innumerable members of Andy's family—who'd been waiting a long time to see this spectacle—and Sam's mother, flown out from the clinic on the Cambodian border, as guests, the two of them repeated their vows, eyes on each other, everyone else melting away.

'I love you,' Andy said as he bent to kiss her lips.

'And I you,' she said on a breath before those lips met hers.

But as they walked into the lighthouse restaurant, she was met by a crowd of men and women, friends from her past, some she'd kept in sporadic touch with and others she'd thought lost for ever.

Andy had found every one of them and had organised for them to come and share their special day.

And suddenly she was home again, among the friends she'd fled three years ago, and home had become a safe haven, a real home, with Andy by her side for ever.

* * * * *

TEMPTED BY THE HEART SURGEON

LUCY RYDER

MILLS & BOON

To my editor, Sareeta Domingo,
who's had an incredibly rough year,
and to Sheila Hodgson, who stepped in
and helped me through my own rough year.

Thank you, ladies.
I wouldn't have made it without your help.

MILLS & BOON

CHAPTER ONE

SAMANTHA JEFFERIES GLANCED over her shoulder and ducked into the hotel bar, relieved to discover the place packed and the lights dim. Hopefully, she could hide from a very handsy and persistent groomsman, and take a break from the Wedding from Hell where she was one of eleven bridesmaids from an adolescent fantasy.

Eleven! Who the heck had eleven bridesmaids?

But then again, at least Stacey had her life together, while Sam's was falling apart. Taking a break from her Life from Hell sounded like an ideal plan. Maybe she could even pretend to be someone else for an hour or two. Pretend she hadn't seen what she'd seen, that she wasn't dressed like a prom escapee or that her own wedding wasn't a thing of the past. Or would be as soon as she informed her grandmother, she thought with a grimace.

And wasn't *that* going to be a thrill a minute. Considering her grandmother had—for once—completely approved of Sam's fiancé, the old battle-ax would blow a gasket.

She didn't want to think about what her brother would say since he'd never *ever* had a life crisis.

Truthfully, it wasn't that her cousin's wedding was that bad, she admitted, heading for the bar counter farthest from the door—although if she had to endure one more girlish shriek and emotional outburst, she was likely to start screaming herself, and never stop.

It was just that she'd very recently—as in two days ago—walked into her fiancé's large and very tastefully decorated office, and caught him *in flagrante* with his PA.

His male PA.

And if that wasn't deserving of a long-overdue freak-out, it was the fact that she was now wearing an off-the-shoulder pink confection—*yeah, strawberry pink!*—its form-fitting bodice showcasing more curves than she was comfortable showing and drawing more masculine attention than she wanted.

The skirt, a short wide explosion of organza, left most of her long legs free and made her look a bit like a gawky flamingo on the lam from the San Diego Zoo.

Samantha Jefferies, granddaughter of Lilian Gilford, CEO of Gilford Pharmaceuticals and doyenne of Boston high society, would *never* be seen dead in something that would fit right into the chorus line of the Folies Bergère—*sans* feathered headdress, of course. Then again, that in itself might have endeared the outfit to her if not for the fact that she wanted to blend in, escape Mr. Hands, take a deep breath without popping the seams— or the strapless décolletage—and process the last three days with the hopes of salvaging her on-the-skids life.

In this dress, there wasn't a hope in hell of that happening.

Drawing on years of conditioning, Sam ignored the amused smirks and speculative glances and tossed her strappy sandals onto the bar counter. With an irritated tug on the stupid skirt, she slid onto an empty barstool.

As a newly advanced-age single, she might want to get with the program but she wanted to do it without flashing her very new, very scandalous pink thong. First thing on the agenda was to sample everything life had to offer before she was forced to trade her strappy highs for comfortable orthopedic lace-ups.

The bartender appeared before her, eyes smiling, brows arched as he took in her appearance. If not for the fact that he looked about twelve, she might have flirted a little to test her newly liberated wings.

"Lose your way to the prom, princess?"

"Not any more than you look old enough to serve alcohol," she drawled, smiling sweetly when she wanted to snarl, because if she had to field one more comment on her appearance, she might scream.

He sighed. Clearly it wasn't the first time someone had commented on his youthful appearance. "So what'll it be?"

"I'd like to see your shooters menu." Heck, if she was going to begin a new life as a swinging single, she might as well start with some "swingy" drink. She'd never set foot in a bar, let alone sampled a shooter. The granddaughter of Lilian Gilford and fiancée of Lawrence Winthrop the Third would never imbibe anything stronger than sherry.

Well that, she decided, wriggling on the barstool, was about to change, especially if it shocked the blue rinse right out of her grandmother's elegant hairdo.

Smirking—and clearly still smarting from the quip about his age—he demanded, "Your mom know you're in here ordering alcohol?"

"The menu, sonny," she drawled. "And make it snappy. You're losing tips here."

He laughed good-naturedly and slid the menu across the bar. "Sure thing, princess. So what'll it be?"

"I want you to start at the top and give me one of everything." Might as well go for broke.

Dr. Adam Knight saw her the moment she walked into the bar in a downtown upmarket San Francisco hotel. Frankly, he would have noticed her anywhere. In a place filled with hockey players and tables of rowdy Saturday-night revelers ready to rumble, she looked as out of place as a giant pink peony in a desert garden.

Nope, he thought, as she moved toward the long mahogany bar. She was all woman—from the top of her upswept, flower-sprinkled dark chestnut hair to smooth naked shoulders, a long elegant and straight-as-a-ruler back and down the mile-long legs to her bare feet. A pair of pink strappy four-inch sandals dangled from one slender finger.

"So," Adam heard his friend and colleague, Wes Kirkland, say behind him as he gestured with his beer to the vision in pink. "Ten bucks says she's from the mansion."

The other occupant of the table, a short slender brunette, took her eyes off her phone to demand, "Mansion? What mansion?" Her eyes narrowed on the object of their interest and after a short pause she snorted rudely. "You guys have a one-track mind. If you ask me, it looks like she's wandered in from a costume party."

Wes scoffed. "Dressed as what? A flamingo?"

Ignoring them, Adam watched as she leaned forward to exchange words with the bartender. Within minutes, he had a line of shot glasses in front of her. From this distance, Adam couldn't identify them but by the second shot, her Vegas showgirl legs were propped onto a nearby barstool. By the third, she was surrounded by hockey players all ordering shots and joining in what seemed to have become a shot party.

He saw the Peony laugh and shake her head, then grab the bar counter to keep from falling off her stool when one guy snaked an arm around her waist and tried to pull her toward him.

Another burly guy stepped in and for a moment Adam thought there would be a violent tussle with her in the middle. She said something that made the guys stop, patted them both on their big arms and slid off the stool to join a nearby group of women on the dance floor. The first guy followed and tried to tug her back, but she laughed and spun away, her long legs flashing as she attempted to lose herself among the dancers.

She wouldn't be lost for long, Adam thought with a grin. Not in that pink dress.

"Bet *I* could get her to dance," Wes announced confidently. "All I have to do is tell her I'm a doctor. Chicks love that."

"I think they love hockey players more," Janice snorted, gesturing to the women crowding around the players at the bar.

Listening to their banter with half an ear, Adam watched as a big hockey player cornered her and wrapped an arm around her waist. She shook her head at something he said and rolled her eyes good-naturedly when he tugged her into a dance, finessing her around the floor like he was weaving a puck through a line of defensemen toward the posts. He must have reached his imaginary goal because he suddenly spun her around and dramatically bent her low over his arm like a cheesy Lothario in a classic movie.

She laughed, the sound low and husky as she tried to shove his face away from her cleavage. Then her gaze locked with Adam's and he felt it like a one-two punch to his solar plexus. The moment caught and held, stretching between them with invisible bands. Bands that abruptly snapped when the guy whipped her upright and around, his hands sliding aggressively over her curves.

Before Adam could object on her behalf, or recover from that odd moment of connection, she shoved the hockey player away and stumbled backward, tripping over the couple who'd moved in behind her. With a startled squeak, she toppled.

Right into Adam's lap.

Instinctively wrapping an arm around her to keep her from landing on the floor, he murmured, "Gotcha."

One minute Sam was wrestling with the clumsy hockey stud, the next she'd tumbled right into someone sitting at a dance-floor table. She gave a startled yelp as one hard arm snaked around her midriff and hauled her back against an even harder, warmer chest, cutting off her air.

In some dark, purely feminine corner of her mind, she enjoyed the sensation of having a man's arms around her again—of a hard masculine chest and muscular thighs cradling her—while she twisted to right herself and find her feet.

Her elbow connected with something hard and the guy behind her exhaled in a softly groaned *oomph*. She froze, the automatic apology dying on her lips. Oh, God, could this evening get any worse? First, the groomsman from hell, then the clumsy hockey stud with one thing on his mind. And now this.

Beneath her organza tulle bottom, hard thighs flexed,

leaving her weak, shaky and shocked that she was reacting physically to a stranger she couldn't even see. Twisting around, she came face-to-face with the guy she'd
locked eyes with for that one startling instant.

And boy, he was even better looking up close and the
right way up. High forehead, straight as an arrow nose,
slashing cheekbones and a strong jaw beneath warm coppery gold skin gave his face a strength and nobility that
more than hinted at his Native American ancestry.

Something within her stilled. And then, as though
drawn by a will not her own, her gaze dropped to his
mouth where a smile tugged at the sculpted lips a couple
of inches from her own. Probably with amusement at suddenly finding a woman in pink giving him a spontaneous
and inept lap dance, she decided dazedly.

"S'cuse me," she gasped. Unable to stop staring at his
mouth, she hoped he'd interpret her breathlessness as a
result of being spun and tossed around, and not because,
even in a room seething with testosterone, his pheromones pinged off her radar like a nuclear blast.

The next thing she noticed was his hair, thick and
straight and jet-black as it fell almost to his shoulders.
Her fingers twitched with an almost agonizing urge to
slide through all that black silk. She curled them instead
into the hard muscles and bones of his shoulders, and she
wasn't the least bit disappointed.

Hmmm, she thought, flexing her fingers experimen-
tally. *Big and solid and—*

Almost as though he could read her thoughts, his smile
grew and strong white teeth flashed in the semi-darkness.
"No harm done," he drawled with a chuckle, his deep
baritone sending a delicious shiver sliding up the length
of her spine. A large warm hand tightened on her hip and

her belly bottomed out, leaving her relieved she was sitting because even her knees wobbled in response to that heated look.

Oh, boy. He was easily the hottest guy she'd ever met, effortlessly oozing sex appeal from every pore that might have had her as tongue-tied as a thirteen-year-old if not for the very lovely buzz she had going.

Whatever it was, the shooters or the champagne she'd tossed back earlier, she found herself incomprehensibly glad for her clumsiness. If she was kick-starting her new life as a single, she couldn't have asked for a better way to test her nonexistent flirting skills.

She slid her gaze over his strong jawline and skimmed up the length of his straight nose to heavily lashed eyes the color of her grandfather's favorite whiskey. And just as it had rushed straight to her head the first time she'd tasted the expensive drink, she lost her breath now as the world tilted.

"S-sorry," she murmured, falling into their potent depths. "I—"

"Hey!" someone complained behind her, jolting her out of the sensual trance she'd been slipping into without a whimper. "Get your mitts off my girl." It was the lumbering hockey stud, closing a hand roughly over her shoulder as he tried to yank her off her perch.

With a shrug of her shoulder, Sam dislodged his hand and wrapped her arms around the gorgeous hot guy's neck. Leaning forward, she begged, "Save me," against his lips and did something she'd never done before. She slid her fingers into thick cool hair and kissed a stranger.

She might have been shocked by her uncharacteristic behavior if not for the two—or was that three?—shooters and two glasses of champagne and the past forty-eight hours. Forty-eight hours since she'd discovered the reason her fiancé had insisted on waiting for the wedding night before he saw her naked. Forty-eight hours of wondering why she hadn't seen what everyone else knew. That her handsome, buff, blond fiancé *was* interested in sex—just not with her, because he was having an affair with his assistant. A guy named Ronnie.

If not for that image stuck in her head, Sam was sure she wouldn't be snuggled in some hot guy's lap, contemplating throwing a lifetime of caution to the wind. Or then again, it could easily be the amused expression in his amber eyes that dared her to plunge right in. She was single after all, and hadn't she just decided to take life by the horns instead of meekly allowing her grandmother to direct her path?

Whatever it was, it was suddenly so hugely liberating that she experienced a moment's dizziness. Besides, she was heading back to Boston in the morning and would never see any of these people ever again.

But staring into his bourbon-colored eyes, the "something" that had stilled within her sparked abruptly to life and for just an instant it was as though—as though she knew him. Before she could tell herself how ridiculous that sounded, her heart leaped and thundered as elation rose within her along with a need that was as frightening as it was wildly thrilling.

The guy stilled. His big hands closed over her shoulders and for one mortifying moment, Sam thought he'd push her away. Then he cupped the back of her head with one hand, the other dropping to nudge her hips closer to his.

And the next instant, he was kissing her back.

The instant that generously sculpted mouth opened

beneath hers and applied a slight suction, it took only a half a dozen frantic heartbeats for her to lose her mind.

And for him to completely own her.

Or the kiss, she corrected dazedly. *Own the kiss.* Because owning her a minute after they'd met was about as farfetched as looking into a stranger's eyes and imagining that soul-click.

In some dim corner of her mind, she heard someone say, "Forget her big boy, I'm a much better dancer," then the heat of his body seeped into hers and the rest of the bar faded away, leaving her in a world she'd only ever dreamed about. It was as though she'd finally discovered fire after wandering through a frozen wasteland for nearly twenty-eight years. Finally experiencing for herself what everyone else knew.

His lips were softer than she'd expected, warmer. A sigh escaped her when his tongue slid along the length of hers, setting off a chain reaction that had her squirming with instant heat. Shifting closer, she reveled in the taste of him—slightly bitter from the beer he'd been drinking and something else. Something dark and delicious and uniquely male.

Uniquely *him*.

Then the kiss turned hot and carnal, and it was all she could do to keep up because her blood caught fire. The heat of the hard thighs against her bottom burned through her awful pink dress to her fluttering core and set all her senses aflame.

In all her secret fantasies, she'd never been kissed like this—with lips and tongue and scraping teeth. Like he wanted to consume her right there in public, in front of all these strangers.

And she was tempted to let him.

It was that last thought that had her jerking away to stare at him in shock. "I…uh… I'm s-sorry," she stammered, rudely returned to reality like she'd been doused with icy water. What the heck was she doing kissing a guy like they were alone and had known each other longer than a couple of minutes?

He stared back at her through heavy-lidded eyes almost black with arousal and murmured, "I'm not," in a voice so rough and tight with lust that she shivered. One of those delicious shivers that started at the base of her spine and rolled over her body in deep luscious waves, leaving her senses heightened and her body humming.

Heat swept up from her jittery belly, filling her chest with the champagne she'd consumed before racing up her throat into her face in a hot wave she wasn't altogether certain was embarrassment. Or maybe not *just* embarrassment.

Then out the corner of her eye, she caught movement and turned to see Mr. Hands, the groomsman, bearing down on her like the IRS intent on an audit.

Dammit, she cursed silently. Trust him to find her here of all places, just when she was finally beginning to enjoy the anonymity of the dimly lit bar.

The condemnation in Jared's eyes had her own eyes narrowing in an uncharacteristic display of temper. Decked out in his vintage wedding tuxedo, he looked ridiculously pretentious in comparison to soft faded jeans and a plain white T-shirt stretched across broad shoulders that needed no padding to look wide and solid and safe.

"Amanda," he clipped out, probably annoyed that she was fondling another man when she'd been evading *his* hot sweaty hands all weekend. "What are you doing here?

I've been looking everywhere for you." *Hoping to maneuver her into a tight corner, no doubt.*

It was on the tip of her tongue to tell him for the thousandth time that her name was Samantha not Amanda when she was gripped by an almost savage need to shock that supercilious look right off his face. She suddenly wanted to rebel against everything in her life that kept her from being the woman she wanted to be. She wanted to be bold and face life head-on instead of timidly letting it control her.

It was tempting to dispel once and for all the prim-and-proper image that had been drummed into her since childhood and behave like a *normal* person for once. A woman with needs and emotions; someone light-years away from the mousey, emotionless and perpetually elegant and dignified woman her grandmother expected her to be.

Well, she thought, wiggling suggestively in the hot guy's lap and giving herself a hot flash in the process. *Damn elegant and to hell with dignified.* She'd left that behind in Boston the moment she'd turned away from the sight of her fiancé and his boy toy to walk calmly from the room, shutting the door quietly behind her, leaving them in no doubt that the wedding was off.

Ignoring Jared, she cupped the hot guy's handsome angular jaw between her palms and smiled into his intoxicating eyes before closing the gap between their lips to place a soft lingering kiss on his mouth. Her blood heated anew when he responded with flattering enthusiasm and smoothed his big hands up the length of her spine.

Shivering deliciously, she gave in to the wild, wanton creature inside of her. After drowning in the taste of him, she reluctantly broke the kiss, her tingling lips remaining on his for a moment longer before she eased back an inch. Staring into his eyes, she memorized the hot potent expression there and the way it made her feel. Like a hot-blooded woman a red-blooded man might desire. Just like a woman bent on experiencing everything life had to offer.

"Duty calls," she murmured, lightly tracing his bottom lip with one finger. Then with real regret, she slid off his lap, grateful for his supporting hands when her knees wobbled and her head spun.

Whoa. No more shooters for you.

Or maybe that should be no more intoxicating kisses from hot strangers. But damn. She really wanted more of that.

"Sure you won't stay?" he asked quietly, his eyes locked on hers. She was tempted—*boy was she tempted.* Then Jared called, "Amanda," in that peremptory tone she suddenly decided she hated, because it was exactly the tone her grandmother used when she felt Sam wasn't living up to Gilford standards. Just as Jared was exactly the kind of man the old battle-ax would approve of: good family, great pedigree, oodles of old money.

And boring as hell.

She shook her head regretfully. "I...can't."

His gaze, dark and seductive, held hers and myriad messages passed between them that she struggled to interpret. "My loss," he murmured, his big hand warm and comforting on hers until her fingers slid free.

CHAPTER TWO

ADAM POCKETED HIS key card and headed for the bank of elevators at the far end of the lobby. After the Peony—Amanda, the stiff had called her—left, the evening seemed to fizzle.

He wouldn't go so far as to say he'd felt bereft watching her walk away but it had been pretty damn close. As if something meaningful was slipping from his grasp. And he was letting it.

His grandmother would have said their souls had clicked but Adam knew just how corny that sounded. Much cornier than if he'd just admitted that his hormones had suddenly awakened from a long hibernation and said, *Mine*.

But that was just his neglected libido talking, he admitted wryly. Besides, he was getting too old for one-night stands, even if tall long-legged women dressed like prom queens suddenly seemed to have become a very personal and surprising fantasy.

He arrived just as the doors were closing and he thrust his hand into the opening, causing the doors to bounce, then jerk back open. He stepped forward, an apology dying on his lips when he caught sight of an explosion of pink and wide startled eyes. Eyes so startlingly blue they seemed to glow beneath their luxurious fringe of dark lashes.

Soft lips parted in a soundless gasp and she stared back at him.

His gaze swept from the top of her tousled chestnut hair to her elegant feet, which were no longer bare. The pink strappy sandals she'd been carrying earlier made her long legs appear even longer. She looked good even in the harsh elevator lights, especially when his frank appraisal caused color to rush beneath soft creamy skin.

That embarrassed self-consciousness was in direct contrast to the bold seductress of a couple hours ago. It caught and held his interest even more than the pink peony dress and long limbs.

Abruptly realizing that he was preventing the doors from closing, and that the elevator's other very pregnant occupant was staring at him with wide-eyed interest, Adam murmured, "Evening ladies," and stepped into the car to punch his floor number. Once the doors slid closed, he propped a shoulder against the wall and studied the woman he'd met in the bar, looking at him as though she hadn't had her tongue in his mouth a couple of hours ago.

"Um…hi again," she said, trying not to squirm even as heat rose up her neck into her face. Her voice, as low and husky as he remembered, gave him a few bad moments when he recalled the way she'd murmured *save me* against his mouth before kissing his socks off.

"I see you escaped your jailer."

She looked momentarily confused. "My jail—? Oh, you mean Jared? Nope." She grimaced. "We're not together," she explained as the very pregnant young woman—also in an explosion of eye-popping pink tulle and organza—snorted.

"No woman in her right mind would *be* with Jared," the young mother-to-be said, as she sucked in a shaky breath and rubbed her enormous belly. "He's an accountant and you know how *they* are."

"Daphne," Amanda whispered aghast, grimacing an apology as Adam's smile widened.

"What?"

Amanda flicked her gaze in his direction as the elevator rose. "Maybe *he's* an accountant," he heard her whisper.

Before he could reassure them that he wasn't, Daphne shook her head firmly. "Nope," she whispered back loudly. "No way. Just look at him. Does any of *that* say accountant to you?"

"How do you know?" Amanda demanded sotto voce, coloring beneath his stare. "It's not like accountants *look* a certain way."

"Of course they do," Daphne argued. "There's Pete and Rowland and don't forget Jared and his brother Mark and oh—"

The last was in response to the jolt as the elevator came to an abrupt and unexpected stop. It swayed violently, prompting the two women to clutch frantically at the rail behind them to keep from being thrown to the floor.

The lights flickered once, brightened and just before they blinked out completely, he saw Daphne's eyes widen as she grabbed her belly. "Uh-oh," she said, and Adam, who'd spent enough time during his internship catching babies, knew instantly what it meant.

"Don't panic Daph," he heard Amanda say tightly. "I'm sure it's only a computer glitch. We'll be on our way in a minute and then you can relax in a nice warm bath while I call Stan—"

"That's not what the uh-oh was for," Daphne interrupted on a thin wail. "I think my water just broke."

"It's all right," Amanda soothed. "No one can blame you for not having control of your bladder at a time like this. I'm sure…um…" She paused and Adam could feel her looking his way.

"Adam," he supplied helpfully.

"Oh. Right," she said in a tone that told Adam she was recalling in perfect detail that she'd been up close and personal with a man whose name she didn't know. "I'm sure…um… Adam will forgive you this one lapse. Besides, it's entirely understandable in a woman who's almost ten months pregnant."

"Eight months," Daphne said with a tight, dry laugh.

Adam drawled, "I think she means she's in labor," turning to feel for the emergency button on the panel.

The emergency lights finally flickered on just in time for him to see Amanda staring at him in open-mouthed horror.

"Labor?" she squeaked, her eyes wide as she dropped her gaze to stare at the other woman's swollen belly. Her expression told him she half expected an alien to pop out any second. "But—but you can't," she said fiercely, clutching Daphne's arm. "It's not time. Tell him," she ordered frantically. "Tell the hunk he's mistaken. Tell that baby it's not time, because if I remember correctly, babies are supposed to stay there nine months. *Nine months, Daph*." She broke off and sucked in a shaky breath. "Besides," she continued tightly after a short battle with her slipping control. "Stan isn't even here. You can't give birth without Stan."

"Yeah, well—" Daphne wheezed out a laugh as she clutched her belly "—I don't think this kid is about to wait for Stan to get here. *Oh, God*," she wailed and grabbed Amanda's arm. "I hope you know something about birthing babies, hon, 'cause you're it."

Amanda yelped as her arm turned white around the younger woman's grip. Adam eyed her curiously, because it was obvious that she was battling to remain in control of a situation that had all the hallmarks of going to hell in a handbasket. "I know zip about babies, Daphne, let alone how to help one into this world."

"Fortunately," Adam said briskly, digging out his cell phone to toss at Amanda. "I do." He checked his watch while she fumbled the catch, finally looking up to find them both staring at him as though he'd suggested something indecent. "I'm a doctor," he told them absently, as he calculated that it had been about four minutes since the last contraction.

Amanda looked relieved. "A doctor? Please tell me you're a gynecologist."

"Call 911," he ordered, ignoring her question and taking Daphne's arm. He didn't think either of them needed to know he was a cardiothoracic surgeon. He gently pushed Daphne to her hands and knees. "This position will help," he murmured, briskly rubbing her back. "Explain the situation," he addressed the woman huddled in the corner with a deer-in-the-headlights look on her face. "Tell them to send an ambulance and the fire brigade."

"Fire brigade?" the two women yelped, staring at him with similar expressions of horror.

"You mean there might be a fire?" Daphne squealed, slapping at Adam's hands as she shot upright to glare at him. "I am *not* giving birth in the middle of a fire!"

"No," Amanda said, her wide blue eyes clinging to his as she punched in the emergency numbers with shaking fingers. "I think it's in case maintenance can't get the computers rebooted in time and they have to break us out of here."

Adam nodded reassuringly. "That's right," he soothed gently, reassessing his Peony as Daphne blew out a long breath and grunted, "Breaking us out sounds good. Can they do it now?"

"Soon," Adam promised. "For now, all you need to do is concentrate on breathing through the contractions. No pushing, okay? Just breathing."

After relaying the information to the 911 dispatcher, Amanda turned narrowed eyes on him. "You better know what you're d-doing," she stuttered in a fierce undertone over Daphne's heaving form. "Because I wasn't kidding. I h-have no idea what I'm supposed to do other than b-boil water and get fresh towels before hiding until it's all over."

Adam grabbed her hand and tugged her down to the floor, guiding her hand to Daphne's lower back. "Trust me," he said cheerfully, a quick grin lighting his face. "I know what I'm doing." Maybe she'd stay calm if he gave her something to do. "Look at me," he ordered softly when he caught the quick panicked sound of her breathing. Her wide eyes flew to his and he said firmly, "Concentrate on breathing evenly. Can you do that?"

She swallowed, a quick spasmodic movement of her throat, before nodding. "Good," he murmured with an encouraging grin. "Now rub. It probably feels like her back is breaking. Keep rubbing and don't worry. Daphne and her baby know what to do."

"I do?" Daphne panted, sounding a little shaky. "I hate

to break it to you, handsome, but this is my first time. I have no idea what to expect."

Amanda gulped, and Adam caught sight of her pink tongue emerging to swipe nervously across her soft plump lip. "I thought you said you went to Lamaze classes?"

"I did," Daphne grunted. "But they didn't say anything about giving birth in an elevator. Nothing," she yelped, squeezing her eyes closed, "in any of the books I read said anything…about…*giving birth in an elevator*." Her voice got louder until she was almost yelling.

Amanda flinched, her eyes wide as she frantically rubbed the other woman's back and flicked a look at him. "Shouldn't she be lying down?" she hissed, but Adam shook his head, enjoying the drama despite himself.

"This position is more natural for now. Ideally, when the time comes, she should be squatting."

Both women looked appalled. "Squatting?" Daphne screeched, "If you think I'm squatting, buster, you're insane. In fact," she batted their hands away and grabbed the railing behind her before hauling herself to her feet. "There is absolutely no way I'm giving birth in an elevator, so just forget it. In fact, I've decided I'm not doing this. Not here, not ever."

"Daphne—"

"Get those paramedics," Daphne snarled. "Because if I can't have this baby in a hospital, I'm not having it at all."

Sam opened her mouth but the next contraction hit and she had to make a grab for Daphne before the girl hit the floor. Once it passed, Sam sank onto the floor beside her and stared at the hunky doctor.

Adam, she reminded herself. His name was Adam and

he had one knee on the floor, his large hands on Daphne's belly. The look of concentration on his handsome face was surprisingly attractive.

"Are you okay, Daph?" Her heart was racing and she felt the edge of hysteria trying to push through her shaky control.

Oh, God. She hoped the EMTs made it in time.

"No. I…am…not…okay," the other woman gritted out, as she dug her fingers into Sam's arm and rode the next wave by huffing, puffing and squeezing out a strangled moan. "I'm about to pass a watermelon through my vagina. What part of that sounds okay?"

Sam winced again, both because Daphne's grip rivaled a muscle-bound logger and she had used the *V* word in the presence of a man neither of them knew—even if he *was* a doctor.

"You're going to be fine," Adam said, a hint of warm laughter in his voice that he quickly swallowed the instant two outraged females turned to glare at him.

Daphne huffed and puffed, eyeing him with intense dislike. "This is all your fault," she snarled through gritted teeth.

A dark eyebrow climbed up his tanned forehead as he eyed her warily. "Me?"

"You're a guy, right?" Daphne snapped, suddenly collapsing against Sam and breathing like she'd run up twelve flights of stairs in stilettos. She pointed a shaky finger at Adam. "If you and your…your *kind* didn't look at women with those hot, sexy eyes, none of this would happen." Sam assumed by the way she said *your kind*— bitten off with more than an edge of teeth—that she was contemplating violence against poor old Stan.

"Look at him," the girl panted, glaring at Adam. "I

just bet he could impregnate some unsuspecting woman at a hundred paces. Better watch those eyes, girl. They're *potent*. One look and he'll have you performing a naked lap dance."

Sam made a strangled sound in the back of her throat and snapped her knees together as though Daphne knew what she'd been up to a couple hours earlier. And as though *he* knew what she was thinking, Adam's amusement grew, his warm gaze snaring hers and holding it captive as his grin widened.

Just when she thought things couldn't get any worse, she heard Adam say, "Can you remove her underwear so I can check dilation?"

Blinking at him uncertainly, she said, "I'm sure you didn't mean what I think you just said because there's no way I'm removing *anyone's* underwear. Let alone someone I only met two days ago."

"*Hey*," Daphne objected through clenched teeth. "We survived two days of the high school histrionics together, so I think we're more than a little acquainted."

Adam's eyes were clear with a message she had no trouble interpreting. His expression said that if he'd asked her to remove *her* panties, she wouldn't have been balking.

Okay, so he might be right. *Maybe*. But she'd need another dozen shooters to contemplate that.

"Oh, for God's sake," Daphne burst out. "It's not like he's going to be seeing *your* lady parts stretched beyond recognition. I'd do it myself but—*Oh, God!*" She squinted at Adam in panic and sprawled onto her back to huff and pant like she was struggling for air. "Tell me they're not getting closer together because I told you we're not doing this here."

"Okay," he said mildly, sending Sam a pointed look. "I won't, but it would help if I could see what's going on."

Sam hesitated for a couple of beats, then sighed in resignation because no amount of pretending was going to change the situation. Besides, she was almost twenty-eight. Practically thirty. Way past the age when she should be over a stupid little thing like embarrassment and panic attacks at the worst possible moment.

Reaching beneath Daphne's bridesmaid dress—the one that made the pregnant woman look like a giant luminous beach ball decked out in a frilly pink skirt, she felt for the hip band and gave a tug.

Apparently enjoying her discomfort, Daphne giggled and tried to lift her heaving body off the floor so Sam could tug her underwear down her thighs. Too busy trying to pretend Adam wasn't controlling a smile and or that she removed people's underwear every day, Sam ended up wrestling with it like a demented squirrel digging for nuts when the swatch of lace snagged on Daphne's two-inch heel.

Oh, God. Face flaming and muttering something about guys being useful for exactly nothing except turning women into giant beach balls with legs, she yanked at the offending garment and shoved it at a giggling Daphne.

Adam was silent for a couple of beats, then said mildly, "Good job," with such a straight face that Daphne's hoot of hilarity smoothed over his next move as he gently nudged her knees apart and bent to look at ground zero.

With perspiration dotting her brow and seeming unconcerned that a man other than Stanley was looking at her naked crotch, Daphne huffed out breathlessly, "Tell me you were mistaken and that I'm not about to—oh," and promptly broke off with a low moan as another contraction hit.

"No mistaking that, Daph," Adam said quietly, sending Sam a narrow-eyed look. "Junior's head is already crowning. Don't push until I say, okay?"

"I thought I told you we weren't doing this here," the laboring woman wheezed as she collapsed against Sam. "Besides, I want to push more than *anything*. Except maybe strangle Stan for getting me this way." Then she grabbed Sam's hand and squeezed as she rode out the next contraction. "And the instant I get out of here," she gritted out, "I'm telling him there'll be no more sex for him...*ever*!"

"Okay, Daphne," Adam said calmly, his eyes gleaming with concentration. "The head's emerging. I want you to push now."

Daphne's body bowed with the force of her effort and her face went red until Sam thought she'd pop a blood vessel. She made a godawful noise that sounded like she was being ripped apart from the inside and Sam's heart clutched in sympathy.

She locked her gaze on Adam's face, the calm in the storm. But—what if something went wrong, she thought suddenly. What if the baby got stuck and they couldn't get it out? Her heart stuttered, a fist closing around her chest in a squeezing grip that threatened to cut off her air because she suddenly wanted more than anything to help.

Her fingers went numb and there was a loud buzzing in her head. What if...what if she froze and Daphne—or her baby—died because Sam was too terrified to move? What if—?

"*Amanda*." A deep masculine voice penetrated the white noise blocking out everything but the tumble of memories that still managed to give her nightmares. Memories that still made her freeze nearly two decades later—

"Hey," Adam said, his voice deep and smooth and soothing.

Sam blinked, realizing that he was talking to her. "Huh?"

He waited until her gaze cleared. "You okay?"

Hiding a wince, she licked her dry lips. "I'm f-fine," she said with grim determination. *Get a grip*, she ordered herself. *It's not like you're the one giving birth.* "I've just never w-witnessed a b-birth before."

After a short silence, he nodded. "It'll be okay," he said briskly, straightening to pull off his jacket. "Women have been giving birth for millennia." She only just prevented the jacket from slapping her in the face when he tossed it at her. She opened her mouth to ask what the heck he was doing when he reached between his shoulder blades with one hand and proceeded to strip his T-shirt over his head in that unique way guys had of undressing, leaving her gaping at him in shock—and admiration, darn it.

"Damn," Daphne wheezed, echoing Sam's thoughts and staring at a whole symphony of muscles bunching and flexing beneath acres of satin-smooth skin. "I'd hate you if you weren't so pretty to look at."

And because Sam was staring at him, she'd swear she detected a rush of color beneath his skin. She blinked. *Had the hot guy just blushed?*

Without missing a beat, he ordered, "Another push, Daph," sending Sam a challenging stare as he thrust his T-shirt at her. "Here, hold this. I'd ask you to sacrifice that dress for what's coming next but I have a feeling you're not wearing a hell of a lot under there."

Sam took the warm soft garment and couldn't resist one last peek at his wide rippling chest, shifting arm muscles and sculpted abs covered in acres of dark coppery gold skin. The perfect distraction from the panic attack hovering at the edges of her mind. But even as her heartrate slowed, he was suddenly frowning and ordering Daphne to stop pushing.

"Stop?" the woman gasped, lifting her head to gape at him. "Are you crazy?" She let rip with an eerie moan that streaked up Sam's spine and set all her hair standing on end. "I can't stop now!"

"The cord," Adam said softly, doing something between Daphne's thighs that Sam couldn't see. "It's wrapped around the baby's neck." He looked up briefly as both women inhaled sharply. "But not to worry," he soothed, transferring his attention back to what he was doing. "As long as you don't push or put pressure on this…" He cursed softly which made Sam's blood run cold and then he was humming encouragement. "Got it. All clear. Just a couple more pushes, Daph, and you'll be able to hold your baby."

By the time they heard the commotion and a frantic man yelling, "Daphne, I'm coming, babe," Daphne was propped up against Sam, gazing with wide-eyed wonder at the miracle in her arms.

Fifteen minutes later, the elevator had reached the lobby and the paramedics were rushing forward to take over the care of Daphne and her baby.

Trembling from reaction, Sam would have tripped in her haste to get out of the elevator if not for the large warm hand cupping her elbow and keeping her upright.

"Don't go anywhere," Adam murmured in her ear,

as he brushed past her to where the EMTs were loading Daphne onto the waiting stretcher. The look of utter pride and joy on Stan's face as he stared down at his wife and child brought tears to Sam's eyes. Thank God Adam had been there to prevent Daphne's baby from strangling himself on his umbilical. Thank God *she* hadn't let Daphne down, she thought as relief washed over her in a knee-weakening rush. And thank God she'd kept herself from losing it. It had been a close call, but other than those brief moments of mind-numbing panic, she'd managed to breathe through the worst of it and help bring a child into the world.

That in itself was a major victory but—

Daphne's sharp, "Wait!" cut through Sam's thoughts and she looked up to see the other woman staring at her. "I don't know how much to thank you for being there. I hope you don't mind."

Sam blinked in confusion. "Mind?"

Looking flushed and serene, Daph linked her fingers with Stan's and leaned into him. "That I named him after you both." She looked briefly up at Stan, who nodded. "Meet Samuel Adam Prescott."

Stunned, Sam could only stare back and manage a garbled, "It's... I... I didn't do anything, Daph. I—"

"You did," Daphne interrupted huskily. "More than you know."

Sam gulped, terrified that she would lose control of the threatening tears "You're w-welcome," she rasped.

Adam, who must have realized that she was holding onto her composure with difficulty said, "It's an honor, Daph and she's right, we didn't do anything. You did all the hard work."

His deep baritone poured over Sam like warm honey,

making her feel as though they'd been partners when she knew he'd been the center of calm.

"I know I acted like a crazy person in there," Daphne continued solemnly, echoing Sam's thoughts. "But I was wrong."

Sam licked her dry lips. "W-wrong?" God knows Sam was starting to sound like a parrot but she couldn't seem to help herself. The combination of adrenaline, a very private sense of accomplishment and the solid male strength and heat seeping into her back had rendered her speechless.

Daphne smirked at Adam's close proximity to Sam. "So totally worth it," she said, waggling her eyebrows. "Even from a hundred paces." She was grinning broadly as they wheeled her away, leaving Sam burning with embarrassment because Adam, who knew exactly what Daphne meant, chuckled softly in her ear.

Her body responded instantly, her skin hot and itchy suddenly felt two sizes too small for her body. Like her hormones were suddenly in overdrive.

What the heck, she thought, aghast. What normal woman emerged from a crisis feeling jittery and turned on enough to contemplate jumping a complete stranger?

Clearly, she needed to get out of there before she did something reckless and crazy.

CHAPTER THREE

ADAM LOOKED DOWN into Amanda's face, noting her high color and ragged breathing.

"You okay?" he asked softly.

She jolted like he'd zapped her with a live current. Nervously licking her lips, she lifted her eyes briefly to his, only to skitter away again at the intensity she found there.

"Uh, excuse me?"

"You're flushed and jumpy."

Her flush promptly deepened, making him wish he could read her mind. Avoiding his gaze, she lifted a hand to fan her face. "It's really hot in here," she said breathlessly, blithely ignoring the blast of cool air from the overhead air vent and the wash of goose bumps popping out across her skin. "I think I'm having a coronary. Maybe I should have it checked out."

"You're not having a coronary," Adam said calmly, having seen her dilated pupils and the rapid pulse in her throat.

She sucked in air and pressed the heel of her hand to her breastbone. "Are you sure? It feels like I'm having a heart attack."

"You're having a panic attack." The panic—coming

on the heels of her bold kiss in the bar earlier—came as a surprise. He'd have pegged her as a party girl if not for the fear he'd seen beneath her pale-faced determination to handle a potential crisis and the way she was currently clutching his jacket as though her life depended on it.

Her eyes cut to him, eyelashes fluttering wildly. "Don't be ridiculous. I am not panicking."

"All right," he said reasonably. "Then tell me that wildly fluttering pulse in your throat is a sign of arousal." One hand flew to her throat. "That your hand is shaking because you want to touch me and your ragged breathing is a sign that you want to be kissed…and touched."

Her eyes widened. "What? *N-no!*" she choked out and spun away, her eyes darting around as though searching for an escape route. He stepped into her and caught her shoulders in his hands, forcing her gaze to his.

"Then maybe," he said gently, shamelessly using his soothing doctor voice, "you should tell me what has you so spooked that you're considering bolting out into the night. Which I would advise against," he said when her gaze flickered in the direction of the street while her body vibrated like a guitar string. "Not in that dress."

Her eyes flew back to his and after a couple of beats, her shoulders sagged, her eyes squeezing shut. She abruptly turned away but he'd already seen her face and could only wonder at the embarrassed misery. Something moved in him then—something hot and tight and unfamiliar. Something that stirred that strange feeling of connection.

Hating to see her suffer, Adam tugged her around and dipped his knees to peer into her face. "Hey." He gave a gentle shake. "It's not that bad."

"Not for you, maybe," she hiccupped on a shaky laugh. "You're not the one who looks like a neurotic flamingo."

"A very cute flamingo," he chuckled, relieved to see the panic fading from her gorgeous eyes. "And everyone has a neurosis or two."

She took a deep breath that threatened the integrity of her bodice, briefly drawing Adam's fascinated gaze. "I bet you don't," she said, releasing her indrawn breath in a long sigh. "I bet you don't let the past freeze you at the wrong moment so that you're useless."

Adam studied her a long moment, wondering what had happened in her past that sent her into panic mode at the hint of an emergency. "You'd be wrong," he said mildly. "I have my demons the same as anyone else."

He could see by her expression that he'd caught her interest. "I bet you don't let it turn you into a shaking mass of insecurities though," she pointed out with a touch of self-loathing.

"Don't be so hard on yourself," Adam chastised gently. "I'm just better trained at handling medical emergencies." Feelings though? *They* usually sent him into a panic. Especially odd feelings for women in pink. Feelings that tempted him to sweep her into his arms so that he could provide the protection of a strong chest and broad shoulders.

Those—those were dangerous and to be avoided at all costs.

"I come from a family of doctors," she burst out in a low agitated voice like she was admitting some deep dark secret. "You'd think I would have learned enough not to freak out when someone goes into labor."

"Hey, *I* nearly panicked when she went into labor," he admitted with a chuckle. "I'm a cardiothoracic surgeon, not an ob-gyn. Heart attack? I'm your guy. But birthing babies?" He gave an exaggerated shudder. "Believe me, I panicked."

"You did not," she argued on a spluttered laugh. "You were great with Daphne." She paused for a long moment, her eyes searching his face. "You're a great doctor."

"Yeah," he agreed so casually that she laughed again. His gaze warmed. "At least that got you to stop thinking about whatever it was that had you wanting to bolt for the door."

For an instant, she seemed startled, then her eyes narrowed speculatively. "Hmmm, you're sneaky too," she muttered and turned blindly, reaching out a slender arm to call an elevator and froze for one pulse beat. Snatching her hand away, she turned in one jerky move, her eyes huge as they met his. "Do you think—?"

"It's probably safe," he said calmly, correctly interpreting her wide-eyed hesitation. "What are the chances of it happening twice in one night, right?"

She backed up a couple of steps, looking alarmed. "Don't say that."

"Why?"

"It's tempting fate." His amusement about tempting fate grew, when he'd all but accepted it.

"Would it help if I joined you?" he asked casually, leaning forward to press the button she'd avoided like it might bite.

Her eyes widened. "I, uh—"

The adjacent doors swished open and after a visible struggle, she drew in a deep breath but didn't move. Adam slapped a hand on the doors to keep them from closing and placed the other low on her back to usher her inside. He could tell by the abrupt tension vibrating through her that she was thinking about bailing.

"It's okay," he assured her when she reluctantly stepped inside. "Seems like they solved the problem." Her look was guarded as she brushed trembling fingers against her upper lip in a nervous gesture. His amusement faded at the sight of that quick tremble she ruthlessly squashed, and he shot out a hand to keep the doors open. "If you're worried, we can take the stairs."

Pursing her lips, she exhaled in an explosive burst that drew Adam's gaze to the generous pink mouth he knew from recent experience was soft and warm and sweet.

"Twenty-five floors?" She quickly shook her head. Shoving his jacket at him, she abruptly brushed his hand away from the touch pad, in a move he was certain was impulsive, and jabbed at her floor number.

The doors slid closed and the car began its silent ascent as Adam shrugged into his jacket. He'd have been blind not to notice the way her shoulders tensed, probably in anticipation of the elevator coming to another violent mid-floor stop.

Turning so that he was facing her, he breathed her in—coolly expensive with a hint of something hot and wild and tempting. Filling his lungs with her scent, he wondered who was the real her. Cool and classy—or hot and wild.

It would be interesting to find out because he had a feeling her cool, classy exterior hid a seething passion that was just waiting to burst free.

"I'm glad you were there to help Daphne," she said abruptly. "If it'd been up to me, we'd have been in serious trouble and—and I'd probably be missing a dress."

His mouth twitched at the image, but his eyes were intent when he told her quietly, "You don't give yourself enough credit. I think you'd have managed just fine."

"I faint at the sight of blood," she admitted baldly.

"Pretty difficult to treat bleeding patients when your eyes are rolling back in your head."

He recalled her going pale at the idea of having to assist in an unexpected birth but despite that, there was intelligence and humor in those striking blue eyes along with a warm softness that drew him in.

He lifted a hand and gently brushed his thumb across her plump mouth. "You shouldn't let other people define who you are," he said firmly.

At first, she appeared startled by his words but her expression quickly turned thoughtful. After a short silence, she exhaled noisily and said shakily, "You're right. I shouldn't."

Before he could draw her out, the elevator dinged, announcing its arrival at his floor. "So," he said casually, reluctant to step out of the elevator and never see her again. "You want a nightcap?"

Sam knew he was offering more than a nightcap. To say she was tempted was an understatement, but the mention of her family had brought her back to reality with an unpleasant jolt.

"I—" She blew out a gusty breath. "I can't." Maybe circumstances—and a cheating fiancé—had brought her to a crossroads of sorts, but that didn't mean she was going to recklessly follow the urgings of her hormones.

Reckless would be pushing him up against the open door of the elevator and taking a bite out of his deliciously sculpted mouth. Reckless would be leaving the relative safety of the elevator with a man she'd spent a couple of intense hours with but didn't know from… well, from Adam.

And reckless would be taking him up on his invitation to a nightcap when she was already drunk on his pheromones.

Physically dragging herself back from that tempting edge, she wrapped her arms around her torso, locked her knees and stared at him helplessly. Oh, God. She wanted to. She really, *really* wanted to.

His eyes darkened seductively at her very obvious inner struggle. "You sure?"

His voice was quiet and deep, a little rough. Not demanding or aggressive, which would have instantly had her shields snapping into place. Despite the almost physical yearning rising up in her to say, *No, I'm not sure, take me anyway,* Sam found herself nodding and shaking her head at the same time.

Yikes. Way to be decisive.

Confused and tempted—so darn tempted, especially when disappointment flashed across his starkly handsome face—she bit her lip and nodded reluctantly.

Sending her one last searching look, he turned away and stepped forward as the doors opened. He was almost through the doorway when something inside her snapped. She gave a strangled gurgle that sounded like, "*Wait!*" And before she could reconsider, she was spinning Adam around and pushing him against the steel frame.

Sliding up against all that warm hardness, she rose onto her toes and for the second time that night, caught his mouth in an awkward, desperate kiss because she suddenly couldn't face the thought of him walking away.

Adam heard her swift intake of breath and had already half turned when she launched herself at him, filling his arms with warm curvy woman. He staggered back against the door, and in that instant, she had her arms around his neck and her mouth pressed to his.

Not about to question his luck, he hauled her closer and slanted his mouth more comfortably across hers. He murmured against her lips and traced the tip of his tongue along the seam, coaxing them open. In the next heartbeat, he was sliding his tongue against the length of hers, drinking in her throaty moans.

God, she tasted delicious, like sweet temptation and decadent sin; like shy eagerness and bold seduction—just as he remembered.

She squirmed, kissing him with more enthusiasm than skill. It didn't matter because in an instant he was rock hard, going from zero to a hundred like a kid having his first French kiss. He widened his stance and slid his hands to her hips, pulling her snugly into his erection in a move that left no doubt about what he wanted.

She uttered a soft moan of yearning and wriggled closer, her nails lightly scraping his scalp as she tunneled her fingers into his hair. A shudder rocked his control, leaving his skin buzzing and his temperature spiking on a wave of pure reckless need.

God, he groaned silently, smoothing his palms from her hips up the slender curve of her waist to the outside of her breasts. He couldn't ever recall wanting a woman with such fierceness before. His instinct was to strip her out of the pink dress and run his mouth all over that soft silky skin.

But first. "Amanda," he murmured, feathering his mouth along the firm line of her jaw to her ear. "Tell me you're sober. Tell me you want this, that you're sure?"

She arched her neck, the move inviting his mouth to explore the long line of her throat. "Sure?" she echoed breathlessly.

"About this," he rasped, planting little nipping kisses

down her throat to her shoulder while brushing the outer curves of her breasts with his thumbs. She gasped—the hitch in her throat the sexiest thing he'd ever heard. Needing to hear the sound again, he moved back a couple of inches so he could see her face and did it again. A shudder moved through her.

"Don't stop," she pleaded softly, fisting his hair and tugging him closer.

With a growl, Adam caught her mouth, ramping up the heat. He fed her hot hungry kisses until his head buzzed and the soft sounds she made in the back of her throat threatened to blow the top off his head.

Something bumped against his back, pulling him briefly out of the haze sucking him under. It took him a couple of seconds to realize that the elevator door was trying to close. It roused him long enough to realize that they were standing in an elevator opening, behaving like horny teenagers. He tried to think about why that was significant but he was too busy chasing her mouth with his.

When the door bumped his back again, he broke the kiss and sucked in a harsh breath in the hopes that it would clear his head. Curling his hands around her thighs, he hiked her up and without being prompted, she wrapped her long legs around his waist.

He blinked to clear his eyes and lurched sideways, hoping he had enough strength to stay upright long enough to get to his suite. It took him a moment to orient himself before he staggered down the passage.

He was shaking by the time they arrived and had to press her up against the wall to fumble in his pockets for his key card. Panting and dodging her seeking mouth, her roaming hands, it took him a half-dozen shaky tries—and double the number of laughing curses—before the door finally clicked open.

Within seconds, he'd shoved it open, staggered inside and kicked it closed to push her up against the entrance wall. The next few seconds were a frenzy of hands as they shoved aside clothing.

Even before Adam found her zipper tab, she'd pushed aside his jacket and her hands were sliding down his back, her nails scraping a line of fire to the base of his spine.

He cursed and tried to slow things down, but she seemed determined to strip him of his clothes as quickly as she was stripping him of his sanity. Pressing her against the wall, he took his hands off her long enough to shrug out of his jacket, not caring where it landed. Instantly her mouth and hands took greedily while he battled to keep them both upright.

"Amanda…honey," he panted when she sank her teeth into the muscle between his neck and shoulder. "Slow… down or—dammit." He grabbed her marauding hands and pinned them against the wall beside her head. "Stop. Or it'll be over before I can get you naked."

The sound of Amanda's name drew Samantha out of her sensual haze long enough to discover that she was in a strange hotel room about to have sex with a man she barely knew. The realization should have shocked her because Samantha Jefferies wasn't the kind of woman to throw herself at strange men or try to climb their bodies.

She nearly told him her name then, but tonight she had rocked a pink-prom wedding dress, given a lap dance to a gorgeous stranger in a bar and kissed him like they were drowning and she was giving them the kiss of life.

Because that's what it felt like—only the other way around. It was as if kissing Adam had jolted her to life. It sounded corny, but at that moment she wasn't Samantha Jefferies, daughter of Vivienne and Edward Jefferies, and this didn't need to make sense. She was Amanda, the woman who ran from high society weddings to kiss hot guys in bars. The kind of woman who helped bring life into the world and the kind of woman who would wriggle against a man's erection and not react like she'd been goosed.

It was a heady feeling to think that here she could be anything she wanted. And deciding that what she wanted was to remain Amanda—for tonight, at least— she dropped her legs and slid suggestively down the front of a gorgeous guy who wanted her as much as she wanted him, hitting all her good spots along the way.

And by the rough sound of Adam's groan, she was hitting all of his too.

Powerful emotions swept through her and for the first time in her life, she understood feminine power. The kind that had men losing control. And suddenly she loved the idea of being the kind of woman capable of getting a man like him to lose control.

But she wanted more, a whole lot more, and with a hungry sound in the back of her throat, she arched up and kissed him wildly, recklessly giving herself over to the feeling of being someone else.

He was by far the hottest man she'd ever met. Toned and sculpted, his shoulders and torso were a work of art. His skin, a lovely warm coppery gold that she wanted to lick up one side and down the other, was stretched over some pretty awesome muscles that bunched and flexed with his every move.

He had a genuine eight-pack, a flat hard belly that could have been sculpted by a master, the delicious ridges angling over his hip bones and drawing her gaze to where they disappeared into his waistband.

Delicious, she thought, feeling her eyes cross a little at the thought of tasting all that toasty skin, of tracing the happy trail with her tongue from his shallow belly button to where it disappeared into the low-slung waistband of his jeans.

And the hefty package beyond. Her mouth watered.

She'd like to trace beyond.

"Are we stopping?"

Only to admire the scenery.

She licked her lips as she made the return trip to his molten gaze. Sleepy and aroused, it sent a bolt of fear and pure lust through her, making something deep in her core clench with longing.

"No," she said, leaning forward to place a hesitant kiss on his heated skin. But that wasn't enough and before she knew it, she was sliding her tongue across the taut surface, sinking her teeth into his muscular neck and nibbling kisses over the well-defined ball of his shoulder.

She reveled in his harshly indrawn breath and muttered curses.

Lost in the salty, exotic taste of him, she shamelessly traced all that masculine perfection, delighting in the way his flesh rippled beneath her mouth. His hands were cupping her bottom again, kneading her flesh and ratcheting up the tension and heat.

Emboldened by his enthusiasm, she scored her nails lightly over his belly before reaching for the metal button on his jeans. Rock hard muscles jumped and jittered beneath the tight skin in concert to the pounding of her pulse. Her gaze followed the path her hands took, coming to a screeching halt when she discovered the long thick length of him straining the jeans' zipper.

"That looks uncomfortable," she said with a husky laugh. She shivered at the promise of that aggressive sign of arousal. She dipped her hand into the gaping waistband, her fingers brushing something broad and hard, yet surprisingly soft. Even without looking, she knew the blunt tip of him was eagerly reaching for her touch.

It didn't seem possible but he was as turned on as she was. The thought sent a shiver of excitement easing up the length of her spine ahead of the rushing heat. Looking up, her gaze locked with his, the blaze of heat prompting her to smooth the pearly bead over his broad tight crown and then lift her thumb to her mouth in a bold move that surprised as much as it excited her. She'd never done anything so daring or suggestive before.

Had never wanted to.

When Adam's gaze flared hotter, a low, ragged curse torn from him, she was glad she had, especially as it sent a rush of heat between her thighs. The sight of his tight features and enlarged pupils made her forget for a fleeting moment that she'd been on a mission to make him lose control.

While she was drinking in the fierce arousal clearly etched on his handsome face, he had both her wrists captured above her head and was breathing like he'd run up the twenty-five flights of stairs from the lobby. A flush of arousal edged his high cheekbones, making his eyes glitter like a tiger's eye. The expression in them had her teetering on a very fine edge; an edge that he nearly shoved her over when he hooked his free hand beneath her knee and hiked it up, shoving his hips against her as he took her mouth in a hungry, urgent kiss.

Long fingers slipped beneath the narrow strip of lace at her hip and followed it to the tiny triangle of material at the apex of her thighs. Her gasp at the feel of his roughened fingers brushing her most intimate flesh turned into a squeak of surprise when one of those long thick fingers drove into her wet heat.

Everything in her clenched and she thought she might climax on the spot. Sam tore her mouth from his to suck in a ragged breath before she lost consciousness.

You can't pass out now, she thought frantically. *You haven't seen him naked yet. You haven't got to the good parts yet.*

Not giving her a moment to collect herself, Adam dipped his head, his mouth hot and damp on her neck, his teeth scoring a line of fire along the large tendon to the delicate skin beneath her ear.

Wordlessly, she clutched at him, tilting her head to the side to give him room to continue doing delicious things to her neck and even more delicious things to the tiny button of nerves between her legs that throbbed in time to her pounding heart.

Swept into a world that was all heat and sensation, Sam threw back her head with a ragged wail when he hiked her leg higher and bent to close his mouth over the tip of one breast. She was unaware that she was moving impatiently until the tip of her breast stretched and then popped free when he drew back.

He growled at her in a voice so low and indistinct that she was unable to distinguish separate words.

"Wh-what?"

"Can you reach my pocket?"

She blinked at him in confusion. "What?"

"Condom," he rasped, chest heaving and looking a little wild. "Now."

Feeling a little wild herself, Sam slid her hands into his back pockets and withdrew a leather wallet with hands that were suddenly all thumbs and impatient need. After a few aborted attempts, she opened it and found what she was looking for. Tossing the wallet aside, she shoved one corner of the foil package between her teeth and ripped.

In one swift move, Adam had swept aside her thong and freed himself from his jeans. Hoping she hadn't damaged the latex, she leaned back and reached for the impressive erection between them.

He snatched the condom from her and brushed her fingers aside. "Next time," he rasped, sheathing himself with a hand that shook. And before she could remind him that there wouldn't be a next time, he pulled her legs up and entered her in one long hard thrust.

Sam's body instantly arched as her inner muscles spasmed around the unfamiliar invasion. His breath whooshed out and he stilled, head thrown back, neck straining and muscles ironhard as he struggled with his runaway control. It was the most erotic thing she'd ever seen.

But then every thought was directed to where they were joined, to where he stretched her to the point of pain. He was huge, bigger than any man she'd ever seen, and while she hadn't had sex in nearly two years, she couldn't ever remember it feeling this good. Couldn't remember *feeling* this good.

Her breasts throbbed as flames licked across her skin, tightening her belly and clenching the muscles surrounding his erection. She'd never been so "in the moment" before that she was blind to everything but the way his body felt invading hers.

Finally, he began to move. Slowly, purposefully, with long slow withdrawals and heavy solid thrusts. Moaning, Sam arched, tilting her hips to take him more fully.

He groaned and thrust harder, deeper. Light exploded behind her eyes and a delicious chaos began to swirl in her belly, edging up the heat and sending ripples of electricity streaking across her skin. She clutched at him to keep from spinning off into deep dark space but with each solid thrust, he sent her spiraling higher and higher.

Just when she thought that she couldn't take more, he changed the angle and speed of his thrusts. The air was filled with heavy breathing, muttered encouragement, ragged curses and the sound of flesh striking flesh.

"Open your eyes, Amanda," he rasped in a tight, hoarse voice. "I want to see you when you come." Incapable of resisting his demand, her lashes fluttered up and she found herself staring helplessly into pools of molten black surrounded by a thin circle of burning gold.

His inky hair fell over his brow, swaying with each pounding thrust, and half concealing his fierce expression. It was the hottest, most erotic thing she'd ever seen and with the next downward thrust and grind of his hips, she went careening over the edge.

Her body arched in a desperate bow and the sound that tore from her throat might have mortified her if she'd been capable of thought. Lost in the fiery ecstasy of her own climax, Sam was only vaguely aware of Adam's pounding race to the finish, the forceful slamming of his hips against hers and finally—the low thrilling sound of his release.

CHAPTER FOUR

Two months later

SAM UNCLIPPED HER seat belt and reached for her phone. Fortunately, the past two months had been a whirlwind of activity that had kept her from thinking too much—about Lawrence, canceling her wedding and San Francisco.

During the day, at least. At night—well that was another story altogether, but she'd have to put that brief chapter behind her because there would be no more tall dark gorgeous strangers in her future.

She shivered, recalling the last time she'd been seated in a pressurized cabin. She'd spent the entire flight back to Boston alternately blushing, grinning like an idiot and then feeling aghast at what she'd done.

Heat rose up from the center of her body like a volcanic pipe of magma when she recalled that she'd bought a hot pink thong and slept with a hot gorgeous man she'd known for all of three hours.

Omigod. She'd slept with a complete stranger! She must be an awful person to have spent the night with a strange guy only a couple of days after breaking off her engagement to a man she'd known and loved for years.

Although, it was clear she didn't know him *nearly* as well as she'd thought.

She was a trollop and she was headed for hell. Okay, so she was actually heading back to California, but according to her grandmother, it was one and the same. Especially after dropping the there-will-be-no-wedding bomb that had put her relative in an icy uproar. She didn't care. There was no way she'd ever consider living a lie like her grandmother.

Something had happened to her during that weekend and now there was no going back. In the space of three days, her life had changed irrevocably. She'd walked in on something she'd give her left kidney to unsee, and then in a fit of furious rebellion, she had entered an upscale lingerie boutique and bought her first thong—heck she'd splurged on an entire bagful of sexy stuff in an attempt to make herself feel like a desirable woman again.

She'd worn a short pink princess dress more suited to a high school senior and entered a bar for the first time in her life to escape the nauseatingly sweet, romantic wedding where she was the tallest *and* oldest bridesmaid. Oh, yeah, and to avoid Mr. Hands.

She'd tossed back shooters with names no self-respecting Boston debutante would contemplate let alone say and given a gorgeous guy a lap dance. Then because he'd looked like temptation, in a sexy dark angel way with his whiskey eyes and potent mouth, she'd kissed him like he was the last man she would taste before the earth was destroyed by an asteroid.

And if that wasn't enough, she'd then been stuck in a lift with a woman who'd gone into labor and practically attacked the hotter-than-sizzling dark angel the moment they were alone.

Who the heck could ignore or top that as a life-changing experience?

It was no wonder she'd felt like a completely different person when she'd returned to Boston. She'd felt as though her entire world had shifted on its axis and she was in the wrong place and time. It was like she'd woken from a cryogenic state to a world that no longer seemed familiar, feeling trapped in a life and body that was meant for someone else.

Fortunately, Colleen Rutherford, her grandfather's mistress of almost forty years, had come to her rescue, offering Sam a job as Operations Director of The Galahad Foundation. Okay, so the job offer had come about a year ago but since Sam had been engaged and planning her wedding at the time, she'd declined.

It had taken a particularly difficult encounter with her grandmother to finally push her over the edge. Summoned to lunch at the Mandarin Oriental, the formidable CEO of Gilford Pharmaceuticals had proceeded to lecture her about her duty to the Gilford name. She'd ordered Sam to get over her childish whining and get her wedding to Lawrence Winthrop the Third back on track.

The command had stunned her, although it shouldn't have since her grandmother had been content to live a forty-year lie all for the sake of appearances. Lilian had brushed aside Sam's objections, ignored her explanations and told her men cheated all the time and that she owed it to the Gilfords to make a good marriage since her mother had let the name down by marrying a Jefferies.

Realizing her objections were falling on deaf ears, Sam had listened politely, then returned to the art museum where she was the outreach coordinator and phoned

Colleen "Coco" Rutherford to ask if the job offer was still on the table.

Upon being assured that it was, she'd promptly accepted, typed up a resignation letter and put her South End house on the market all in the space of one afternoon.

Now here she was, one month later, winging her way west to start a new life. Pity she couldn't leave behind the images that had been burned into her brain because now that she was finally motionless—and heading to the scene of her fall from grace—all she could think about was the night she'd spent with Adam. And while there would never be a repeat, she regretted not staying a little longer. Regretted sneaking out of his hotel room while he'd been in the shower. Because as liberating as her taste of rebellion had felt at the time, Sam wasn't really cut out for the guilt and panic of one-night stands with gorgeous strangers.

She'd woken sprawled naked across a queen-size bed, feeling wonderfully lethargic and decadently used. Then, in the space of two heartbeats, reality had struck and she'd freaked out. She had absolutely no experience with morning-after etiquette—and she knew a heck of a lot about etiquette thanks to her grandmother—so while he was in the shower, she'd scrambled off the rumpled bed that smelled like a combination of them both, almost landing flat on her face when she tripped over the tangled bedding.

Carefully avoiding the empty foil squares littering the floor like anti-personnel mines, she'd gathered her pink dress and strappy heels—there'd been no sign of the hot pink thong—and bolted.

While nervous of her ability to handle all the impulsive life changes that she'd made over the past few weeks, she couldn't help the dizzying relief and the feeling of lightness at having discarded her old life. At having finally taken control.

Where she was going, no one cared about the Boston Gilfords or that she was the awkward underachiever in a family that made the Rockefellers and Oppenheimers look like a bunch of slackers.

Feeling deliciously free for the first time in her life, Sam opened a new document on her smartphone and typed *The Plan* in the heading. She might be a late bloomer, she admitted, but she was doing things differently this time. Instead of letting other people orchestrate her life and weigh her down with their expectations—and disappointments—she was going to direct her own destiny. And to do that she needed a plan.

Frowning in concentration, she began to type.

No more engagements to "suitable" men at least in Gilford terms
No more caving to familial pressure
No more trying to be someone I'm not
No more trying to hide my curves, hair or unfeminine height
No more sedate, tasteful underwear or low-heeled shoes
No more panic attacks
And definitely no more one-night stands with hot dark angels

She was going to take charge of her destiny. Or die trying.

Adam leaned back in his chair and stifled a yawn that was more boredom than fatigue, although there was a large portion of the latter from spending the past ten hours in surgery. He was tired, hungry and the last place he wanted to be was in a meeting at—he surreptitiously checked his cell phone—8:00 p.m. on a Tuesday night.

As a founding member of The Galahad Foundation, he was expected to attend board meetings but tonight he was drifting while Dr. Rutherford listed the virtues and accomplishments of the foundation's newest operations director—who was glaringly conspicuous by her absence.

He'd already heard all about Samantha Jefferies of Boston from Coco Rutherford, having voted in favor of the new appointee a month ago. As long as he could concentrate on the reason for the foundation—consultations, transplants and surgeries for people unable to afford the huge medical costs—he was happy for anyone to take over the running of it, especially someone more experienced and suited to the position than a bunch of overworked doctors.

Up until now, Coco Rutherford, mentor and boss, had taken on the day-to-day duties with the rest of them pitching in as needed. Adam was a busy surgeon and hated drafting letters, deciding what fundraiser to host next or organizing organ-donation drives. He hated having to decide who was more deserving of transplants or surgical procedures—there were just so damn many who needed them—and he loathed hospital policy and red tape that prevented them from doing more. That was Coco's forte.

Stifling another yawn, Adam ignored the cup of coffee cooling at his elbow and let his mind wander—right down the path it insisted on wandering every time he had two minutes to himself. Ever since the weekend he'd presented a paper at UCSF School of Medicine, he'd thought about his Peony. Despite their unspoken agreement that it was just a one-night stand, he'd found himself wondering where she was, why she'd left without saying goodbye and if he'd ever see her again.

After that first explosive encounter, he'd taken time to explore her long lush body and had noticed the pale band of flesh on her ring finger. He'd wondered if she'd removed her rings to pretend she wasn't married, if she was recently divorced or wanted one last wild weekend fling before tying the knot with another man.

Maybe her leaving while he was in the shower was a good thing because he wasn't in the habit of sleeping with married women or being some engaged girl's last wild fling. He'd been the result of an engaged debutante's final rebellion and had spent his entire life not belonging in either his father's or his mother's worlds.

Although he didn't know if Amanda was from a rich and powerful family, he'd been pretty sure that he'd been her big rebellion against something. And yet he'd woken hoping to talk her into spending the day with him because he hadn't wanted to let her go.

He knew nothing about her except her first name and that she panicked in a crisis.

Oh, yeah, and she had a tiny velvety mole on the outer curve of her left breast where it met her ribs, sexy dimples at the base of her spine and that she was the most responsive woman he'd ever been with. He also knew her lips were soft and full and that she enjoyed kissing more than any woman he knew. And when she was aroused, her startling blue eyes darkened to cobalt. Just the memory of her biting her lip to hold back the throaty moans and sexy sighs she'd made when he'd taken his mouth on a torturous exploration of her body, made him shift uncomfortably in his seat.

Adam was just about to suggest they postpone meeting the new recruit when he became aware of voices coming from the outer office.

The hair on his arms and the back of his neck rose in premonition and he looked up from where he'd been doodling peonies just as the door was flung open and a feminine whirlwind entered in a cloud of familiar perfume and breathless apologies.

"I'm so sorry I'm late," she murmured huskily, sliding into the nearest available seat—which just happened to be directly opposite Adam. "My flight was delayed in Boston and then the airline lost my luggage."

Everything inside him came to a screeching halt and he missed the rest of what she was saying, what Coco Rutherford said, as well as the murmurs from other board members. He missed everything because there in the flesh was the very woman he'd just been thinking about.

Or was it?

His gaze sharpened as he studied the newcomer, because although she bore a striking resemblance to the woman he'd spent a passionate night with, this woman looked more like an elegantly cool and well-put-together professional and less like his wild, flushed Peony.

Gone was the tousled hair and short pink princess dress and in its place was a just-above-the-knee wraparound turquoise dress edged with black piping that molded to her body and drew attention to the spectacular curves beneath. Her chestnut hair had been drawn back into a severe bun that showcased her startling blue eyes and creamy complexion. Her makeup was perfect despite the long flight delays and the frustration of missing luggage. Her lips were a soft pink and those long,

long legs that ended in sexy black sling-backs, brought back some very pleasant memories.

Adam heard a loud buzzing in his ears and completely missed Coco's introductions to the rest of the board members.

If he'd wondered whether there were two women in the world who could look and sound exactly the same, down to a familiar soft gasp and the hint of a dimple in her right cheek, the moment he met those wide shocked blue eyes, he knew this cool, put-together stranger and his passionate, rumpled Peony were one and the same.

Rising languidly, he leaned across the table to offer his hand, forcing her to take it or appear rude. Her skin was cool as she slid her hand into his and he had to admire her game face, because even as he felt the little jolt move through her, she didn't pull away. He knew she wanted to. It was there in her eyes.

He held on a little longer than was polite, and when her eyes gave the barest flicker and she tugged on her hand, he let his mouth curve before releasing her.

"So it's… *Samantha*?" he asked politely, deliberately trailing his fingertips over her wrist and across her palm, his gaze dropping to where her fingers curled into the palm he'd just caressed. She blinked, and for just a second appeared too flustered to speak.

She finally gave a jerky nod. "That's right," she murmured, quickly turning away to face Coco whose speculative gaze was bouncing between them. That shiver of premonition he'd felt earlier was nothing to the one that moved through him now. It was as if Coco had caught the abrupt tension and was amused and oddly pleased by it. Sitting back, he folded his arms across his chest to stare at his mentor in silent challenge. Her reply was an arched brow and a quick grin before she went back to addressing the meeting.

Adam pretended to listen but heard nothing. He was too busy watching out of the corner of his eyes as Samantha pretended he didn't exist. He knew it was a pretense because he caught her sneaking peeks at him when she thought no one was looking. He could practically see the tension shimmering off her body.

Hugely enjoying himself, he turned his head and let their gazes lock. He didn't know what she saw in his expression but she quickly looked away, picked up the folder containing the latest financial report and fanned her flushed face.

Finally, when Coco announced that the meeting was closed and invited everyone for refreshments, the room cleared of all but Adam and Coco in less than a minute. Slowly shoving back from the table, he followed Samantha's quick escape with his eyes. He wanted answers. But first things first, he thought, as Coco picked up her cell phone to either check her emails or to pretend she was in an effort to discourage conversation. However, Adam had known her since she'd elected to be his med school mentor and he wasn't easily put off. "What are you up to?" he asked when they were alone.

She lifted a finger in a brief give-me-a-minute gesture, then continued to tap away before finally lifting her head. Her expression was coolly enquiring but Adam caught a glint in her gray eyes, as well as the quickly suppressed smile at the corners of her mouth.

"I have no idea what you're talking about, Dr. Knight. Perhaps you could be more specific."

"I'm talking about that look," he said, jabbing a finger in her direction. "And the fact that I've known you long enough to know when you're up to something. Why do I have the feeling the other shoe is about to drop?"

Coco chuckled. "You're getting paranoid, my dear boy. Perhaps you've been working too hard. Come," she said, rising from the table. "You look hungry and I know you must be dying to talk to Sammie."

Geez, was he so damned transparent? "I am?"

"Of course you are." A smirk flashed across her face. "She has a million ideas for fundraisers that are bound to make us a lot of money."

He narrowed his eyes as she swept from the room, leaving him to follow. *Yep*, he decided, she was definitely up to something. And yep, he *was* dying to talk to *Sammie*, but not about her fundraising ideas. First, he was going to ask why the groomsman had called her Amanda—he'd neglected to ask, having better things to focus on during that heated night they shared—and then he was going to—heck, he didn't know what, he thought with a buzz of frustration. He only knew that all he could think about was undoing those four large buttons holding her dress together and sliding his hands up her smooth thighs. He wanted to taste her mouth to see if it was as sweet as he remembered and maybe muss her up a little.

Okay, he decided when his gaze instantly found her laughing at something someone had said, so maybe he wanted to muss her up a lot. He wanted to get her alone and put his mouth on that spot beneath her ear that gave her a full body shiver and hear her breath catch in her throat.

For the next half hour, Adam pretended to enjoy the food and conversation as he stalked Samantha around the room. He'd casually work his way to the group she was with and watch in amusement as she quietly excused herself. Just as he was beginning to lose interest in the game, she murmured something to Coco and slipped from the room.

Taking it as his cue, he followed, catching sight of a flash of turquoise as he got to the door. By the time he pushed through the outer suite door, the ladies' bathroom door halfway down the passage was closing, telling him where she'd disappeared.

After a quick over-the-shoulder glance to make certain they were alone, he followed.

Sam stumbled into the ladies' room and collapsed against the rich cream-and-sage-green wall. Gulping air, she pressed a shaky hand to the awful cramping in her belly. *Oh, God, oh, God, oh, God.* The man she'd spent a reckless night having hot sex with in San Francisco was an executive member of the foundation she was now running—*in San José.*

Granted, the two cities were close, but never in her wildest dreams—fine, nightmares, she corrected a little hysterically—had she thought she'd see him again.

She squeezed her eyes closed, hoping that when she opened them everything would be back to normal because this was the worst thing that could have happened. She was supposed to be starting over with a clean slate and having her past come back to bite her in the ass wasn't part of her pla—

"Running away again, *Amanda*?" a deep voice asked quietly.

CHAPTER FIVE

SAM JUMPED SO high she was surprised she didn't give herself a concussion on the ceiling. Her eyes flew open to where Adam leaned against the door a few feet away. Hands thrust into the pockets of his black scrub pants, he looked casual and relaxed. She hadn't heard him enter, but then again the entire fifth battalion could have entered guns blazing and she wouldn't have heard anything over the wave of panic rushing over her.

She lifted a shaky hand to press against her racing heart and hoped he couldn't hear it flopping around in her chest. "I have no idea what you're talking about."

Despite her denial, memories of the night they'd spent together assaulted her and she suddenly wanted to thrust her hands into all that cool black hair and pull his mouth to hers. Or maybe slide them beneath his black scrub top so she could feel those fabulous satin-covered abs.

Aghast that she was imagining stripping him naked, Sam stayed where she was and eyed him warily. He looked even better than she remembered and that bothered her because she'd remembered plenty.

For long moments, they studied each other until Sam pushed away from the wall, annoyed that she was letting old insecurities surface. She went straight to the vanity counter, hoping the distance would clear her head.

"My name is Samantha."

One dark brow arched up his tanned forehead. "Uh-huh and was that just for the benefit of the board members or are you really going to pretend we haven't met? That you have a twin somewhere in Frisco who looks exactly like you," he murmured, his eyes sliding across her face. "Right down to the freckles sprinkled across your nose?"

"Freckles?" she gasped in outrage, totally forgetting that she'd decided to pretend they'd never met. "I do not have any freckles."

"Wanna bet?" he challenged softly. "There are fourteen across your nose, five on your—" His gaze dropped to the reflection of her breasts in the mirror, causing the breath to back up in her lungs when her nipples tightened. "A dozen scattered down your back and three on the inside of your right thigh." He reached out to run a teasing finger slowly, tortuously, down the length of her spine, scattering her senses and sending goose bumps stampeding across her skin, racing down the center of her back to the base of her spine. "I know," he murmured wickedly, "because I tasted every one of them."

Heat spread outward at the careless sensuality of that caress but she suppressed it. "N-not everyone is lucky enough to have s-skin that doesn't blemish in the sun," she managed to say through the rush of sensation.

He stilled, and for a moment she thought she'd offended him, but then he leaned forward to blow on her neck. And heck if her scalp didn't prickle along with the soles of her feet. For an instant, she wondered if her hair was smoldering, but a quick glance assured her she was still Samantha Jefferies, cool and elegantly professional.

Except for the wild flush staining her cheekbones, wide eyes and dilated pupils. *Oh, God*, she thought spinning around to avoid the truth staring back at her. But when she found him close enough to feel the heat pumping off him like a nuclear reactor, she wondered at the wisdom of the move because he was so close she could see each individual speck of gold glinting behind the thick fringe of sooty lashes that drooped over his shimmering eyes. Eyes that abruptly reminded her of a stalking lion.

Her pulse jolted, because that's exactly what he'd been doing. All through the meeting, he'd watched her watching him, and once it was over, he'd subtly stalked her from one group to the next until the only thing left was to escape into the ladies' room.

"What are you doing here, Adam?" she demanded, attempting to infuse her voice with cool outrage and cursing inwardly when it emerged husky and breathless instead.

Amusement came and went in his expression, infuriating her because he was too close, too disturbing, too— *everything.* She lifted her hands to his chest, intending to push him back a couple of inches but it was like moving a boulder.

"This is the ladies' room," she pointed out, ignoring the heat seeping into her palms and spreading up her arms; ignoring the very basic need to spread her fingers and feel all those amazingly hard planes and dips. "And the last time I checked, you don't qualify."

"So," he murmured, taking advantage of their proximity to toy with her earring. "You admit there *was* a last time, that you were the woman in Room 2014 who used her tongue to—"

"*Stop!*" she interrupted on a breathless squeak when she recalled exactly what she'd been inspired to do. Dammit, she was never mixing shooters and champagne again because that was the only explanation for the things she'd done that night. "Okay, so maybe I let you um…think my name was Amanda, but only because I never expected to see you again and didn't think it mattered."

His eyes darkened. "You don't think it matters to a man that he knows the name he groans whilst buried deep inside of that woman's body?"

She felt her core shudder at the memory of him doing just that in a voice so deep and rough her body instantly heated and melted in anticipation. "I…um—it does?"

His hands dropped to her hips and he tugged her against him, the move—and the feel of his substantial erection—leaving her in no doubt about what he meant. "Why don't we put it to the test, hmm?" he murmured, dropping his head to feather his lips along the soft underside of her jaw.

A painful rush of yearning gripped her and she found herself curling her fingers into his scrubs, tilting her head back to give him room to explore. She'd only spent a few hours with him and yet the way he touched her, skated his mouth and tongue across her skin, seemed achingly familiar.

"I d-don't think this is such a good idea," she heard herself say, heard the soft moan and wondered at the war going on inside her; to climb all over him or push him away and see that he stayed there.

Her mind yelled at her to step away while her body urged her closer.

Horrified that she might do something reckless, like rip off his shirt and sink her teeth into some part of him,

Sam shoved him back and scuttled out of reach. She spun around and automatically reached out to turn on the tap and dispense a blob of foam hand soap into her palm.

"I—uh, this isn't what I want," she said in a voice she didn't recognize as her own. It sounded husky and throaty, as if they were stretched out on a bed in the dark.

Rubbing her hands together to spread the foam, she cleared her throat, not daring to look at him in case he saw past the desperate attempt to appear professional and in control. Heck. How was she supposed to act with a man who in many ways knew her better than the man she'd been engaged to?

"I left Boston because I needed a change," she explained, rinsing her hands and turning to address his chest because she couldn't look him in the eye. After a couple of beats, he wordlessly pulled a length of paper-toweling from the dispenser and held it out. Not seeing any other option, she took it and began to dry her hands. "Coco offered me this job about a year ago but I was um—occupied with other things at the time."

Dropping the damp mess into the trash, she leaned her hip against the counter and folded her arms beneath her breasts in a move she knew was defensive but hoped looked casual. Just being in the same room with him made her nervous and edgy, because she couldn't recall ever coming across a situation like this in her grandmother's etiquette book.

Grimacing inwardly, Sam finally lifted her head and forced herself to meet his hooded gaze. "Then something happened and—" Pausing, she bit her lip and let her gaze slide away from his. It was one thing to admit how hurt she was at the discovery that Lawrence had been satisfying *his* physical urges all the time he'd been preaching abstinence until the wedding night, and quite another to have the man she's supposed to spend the rest of her life with lie to her.

"San Francisco."

Lost in thought, it took Sam a few moments to mentally catch up with the conversation.

"What? Yes—no." She paused to breathe in, then exhaled in one long shuddery breath. "Partly," she admitted shakily, rubbing at the tension between her eyes. "I, uh, realized that I was trying to please too many people and it took certain um—" she paused and flushed as one dark brow rose up his forehead "—events," she said more briskly, straightening her spine and glaring at him. "Before, during and after that weekend to show me I needed a change." She paused to swipe her tongue across her bottom lip and smooth a loose curl off her forehead. "I, uh—I didn't intend to have a one…um…night stand with you…or anyone else, for that matter. I want—no, I *need* to make a success of this to prove to myself that moving wasn't a mistake."

"And you think everyone knowing we slept together will jeopardize that?"

He sounded so amused, damn him, that Sam narrowed her gaze. "Yes—no." She broke off and lifted her chin at the open skepticism in his gaze. "Maybe. I don't know, but as we'll be working together, I don't want to muddy the waters with um—" She broke off and sucked in an unsteady breath.

"Sex?"

It was only when her breath whooshed out that she realized she'd been holding it.

"Yes."

After a long silence, during which Sam had to force

herself to hold his stare, Adam's gaze dropped to her mouth, scattering all her good intentions. Her lips tingled and parted, her breath hitching softly in her throat.

The air thickened and warmed, swirling around them like a firestorm of sensation that she couldn't ignore no matter how much she wanted to. A warning buzzed through her the instant his gaze returned to hers. Sensuality curved his mouth and blazed in his amber gaze, all but hypnotizing her.

"Okay," he murmured, shifting closer in a move that had the warning buzzing louder. "I'll be the soul of discretion in public." He paused to let his words drift between them before continuing. "But in private—" he lifted a hand to toy with the large button above her left breast "—I have no intention of letting you forget anything."

Distracted by his proximity, it took her a moment to realize that he'd very sneakily issued a challenge while her body and mind were in meltdown.

Sucking in a shocked breath, she lurched backward, knocking his hand aside. "Excuse me?" she demanded, outraged. "There won't be anything *in private* and there certainly won't be a repeat of...of..." She broke off to blush and curse at the dark brow rising up his forehead. "Of whatever it is you're thinking about. I told you. I'm done living my life to please everyone else. From now on, I'm going to please myself. I've got a plan and—and you're not in it."

In an instant, his eyes went flat and his jaw hardened. On a roll, Sam waved her hand in his direction. "And don't give me that look," she snapped. "Because it has nothing to do with your...your—" She broke off abruptly, unsure how to explain without offending him.

"My what?" he drawled smoothly, a muscle ticking in his jaw. "The fact that you had a wild steamy night with a man whose skin is too dark to fit into your rarefied blue-blooded world?"

Her mouth dropped open at the bitterness in his tone and she had to blink past the hot tears burning the backs of her eyes at the implied insult. Pressing a hand to the painful tightening in her chest, she sucked in air that felt like ground glass. "You r-really think that? You think I s-slept with you because…because—" She ground to a halt and swallowed convulsively.

"It's exciting to have a reckless fling with someone from the wrong side of the tracks before heading off to marry someone from a more suitable family?" His brow arched up his forehead. "You wouldn't be the first, *Sam*."

"Well, I'm not the latest either," she snapped, incensed that he would accuse her of bigotry when he didn't even know her. "For your information, it has nothing to do with your ancestry and everything to do with the fact that I'm not looking for a relationship right now, especially with a *doctor*." She said the word like it was something offensive and turned to fling herself away from him. When he said nothing, she spun back around to find him staring at her incredulously.

"All this is because I'm a doctor?" he demanded skeptically. "You can't be serious."

"My entire family consists of doctors and surgeons," she said heatedly. "I was an unplanned late-in-life baby and spent my childhood wishing I had some mysteriously interesting medical condition that would get my parents to notice me. And don't smile," she fumed. "It was awful. I was foisted onto nannies, housekeepers and finally my grandmother who had as little time for me as my parents did."

She sucked in a steadying breath because the last thing she wanted was pity from anyone. Especially him.

"I used to think that I'd been abducted by aliens at birth and given to the wrong family, because that was the only explanation for the fact that I had no aptitude when it came to medicine and panicked at the sight of blood."

"Aliens?"

"My point *is*," she said, rolling her eyes in exasperation. "I get that doctors are driven to save people with their superpowers but I'm not interested in anyone determined to prove he's God's miracle worker. It's too— lonely."

"So you're what? Looking for a man who stays home and rubs your feet?"

"Who says I'm looking for a man at all?" she snapped, incensed.

Adam's eyes gleamed with amusement. "Seriously?" His mouth curved into a wicked smile. "After San Francisco, you're trying to sell me that?"

Sam felt her face heat and huffed out in annoyance. Trust a man to twist her words into something sexual. "I'm not trying to sell anything," she informed him primly. "I'm merely explaining why I'm not looking for a relationship right now. Besides, with my track record with men—look, it's nothing personal," she added hastily.

"Nothing personal, huh?" he demanded softly, his eyes gleaming a sensual warning that skittered down her spine. He gave a short laugh and propped his shoulder casually against the wall. "I'm not supposed to take it personally that I'm good enough for a hot night of rebellion against your family but nothing else?"

"I didn't sleep—" She gulped at the look on his face. Drawing in a shaky breath, she tried again. "I didn't have sex with you to get back at my family."

"Who then? Your husband? Your fiancé?"

Sam felt herself go pale. "Who—who told you I had a fiancé?" she demanded hoarsely. For several beats, Adam stared at her, then reached out and caught her left hand. She tried to pull away but he easily lifted it and turned her hand so her ring finger was visible.

"This," he said, indicating the pale band of flesh where Lawrence's ring had rested for two years. "Although that night the indentation left in your finger looked fresh. As though you'd recently removed your ring."

Powerless to deny the truth, Sam sagged against the wall and studied the differences between their hands; hers pale and delicate against the large dark masculinity of his. "I *had* recently removed it," she admitted softly, her gaze flying up when his fingers tightened. It was her turn to wrap her hand around his to prevent him pulling away. "But it's not what you think," she added hastily, suddenly hating that he thought the worst of her.

"And exactly what *do* I think, Samantha?" he growled, his gaze shuttered against her.

"That I slept with you while being engaged to another man." After a moment, one brow rose up his forehead in query. "I um—" She licked her lips nervously and tried to think but it was more difficult that she'd anticipated. Finally, unable to utter the words with his amber eyes watching her with the intent of an eagle poised for attack, she dropped his hand and slid away.

When she could breathe, she said, "I'd already broken it off two days before we met," over her shoulder without meeting his eyes.

"Why?"

The question jolted her around. "W-why?"

Propping his shoulder against the wall, he folded his arms across his chest. "Why did you break it off?"

Realizing that he probably deserved the truth, Sam blew out a breath. "I walked in on him and his—assistant having sex." He grimaced but said nothing. Goaded, she added, "His assistant's name is Ronnie, which is short for Ronald."

Understanding flickered in his gaze. "Oh."

"You got that right," she muttered and then sighed. "I felt—betrayed."

"Of course you did."

"No, you don't understand," she said heatedly, pushing her hair off her face. "I've known him forever. I believed him when he said he loved me. I thought he wanted to wait for the wedding night before we—um, before we—" She broke off, face heating with embarrassment when Adam's eyes narrowed.

"How long were you engaged?"

She finally muttered, "Almost two years," sighing with resignation when his eyebrows shot into his hairline.

"You were *celibate* for two years?"

She glared and folded her arms beneath her breasts, daring him to comment on her stupidity. "*I* was," she muttered. "*He,* however, wasn't."

His face was a mix of emotions that might have been comical if the situation weren't so mortifying. "Do you mean to tell me that night was your first time in two years?"

Her face flamed because it had been way longer than that. Embarrassed, annoyed and wishing she could escape, she set her jaw and demanded irritably, "What's that got to do with anything? I was just trying to explain why rebound sex is a bad idea and—"

"Have you heard of destiny?" he interrupted mildly.

She blinked, confused by the non sequitur. "Destiny?"

"Fate, providence, predestination, chance, karma or kismet, if you will."

"I know what it means," she said through clenched teeth. "I'm just not sure how it relates to this discussion."

He pushed away from the wall and stalked toward her until she found herself backed against the tiled wall. Annoyed that she'd allowed him to put her in retreat, Sam lifted her chin and met his gaze head-on.

"Did you know," he murmured, planting one hand flat against the wall beside her head, "that this is the fourth time we've been thrown together by *events*?"

"Events?"

"Yeah, you know destiny, fate."

She made a sound of annoyance. "There's no such thing. It was a coincidence."

"That we were in the same bar, in the same hotel at the same time? That you tumbled into *my* lap and not one of a dozen men surrounding the dance floor? That we decided to call it a night at the same time and ended up in the elevator together to help bring a child into the world? And then two months later, you cross the continent to work on the *same* foundation because we're both acquainted with Colleen Rutherford?" He paused to let his words sink in before leaning closer. "Not only don't I believe in coincidences, *Samantha*," he said softly, "there is no way I can ignore the fact that I already know you intimately."

Her throat moved convulsively as she swallowed. "You don't know a thing about me."

"Don't I?" he asked softly.

"That's just ph-physical stuff," she rasped, her body going hot at the reminder of how much he'd learned that night. "But that's beside the point. Rebound sex—"

"Is a bad idea," he interrupted roughly. "Yeah, I know. But here's the thing." He ran questing fingers up her arm, across her shoulder and down the neckline of her dress to where the two sides of her dress overlapped. "Rebound or not, I look at you and I can't forget."

"Well, I certainly won't have any problem forgetting anything," Sam lied, desperately ignoring the rush of sensation spreading out from the barely-there touch. "In fact, I'm really good at ignoring things that aren't good for me." For too long, she'd been really good at ignoring her own wants too, doing what was expected of a Gilford.

She pressed her hand against his chest in the hopes that he'd get the message and back off. "You're in the ladies' room. Now, please leave so I can get b-back to my p-plan."

Adam's eyes darkened and before she could squeak out a protest, he gently pulled her against him and brought his lips close enough to shock her into stillness and then strain for more. She yielded to temptation, slanting her lips against his and opening them to receive his invading tongue before she could remind herself that this was the last thing she wanted, that *he* was the last man she wanted.

But she did. Oh, God, she did. She'd wanted him in San Francisco and she'd wanted him while sitting across the boardroom table, pretending interest in what Aunt Coco was saying. She hadn't heard a thing over the panicked embarrassment and excitement pounding through her blood.

She shouldn't be kissing him. But she was and she didn't want to stop. Oh, God, she thought as she closed her lips around his tongue and sucked it into her mouth. She didn't want to stop the wild recklessness rising within her to give and take and then take some more.

And then, just as the edges of her vision grayed, he broke off the kiss with a ragged curse and backed away, leaving Sam clutching the vanity counter. Opening heavy eyes, she stared at him in confusion. He was half a dozen feet away, dragging air into his heaving lungs. After a slow burning stare, Adam turned and pulled open the door.

"Ignore *that*, if you can, Ms. Jefferies," he growled over his shoulder in a voice that was hardly recognizable, and then he was gone.

CHAPTER SIX

"Suction," Adam said, pausing to allow the surgical nurse to remove the blood pooling in the chest cavity. "Release the clamp and test the vessel for integrity," he instructed the surgical intern. "When you're certain the graft will hold, we can proceed with closure."

Satisfied that the young surgeon was coping, he looked up at the real-time image on the fluoroscope screen. So far, he couldn't detect any leaks. The new bypass seemed to be holding steady but the next forty-eight hours would be critical.

Out of the corner of his eye, he caught sight of movement in the observation window overlooking the surgical suite and turned as a figure rushed from the room. He didn't need to see her face to know who it was. That straight-as-a-ruler back and the warm fire of upswept chestnut hair gave her away.

His skull tightened and a tingle worked its way down his spine. Since the foundation meeting a fortnight ago, giving Samantha the space she'd wanted had been both easier and more difficult than he'd imagined. Easier because there'd suddenly been a spate of new patients and he hadn't had time to sleep let alone follow his instincts. Which was where the difficulty had come in.

Now that he knew the woman who'd dropped into his lap and shaken his world with her bright blue eyes and enthusiastic kisses was right here in San José, giving her space had been the last thing he'd wanted, especially with her habit of appearing in the observation room in the middle of intricate procedures.

If he were honest with himself, it had stung having her call what to him had been the best sex of his life a rebound mistake, and he'd reacted like a nerdy adolescent experiencing his first rejection.

"How's the temperature holding, Mr Davis?" he asked the perfusionist, deliberately pushing thoughts of Samantha from his mind. The assisting surgeon had released the clamp and there was a collective inhalation as all eyes went to the fluoroscopy monitor. He caught the thumbs-up as everyone watched blood fill the graft section, then flood the heart. After a couple of shudders, it settled into a sluggish rhythm.

"Vitals?"

"Holding steady." This from the anesthetist.

"All right then, bring the temp up, Mr. Davis. Dr. Guthrie, let's proceed with closure." He waited while the two halves of the sternum were brought together. "Talons ready?"

Six hours later, Adam left the elevator and headed down the passage toward the children's ward. Four-year-old Katie Ross had undergone an atrial septal repair that morning and he wanted to check on her before calling it a day.

Although the procedure was a relatively simple one requiring a transcatheter repair and a tiny device—folded up like an umbrella in the catheter tube—deployed and attached over the hole, she would need careful monitoring over the next few weeks to ensure it did not detach and cause an embolism. Despite the septal defect, the little girl was a bouncy, bright-eyed little imp and keeping her quiet was going to take some doing.

He paused to check the ward register, then moved past the nurses' station toward the wards, wondering why it was so quiet when the children's ward was usually filled with the wails of distressed children and the murmured reassurances of nurses and mothers.

He caught the sound of murmured tones spoken into the hushed, expectant silence followed by a chorus of childish gasps. A low familiar feminine laugh sent him spinning back nearly three months.

He paused in the doorway to Katie's room, finding a group of children, ranging from about three to nine, gathered around Katie's bed. Some were leaning against their mothers while others practically bounced up and down in their excitement as the story unfolded.

Nurses quietly checked their vitals and the person using different voices to bring the story alive for the wide-eyed audience was none other than the woman he'd spent way too much time thinking about.

Samantha Jefferies. Not looking as out of place as she might with her upswept hair and off-the-shoulder half-sleeved rose-colored dress more suited to a fancy ladies' luncheon than the children's ward. Snuggled in her lap was a small boy with messy dark hair and sleepy eyes. Adam watched as she absently smoothed the overlong strands off his forehead before turning the page and continuing the story.

Disinclined to draw attention to himself and break up the story hour holding the children spellbound, Adam propped his shoulder against the open doorway and watched the engrossed little faces while a husky voice brought the story to life.

He sensed someone come up behind him and turned to see Janice Norman. The Paeds APRN arched her brow at him before turning her attention to the gathering around Katie's bed. "She's great, isn't she?"

Adam turned back to the scene, his expression neutral. Janice had been in San Francisco the night he and Samantha had met and wasn't anyone's fool. She'd spot a weakness a mile away and take unholy delight in needling him.

"Ms. Jefferies come here a lot?" he murmured casually.

"Usually about this time," she said absently. "And sometimes in the afternoons when the kids are restless. They love her. She's a natural, and her stories distract them from all the poking and prodding."

Adam scratched his jaw and wondered if Janice knew that his heart was pumping a little faster, that a buzz had started at the base of his spine and traveled all the way to the top of his head at the sound of that husky voice. A voice he recalled urging him on. *Don't stop*, she'd ordered, *Harder*, and then on a sexy little hitch, *Oh...oh... right there*.

Just the memory had his body hardening, and by the knowing little smirk on Janice's lips, she recognized Sam and wasn't about to pass up the opportunity to rag him.

"You know," she remarked idly after a couple of beats, confirming Adam's worst fears. "I can't help noticing how much she reminds me of someone." Having known her since his intern days, she knew him better than anyone and enjoyed making him squirm. Schooling his features, he just grunted even as Samantha finally looked up and noticed she had another audience member.

She stopped abruptly mid-sentence, her eyes widening as she stared at him for a couple of beats before flushing and looking away. But in that moment, Adam had seen both anxiety and vulnerability beneath the surprise. The vulnerability got to him in a place he hadn't expected. His chest. Or more specifically his heart. It clenched hard and all he could do was rub the heel of his hand against the sharp ache.

Dammit, he snarled silently. The last thing he needed was to feel anything for the woman who'd relegated him to a rebound mistake. Even if he'd never thought to see her again.

"So..." Janice said casually. "You and the Prom Queen, huh?" Without waiting for him to reply, she glared at him and demanded, "When were you going to tell me that the woman from the bar in San Francisco is related to Dr. Rutherford and working for the foundation?"

Amused by the censure in her tone, Adam shrugged because he hadn't wanted to talk about Samantha with anyone. He wasn't sure why; what had happened between them was just too private to discuss. Even with friends.

"They're not actually related," he said absently, before hitting her with what he hoped was a look of male bafflement that he didn't for a minute think she bought. "I think the connection has something to do with her grandfather." He let his gaze drift over the yawning kids, then squinted at his watch. "It's a bit late for story time, don't you think?"

Narrowed eyes promising retribution, she growled and shoved past him, leaving Adam relieved that he'd narrowly escaped a grilling. The relief was short-lived, however, when his gaze drifted back to Samantha and their eyes locked again. Hers widened and darkened as wild color rushed beneath the creamy skin, making him wonder if she was remembering that night too.

But did her determination to ignore what he felt between them stem from the fact that he was a doctor; that she'd only recently broken off her engagement and didn't want to jump into a new relationship too quickly; or because of his background? Not that he was looking for a relationship, he assured himself. She wouldn't be the first woman to sleep with a man because of the thrill of the forbidden and she probably wouldn't be the last.

His own mother had treated his father as a temporary thrill while she sowed her wild, youthful oats before marrying a man worthy of her blue-blooded status. He'd often wondered if falling pregnant had been a way to rebel against the strictures of her family or if she'd just been young and stupid. Whatever it was, he'd ended up collateral damage and spent most of his life fighting the prejudice of having one foot not only in his mother's culture but in his father's too.

He had no desire to repeat his parents' mistakes or be anyone's rebellious one-night stand. He thought too much of himself for that. He'd had to work twice as hard to be given even half the respect other students or doctors expected as their right. He'd never minded the hard work since it had put him on Coco Rutherford's radar and helped him become a top cardiothoracic surgeon.

He certainly didn't need a curvy chestnut-haired woman reminding him of his childhood and making him feel as though he was always on the outside looking in. As though he was good enough for wild rebound sex but not for anything more open or long-term. He refused to yearn for scraps of attention the way his father had, finally hitting a spiral of depression and alcohol because some vain, shallow debutante had only wanted a quick thrill.

Reminding of a past he had no intention of repeating, Adam pushed away from the door frame, suddenly needing fresh air. He would come back later, he told himself as he left the ward. He'd return to check on Katie when the ward was quiet—when he could think past the urge to mess up Samantha's sophisticated perfection in an effort to find the warm sexy woman from San Francisco.

Pulse jumping, Sam saw Adam's eyes change—narrow and cool—before he turned and disappeared. It was as though he'd come to some decision that she knew should have relieved her, but didn't.

Oh, boy, it really didn't.

And with that realization, she sucked in a sharp breath and cringed as her thoughts tumbled one over the other inside her head. Had she—had she secretly *wanted* Adam to ignore what she'd said about rebound sex and not give her the space she'd said she needed?

Her belly bottomed out and a rush of heat washed over her at the images that popped into her mind. Oh, God, she had, she thought with horror. In some silly feminine part of her, she'd secretly hoped that he wouldn't be able to stay away. That he'd ambush her, push her up against the nearest wall and kiss her senseless.

Her lips tingled but she ignored it, because it made her a vain and shallow person who said one thing while meaning another because he was hot and buff and made her feel like a sexy, desirable woman. Which meant, *dam-*

mit, that for all her talk of changing her life, changing *herself*, she was still not taking charge of anything.

Cringing at the knowledge that she was falling back on old habits, she dispensed a few hugs with a promise to be back the next day. A headache squeezing her forehead, she returned Janice Norman's greeting with a wan smile and headed for the exit, eager to escape the woman's speculative gaze.

It was only when she was alone in the elevator that she recognized the roiling emotions for what they were. Jealousy. She was jealous of the closeness she'd sensed between Adam and the head paediatric nurse.

And if that didn't make her a pathetic fool, she didn't know what did.

It should have been easy for Adam to put Ms. Boston Socialite firmly out of his mind. He'd learned early on that he couldn't control everything and then put all his energy into doing just that. He'd focused on acing high school and then med school, needing to prove to himself that he'd been awarded the Stanford scholarship because he deserved it.

He'd worked two jobs until Coco swept into his life, becoming much more than a mentor. She'd arranged for him to work at the hospital so he could focus on medicine and bullied him to eat properly. At first, he'd been too proud to accept her help, but she'd simply told him that she was protecting her investment. When he'd realized that helping him was helping her get over the death of someone she'd loved, he'd accepted—albeit reluctantly—then worked his ass off to prove she hadn't been wrong about him.

There'd been women, of course, but he'd never allowed

anyone to become a distraction from what was important; and *that* was overcoming his past and becoming the best cardiothoracic surgeon on the West Coast.

He'd been perfectly happy with the status quo, seeking out women when the need arose, all the while focusing his energies on professional goals. Then he'd met *Amanda*, who'd turned out to be Coco's Sammie, and his focus had shattered.

Okay, maybe not shattered, but she'd jolted him out of the nice little groove his life had become and made him want something he hadn't let himself want in a very long time.

He wanted a connection.

Ironic as hell, considering the woman wanted nothing—except distance—from him. Even worse, he hadn't realized how much he'd come to look forward to seeing her in the surgical observation room until she stopped coming.

And damn if he didn't miss her.

He scowled at the thought. Damn the woman, and damn the effect she had on him.

Then, before he'd realized he'd come to the decision, he found himself heading to the floors housing the hospital's top management late the following Friday. He'd been on his rounds when an idea had popped into his head fully formed.

The best way to get Samantha out of his system, he decided, was to spend some time with her and see how she handled a day in Juniper Falls where he was due for his monthly outreach visit. It was where the foundation had been conceived—and where he'd grown up. He was hoping the differences in their upbringing would cure him of his growing obsession with a woman that was way out of his social league.

It was only when he saw Coco sitting in reception, frowning at the computer screen, that he realized how late it was. The only other illumination came from one corner lamp.

"Adam," Coco said when he opened the door. She looked surprised to see him. "Is something wrong?"

"No, I uh—" His mind went blank for a couple of beats before abruptly coming back online. "Nothing's wrong but I was looking for Samantha and only just realized how late it is."

Coco frowned and turned her attention back to the screen. "Sammie? Why?"

He thought about leaving but then firmed his jaw. *Dammit*, he wasn't that awkward kid he'd been at fifteen screwing himself up inside over the most popular girl in school. Giving in to the discomfort, he rubbed the back of his neck and said as casually as he could, "I'm flying out to Juniper Falls in the morning and thought she might like to see what Galahad is all about. She's been here over a month and aside from meeting some of our recipients, she knows next to nothing about the foundation."

"Great idea." She waved her arm to the passage that led to the offices before resuming her keyboard clacking. "Don't know why I didn't think of it myself." She paused and sent him a quick grimace. "You just missed her though. She went out to dinner on a—"

"Date?" he interrupted so sharply that Coco looked up, her expression oddly arresting. Embarrassed by his outburst he brushed it aside with, "Never mind," his brows drawing together over the unpleasant emotions tightening the back of his skull at the realization that while he hadn't had a date in—heck, he couldn't remember—Samantha was out to dinner.

He knew exactly what the emotion was but it had been at least twenty years since he'd felt it, and he couldn't understand why it was emerging now.

"Do you have her cell number? I need to get an early start."

Coco grabbed a small notepad off the receptionist's desk and scribbled something. She tore off the top sheet and thrust it at him.

"What time do you plan to leave?"

"About five, why?"

"Better pick her up at four thirty with hot, sweet coffee. She's not an easy morning person. Oh, and Adam—" She waited for him to meet her gaze and after a couple of beats said, "Give her a chance."

Confusion tightened his forehead. "What are you talking about?"

"Sammie isn't anything like your mother," she said gently, her eyes dark and soft with a compassion that he abruptly wished wasn't focused on him. *Dammit*, he wasn't some orphan.

"I know that—" he began irritably only to have Coco interrupt.

"Do you?" she drawled softly, one brow arching up her forehead as though he were a little dense.

Frustration grabbed him by the throat. "What's that supposed to mean?" He wanted to tell her to mind her own business but she'd been mother, mentor and friend to him when no one else had cared.

"It means I know you too well," she said gently, pushing away from the desk, a challenge gleaming in the eyes that locked with his. "It means that every relationship you've had since we met has been with social butterflies. Relationships that had an expiration date even before they started."

"That isn't relevant," he growled. "Besides, Samantha and I do not have a relationship outside of the foundation."

Coco clucked her disappointment. "Do you think I haven't seen the way you look at each other when you think no one is watching? You're interested, Adam, but you're so determined to paint all socialites with the same brush as your mother that you'll overlook the fact that Sammie is warm and generous and funny—absolutely nothing like those other women."

What could he say to that but, "This is for the foundation," before turning and walking away.

Of course, Coco had to have the last word but she let him get to the door before saying smugly, "Oh, and in case you wondered—she's interested too."

CHAPTER SEVEN

SAM BLINKED BLEARILY up at the man leaning casually against the wall outside her apartment, looking alert and rested like it wasn't the middle of the night. His eyes took a leisurely journey over her and by the time they returned to her face, a smile tugged at the corners of his mouth.

The expression in his gaze sent a buzz of sensation zinging through her, clearing away the last remnants of sleep. Wondering if she was still dreaming about seeing him, standing in the exact same spot and with the same predatory expression in his eyes, Sam shoved the wild tangle of hair off her face and rasped, "Adam?"

One dark brow arched and his eyes darkened. "Expecting someone else?"

Even in her befuddled state, she caught the bite in his words and wondered what the heck he was mad about. It wasn't like *she'd* arrived on *his* doorstep in the middle of the night, dragging him from a deep sleep, then looking at him like he'd committed some heinous crime.

Shaking her head to clear it, she inhaled, swearing she could smell coffee. She must be dreaming or maybe it was part of the same Adam hallucination? "What are you doing here?" she rasped.

He was silent a beat before saying, "Our field trip."

And when she continued to stare at him, said, "You did get my message, didn't you? I tried calling but your phone was off."

"Wha—?" She inhaled, hoping the cool air would clear her head. It had been a while since she'd been this close to Adam and it was messing with her head. "Oh, right. Yes, I—" At his arched brow, she broke off. Her hand tightened on the doorknob and she exhaled with a whoosh. "Sorry, you'd better come in."

He narrowed his gaze but didn't move. "You alone?"

"What?" She scowled her confusion, and when he just looked at her, scrubbed a hand over her face and muttered, "I need caffeine. I can't think this early."

Stepping back, she blinked a large to-go cup from a local coffee outlet into being. At first, she thought it was an apparition until it was followed by a large male that smelled even better than the hot beverage. For a scary moment, she worried that she might be tempted to drag him inside and gulp him down.

"Earth to Samantha." He chuckled, waving the coffee beneath her nose, and she realized she'd gone a little glazed with lust. She licked her lips and hastily assured herself that it was for coffee. Definitely for coffee.

"Looking for this?"

"Um—yes?"

When she continued to stand there and drool, he chuckled and caught her hand to wrap her fingers around the large cup. Warmth instantly infused her palm and traveled up to the inside of her elbow before spreading to the rest of her in insidious waves of pleasure.

"Late night?"

There it was again, that edge suggesting he was annoyed with her. Her brow tightened in confusion but the heat of his hand around hers was kind of distracting. She'd forgotten how large his hands were with their wide palms and long strong fingers; and she'd forgotten how they could make her feel.

And that wasn't good, she decided, when a shudder accompanied the memory. "It's not the late night," she blurted out, a little freaked that he just had to show up and she turned into a woman who couldn't recall her name or that she had a plan. One who'd danced barefoot in a five-star hotel bar, tossed back shooters like a pro and then helped deliver a baby in an elevator. "It's y-you."

"Me?"

Oh, great, now she was stuttering and about to admit that after seeing his missed call and listening to his deep voice inviting her on a field trip for the foundation, she'd hardly slept. She'd wished he were inviting her because he wanted to spend time with her and not because he wanted her to meet people connected to the foundation.

When she had slept, it had been to dream some pretty hot stuff that made her blush just recalling it. No way would she tell him all that though. Especially not with the way he was acting.

Then again, he had brought coffee.

"Ignore me," she muttered. "My brain always struggles to wake up in the middle of the night." She let him guide the cup to her mouth. Forced to take a testing sip of hot, sweet brew, she felt her system shudder and was pretty sure it was the infusion of caffeine.

"It's nearly five," he murmured. His voice, a little rough around the edges, reminded her of the way he sounded when he was aroused. "We should go."

Fighting memories of San Francisco, Sam tightened her grip on the to-go mug and finally found the presence of mind to step back. It was more of a stumble but she couldn't think with him so close, not when he looked and smelled so good that she contemplated testing to see if he tasted better than coffee. She licked her lips, afraid that he did.

"Go...?" Her brow creased in confusion. "Oh—right," she said on a rush of air and gestured out the door. "Let's go then."

He didn't move, just rocked back on his heels, his hot eyes lightening until he was smiling.

"What?" Annoyance tugged at her brows. *Yeesh*, it was bad enough that she was expected to think before the sun was up and now she had to deal with his annoying masculine amusement.

Annoyance she promptly forgot when he gave her a slow down-up look, his eyes a little heated as they returned to hers. "Not that I'm complaining," he drawled huskily. "But you might want to dress first."

"Wha—?" Sam looked down and realized that she was in her skimpy pajamas and a light summer robe that left very little to the imagination. Heat rose into her cheeks because the cool early morning air had tightened her nipples into visible buds. "Oh, boy," she muttered, rolling her eyes and spinning away to hurry through the arch toward her bedroom, calling, "I'll be right back. Make yourself at home," over her shoulder.

She took the fastest shower on record and returned twenty minutes later wearing a dress that she'd bought at a little gem of a boutique she'd found close to the hospital. It was part of her new-me makeover, and she had no idea why she'd chosen to wear something so outrageously feminine today of all days.

Adam, leaning against the French doors that opened

onto the complex's communal gardens and swimming pool, turned at the sound of her heels clicking on the tiled floor and stilled. For one horrifying moment, she thought she'd made a mistake in her choice of white flowing midi sundress covered with large scattered red camia. Then he moved and the expression in his eyes had wariness and awareness rolling over her like a tidal wave.

Abruptly self-conscious, she had to force herself not to back away as he neared. Lifting her chin defiantly, she dared him to comment on her appearance because *dammit*, she had to stop feeling as though she were constantly being judged and found wanting. She had to stop worrying what other people thought and start pleasing herself.

That was the reason for moving across the country, wasn't it? To move out from the shadow of her grandmother and find herself. Find her own mojo. Be her own person.

Besides, the dress, with its tiny capped sleeves, form-fitting bodice and full skirt had pleased her the instant she'd seen it and even in her half-awake state, she knew she looked good.

Adam paused less than a foot away and lifted a hand to tip her chin up with one long tanned finger. The expression in his eyes was hooded and impossible to read. Heat, most definitely, and maybe a little amusement but she thought she caught the same sharp yearning that lanced through her.

"Good morning, Samantha," he murmured before dropping a kiss on her startled mouth. The first kiss was featherlight. The next lingered. The third turned into more than a hello. A *lot* more.

Her reserve melted away and she gave a soft mewl that was a mix of surprise and longing. Before she knew it, she was plastered up against him, her mouth clinging enthusiastically to his. Once her ears were buzzing and her skin tingling, Adam drew back, his eyes dark and slumberous.

Sucking in air, she then let it escape in a shuddery gush before realizing that her hands had fisted his shirt as though she were afraid he'd vanish. It took a concerted effort to unclench her fingers one at a time and smooth the wrinkled fabric with hands that shook.

All she could manage was a hoarse, *"Wow."*

"Yeah." His voice was deep and raspy, his breathing almost as ragged as hers. "That was some hello but maybe we should leave before it turns into something else."

"Something—?" She blinked his face into focus. "Oh...um—right." Color high, she stepped back on wobbly legs and nervously slid her tongue along her bottom lip. "That might—um, be for the b-best." Spinning away to reach for her shoulder bag with hands that trembled, Sam rolled her eyes because even to her own ears she'd sounded disappointed. Disappointed that he hadn't ravished her like the last time.

Her breath escaped in an audible whoosh. *Oh, boy.*

Adam chuckled and when she straightened, dropped a friendly kiss on her neck. He slid his palm down her back to the base of her spine and even though she knew it was just to guide her out the door, she shivered because she had a feeling all her good intentions—her careful planning—were about to go up in smoke.

And she couldn't have cared less.

Studying him out of the corner of her eye, Sam couldn't help noticing that he drove as he did everything else, with casual competence and complete mastery. She'd told herself that sneaking into the surgical observation rooms to watch him had simply been professional curiosity when the truth was she hadn't been able to stay away.

Before she could stop it, a tingle began at the bottom of her spine and worked its way up to the base of her skull because she knew from experience that he did other things just as masterfully. Things she'd told herself her memory had exaggerated. Things that would be easy to forget. That *he* would be easy to forget.

Fat chance. Especially after that kiss.

She'd told him she needed space and then ignored her own protestations because she'd had an almost overwhelming need to see him. She was rabidly curious about a man who could look at her with hot intensity one minute and then deliver a baby the next; a man who'd said he wasn't about to ignore what had happened in San Francisco and then promptly did.

Huddling against the door to put as much distance between them as she could, Sam realized that he was dressed pretty much as she remembered him in San Francisco—faded jeans worn almost white in places and a black T-shirt that emphasized his warm coppery skin.

It had something very un-Sam-like stirring beneath her skin. Like "Amanda" was restless to emerge. Like her alter ego was lifting her head, sucking in air as she closed her eyes to concentrate on identifying the deliciously heady scent of him—warm and spicy with a subtle hint of bergamot.

A little freaked by the realization that she was starting to sound crazy even in her own head, she sneaked another peek at him and found him studying her with eyes as warm and spicy as he smelled. Her pulse gave a funny little lurch, and for an instant, her belly went airborne.

"So. Where are we going again?" she asked a little desperately.

"Juniper Falls."

"It sounds rustic."

Adam's grin was quick and white in the predawn darkness as he took the interstate on-ramp and accelerated south. "You sound worried."

She nibbled on her lip and nervously smoothed her skirt over her thighs. "Should I be? Worried, I mean?"

She felt his eyes on her profile. "Are you?" His voice reached across the Jeep's darkened cab, a rough and tempting challenge that scraped at the sensual nerve endings she hadn't thought she had.

"Well," she rasped, a little light-headed. "Only if you're kidnapping me."

His soft chuckle soothed the little pulse bump. "As tempting as that sounds, that isn't the reason for our field trip."

"Oh?" Heck, had that sounded as disappointed as she felt?

Instead of replying, he checked his side mirrors before accelerating around a truck. Once they were some distance away, he said casually, "Coco thought you might like to see where the foundation started."

Perturbed by the disappointment that it had been Coco's idea, all she could say was, "Why Juniper Falls?"

"I grew up there," he announced, and her disappointment morphed into curiosity. "Since it relies mostly on tourists all year round there isn't—wasn't—a proper hospital, which meant no medical care, especially for the folks who can't afford to travel to larger centers. I started the outreach program for people who can't afford specialist care."

She sat up slowly and studied him curiously. "*You* started the foundation?"

He grimaced. "Unofficially. It was just an idea until I took the concept to Coco," he corrected. "She has all the contacts. So we set things up and now it's not just about Juniper Falls anymore. There are dozens of people who donate their time and skills to the foundation in other small towns."

"Maybe," she conceded. "But *they* don't have a foundation named after them, do they?"

He made a sound of exasperation in the back of his throat. "How on earth did you reach that conclusion?"

"Oh, come on," she snorted, turning to grin at him. "Surely, I'm not the only one to make a connection between Galahad and Knight?"

He met her gaze for just a moment and she lost herself in the warm amber depths of his eyes.

"You know," he said, when her amusement faded beneath his intense scrutiny, "that's the first time I've heard you laugh. Really laugh, I mean."

"That's ridiculous," she scoffed, smoothing her hair off her forehead in a move she recognized as nervousness. "I laugh all the time."

He shook his head. "Not with me." His gaze caressed her face, coming to land on her mouth before returning to the road. He was smiling when he said, "I like it."

A shocked little bubble grew in her chest. Something that felt very much like pleasure. Horrified by how much his words affected her; how much she'd needed that brief acknowledgment of an attraction that went beyond the physical, she rasped, "You're changing the subject, Dr. Knight."

He chuckled, the deep warmth of it reminding her that she might have said he'd been her rebound rebellion but she hadn't been able to forget how he'd made her feel and she hadn't been able to stay away despite her determination to treat him as nothing more than an occasional boss or colleague.

To distract herself from the direction her thoughts were heading, she finally asked, "Are you going to tell me what prompted you to start the foundation?"

He flicked a hooded look in her direction before returning his gaze to the road. After a long pause, he said, "My grandmother died of a heart condition that shouldn't have killed her." He was silent for some time before adding, "My father was an artist, more concerned with the contents of a bottle than with making a living—at least after I was born. Needless to say, there wasn't a lot of money and she kept quiet about her condition until it was too late."

She heard what he didn't say. "And your mother?"

His mouth twisted an instant before he gave a short hard laugh. "She wasn't around."

"Oh?" she said carefully, wondering if his mother had died. "I'm sorry."

"Don't be," he drawled dryly. "She wasn't."

"Oh?" she said again, her brow tightening at his tone more than his words. "Why do you say that?"

After a short pause, he admitted, "The instant I was born, she handed me over to my father and told us to have a nice life."

Sam couldn't hide her shock. "He—he *told* you that?"

"Every time he got drunk," Adam said casually, as

though he were talking about some acquaintance. "He'd lock himself in his studio and stare at the paintings he'd done of her. And then he'd cry and quietly put away the contents of an entire bottle of whatever he had in the house."

Sam swallowed past the lump in her throat at the image he'd painted of a man devastated by the loss of someone he'd loved. "He must have loved her very much."

She wasn't sure what to make of his dry snort.

"He was obsessed with a woman he couldn't have," he said dispassionately as though he were talking about a stranger. "Her parents wanted a commemoration of her coming of age. Apparently, it's a thing among socialites of wealthy families, but then I suppose you'd know more about that than I would." He sent her an unreadable glance, but before she could say that she hadn't run with that crowd, he continued, "Anyway, they heard about this up-and-coming Native American artist and decided to one-up their friends. Of course, he didn't do portraits and initially refused the offer, that is until he got a look at his subject. She was everything he wasn't—a blue-eyed blonde that simply drew everyone in with her bright and bubbly blue-blooded gorgeousness." This time Sam had no trouble interpreting his snort.

"Well, long story short, he fell like a rock and thought she'd fallen too. When she announced that she was pregnant, he was over the moon because now her family would surely allow them to be together." He gave a hard laugh. "Yeah, well, the laugh was on him because it turns out she was already engaged to some rich blue-blooded guy and had no intention of giving up her bright and golden future for a struggling artist from the reservation. She'd only been having her last fling before tying the knot. A baby with him didn't exactly feature in her plans other than to punish her parents."

Sam's mind whirled as she considered his words. "She—she was a debutante?"

"Coincidence, huh?"

Sam didn't know what he meant, but before she could ask, he whipped into a small local strip mall. He parked and with a terse, "Wait here," slid out of the car and disappeared into the bakery, leaving Sam with her thoughts whirling.

Minutes later, he was back, handing over a large to-go mug and a small bakery box. Conscious that he'd used the stop to close the subject, she took the coffee and peeked into the box at the assorted pastries. They smelled fresh, warm and very tempting, but in that instant she couldn't have swallowed one mouthful if her life depended on it.

"You eat pastries for breakfast?"

He backed out of the parking spot and headed for the exit. "They're for you."

"I don't normally eat breakfast," she said absently, as he turned onto the road heading east again, studying him out the corner of her eye.

She caught sight of his wry half smile before he said, "Maybe that's why you're so cranky in the morning."

"I am not cranky," she said primly, unsure whether to be relieved or disappointed by the subject change but willing to give him space. Heck, she understood all too well the baggage that came with family. "I'm just not a morning person." His answer was a low chuckle that eased her clenched gut. Apparently, talking about his family made him as cranky as he accused her of being. "At least not when I'm rudely awakened before the birds."

He flashed her a sizzling look, his mouth curving

with sensuality. "I could help with that," he drawled, the deeply sensual timbre of his voice sliding into her belly like a heated promise because there was absolutely no doubt about what he meant.

She snorted and inhaled sharply at the exact moment she took a sip of coffee and everything went down the wrong way. She instantly went into a paroxysm of coughing. Preoccupied with hacking up a lung, she felt the car pull over and the to-go cup whipped out of her hand, the next instant receiving a couple of hard whacks to her back. It finally did the job, and after a few more splutters, she managed to drag in a shuddery breath as she held up a hand of surrender and collapsed back into her seat.

A large hand gently cupped her chin and tipped her face sideways. "You okay?" he murmured, his eyes quickly assessing her in a way that was both professional and intensely personal, leaving her feeling exposed.

"Define okay?" she rasped, brushing his hand away before she decided she liked it there. She sat up and reached for her shoulder bag to look for a tissue.

Adam snagged it from her nerveless fingers and again tilted her face toward him. She was surprised enough by his move that she let him gently and efficiently dab at her face and wet eyes. His mouth quirked as he caught her gaze.

"Interesting that the idea of my helping to improve your morning mood makes you choke," he said, studying her intently in the light from the dash. "Why is that, I wonder?"

Her face heated. "You had your chance and blew it," she dismissed loftily, snatching the tissue from his hand and stuffing it back in her purse. Then because she was tempted to crawl into his lap and bury her face in his throat, she shifted back, hoping to put a little distance between them. "I was just a little stunned by your arrogance, that's all. Besides—" she waved her hand flippantly as he pulled back onto the road "—many have tried and failed."

Now why had she said that, she wondered when one dark brow rose up his forehead and his eyes turned almost black. She shivered. Heck, he must know from her behavior that she wasn't nearly as sophisticated as her words implied. Or, at least, *suspect* that she wasn't.

"Many huh?" he drawled—and there was that bite of annoyance again—studying her in the light from the dash. "Does that include last night's date?"

Sam frowned, confused. "Last night's—? What are you talking about?"

"Coco said you were out to dinner last night." He paused, his eyes unreadable, mouth unsmiling.

"Oh," she said, thinking back to the subtle bite of displeasure in his voice when he'd arrived at her door. As though he were jealous of her *date*, which had actually been a business dinner and had not exactly gone well. Blake Lowry had kind of hinted that any sizeable donation he made came with strings. The kind that led to the bedroom. Needless to say, she'd cut the evening short.

"Blake is a wonderful man." No, he wasn't. But she wasn't about to tell Adam that. Anyway, let him think what he wanted. Sam didn't have anything to hide.

"Blake?" He grimaced as though the name pained him. "So he's what, some male model or something?"

Sam snorted out a laugh. "Don't be snide," she chastised mildly. "He's actually a financial director at the tech company his father owns."

"Uh-huh," he said finally, sending her a hooded glance

as he flipped his indicator and turned onto a gravel road, the Jeep's headlights slicing through the darkness. "And does this financial director fit into that ridiculous plan of yours?"

Alerted to something in his voice, Sam paused in selecting a cinnamon-covered doughnut hole from the bakery box and slid him a curious look. "Actually, no," she snapped. "For your information, my plan is *not* ridiculous." He didn't comment but the glance he sent her spoke volumes about his opinion. "It makes perfect sense when you're changing your life."

"Uh-huh. So Jake's—what?"

"A potential donor," she snapped, shoving the doughnut hole into her mouth. "And it's Blake."

"Ah. So it was a business dinner."

She looked up and narrowed her eyes when she caught the amused curve of his mouth, as though the news pleased him. Annoyed with that smug look, she opened her mouth to deny it out of irritation but was distracted when the headlights picked out an arched-stone-and-iron gateway over which the words *Copper Creek Aviation* were displayed.

Her mouth closed with a snap and an uncomfortable feeling settled in her belly. It might have been the result of the three doughnut holes she'd just wolfed down, but was more likely the uneasy feeling that they were about to board an aircraft that in no way resembled anything she'd ever flown in.

"Please tell me that we're about to board a large commercial jet with in-flight attendants."

He laughed as though she'd made another joke, when she'd been serious as a heart attack. "Nope, Miss City Girl. Where we're going, there's no place for anything larger than a twin prop." Fried dough abruptly churned in her belly as he pulled up in front of a sprawling building. With the sky only just beginning to lighten, the place appeared deserted. "But not to worry," Adam assured her lightly, "I have a couple hours flying time, and last week I learned how to land without the instructor."

Sam felt her eyes widen and tightened her grip on the rapidly cooling coffee. "You mean—*you're* flying?"

He must have heard something in her voice because he turned to study her face in the darkened interior of the cab, his gaze abruptly serious. "Yes, I'm flying." After a short silence, during which she struggled to absorb the news, he asked quietly, "You trust me?"

Sam gave a strangled laugh. "If I needed heart surgery, maybe," she managed, exhaling on a gusty whoosh. "But this—this is something completely different. I, uh—"

"Hey," he interrupted gently, lifting a hand to cup her face and gently swipe his thumb along her tight jaw. The gesture was both an apology and intended to soothe. While it did just that, it also sparked a host of sensations that weren't the least soothing.

Dammit, she thought, struggling not to lean into his touch. She was in a bad way when just the touch of his hand on her face had the hard knot of fear melting. His deep voice slid across the space, settling alongside the feelings she was already fighting for this complex man. Feelings that were as thrilling as they were terrifying.

"I was kidding," he said softly. "I've logged over thirty-two-hundred hours in the air and I've been doing this since I was in high school."

"Doing what exactly?" Sam choked out. "Abducting women?"

He traced a finger along her collarbone. "Nope," he

said with a grin when she shivered. "I've never had to do that before."

She could believe it. Just take her for example. Ever since she'd fallen into his lap in San Francisco, she'd been fighting the urge to follow him anywhere. She might say that she was annoyed to be dragged out before the sun was even up but the terrifying truth was that something deep inside had shuddered awake when she opened her door to find him on her doorstep looking better than coffee and doughnuts.

If *that* wasn't a sign she was in *big* trouble, then she hadn't been paying attention.

CHAPTER EIGHT

ADAM SLID HIS gaze to the woman white-knuckling it beside him. She was pale and tense but had uttered not one word since that strangled gurgle back when she'd first caught sight of their ride.

"Hey," he said softly, infusing his voice with confidence. "I know this isn't what you were expecting, but this is a solid little plane and the mechanic keeps her in tip-top condition."

With her fingers digging into the seat, Sam looked around the tiny cockpit. "There's not a lot of plane between me and the ground," she admitted into the headset. A visible shiver moved through her. "And those propellers look kind of flimsy. In fact, this whole aircraft looks flimsy."

"Relax," his deep voice soothed. "This girl is the best twin turboprop on the market. She's solid and reliable and can withstand anything but major weather. Besides—" he said, gesturing to the landscape below "—you don't see scenery like this from a commercial jet."

Instead of agreeing, Sam ignored the view and kept her eyes locked on him. "Did you know that nearly four-hundred people die in private plane accidents every year?"

"That fatality rate is negligible compared to the thirty-thousand road accident deaths," he pointed out, hoping facts would ease the hollow-eyed fear. "That works out to be about one per one-hundred-thousand flying hours, which is nothing. You have a better chance of dying walking across a street than you do in an aircraft." Unable to keep his hands to himself, he took one hand off the controls and smoothed the wrinkle between her brows, enjoying the softness of her skin. "We'll be fine, Miss Worrywart. Just sit back and enjoy the new experience."

For reasons he couldn't think about now, he wanted to share his love of flying with her.

Grabbing his hand, she returned it to the controls. "Hands back on those controls, buster," she squawked, making him chuckle and link their hands. He enjoyed her surprise and the perceptible tremble in the pale elegant fingers and the way her eyes darkened and her breath caught as her fingers clenched in his.

Looking down at their entwined hands, he marveled at how different they were, at how good her hand looked and felt in his—his large and dark, hers pale and slender. It was as if they'd been molded to fit together like pieces of a puzzle.

He gave her hand a last squeeze before releasing it, because not only was that kind of thinking sappy and *way* out of his comfort zone—probably because it reminded him of his father—he felt like he was free-falling through space without a parachute.

It would be wise to remember that wanting something didn't always make it happen.

Just ask his old man.

Ninety minutes later, Adam pulled into the tree-shaded parking area of a two-story building tucked against the side of the mountain, overlooking the narrow valley below.

"What is this place?" Sam asked curiously, taking in the surroundings, the neat gardens and sprawling green lawns.

"Juniper Falls Medical Center. It's pretty basic but handles all local medical and emergency care. Anything they can't cope with gets flown to the closest large center."

It looked more like a ski lodge than a hospital. "A hospital?" she asked, studying the building and wondering why she got the feeling he was waiting for her reaction. "Why does it look like a ski lodge?"

Adam laughed, and for the first time seemed relaxed. "That's because it is. Or was. With the town growing to accommodate the increase in tourists, the lodge owners needed more space, so they sold and moved farther out of town. Since the building was already here, it made sense to renovate instead of starting from scratch."

Sam was quiet as she studied the view of the town nestled in the valley. It was a gorgeous, tranquil setting that tugged at a memory buried deep inside her.

"Do you remember when I told you I used to think I'd been abducted by aliens as a child?" She saw his lips curve into a smile and laughed at the memory. "Well, I used to fantasize they'd taken me from a place like this."

Pulling his keys from the ignition, he turned toward her and Sam felt the brush of his gaze. It made her feel vulnerable and exposed so instead of meeting his eyes, she kept her face averted.

After a moment's silence he said, "You didn't like growing up rich?"

Sam nibbled on her lip because she sensed that to dismiss her affluent childhood would be to denigrate his. "I think—I think I would have preferred a mom who baked cookies and tucked me in at night," she admitted quietly. "A mom who wasn't always too busy to attend my ballet recitals."

"Yeah," he said quietly after a short silence. "Me too." She turned and caught his quick mouth quirk as he shook his head. With a soft laugh, he opened the door and got out. Before closing it, he looked at her. "But I'd have skipped the ballet recitals too."

Only mildly offended because she had a feeling he was deliberately trying to lighten the mood, Sam scrambled after him. "You're such a *guy*," she accused, clamping down on the inexplicable emotion grabbing her by the throat when his deep chuckle resonated deep inside her. Emotion she had no business feeling for a man she'd insisted on labeling a rebound rebellion.

Inhaling the fresh mountain air, she let her gaze drift to the shifting muscles in his back, down to a really world-class ass cupped in soft worn denim and felt her chest ease. Physical attraction, it seemed, was easier to handle—and ignore—than emotions.

"So," she said lightly, "what *did* you do as a kid?"

He turned and nearly caught her ogling his body. Cheeks warming, Sam met his gaze with big innocent eyes. With a knowing look, he handed over a bulging briefcase. "Hold that, will you." She took it, pretending the brush of his fingers didn't send tingles shooting up her arm.

He looked toward the mountains, then scratched his jaw and shrugged as his gaze returned to hers. "What every kid out here does, I guess."

"And that is?"

"My cousins and I ran wild. Fishing, hiking, skiing,

riding, camping and—" he chuckled "—chasing girls, of course."

She grunted softly at the image of a young Adam chasing girls and dismissed the little shaft of jealousy that lodged right beside her heart.

"Of course you did," she muttered dryly, imagining him at seventeen sending young girls aflutter with a heavily lashed amber-eyed look. Heck, she wasn't even an impressionable adolescent and he made *her* flutter.

She imagined the little boy whose mother had waltzed off to her fairy-tale life, uncaring how much her actions had hurt her lover and the infant she'd blithely given up. She couldn't conceive of abandoning a child she'd carried—and come to love—for nine months, even if she didn't want to be with the father.

For a moment, she let herself imagine what would have happened if her weekend in San Francisco had resulted in a child. A warm little glow sparked in the center of her chest even as her belly dipped at the image of a dark-haired, dusky-skinned baby staring up at her with serious amber eyes.

God, she thought as her heart clenched with yearning. *How could anyone walk away from that?*

It was on the tip of her tongue to ask if he'd ever met his mother but he'd already turned away to reach for a large box and the moment was lost. Finally, with a hooded look in her direction, he shut the door and took off toward the portico entrance of Juniper Falls Medical Center.

Lifting her face to the crisp mountain air and warm sun, Sam paused a moment before following more slowly. She was bewildered by the emotions swirling inside her and needed a moment to steady herself. Despite her growing unwanted feelings for a man who was way out of her league, she felt happy—perhaps for the first time in way too long—which was reason enough to be cautious.

He stirred up emotions she didn't have a clue how to handle or interpret and wasn't sure she liked.

Seriously though. She'd recently broken off a relationship with a man she'd thought she'd spend the rest of her life with, so how was it that she was feeling things for another man that she'd never felt for Lawrence?

No sooner had they crossed the parking area than the front doors flew open and a slight figure emerged at a run to fling herself at Adam. Since he was carrying a box of medical supplies, he caught her one-handed before she knocked them both to the ground.

"Adam." The girl laughed and hugged him tightly. "We've been waiting for ages. What took you so long?"

"Since it's barely seven, it can't have been that long," he chuckled, dropping a kiss on her forehead and turning to introduce Sam who'd been standing there, feeling a little stunned. "This is Samantha Jefferies," he said to the girl. "She's the angel who's taken over running the foundation. I wanted to introduce her to everyone and show her where it all started."

Studying the way Adam tucked the young woman against his side, Sam wondered at the sharp pain in her chest. He'd introduced her as nothing more than a colleague. Which was fine, she told herself as she unclenched her fingers from the briefcase to transfer it to her other hand. It was exactly what she wanted. Wasn't it?

"Hello."

"Hi, I'm Leah," the young woman said, stepping away from Adam to grab Sam's hand between hers and Sam couldn't help but notice how beautiful and delicate she was, with long glossy dark hair, dusky skin and large almond eyes. The sight of her beside Adam, slender and graceful as a deer, made Sam feel like a clumsy Amazon in comparison.

Before she could reply, Adam checked his watch. "Leah's a med student at Stanford," he said briskly. "She's been working summers here in one capacity or another since high school. No one knows this place better, so I've asked her to give you the VIP tour since I have a full day ahead. Don't let her talk your ear off." With that, he shifted the box and leaned toward her.

For an instant, she thought he might kiss her but he simply relieved her of the briefcase and turned away, leaving Sam staring after him in bewilderment, a hollowness blooming in her chest because he suddenly seemed like a stranger.

Because there was something between him and Leah?

Feeling hurt and ridiculously like she'd been abandoned, Sam schooled her features and turned to find Leah frowning at Adam's disappearing back.

"What's up with *him*?" the younger woman muttered before turning speculative eyes Sam's way. She shrugged, as baffled by his odd behavior as she was embarrassed by her own. She'd almost—*almost*—leaned into him for that "kiss" and cringed inwardly at the thought of how he would have handled it if she had.

Oh, God. She really needed to get a grip.

There was an awkward moment as Sam tried to ignore the other woman's curiosity before finally exhaling in a long gush. "Look," she said, turning to look the girl in the eye. "I'm really sorry to be dumped on you like this. You're obviously busy so maybe I should just head back to town. I'm sure I could keep myself busy until Adam is ready to leave." Either that or she could hire a car and return to San José.

"No way." Leah's response was immediate and fierce. "That'll be hours. Besides," she said, studying Sam openly with her large almond-shaped eyes, "I've been dying to meet you."

Surprised, Sam blinked at the young woman and wondered if she'd heard correctly. "You…have?"

"Uh-huh." She laughed when she caught Sam's expression. "Oh, not from Adam," she snorted cheerfully. "He *never* talks about his private life. I heard all about you from Dr. Rutherford."

Sam's eyebrows shot into her hairline. After a couple of beats, she gave a tight laugh, wondering what Aunt Coco had said and why she hadn't prepared Sam for this girl, this town—well, this field trip. "Oh. Well, don't feel bad." To give herself a moment, she lifted a hand to tuck an escaped lock of hair behind her ear. "He's told me nothing about you either." She gestured to the hospital and the town. "Or any of this."

Leah's dark eyes twinkled. "That's okay." She grinned. "I'm sure you have other things to talk about."

"Wh-what?" Sam blinked as her mouth dropped open. "Oh, no," she said hastily, wondering at the relationship between Adam and this gorgeous creature. "It's not what you think. We work together. Sort of." She sighed. "It's complicated."

"Isn't love always?"

"Love?" Sam said aghast. "Oh, no. No," she said again when Leah cocked her head, long silky dark strands brushing a slender shoulder. "We've just kind of met," she explained, ignoring the heat rising in her cheeks at the girl's expression. She ended with a lame, "Besides, we work together."

Leah snorted. "I've known Adam a long time and

I've never seen him look at anyone the way he looked at you just now." She gave a dramatic shiver that made Sam roll her eyes.

"Like he couldn't wait to get away?"

Leah's brow wrinkled and her eyes narrowed on Sam's face. "No," she said slowly, contemplatively. "It wasn't like that at all."

Not wanting to think about what it was, Sam used the moment to shove the hair off her forehead. "Why are you doing this?"

"Adam asked me to."

Sam's eyes widened in surprise. Okay, so maybe it was closer to shock, but what the heck? "Adam asked you to interfere in his personal life?"

For a couple of beats, Leah stared at her uncomprehendingly, then she burst out laughing. "Heck no," she giggled finally. "He'd skin me alive if he knew."

"Then why, when you're clearly in love with him yourself?"

"*What?* No." She gave an amused snort and caught Sam's hand in hers. "I love Adam, sure," she said tugging her in the direction Adam had gone. "But like an honorary uncle or something. I'm only twenty-two so he's way too old."

"He's not that old," Sam defended him hotly.

Leah grinned knowingly and steered Sam across the lobby. "Much older brother then," she said cheekily. "But it's interesting how quickly you defended him."

It was mid-morning when Adam decided to take a detour to the wards before hunting down some food. Most of the patients he treated here had little or no health insurance and many came from the tribal lands nearby. They were people who would probably die without the procedures and hospital care the foundation covered. And because today was mainly follow-ups, part of his mind had been occupied elsewhere.

In truth, he'd kept seeing Samantha's face. Firstly, when he'd deliberately pulled Leah close, hoping the move would put a little distance between them—especially after the stuff he'd revealed about his past—and then as he'd reached for his briefcase. For just a moment, she'd stilled as though he'd been about to kiss her. He'd seen it in her widening eyes and the hitch in her breath. And damn if he hadn't been tempted. So tempted that he'd had to leave before he'd shocked both her *and* Leah.

He'd caught her embarrassed mortification as he'd spun away and had almost turned back. But he didn't want an audience for what he wanted to do with Samantha Jefferies. He was done giving her space and he was done pretending they didn't know each other.

The nurses' station was deserted. Hospitals tended to empty out ahead of the weekend, leaving only those too sick to be sent home. And since Juniper Falls wasn't a bustling metropolis, weekends at the medical center tended to be quiet.

So quiet that over the muted beep of equipment, he heard the low murmur of voices and then the unmistakable sound of throaty laughter that dug claws of lust and awareness into his gut.

Damn. He was in a bad way if just the sound of her voice had his skin itching and tightening. He'd tasted her again and wanted more. He wanted to wrap himself in her sweetness and was pretty sure after this morning that she did too.

"When I'm finished with you, Mrs. Jackson," he heard her say. "You'll be the belle of the ball."

"Call me Ida, dear," he heard, as he headed around the counter to access the computer. "Can I let you in on a little secret?"

"What's that?"

"In my day, I had a dozen beau all competing for my attention."

"I can believe it. You look gorgeous," Samantha declared with a chuckle. "Bart won't know what hit him."

"Oh, pooh." The woman snorted. "Bart Schmart. I was thinking more along the lines of that hunky Dr. Knight. He was here earlier and *hoo-wee*, that boy is hot tamales." Sam's warm laughter drifted seductively down the passage and Adam felt the back of his neck heat that he was eavesdropping on a discussion about himself.

"What do you think, Gladys?" the voice continued. "Should we introduce Samantha to our new beau and risk him falling for her?"

He was thinking that it was way too late for that when an odd sound sent a shaft of foreboding spearing through him.

"Gladys, are you all right?" Mrs. Jackson demanded, then a more peremptory, "*Gladys!*"

He was rounding the counter when he heard, "Samantha, get the nurse and tell them to page the doctor. Hurry!" Her voice was strident but Adam caught the fear in the woman's voice. "Gladys, hang in there, you hear me. Don't you dare die on us. *Nurse!* Oh, Lord—"

Adam broke into a run, nearly colliding with Samantha on her way out of the ward. He instantly spun around, his hands closing instinctively around her arms to steady her before his forward momentum sent them both sprawling.

"*Adam!*" she gasped, her eyes huge and startlingly blue in her white face. "Oh, th-thank God. It's Mrs. Roscoe, she's—"

"Having a heart attack. Where is everyone? Where is Leah?" he demanded, pushing her firmly aside to stride into the room. He took in the situation at a glance. "Mrs. Jackson, you need to step aside."

"She was fine," the woman insisted, blinking rapidly as she scuttled out of the way. "Gladys was fine and all of a sudden she clutched her chest and made this awful sound. You're a doctor," she insisted, her voice wobbling alarmingly. "She isn't breathing. *Fix* her."

The woman on the bed was in her late seventies and clearly in distress. She was gasping and clawing at her chest, her throat. Adam snatched the oxygen mask from the wall and covered her nose and mouth, turning up the flow to full throttle. "Samantha," he rapped out, turning to see her hovering uncertainly in the doorway. "I need you to hold this."

"What—what about the n-nurse?" she croaked, looking a little wild-eyed as she hurried over to the bed.

"No time," he growled when Gladys abruptly went limp. "Hold this."

A slender hand instantly reached out, fingers visibly trembling and icy cold when they briefly covered his. He slid his hand free and began CPR, his gaze holding Samantha's. "Mrs. Jackson," he said calmly. "Could you please press the button on the wall above your bed?"

The other woman quickly reached over and activated the alarm. "I'll do one better," she told him briskly. "I'll find you a nurse."

"Tell them it's a code blue," he called out, as she hurried from the room. And with the sound of her slippers slapping smartly against the linoleum, Adam looked back to find Samantha's attention now locked on the still face in the bed. Her lips were pressed into a distressed line.

"Sam, honey," he said calmly and waited until she looked up. His heart clenched at the sight of overly bright glassy eyes and the waxy complexion. "I know this is scary but I need you to listen carefully, okay?"

She sucked in a shaky breath and gave a jerky nod.

"Good girl. I can't stop chest compressions, so I want you to slip the face-mask elastic around the back of Gladys' head and tighten it." He waited patiently while she followed instructions, gently lifting the unconscious woman's head to fit the elastic band around the back of her head. "Now adjust it at the side where it joins with the mask. That's great," he encouraged when she tugged on the elastic until the mask fitted snugly to Gladys' face. "Okay, I want you to go to the nurses' station and find the crash cart and bring it here." She paused for an instant, her eyes sweeping up to meet with his. "It looks like a trolley with a lot of drawers."

She gave another jerky nod and hurried away, leaving Adam worried about her ragged breathing and the expression in her eyes. She was teetering on the edge of a panic attack and there was little he could do except try to talk her out of it while he worked to keep Gladys' heart pumping.

He paused to check the woman's carotid pulse, his mouth tightening when he found it weak and fluttery. She needed meds, he thought, as well as an emergency transfer to the nearest center equipped with a cardio-surgical unit or she wasn't going to make it.

The best he could do for Gladys now was to administer a series of drug cocktails to stabilize her heart and dissolve clots. The hospital didn't have a catheterization lab, an MRI or a surgical suite equipped to perform complicated heart surgery. All they could do, he thought as the sound of the trolley drew closer, was do a sonar and EKG before flying her out because most of the hospital's lab work was flown to Fresno.

He turned as Samantha rushed into the room, pushing the trolley ahead of her. "That's great," he said as she pulled the trolley up to the bed. "Now open the third tray and remove the bag that says dextrose and a five-ml syringe package."

CHAPTER NINE

EVERYTHING AROUND SAM FADED. Her muscles quivered with the need for flight but she forced her world to narrow to just her hands and the calm voice filling her head. Hands shaking uncontrollably, she followed Adam's instructions, fighting not to be sucked back into a past she thought she'd overcome.

Breath lodged in her throat, she was abruptly ten again and home alone with the housekeeper for company. As if she were experiencing the events of that long ago night, she heard again the loud thump over her thundering heartbeat; the sharp cry of someone in distress and then freezing with terror because there'd recently been a spate of home invasions…of finally creeping down the stairs to find Mrs. Hopkins collapsed on the kitchen floor…dialing 911…the house filling with police and paramedics—

"Samantha. *Sam!*" A sharp voice came to her from a distance. Barely aware that she was gasping for breath, she felt herself jostled aside as hands suddenly took over.

"We'll take it from here, hon."

Sam blinked and looked around, shocked to see people filling the room. When had they arrived? She'd heard nothing over the panicked rush of blood in her head as she'd automatically followed Adam's instructions.

Blinking away the black spots invading her vision, she backed away jerkily as several nurses blocked her view, the flurry of activity making her feel useless and inept. A fragile hand crept into hers and Sam dragged her eyes off the drama to see Ida Jackson looking as shaken as Sam felt.

"Let's g-go find some t-tea," she rasped, squeezing the old woman's hand and nudging her toward the door.

"Do you think we could add a d-dash of b-brandy to that?" Ida wobbled, her hand trembling uncontrollably. "Or maybe two?"

Fighting the chaotic emotions battling for control, Sam gave a ragged laugh that sounded a little too close to hysteria for comfort. She squeezed Ida's hand again and sent one last look over her shoulder at the tableau surrounding the bed where Adam, in the midst of the chaos, looked calm, skilled, in control and very much in his element.

At that moment, he looked up and their eyes met across the distance. Sam's breath caught in her throat. Everything in her stilled at the fierce emotions burning in Adam's amber gaze. His passion for his job. His grim determination to save the woman and the flash of awareness that it might not be enough.

With her heart clenching hard in her chest, she mouthed *I'm sorry* before hurrying from the ward, desperate to escape the feelings of inadequacy and shame that came in the wake of a panic attack.

Dammit, she'd thought she was getting over herself; thought she was overcoming the debilitating childhood affliction. Despair washed over her because she'd once again let everyone down because the insecure little kid inside her was terrified of failing. Terrified of losing someone else she cared about.

Oh, God. What must Adam think of her? That she couldn't even keep it together long enough to forget her insecurities and help save a dying woman.

Ten hours later, Adam drew the Jeep to a sliding stop before his cabin. The earlier hail had turned to snow, which was gusting around his Jeep, dropping visibility to a few feet. The weather forecast's predicted turbulent conditions had brought typical wild Sierra weather, and even if he hadn't flown to Fresno with medevac, the winds would have grounded his plane.

On their return, the pilot had been forced to make a detour when a group of hikers became stranded. It was now almost nine o'clock and he should have been exhausted. Yet, there was a low humming beneath his skin at the thought of Samantha waiting for him in his cabin.

Right. It somehow felt right.

Stilling, he studied the light spilling from the cabin windows and wondered if he'd somehow planned for this to happen. Although there hadn't been any question about accompanying Gladys to Fresno, he couldn't deny that he was glad the weather had grounded the plane.

He'd told Leah to book Samantha in at one of the numerous B&Bs but the girl had sent him a message that she'd dropped her off at his cabin. Instead of being elated at the thought of Samantha surrounded by his things, he should have been questioning Leah's motives.

His cabin was basic at best, not exactly the kind of place one took a blue-blooded princess.

Instantly, images of her earlier filled his mind. She'd bitten her lip, stiffened her spine and followed his instructions even as her fingers shook so badly she'd barely been able to hold the syringe. Yet, she'd held it together long enough for the nurses to arrive when he knew the panic attack had swooped over her like a dark cloud.

That last look over her shoulder had been filled with emotions that sliced right through him as she'd mouthed the words *I'm sorry*, and he wondered what had happened to put that look of shame and self-disgust in her eyes.

Adam reached for the bag of groceries, hoping she'd started a fire and helped herself to some of his clothes. It might be summer but up here in the Sierras, the weather could change in a matter of hours.

He shoved open the driver's door and was instantly assaulted by wind-driven ice and snow. Lurching from the Jeep, he slammed the door behind him and made a dash for the safety of the front porch. The little pellets of stinging ice were giving way to flakes that melted the instant they settled. *That could change*, he thought, shaking himself off before quietly slipping inside and shutting out the storm.

Once inside, Adam slid the bolt home and wiped moisture off his face. The faint glow coming from the fireplace did little to dispel the cold. Setting the groceries aside, he realized that Samantha hadn't added enough logs to heat the room.

He grimaced, reaching back to pull at the damp material clinging coldly to his skin. She had to be freezing, he thought, as he stripped off his shirt and used it to dry his face. Hell, *he* was freezing.

"Samantha?" he called softly, not wanting to startle her. "Sam?"

The only sound in the cabin was the shifting of logs in the fireplace and the lazy crackle of wood. For one horrible instant he thought that the cabin was empty, that she'd become tired of waiting and left. His gut instantly tightened. Maybe she'd thought she could walk into town and became disoriented. Maybe she'd wandered off the road and tumbled down the mountain or maybe—

He stopped when he realized what he was doing. Hell, he was losing it. Losing it over a woman who pulled him closer with one hand while pushing him away with the other. A woman, who despite the trappings of her childhood, was warm and sweet. A woman who was vulnerable but not stupid.

Of course, she wouldn't leave. She was smart and resourceful—but she was a city girl completely out of her depth in the wilderness, and would hardly go wandering off alone in the dark.

He knew this, yet he couldn't stop the images flashing through his mind of her out in that, alone. Lost, cold and afraid. He would never forgive himself if anything happened to—

A soft sigh interrupted his self-directed anger, drawing him into the room like she was a magnet and he slivers of iron filings. His relief at finding her curled up beneath the afghan that was usually draped on the back of the sofa, nearly brought him to his knees. He had to rub his face a few times before he could look at her and not completely unravel. Because there she was, face flushed and peaceful beneath the wild tangle of hair that reflected the flickering light from the dying fire.

Something wild and sweet and alien moved through him then; something so powerful that he had to turn away before he scooped her up and crushed her against him. The intensity of the primitive impulse left him shaken and drove him to the fireplace where he began to build a fire that would drive away the chill.

He could do that, he thought, rattled by more than the

emotions bombarding him. Alien emotions he had no idea how to handle.

Once the flames licked greedily at the tower of logs, he rose with every intention of heading to the kitchen to begin preparations for their dinner. But the moment he turned, his gaze was drawn inexorably toward the sleeping woman now half on her back, one arm flung above her head, the throw pooled at her waist.

His eyes traced her creamy features, the heavy lacy crescents of her eyelashes resting against her flushed cheeks. The tousled mass of hair, tumbling across the cushion in wild disarray invited him to bury his face and hands in the fragrant cloud—and just breathe her in.

Her mouth, a full soft bow, parted on a quiet sigh as though she were dreaming. A heated spike of longing arrowed through him, and even as he instructed himself to move away, he was dropping to his haunches beside the couch.

God. She looked so lovely with firelight gilding her flawless skin and setting fire to the heavy spill of warm chestnut locks. His breath caught and he could not resist reaching out to trace the elegant arch of one eyebrow; smooth a silky lock of hair off her forehead with a cautious finger.

Almost imperceptibly, her breathing changed, her eyelashes fluttering as though she'd felt that whisper-soft touch in her sleep. She shifted languorously, her head rolling toward him. He was unable to resist touching her again—just the brush of his thumb across her cheekbone.

A low sound of yearning hummed in the back of her throat and more than anything, Adam wanted to cover her mouth with his and catch that husky sound for himself. He wanted to taste her need and let her taste his.

"Hey," he murmured, and her eyelashes fluttered again, then rose a fraction of an inch. The usually vibrant blue depths of her eyes were hazy and soft with sleep. He held his breath because watching her awaken was the most erotic thing he'd ever seen.

"Adam?" She breathed out a husky question that had something primal slamming into him like a one-two punch to the solar plexus; violent feelings he'd never felt for anyone let alone a woman from a world he despised. Feelings of need, lust, possessiveness and the overwhelming compulsion to protect.

Inhaling to clear his head, he drew the scent of her into his lungs instead. She smelled of soft warm woman with a hint of something fresh and clean. Like something he'd yearned for his entire life.

His throat tightened along with his gut. "Yeah," he said roughly. "Sorry I'm late. I tried to get here sooner but we had to rescue a couple of stranded hikers on the way back."

Awareness sharpened her gaze and she sat up abruptly, forcing him back a couple of inches. "*Ohmigod*," she burst out. "You flew in *that*? How's Gladys? When did you get back? Are the hikers okay? Are *you* okay?"

She shoved her hair off her face, eyes huge and distressed as they swept over him, presumably to check for injuries, before coming back to his. Completely against his will, Adam felt the pull of those endlessly blue depths and couldn't recall the last time any woman had expressed such genuine concern for him. Coco maybe, but then again she'd been more mother than mentor.

"Gladys is hanging on, the hikers will be okay and I'm good," he murmured. *Now.* Now that he was inches away from her and breathing in the scent of her skin, feeling the gentle heat pulsing off her body and the siren call that he'd tried but could no longer resist.

With his gaze locked on hers, he shifted closer, lifting his hand to gently trace the elegant line of her jaw and neck. He settled his thumb gently over the pulse beating a rapid tattoo in her throat, feeling it throb with life—and excitement.

It lit an answering call in his blood.

"You sound as though you were worried about me."

"I—of course, I was worried," she burst out indignantly. "I'd be worried about anyone caught in that."

Adam chuckled and brushed his thumb repeatedly against the delicate skin covering that fluttering pulse. She might deny there was anything between them but she couldn't control that little telltale response.

"Anyone?" he murmured deeply. "Are you sure you weren't just a little bit worried I might end up smashed against the side of the mountain?"

Her breath caught and she tried to jerk away in protest. "That's not funny, Adam," she rasped, wrapping long elegant fingers around his wrist. Her eyes flared with anger and something that instantly roused his blood. Instead of pushing him away, her gaze locked with his and, abruptly tired of hiding his feelings, he made no attempt to disguise the heat and emotions pumping through him.

Seconds ticked by as they breathed heavily into the heated silence until with a shuddery exhalation, her gaze dropped to his mouth with a sweep of heavy lashes. Beneath his thumb, her pulse stuttered, then sped up and she finally made a jerky, involuntary little move that brought her mouth closer to his. Then she stilled, tension humming in the air.

Her throat moved in a convulsive swallow that told

him she wanted his mouth but was waiting for him to make the move and when he didn't, waiting for her to come to him, she made a hungry little sound in the back of her throat and jerked her gaze to his. The move had her parted lips brushing his, her eyes darkening until only a thin circle of cobalt surrounded large deeply black pupils. And because he was still touching her, he felt the helpless shudder move through her.

Whether she was deliberately drawing out the tension, ratcheting up the need, Adam wasn't certain. He wasn't a green boy but a jolt moved through him at that barely-there touch. His skin buzzed with the growing compulsion to crush her mouth beneath his and take what they both wanted.

"Adam?" she murmured on a shuddery gust of yearning that had his awareness narrowing until the rest of the world faded. In that moment, the entire mountain range could have slid into the Yellowstone magma chamber and he wouldn't have noticed or cared.

"If you want it, Samantha," he growled hoarsely. "All you have to do is take it," he huffed out, when she blinked, looking drugged. Hell, he felt a little drugged himself. "You want it?" he taunted softly. "*You* take it."

"Just—take?" she breathed, sounding as though the idea had never occurred to her. And because he already knew that she wasn't nearly as self-assured and experienced as she appeared, Adam felt another crack appear in the wall he'd built around his heart.

This woman, he thought with surprised affection, for all her apparent sophistication and poise, was anything but. There was a vulnerability, a softness, that she couldn't quite hide from anyone paying attention. She felt too much and too deeply while pretending to be coolly reserved, and he suddenly understood that she'd shied away from medicine because she didn't know how to shield herself from the heartbreak that often accompanied the knowledge that not everyone could be saved.

She'd want to do that, he realized, recalling the way she sneaked into the children's ward to read to them, to give them a few moments of joy. Then he recalled how she'd given Gladys and Mrs. Jackson a makeover because being ill chipped away at one's self-esteem.

She'd want to save everyone and when she couldn't, it would devastate her.

A rush of emotion squeezed his chest in a vice-like grip. She was sweet and feisty and so desperate to hold herself aloof, hide her vulnerability. But he wanted her vulnerability and sweet warmth. He wanted her to give them to him.

Hell, he wanted her to give him everything.

Planting his hands on the sofa, on either side of her hips, he leaned closer and gathered the cool material of her dress in both hands.

"Take it," he taunted softly. "Take what you want." He waited a couple of beats before closing the distance between their mouths and then adding, "I...dare...you," so softly the words puffed against her lips.

She was so close that he could see each blue, silver and turquoise striation in her irises. Her eyelashes fluttered once before her chin dipped and with a shuddery breath, settled her lips lightly on his. After a couple of heartbeats, her gaze lifted and something warm and mischievous sparked in the darkened depths, bewitching him. Her lips parted on a quick grin and before he could anticipate her intention, she closed her teeth on his bottom lip and tugged gently.

The unexpectedness of that cheeky nip jolted him, sent fire racing across his skin. His hands clenched into fists to keep from yanking her closer. Locking his muscles, he hummed in the back of his throat.

Again, she surprised him. Closing her lips around his bottom lip, she sucked it into the moist warmth of her mouth before releasing it with a quiet pop. Then she began brushing her lips lightly along the length of his, flicking her tongue out in teasing swipes, making him wonder if she knew how close he was to losing control.

His skin buzzed, muscles tightened until he thought her next move would shatter his rapidly fraying control. Before long, he was growling low in his throat and sliding his tongue out to flick at the seam of her lips, tangle with her teasing tongue.

Unable to keep his hands to himself, he slid them beneath her skirt to smooth his palms up her thighs. Material bunching at his wrists, he headed north. Her breath hitched and she shivered, the long slender muscles quivering beneath silky skin. With a soft growl, she smoothed her palms up the slope of his arms, across the line of his shoulders to bury her fingers in his hair.

Then it was his turn to shudder, the sensation of her nails scraping his scalp, streaking the length of his spine, sending heat and lust clawing at his belly. He was rapidly spiraling out of control and he worried that when he did, he would be forever changed.

Unaware of the impending collapse of his iron control, Sam playfully evaded his teasing attempts to pursue her mouth, building the tension while he tamped down the primitive impulse to crush her close, to take what she was offering.

He knew the instant her teasing turned serious. Her

fingers tightened and she murmured a command that finally snapped the fraying edges of his control. He opened his mouth and caught hers in a ravenous kiss the same moment his hands closed over her hips and tugged, rolling backward as she fell against him.

In an instant, he'd rolled her onto the thick rug before the fire, one thigh nudging hers apart as the kiss exploded. Wild and ravenous, then slow and deep, he took and gave back in equal measure until they were both breathless, writhing with need.

Frantic for the feel of smooth feminine skin sliding against his, for the hot intimate dampness of her need, Adam swept his hand up one long thigh until he encountered the narrow band of lace at her hips. Slipping his fingers beneath the elasticized lace, he tugged and quickly stripped the garment away, tossing the lace aside before cupping the soft firmness of her bottom in his hand.

He squeezed, and she moaned, arching into him as her nails trailed a torturous line of fire down his torso in retaliation. Her fingers curled into the waistband of his jeans, brushing his erection. He jolted at that teasing touch and, fearing he was seconds from embarrassing himself, he grabbed her hands.

"I've got this," he rasped in a voice he barely recognized as his own. *God*, he was so aroused that just the accidental brush of her finger across the wide sensitive crown had him shuddering like a kid.

Cursing the need to get naked, he yanked at the zipper and shoved his jeans and underwear down his legs. Even before the material cleared his ankles, she wrapped a hand around him and squeezed firmly enough to have his eyes roll back in his head.

"Not yet," he growled, gently removing her hand before he lost the last of his control and tore her dress in his desperation to get her naked. And he wanted her naked. He wanted to rediscover every inch of her lush body— every curve and dip and secret place. He wanted to taste the underside of her breast, curl his tongue around the tight pink bud and feast on her velvety skin. He *needed* to slide his mouth down her body, dip his tongue into her shallow belly button and then kiss her more intimately than any other man.

Adam's senses swam. Every touch felt new. Every hitched breath an aphrodisiac. He couldn't seem to decide what to sample next; what would elicit the most delicious shiver, the hungriest moan or the throatiest sigh.

San Francisco, it seemed, didn't count because he hadn't known her. Hadn't known the sound of her voice, the curve of her jaw and the way her eyes darkened when she was aroused. Now he could tell when she was nervous by the way she first licked and then nibbled on her bottom lip, the way warm color raced up her throat into her face.

Now he welcomed the hitch in her voice and the tiny shivers that moved across her skin. He wanted to fill his hands with her breasts and swallow the low sounds of her arousal because no woman had ever taken him from zero to a hundred in less time that it had taken for him to yank down his zipper.

"Adam—" she protested, and he quickly covered her mouth with his, snatching her breathless protest before it could fully form. He fed her kisses that were ravenous and just a little desperate, kisses that stripped him of his sanity and her of her protests.

She fisted his hair as their mouths tangled, giving him access to the rest of her body; access he ruthlessly exploited by bringing her to the edge over and over again until her breath was a ragged moan and her muscles quivered with the effort to reach for that elusive peak.

Glorying in her taste, the slide of her skin against his as she moaned and writhed, Adam mercilessly whipped the tension higher, tighter, until he was blind and deaf to anything but her pleasure. And when he joined their bodies with one hard thrust, she gave a sharp ragged cry, her body arching beneath his, her inner muscles clamping down on him like a hot fist.

He froze, panting roughly as she spasmed helplessly around him. "Did—?" he huffed tightly. "Are you okay?"

Sam opened her mouth but the only sound to emerge was a low breathless moan. She bit her lip and gave a quick jerky nod, her eyes blind and turned inward as her body undulated helplessly beneath his. "Don't stop," she gasped, wrapping her long legs around his hips and clutching at his shoulders as though she would bind him to her.

He wanted to tell her that there was nowhere he'd rather be but the sight of her beneath him, the feel of her around him fascinated him. It was nothing like he remembered. It was hotter...better...and in that moment she was the most beautiful thing he'd ever seen.

A flush of arousal stained her breasts, rushed across her chest and rose up her neck into her face. He wondered briefly how any man could look at her as she was now, head thrown back, lush curves and long slender limbs entwined with his, and want anyone else.

Slowly pressing deeper, Adam growled when she gasped and squirmed, yanking at his hair. "*Move!*" she ordered in a tight demanding voice, even as she arched her back and wrapped her limbs around him.

He simply tightened his grip and pressed her into the

rug. "Look at me," he murmured deeply, and when her eyes fluttered open, the dazed expression in them nearly had him climaxing. "I want you to see *me* when you come."

"Adam—"

"Yeah," he growled roughly, leaning down to nip at her mouth. "*Me*. Only me."

And with his eyes locked on hers, he began to move. Slowly at first with long measured strokes meant to gradually build the tension. But Sam wasn't interested in gradual and tried to force him to increase his pace when he wanted her blind to everything but him. He wanted her to see him, feel him, breathe him as he took her over.

And when her blue eyes went hazy and dark, those sexy little sounds that he'd never thought he'd hear again bursting erratically from her throat, he changed the tempo to shorter, harder strokes that jolted her and had her clenching even tighter around him.

He saw her eyes go wide the instant before her body bowed and shattered, the long low moan tearing from her throat.

The sight and sounds of her release triggered his own and he followed her over, pounding his way through his own climax until, with a grunt, he slammed home one last time and stilled, emptying himself into her shuddering body.

CHAPTER TEN

"So that's a yes?" Samantha asked calmly into the telephone while inside she was doing a little victory dance. She had one more donation for the foundation's first fundraising event with her at its helm. That it was a life-size sculpture—the centerpiece and drawcard she'd been looking for—meant it was guaranteed to generate a lot of interest. *And money.*

"That's very generous of you, Jack. I'll call you next week to arrange collection." She listened to his reply and then said, "Oh, no, it's the least we can do."

She thanked him again and disconnected, flushing at the memory of standing in his studio with her mouth hanging open after he'd asked if she'd consider modeling for him. It had been hugely embarrassing as the man was well-known for his erotic nudes.

Okay, so Jack Cesar was hot and fast becoming famous for his art, but there was no way she could get back to her plan with the memory of Juniper Falls so fresh in her mind. So she'd told him she was seeing someone, although she hadn't seen Adam since he'd dropped her off after that weekend.

From the moment she'd opened her eyes to find herself naked in an empty bed and the sounds of activity coming from the cabin's small kitchen, she'd started freaking out because their one-night stand had just become two. She could no longer tell herself that it had been the result of too much alcohol or the reaction of a woman discovering her fiancé with another man.

This time there was no rebellion to blame her actions on, only—oh, God, she was afraid to even think about *what* it was. She only knew that the previous twenty-four hours had irrevocably altered her opinion of Adam and wrecked the stability of her world.

When he'd dropped her off, she'd thanked him politely for the weekend, and belly cramping with nerves, told him nothing had changed when *everything* had changed.

For several heartbeats, he'd just looked at her and then the worst had happened. He calmly accepted her explanation, a hint of amusement in his eyes as he'd gently pushed her back against her front door, trapping her with his big body. Captured by his mesmerizing gaze, she hadn't put up even a token protest when his head had lowered and he'd caught her mouth in a kiss so potent it had scorched the bottom of her feet.

Just when she felt her body melt against his, he'd stepped back. With a, "See you soon," he'd casually descended the stairs, leaving her head buzzing with confusion.

Then she'd gotten mad, which had her even more confused because she had no right to be angry with him for giving her exactly what she'd said she wanted. It wasn't logical, it wasn't fair but she was learning firsthand that her feelings for him had no roots in logic.

Where they came from she wasn't sure—only that they were deep and terrifying.

Fortunately, she was busy planning her first charity

event or she'd probably have gone insane obsessing about
what he'd meant by that kiss and his parting remark. It
was something she thought about constantly when she
was alone at night, her body and her soul yearning for
something she told herself she didn't want.

But she did. Oh, God, she did. And it scared her. Especially as the most she'd seen of him had been in passing
and then briefly during a foundation meeting before he'd
been paged. His gaze had been hooded and intense when
it settled on her, and horror of horrors—she'd fluttered.

She still wanted Adam with an intensity that made
her ache.

And she was lonely, dammit. When she'd never been
lonely for a man before.

Glancing at her desk monitor, she was surprised to
find it was nearly seven o'clock. Reaching up to remove
the hairpins digging into her scalp, she shook her hair
free and sank her fingers into the heavy mass to give her
beleaguered scalp a good massage. Closing her eyes in
relief, she let out a long sigh and sank back in her chair
only to jolt upright when a familiar voice drawled, "Finally letting your hair down?"

Her pulse jumped and her darned heart fluttered at
the sight of the man she'd just been fantasizing about
lounging in the doorway. He looked even better than she
remembered, and for just an instant, she struggled to recall exactly why she was so determined to keep him at
arm's length.

"Literally speaking," she murmured, trying not to recall the last time she'd *let her hair down* with him or the
way her body began buzzing like she was plugged into
a transformer. "It's been a crazy week."

He scrubbed a hand down his face, his rough laugh

drawing her sharpening gaze. He was still the hot, hunky Dr. Knight women sighed over, but something was very wrong. She could see it in the bleak amber gaze, the paleness of his normally coppery gold skin stretched tight across high cheekbones and the tension around his mouth.

"Yeah," he rasped, his gaze locked on her with burning intensity. "A bad one too."

Alarmed, Sam straightened in her chair, heart tripping over itself as her planned apology for her behavior slipped away. "What happened?" she asked, her gaze searching his.

For several beats, he stared at her, then his breath escaped in an audible whoosh. "We lost a patient today," he admitted quietly, lifting a hand to rub his chest and then grimacing as though he were in pain.

Alarm morphed into terror.

Lurching to her feet, she rounded her desk, her mind desperately skittering over everything she knew about treating a coronary. If she hadn't panicked in Juniper Falls, she railed at herself, and paid more attention with Gladys, she would know what to do now.

And God, she thought, when the blood drained from her head, she didn't want Adam to die. *Anything*...anything *but that*.

"T-tell me what to d-do," she babbled, grabbing his wrist to search for a pulse and panicking because she couldn't find one. "I can't p-promise not to f-freak out but I'll do exactly as you s-say—"

The next thing she knew Adam grasped her chin in warm fingers and firmly lifted her face to his. "Hey, *hey*," he repeated firmly when her breath hitched on a sob. "Look at me, Samantha. I'm not having a heart attack, if that's what you're thinking."

She froze and stared at him, *her* heart feeling like it was going into spasms and would burst out of her chest any second. Her vision began to fade around the edges.

"*No!*" She shook her head violently, dislodging his touch as she tried to push her hands against his chest right over his heart. "I—I've seen it before and—"

"*Samantha!*" The gentle firmness of his voice finally reached her. She froze as he cupped her face firmly in his hands and gave her a little shake. "Look at me," he ordered softly and waited until her gaze met his before assuring her calmly, "I'm fine. I promise. Now breathe."

She blinked and finally noticed that his skin didn't have the same gray color of Gladys's and Mrs. Hopkins's and his lips weren't blue. Needing something to hold onto, she wrapped her hands around his brawny wrists and focused on his mouth as her world slowly settled.

Finally, she lifted her gaze to search his. "You're— sure?"

He reached out to smooth an unruly lock of hair behind her ear. "Yeah," he murmured softly. "I'm sure. It's just—" He sucked air into his lungs and tugged her against him, wrapping her up in his embrace and burying his face in her hair.

Shocked by the move—the raw emotion in his voice— Sam could only slide her arms around him and press her body close in an instinctive need to offer comfort. She was glad of the support too since her knees wobbled alarmingly.

"It's just what?" she murmured, her throat working furiously as she burrowed close.

His big body shuddered and he tightened his hold, pulling her impossibly closer. "It was a long shot but we were hoping—" He broke off and sighed.

"I'm sorry," she offered lamely, turning her face into his throat to press her lips against his warm skin. "I know how awful it can be. It's terrifying having someone's life in your hands. I don't know how you handle that every day." She pulled back a couple of inches to look up at him, experiencing an odd little thrill that he would seek her out when devastated by a loss.

He gently nudged her back and took her hand, guiding her to the desk.

"Something happened, didn't it?" he asked quietly, sitting on the edge and pulling her between his legs, his hands a warm weight on her hips. "Is that why you didn't follow the rest of the family into medicine?"

Damn. The last thing she wanted was to rehash old demons. But then maybe he deserved to know after talking her down from not one but three freak-outs. It was her turn to sigh as she slid her hands up his muscled arms to his shoulders, forgetting that she'd told him not a week ago that nothing had changed.

Everything had changed; she was just terrified of what it meant.

"I was ten," she admitted with a ragged laugh, abruptly turning sideways in his arms so she didn't have to look at him when she confessed her deepest darkest secret. "My parents had died about a year earlier in an accident and we were already living with my grandmother," she said quietly, thinking back on those awful years. "My brother and sister were rarely home because being much older, they were already in med school. Grandmother often went out at night and I was left alone with the housekeeper. Anyway—" she sucked in a shuddery breath before continuing "—one night Mrs. Hopkins had a h-heart attack. A huge storm had knocked out the power lines and I'd hidden in my closet with a flashlight. I ex-pected her to come and find me and when she didn't, I went downstairs and f-found her—on the kitchen floor." She realized she was holding her breath and exhaled on a rush. "If—if I hadn't been afraid of the dark, I might have been able to save her."

"You were a kid," he reminded her gently. "What about 911?"

She shook her head. "Because of the storm, they took almost two hours to arrive. I s-spent almost two hours alone with—" She broke off and shuddered at the mem-ory.

"With a dead body," he finished quietly, tugging her closer. She nodded and rested her head on his shoulder, glad of its solidity and width.

"Yes."

"Hell," he cursed on an explosive exhale. "No wonder you have panic attacks. It would have traumatized any-one, let alone a ten-year-old."

"I'm not ten anymore, Adam," she said tiredly.

"Yeah," he murmured, turning her into his arms. Slid-ing his hand beneath her hair, he tipped her face to his, eyes gleaming with warm amusement as he slid his lips along her jaw to her ear. "I noticed." She shivered and arched her neck to give him more room, enjoying his warmth and strength. "Fears don't always make sense, Sam, but everyone has them."

"I can't see you letting some childhood trauma para-lyze you," she murmured, sliding her hands up his hard abdomen and melting inside when the flesh beneath bunched and rippled.

"You'd be surprised," he growled, brushing his lips against the pulse in her throat that felt like it bumped against her skin, yearning to get closer. "The thought of asking you on a date terrifies me."

She stilled as the words registered and he took the opportunity to nip her jaw. "A d-date?" she squeaked moving back to gape at him, unsure why she was so shocked by the concept of a date. With Adam.

"Yeah," he murmured with a soft chuckle. "We've done things a little backward. So, what do you say to dinner and—" He paused, a look of annoyed resignation passing across his features, and it was then that Sam realized the buzzing she felt where their bodies were pressed together had nothing to do with sexual tension vibrating between them.

With a heavy sigh, Adam silenced his pager. Instead of moving away, he tightened his arms around her and dropped his forehead to hers. "Looks like our date will have to wait," he murmured softly, and Sam had to squeeze her eyes closed so he didn't see her disappointment.

Damn. Since when had she been yearning for something as simple as a date?

"Looks like," she agreed, the tightness in her throat way out of proportion to the situation. They didn't know each other well enough for her to feel the loss even before he left to attend to his patients. As though something deep within her needed to cling to this new closeness between them, the unfamiliar emotions flooding her that went beyond the physical. It should have terrified the woman who'd learned early on to hide her emotions from a grandmother who'd neither the patience nor the empathy for a little girl who'd been torn from everything familiar.

It did terrify her, she admitted silently, but not as much

as the knowledge that he might not feel the same way. Because it meant that despite her plans, despite her recent experiences, she was headed for heartbreak that made Lawrence's betrayal feel like nothing more than disillusionment in someone she'd thought she'd known.

This close, she couldn't hide the tremor that went through her and when he wrapped a warm hand around her neck and tipped up her chin, the query in his warm whiskey gaze had her lashes sweeping down to hide the prick of tears that surprised as well as baffled her.

"Hey," he murmured softly, bending his knees to frown into her eyes. "You okay?" So much for hiding her emotions.

Sam gave a watery laugh and pushed away from him when all she wanted to do was cling. "I'm fine." Without looking at him, she patted his chest absently and moved behind her desk, abruptly needing space to think about the emotions currently tying her in intricate knots. "Go use your superpowers, Dr. Knight, while I use mine to see how much money I can make for your foundation."

He was silent a long moment, and when she sneaked a peek at him, he was studying her intently, his mouth somber, eyes unreadable. "This won't take long and we'll—"

"Adam," she interrupted softly. God, she needed him to go before she embarrassed herself. "It's okay. We'll make plans for the next time you're not on call and *I'm* not crazy busy with the gallery evening." He opened his mouth just as his pager buzzed again. "Go," she laughingly ordered when he spun away with an impatient growl and headed for the door. "I have work to do."

When he got to the door, he planted one hand on the frame and sent her a heated look over his broad shoulder. "This discussion isn't over," he promised, his voice deep and rough with just a hint of warning that sent caution twisting up her spine. "I shouldn't be long. We can have a late dinner."

She waited until she heard the outer door close before sinking into the chair, her breath an audible whoosh in the silence. Her knees wobbled and her hands shook, her heart thundering in her ears.

"What the heck was that?" she demanded, when she was very much afraid she already knew. Her emotions were rapidly becoming difficult to ignore. Adam though? Who knew what he thought, how he felt about anything, especially her. But then again, hadn't she constantly told him he was a rebound and that she had a plan for her life? A life that didn't include him?

Of course, he wouldn't verbalize his feelings when he found so many similarities between his mother and Sam. And he was determined not to become like his father, which meant he'd never let himself feel anything deeper for her than hot lust and mild affection.

Pressing the heel of her hand to the pinch beside her heart, Sam shut down her computer and tidied her desk. She would go home, pour herself a glass of wine and pretend that her life wasn't spiraling out of control. She would pretend that being judged by someone else's actions didn't shred her heart and she wouldn't let herself be devastated when Adam grew tired of her inconsistent behavior and moved on.

Because he would. She wasn't gorgeous and exciting like the women he probably usually dated and she was too old to wait around for someone too busy living for other people. She'd waited for Lawrence to find time to be with her, to love her, she realized with a flash of insight. As though she hadn't deserved more. She was done with that.

But could she believe that Adam really wanted something as simple as a date when they'd already done so much more? And if so, why?

Why now?

And why the heck did it matter so much?

Sam had been asleep for only a short while when she heard pounding. She tried to turn over and pull a pillow over her head but it didn't shut out the noise. Finally, with a sigh, she got up because the crazy person clearly wasn't going away and she didn't want the noise waking her neighbors.

She opened the door to find Adam, hands shoved into his jeans pockets, leaning against the wall, looking hot and brooding, and more than a little dangerous. In an instant, her exhaustion and depression vanished.

For long tense moments, they stared at each other while her jittering pulse jerked, stumbled and then took up a slow sluggish rhythm. The last thing she'd expected when she'd left the office was that he'd follow—especially after her embarrassing meltdown. She'd admitted more to him than the therapist she'd seen as a child.

His thick hair shone blue-black beneath the overhead light, his chiseled features seemingly cast in granite. Eyes, hooded and slumberous, gleamed like light-shot bourbon between his sooty lashes making it difficult to interpret his thoughts.

Struggling against the conflicting emotions she had no idea how to handle, Sam was tempted to slam and lock the door before she did something stupid. Like yank him inside so she could get her hands and mouth all over him.

"Dr. Knight," she said breathlessly, her fingers tightening on the door because she'd discovered that she was achingly vulnerable when it came to this man and her instinct was to protect herself.

Her formality had one eyebrow rising up his forehead to disappear into the lock of hair that refused to be tamed. *Kind of like him*, she thought. Kind of like the way he made her feel.

"Miss Jefferies," he drawled with an ironic twist of his lips. He hadn't moved but she could feel the pull of his magnetism and it scared as much as it excited her. "You opened the door without checking the peephole," he accused, his voice a rough slide of velvet against her skin.

"You're the only crazy person I know who likes to wake people up in the middle of the night," she said, wildly pleased that she managed to sound coolly amused and thought, *Oh, look, I learned something useful from Lilian after all.*

His gaze drilled into hers and after a couple of silent beats, he pushed away from the wall to crowd her in the open doorway. Her heart bumped against her ribs and her breath backed up in her lungs, everything within her stilling at the crackling tension he brought with him. And suddenly channeling Grandma Lilian fizzled like a wet cracker.

Dammit, the man was too potent for her own good.

"Yeah, crazy," he murmured, his deep sinful voice wrapping her in heady sensations. When she refused to move, he placed a large palm against her belly and gently propelled her backward into her condo.

She didn't resist because the awful truth was she was emotionally attached in a way she'd never been before and was afraid it was deep and permanent. But she couldn't think about that right now, not when he'd crowded her against the small foyer desk with his big warm body.

Staring up into his boldly handsome face, she couldn't help noticing how the warm glow from the sitting room lamps slanted across his features and threw them into stark relief. The shimmer of light through his remarkable eyes took her breath away, watching her with predatory intent and more than a little impatience.

She curled her fingers around the edge of the desk, hoping the sharp pain would keep her grounded. But then he slowly leaned forward and the breath backed up in her throat. Anticipation ratcheted up a thousand notches and just when she thought he'd kiss her—her lips had parted on a soft anticipatory gasp—he angled his head to brush his mouth against her ear, tugging a gasp from her lips, before dropping to press an openmouthed kiss against her throat.

"You left," he murmured before sucking a small patch of sensitized skin into his mouth. Her breath hitched as her mouth opened but all that emerged was a strangled laugh.

"You expected me to…to wait?" she finally demanded, the query morphing into a startled squeak at the tiny punishing nip he inflicted on the muscle joining her neck and shoulder.

"Why not?" he growled, nudging her thighs apart and pressing up against her heated core, covered in the thinnest stretchy lace. "I've waited a lifetime for you. But I'm done waiting, Samantha."

Before she could ask what he meant, Adam took her

mouth greedily, his hands filling with her breasts, and when her head finally cleared enough to recall those words, his big body was sprawled across hers in exhaustion.

CHAPTER ELEVEN

SAM REARRANGED THE remaining canapés on the platter to make room for a new batch as the servers rushed around her. Fine wine and conversation flowed freely in the art gallery she'd managed to charm into hosting the charity event, along with artworks donated by local artists. The caterers she'd hired were worth every dollar they were charging and the evening was to all intents and purposes a huge success.

So what the heck are you doing hiding out in the kitchen when the results of all your hard work are out there?

She paused and thrust out her bottom lip to blow cool air into her hot face. She should be reveling in her success. Instead, she was hiding in the kitchen, hoping no one would notice she was having a breakdown. Because that's exactly how she'd felt ever since Adam had uttered those cryptic words, stolen her breath along with her mind and then fallen asleep.

That was two days ago.

Two days since she'd heard his pager go off; two days since he'd grunted irritably as he'd rolled away from her and she'd curled around his pillow to hold his heat to her a little longer. Exhausted, she'd been vaguely aware of him smoothing the hair off her cheek with a gentle hand before kissing her softly.

"Gotta go," he'd murmured against her mouth between kisses, and when she'd moaned and let her lips cling sleepily to his, she thought he'd murmured something that sounded like, "We can't go on like this, Sam. We need to talk," but she must have dreamed it because other than a bouquet of wildflowers that had appeared on her desk the following day without a card—from Adam?—she hadn't so much as received a call or text message from him.

There'd been no talking and things had gone on exactly as they had. One of them disappearing after a hot night of sex and then...*nothing*.

Or maybe—maybe he'd been kissing her off. Had the flowers and the cryptic message been his way of saying they were done? Is that what he'd meant by *we can't go on like this*?

She had no idea and the suspense was killing her.

Fortunately, organizing tonight's event had kept her too busy to obsess and she'd managed to push everything firmly to the back of her mind. Until *he'd* arrived, looking Hollywood handsome in a dark designer suit over a white T-shirt that emphasized his tall rangy build, overlong inky hair and coppery gold skin. It had also emphasized the glowing amber eyes that reminded her of a large mountain cat lying in wait.

Like a besotted adolescent, she'd known the instant he'd arrived by the shiver that had raised the hairs on the back of her neck. Engaged in a spirited debate about the stereotypical views that persisted in discussions on Native American art, Sam had looked up and locked gazes with him. That seemingly endless moment of connection had sent a wave of heat and longing storming through her and she'd promptly forgotten what she was saying.

In truth, it had lasted only a second before he was swamped like a celebrity, and she'd been left feeling hollow and alone in a roomful of people. A feeling so common that she'd run and hidden. It was mortifying to discover that she was still that insecure little girl desperate to belong. It made her angry and emotionally raw.

Fine, she admitted, thrusting out her bottom lip and exhaling explosively. It was seeing him surrounded by all those beautiful women that had all her insecurities swamping her. *God.* She wished she had more experience on how to handle these kinds of situations but she was an emotional coward; preferring to lock down her emotions. And hide.

Besides, did she go out there and demand to know what he'd meant or pretend that everything was fine? Pretend that seeing Tiffany Travers, legendary maneater and celebrity tech-heiress, wrapped around him like Christmas ribbon didn't send shards of hurt and anger ripping through her?

Or did she—?

"Darling, what on earth are you doing hiding in here?" Aunt Coco's voice jolted Sam rudely out of her silent self-debate. "Are you all right?"

Hastily composing herself, Sam turned with a smile she hoped appeared genuine. "Of course I am," she assured the older woman. It wouldn't do to let the other woman know just how ragged her nerves were or *worse—* why. "Have you seen all those red stickers? I don't think there's one item left for sale."

"I have and I also know that the caterers are excellent

and can handle everything in here," Coco said. "Now come, everyone's asking for you."

"In a minute," Sam promised a bit vaguely. "It's been so insane the past week. I just need a quiet moment."

Aunt Coco frowned and after a couple of beats, reached out to cup Sam's face between her elegant hands. "You look unhappy," she murmured, studying Sam with gentle intensity that had Sam wishing she were better at hiding her feelings. "You've been quiet and withdrawn the last few days. Are you regretting moving here and taking over the foundation?"

"Oh, no," Sam hastened to assure the older woman. "Not at all." That was the one thing she didn't regret. "I'm enjoying the challenge. It's much more rewarding than babysitting artwork and I like feeling that I'm helping make a difference."

"You are, but I can't help but think that I've made a mess of things by encouraging you to break away from Lilian."

"You haven't," she insisted firmly, giving Coco a quick hug. Leaving Boston was the best thing she could have done. "And I'm not unhappy. It's just a headache, that's all." Yeah, he was a *big* headache. Then because she needed to stop thinking about him, she said, "In fact, I'm really glad we've had a chance to reconnect. I missed you and grandpa."

"And we missed you, darling," Coco murmured, her green eyes misting with tears. "You are *so* like him, you know. Sweet and caring and so full of life and vitality. With your gentle nature, we were worried Lilian would crush you."

"She nearly succeeded," Sam muttered, ashamed to recall all the times she'd buckled to her grandmother's dictates, giving in rather than fighting for her own identity.

"I couldn't be happier that you accepted the job. For me, for the foundation and for—Adam."

Sam stilled a moment, then returned her attention to arranging canapés, hoping that Aunt Coco bought the casual move, knowing she wasn't fooling anyone. "Adam?"

There was a short pause before Coco's softly chiding voice said, "I know you and I know Adam, sweetheart. Something happened in Juniper Falls that's making you unhappy."

"Nothing happened," she lied, desperate for it to be true. "And I'm just tired. *Really.* The past two weeks have been hectic with all the details for tonight." She sent Aunt Coco a preoccupied smile she hoped the other woman bought. "I wanted this evening to be a success."

"Well, it certainly is that," Coco said with a chuckle. "In fact, we're all in agreement that this should become an annual event. With a little more time, I'm positive you could badger even more artists into contributing. You're doing a wonderful job, just as I predicted. I couldn't be prouder of you."

She reached out and hugged Sam. "Oh," she said archly as she released her. "And just in case you were wondering, Tiffany Travers came with Paul Gilberts and abandoned him the instant she saw Adam arrive alone. She's been after him since before her divorce." She paused as though to let her words sink in before continuing. "Are you going to let her get her hooks in your man?"

Sam's startled gaze jumped to Coco's. "He's n-not *mine*," she protested quickly, ignoring the sudden pressure in her chest that felt very much like panic, especially when Coco's eyebrow arched. "Really, Aunt Coco, *noth-*

ing happened." Well, nothing other than a few hot nights of sex—and maybe a looming heartbreak for her.

Coco cocked her head and studied Sam in a way that made her nervous. Casually turning away from that shrewd glance, she reached for the container of canapés.

"Does this have something to do with your plan?" Coco demanded, clearly not done.

"What plan?" she asked absently.

"That ridiculous life plan you concocted," Coco said briskly. "The one that stops you from throwing caution to the wind and grabbing life with both hands."

"That's not why—"

"Adam is not Lawrence," Coco interrupted smartly, clearly not done having her say. "He would never have a relationship based on lies and deceit. He values family more than anyone I know. He's fiercely loyal and feels deeply even if he'd like to deny it." She sighed, cupping Sam's face. "Oh, darling, that plan isn't you. What happened to emotion and joy? Whatever happened to spontaneity and taking a risk on life and love?"

Sam's eyes widened at the woman's vehemence. "Love?" she gasped, appalled. "Aunt Coco—"

"Dammit, I could shake you," the other woman snapped. "Your grandfather would be ashamed of you for being such a coward."

Coming on the heels of her own self-flagellation, the accusation stung and Sam took a step back only to ram her hip into the counter behind her. She sucked in a sharp painful breath and curled her fingers around the edge to steady herself. "C-coward?"

Oh, damn. Did Coco know she still had panic attacks and avoided anything that would cause them? Did she see the pain and panic threatening to break her apart inside at the thought of Adam moving on to someone like Tiffany Travers—or one of the other gorgeous, sophisticated women surrounding him?

"Yes," Coco affirmed firmly, and for an instant, Sam wondered if she'd spoken out loud. "For hiding and ignoring what's in front of your nose." And with that parting shot, she spun away and left Sam gaping at her retreating back, too shocked to admit that she hadn't thought of her plan in weeks.

"You okay, Ms. Jefferies?" the head server enquired. She nodded quickly, embarrassed that anyone had heard her being called a coward. "I'm fine," she said firmly, returning to the job she was making a complete hash of when he looked unconvinced. "Rough day."

Hell, rough year. But she would be fine, she vowed fiercely. Soon. Maybe. All she had to remember was that she wasn't the kind of woman to inspire grand passion or loyalty in men and she'd be fine. Lawrence, whom she'd known most of her life, had been promised the position of CEO of Gilford Pharmaceuticals once Lilian retired if he married her and had been quite happy to live a lie to gain access to the Gilford billions. She felt like a complete idiot for not seeing that sooner. *Or* that he was gay.

Adam? Well, who knew what motivated him? Because she had no idea. Maybe the gossip was right. Maybe he had a thing for socialites—a very *temporary* thing that allowed him to exorcise his demons without engaging his heart.

Scowling at the platter, she forcibly moved a couple of canapés. Not that *she* was a socialite. Far from it. She'd always had a job, wasn't exactly known for being fashionable and was rarely seen at the "right" parties with the "right" people.

As much as she hated to admit it, she was more Samantha than Amanda. Amanda was fun and spontaneous, full of courage and vitality. Amanda was sexy and exciting while Samantha was...*meh*. She was bland, uninteresting and—*bleh*.

Was it any wonder, she asked herself when she returned to the party and immediately caught sight of Adam, head bent intimately toward Tiffany and laughing as they shared a joke, that he would prefer being in the company of gorgeous, exciting women?

Ignoring the knife-sharp pain spearing through her body, she spun away only to lurch into someone right behind her. She stumbled back a step, an automatic apology on her lips.

"Oh," she gasped when she saw exactly who it was. Her heart sank. The last time she'd seen Blake Lowry had been their dinner date where he'd hinted that a donation came with a price. A price she wasn't prepared to pay.

"Mr. Lowry. I—I'm sorry, I didn't see you."

"Samantha," Blake Lowry drawled smoothly. He lifted his wine glass and took a sip of excellent Zinfandel, his eyes glittering as they swept over her in a way that made her uncomfortable. "I thought you'd agreed to call me Blake?"

"Yes, of course," she said graciously, pasting on her social smile as she edged away under the guise of facing him. Blake Lowry, it seemed, thought every woman was flattered by his attention, one of those obnoxious men who thought their money and social status gave them permission to take what—and whom—they wanted, regardless. "Have you tried the lobster rolls or the salmon and watercress wraps? The caterer's recipe is—"

"As excellent as they are," he drawled, lifting his hand

to brush intimately at a tendril of hair that had escaped her updo. "I'm not interested in swapping recipes, Samantha."

"What about the artwork?" she asked, dislodging his hand by turning to the large painting of the New Mexico landscape beside them. "I noticed earlier that you were interested in the sculpture. Have you met the artist?"

His eyes dropped to her breasts and she had to force herself not to recoil, reminded that she was more than adequately covered—in the front, at least. "I'm much more interested in why you've been avoiding me."

"Not at all," she said sweetly. "As hostess, I've been busy and—"

"Too busy to spend time with a potential donor?" he interrupted softly, catching her hand and tucking it into the crook of his arm. Sam's instinct was to snatch her hand away but she resisted the urge, especially when he tightened his grip on her fingers. What she couldn't stop, however, was the irritation that stiffened her spine.

"Of course not," she said graciously, all but gritting her teeth. "I—"

"I'm delighted to hear it," he interrupted again, much to Sam's growing annoyance. He'd done that during their dinner too, reminding her that he was the kind of man who wasn't interested in anything a woman had to say, only that she made him look good. "Why don't you tell me more about your little foundation while we admire the artwork?"

Adam looked down at Tiffany Travers, who was practically bonded to his side, and wondered how he was going to pry her off without causing a scene. For years, petite blondes had kind of been his type—a shrink would have

a field day with that, considering his mother was one—
but now all he could hear was the sound of husky laughter
drifting over the noise of the crowd. Husky laughter that
had the power to make him smile even when he didn't
feel like smiling.

Especially as she was purposely avoiding him; which
made as little sense as the emotion he'd caught in her
expressive eyes before her public mask had slipped into
place. As a foundation board member, he was forced to
play the social game when all he wanted was to hunt her
down and demand to know what game *she* was playing.

Watching her out of the corner of his eye while pretending interest in the conversation around him, Adam
decided that dealing with Samantha was like tracking
the elusive spotted lynx. As frustrating as it was, those
rare glimpses he had only made him more determined
to catch her.

Her back was to him and the sight of her long slender,
naked spine had his blood pressure hiking to dangerous
heights. And not in a good way. Especially with pretty
boy's hand straying to the dip in her waist just above the
shallow dimples at the base of her spine. He wanted to
march over there and physically remove the offending
touch but since she didn't seem to mind, he couldn't very
well toss her over his shoulder and drag her into his cave
like a Neanderthal.

He wanted to publicly claim her as his but he was all
too aware that she'd chosen the golden god with his casually tousled blond hair, careful bronzed tan and elegantly
expensive suit. Teamed with the effortless confidence the
social elite seemed to be born with, it identified him as
someone who'd grown up in the same world as Samantha. Together, they drew the eye, standing out among

the other couples filling the gallery. Smooth, polished with the kind of class that shouted money—and lots of it.

It was something Adam would never have and could never offer Samantha. Not the billions her family was reputed to be worth. He was who he was and he'd long since come to terms with it. Living in San José, rubbing shoulders with the upper classes and dating socialites would never make him one of them and he was fooling himself if he thought he had anything to offer Samantha other than the brutal hours of a busy surgeon.

None of that seemed to matter, however, because the sight of another man touching places where Adam's lips had been was eliciting some pretty fierce emotions that smacked of jealousy. Since he'd never been jealous over a woman before, the roiling emotions were as unwelcome as they were unexpected.

Which is probably why he stayed where he was surrounded by women he had little interest in while visually tracking Sam's movements and tracing the delicate line of her spine, the pale creamy skin between the wide V of silver-shot black. Most of the women present were dressed far more provocatively than Samantha, but none of them looked as sexy or classy.

With determined effort, he tried to ignore the swirl of anger and confusion, and focus on Tiffany's high titters and breathless account of her week in Cabo San Lucas. Frankly, he couldn't have cared less about her topless bathing or the new micro bikini she was offering to model for him.

All he could think about was watching the guy dip his head to whisper something in Sam's ear. All he could wonder was if she was shivering the way she did when Adam kissed the soft skin beneath that same ear. And all he could imagine was punching the guy in his perfect nose.

Damn the stuffed shirt for looking like he was anticipating molding Samantha into something as erotic as the sculpture they were studying, he thought with a burst of fury as the guy suddenly tugged her toward the dark hallway that probably led to the owner's offices. Empty and quiet this time of night.

Abruptly excusing himself, Adam ignored Tiffany's shocked protest and wended his way between the wine-guzzling crowd discussing everything from the San José Sharks' recent win to the price of tech stocks.

With his gaze locked where he'd last seen Samantha, Adam didn't stop until he stepped into the passage, just in time to hear a husky voice say, "Mr. Lowry—Blake, stop. As flattered as I am by your offer, I really need to get back and...*oh!*"

Adam heard a faint scuffle, an outraged squeak and took a couple of long strides down the darkened passage, arriving in time to see Samantha pinned against the wall, trying to avoid the man's hands and mouth.

By the time he reached them, Samantha's dress had been ripped off one smooth shoulder and the guy's hand was up her skirt.

"Blake, *stop.*"

Her shocked squeak had fury exploding through Adam's skull, and before he knew he'd moved, he'd grabbed the other man and flung him against the opposite wall. After one quick glance at Samantha's shocked face, he turned to face Lowry, taking care to block her body with his.

"I distinctly heard the lady say stop," he drawled, tamping down the fury that darkened the edges of his vision. If there was one thing he hated, it was men forcing themselves on unwilling women.

"Who the *hell* are you?" the man demanded, looking furious at the interruption. With a jerk, he adjusted the jacket Adam had practically ripped off him and smoothed his hair back into its preppy neatness.

"A witness if Miss Jefferies decides to press charges," he said, ignoring Sam's soft moan of humiliation.

"Charges?" the guy drawled, one eyebrow arching arrogantly as he flicked imaginary lint off his jacket sleeve. "For what exactly?"

"Assault," Adam snapped coldly, his eyes narrowing dangerously as the other man began to laugh, gaze scathing as it swept over Adam.

"You seriously think anyone's going to believe the word of a redskin over *me*?" His insulting emphasis reminded Adam of all the times he'd been called redskin and half-breed. "Do you know who I am, *Tonto*?"

Adam's muscles hardened, and as though she knew he was imagining lashing out at the man's smug face, Sam grabbed hold of his jacket. "Please, Adam," she murmured, tightening her grip. "Let it go." And when he and the other man continued their stare-down, she rasped in a low intense voice, "*Please.*"

After a tense silence, Blake gave a bark of mocking laughter, his gaze flicking over Sam with insulting lewdness. "You're welcome to her, Cochise," he drawled insolently, pushing away from the wall where he'd been lounging. "Mousy ice queens aren't my thing anyway, but it was fun seeing if I could get her to melt."

With a contemptuous smirk that said, *My proposition still stands, babe. Let me know if you're willing to trade a nice chunk of change for your little charity*, Blake

Lowry turned and sauntered off, leaving a tense silence in his wake.

Furious that she would put up with being mauled and insulted by a smug, arrogant jerk because of his money and social standing, Adam spun around abruptly, forcing her to release her grip on him. Startled by his abrupt move, she backed away, looking wide-eyed and wary. Not that he could blame her since aggression pumped hot and fierce through his veins.

Unable to help himself, he raked his gaze across her disheveled appearance, taking in the way her dress sagged on one side, exposing a pale shoulder and the tempting swell of her breast. Her elegantly upswept hair looked a little mussed and Adam hated that the other man had seen her like this—soft and tousled and anything but ice-queenly.

Fury rolled through him again.

After a long pause, he lifted a hand to slide the dress back over her shoulder with fingers that shook.

A visible tremor moved through her as her head jerked up, her eyes wide and liquid as their gazes locked. Suppressed emotion darkened her eyes and one lone drop of liquid clung to her lashes. The sight of it tilted the earth on its axis and something clenched hard in his chest.

Feeling abruptly off balance, he fisted shaking hands and shoved them into his trouser pockets to prevent himself from reaching for her. "You okay?" he rasped, telling himself fiercely that nothing had changed. When suddenly *everything* had.

Seeing her in her social element among other beautiful people had brought home to him how little he had to offer her. He refused to be like his father and he'd been kidding himself thinking there could be a future for them.

He didn't fit into her world any more than she fitted into his and he'd be damned if he'd beg.

Her throat worked spasmodically before her voice emerged low and husky as she said, "I'm fine…thank you," in a tone so polite his jaw clenched.

And because he felt as though his life were spinning out of control, he gave a brief nod and walked away before the crushing need to yank her into his arms and beg her to love him overwhelmed his common sense.

CHAPTER TWELVE

As ADAM WALKED AWAY—the expression in his suddenly remote eyes telling her this was the last time—Samantha blinked back the burn of tears and pressed a hand to the cramping in her belly.

Her breath escaped in a long shudder as she sank back against the wall, grateful for the support, the moment of solitude. The relief, however, was short-lived as nausea abruptly rose, sending her rushing into the bathroom.

Fortunately, she was alone when she burst into the ladies' room, heading for the nearest stall where she promptly lost the contents of her stomach. Not that there was much to lose, she thought with a grimace. Confrontation had always made her feel sick but Blake's attack—and Adam's awful remoteness—left her shaking so hard she could barely stand. How did other women handle such situations? And why had Adam reacted as he had?

Staggering from the stall, she caught sight of her reflection in the vanity mirror and froze. Her eyes were huge, stark in her pasty white face and a sheen of perspiration dotted her brow. She looked like she would fly apart at the seams at the slightest encouragement.

It was at that moment she saw herself clearly for the first time. And what she saw had anger abruptly flashing through her, snapping her spine straight and flooding her cheeks with color.

Blake was right, dammit, she thought with a rush of self-loathing. He was a bigoted ass, true, but he was right. About her, at least. She *was* a mouse and it was time she became a lioness—like the rest of the women in her family.

She was a Jefferies and a Gilford. Her mother—who'd defied Lilian Gilford to study medicine and marry a doctor with no pedigree—would be ashamed of the woman she'd become. Heck, *she* was ashamed of the woman she'd become. No wonder her grandmother had found it so easy to manipulate her into a relationship with Lawrence.

She was a wimp and it was time she grew into her own woman.

Hands shaking, she stomped over to the basin and glared at the woman reflected there. "I'm done," she told her reflection fiercely. Done being a mouse and she was done being *meh*.

Ripping off a section of paper towel, she dampened it and began to pat her face. For heaven's sake, she looked like she'd been dragged through a hedge backward. If she was going out there, she was going to do it armored, she told herself firmly.

She'd repair her flawless makeup and pretend she had her life together. She'd march out there and demand to know what Adam had meant when he'd sent her flowers after saying they needed to talk. He'd left in the middle of the night; he'd kissed her as though he'd wanted to slide back against her body—and then nothing.

Not a phone call or even a text message. And dammit, she deserved to know why he constantly blew hot, then cold. The stress was killing her, tying her stomach into knots. If he told her they were finished, she'd face the heartbreak with cool dignity.

Or pretend anyway, because the Gilford and Jefferies women were tigresses.

With anger and a new determination fueling her, Sam repaired her appearance and left the bathroom only to discover that Adam had already left.

Dammit, she thought, stewing, you'd think he'd at least have the courtesy of cooperating when she finally had her "moment of truth." What the heck was she to do with all this roiling determination and energizing anger if she had no one to direct it at?

Fortunately, Blake Lowry had also left because with Adam gone, Sam had been tempted to hunt down the smug bastard and punch him in the face for the racist insults he'd aimed at Adam. And another one for attacking her.

Aunt Coco offered to help with the cleanup but Sam sent her home. Coco may not look it but she was nearly seventy. Besides, left to thank their guests and handle cleanup meant she had no time to focus on her problems or the crushing disappointment and looming heartbreak.

It was only on her way home that she suddenly recalled Adam's expression as he'd turned away and stomped off. There'd been something fierce and hot in his eyes and she wanted to know what it was. Even if it meant that expression had been anger directed at her, she wanted him to look her in the eye and tell her she was a mess he wanted no part of.

She tried calling him once she got home but his phone was off, and despite waiting all night for him to return her call, her phone remained stubbornly silent. At dawn, she dressed and headed to the hospital, determined to catch him before he went into surgery only to discover that he'd taken a leave of absence and left town.

Stunned, Sam shut herself in her office and pretended to work all the while wondering what the hell had happened. Aunt Coco left a message that she'd be in hospital board meetings the entire day and Sam couldn't pretend she wasn't relieved. She wasn't up to dealing with questions or the other woman's shrewdly perceptive gaze.

She was wired and looked awful—as if she hadn't slept in days and was subsisting on caffeine. It was hard enough convincing herself she was fine without having to actually face Coco.

It was only when she got home that night and switched on the news that she realized where Adam had gone. The Sierras was burning and Juniper County was directly in destruction's path. She might be mad at Adam but he wasn't the kind of man to lie on a beach somewhere while his hometown was in danger.

For several long minutes, the images flashing across the screen held Sam spellbound with horror. Towering flames, fed by the hot air rushing up from the south east, greedily swept across the mountains, consuming everything in their path.

She'd seen television footage of wildfires before, but never when she'd been personally invested in the victims. She knew them and it was horrifying.

Cell-phone footage showed people risking their lives to save their animals; long lines of firefighters clearing fire control lines; specialized vehicles digging dozer lines in the vain hopes of containing the blaze; and people watching helplessly as their properties went up in flames.

The reporter said trained personnel were stretched

thin and the local Incident Command Center was calling for volunteers even as smoke jumpers from all over the world began converging on the Sierras. It was a desperate attempt to save people's homes, their livelihoods caught in the wildfire's path.

Even before she'd realized she'd made a decision, Sam was reaching for her phone. Adam had flown into danger to help the people of Juniper Falls. The hospital and Leah were in peril, as were Gladys and Ida—along with all their friends and family. They needed help.

Maybe she couldn't fight the fire or help the injured, but she was an ace at organization and she had a ton of contacts. Juniper Falls needed help and she was going to get it for them.

Adam drove through the darkness, his eyes gritty with fatigue. He'd gone nearly three days without sleep and it was beginning to tell—slowing down his reflexes. *Dammit*, he thought, wrenching at the wheel as he struggled to keep his vehicle on the road, he'd better pay attention before the wind blew him off the pass.

Coming around that last bend, he'd barely missed a family of black bears walking in the middle of the road. To the east, a smoky red glow illuminated the night sky and every few miles he had to slam on the brakes to avoid the animals fleeing the approaching inferno. He'd already seen so many charred remains that he'd probably have nightmares for years.

He'd been closer to those flames than he'd liked and would never forget the sound of them chewing up his cousin's ranch. That jet engine roar would stay with him for the rest of his life—as would the heat and the smell of burnt, devastated landscape.

His cousin was lucky to be alive and had his ranch hands to thank for yanking him to safety. In the chaos of trying to save his horses, Ben had fallen into a gulley, broken his leg and given himself concussion, a dislocated shoulder and minor burns down one side of his body. With Ben in the hospital, it had been up to Adam and the two ranch hands to save what was left of the place and retrieve the scattered horses.

The house, mostly built of stone, had barely escaped the inferno but the stables, barn and bunkhouse were burnt out shells of still smoking ash. They'd have to rebuild but having the house mostly spared was a small price to pay for maintaining substantial firebreaks and having other measures implemented. Others hadn't been so lucky and Adam had spent the past few days helping the neighbors and providing emergency medical care to those in need.

But the fire was gaining speed and it was heading straight for Juniper Falls. With tourism its main source of income, the townspeople couldn't afford to lose their revenue. Many would probably refuse to be evacuated and the medical center would be overwhelmed. Even without the added danger of being in the path of the fire, they didn't have the facilities, staff or equipment to handle disasters of such magnitude. The only thing he could do now was get them the help they needed.

As though thinking about the medical center was the excuse his exhausted mind was looking for, an image of Samantha popped into his head as vividly as if she were sitting next to him, rumpled and tousled, her beautiful eyes swimming with hurt.

He'd tried not to think about her the past few days, but

thoughts of her ambushed him when he least expected it. And each time, it twisted his gut tighter and tighter.

That last night he'd spent with her, he'd had every intention of talking about where their relationship was going—where *he* wanted it to go. Instead, she'd opened her door, looking all sleepy and warm, and he'd completely lost his head. He'd briefly thought they'd wake up together and talk over breakfast but that hadn't happened either.

In the days that followed there'd been one emergency after another and he hadn't been able to get away. What he'd wanted to say couldn't be said over the phone, so he'd waited for the gallery evening with every intention of whisking her away afterward and having their discussion—before they ended up in bed.

It had been all planned out in his head and then— dammit, he still had no idea what had happened. He'd taken one look at her and felt as though he'd been kicked in the chest.

He'd seen her in any number of settings and the pull had been strong but seeing her among San José's rich, social elite had forced him to acknowledge that she was completely out of his league and he was reaching for a beautiful unattainable star.

Elegant and sexy, she'd looked very much in her element, eclipsing many of the other women there. Her animation—and that damned laugh of hers—had drawn not just his but every man's attention in the room. Then she'd turned, their eyes meeting across the room and he'd felt that cool blue gaze like a blow to his soul. The force of it had made him turn away, reeling from the realization that she'd burrowed so far beneath his skin he would never recover once she was gone. Because let's face it, she belonged more in that world than slumming it with the folks of Juniper Falls and a man driven to help others because he felt empty inside.

The shock had been discovering that she filled him—filled all those empty dark and lonely places. When next he'd seen her, she'd been with Lowry, looking like she belonged with the wealthy businessman.

And he'd been gutted.

It had been sheer self-preservation that had kept him from wading through the crowd and snatching her up. Seeing the man's hands on her had had something dark and ugly swamping him. Walking away had been the hardest thing he'd ever done but he'd had to before he said or did something he could never take back. He'd stalked off, fighting a wild need to go back and wipe that look of hurt accusation from her eyes; but knowing she had the power to shred his soul had spurred him to escape.

The call from Ben's ranch hands had been the excuse he'd needed. Racing to his cousin's side had given him the perfect out and seeing the chaos and devastation had pretty much wiped everything else from his mind.

With cell towers down it had only been when he'd reached the outskirts of Fresno on that first medevac that he'd seen the missed calls from Samantha. He'd been about to call her back, his thumb hovering over her number when he'd abruptly shoved the phone back into his pocket.

What the hell was there to say? That he'd followed his father's footsteps by falling for a woman whose world would never accept him? Hell, he thought with a snort, he lived with that kind of prejudice every day, pretending it didn't affect him. Knowing that Samantha could very well be like his mother did affect him and seeing her with Blake Lowry had forced him to acknowledge that he would never fit into her world or her life.

Women like Samantha didn't fall in love and marry someone from the wrong side of the bedsheets or leave their world for his. It wasn't done. His mother—and every debutante he'd ever dated—had made that more than clear. They had wild, exciting flings with bad boys but married their social equals. Equals like his mother's senator husband—and Blake Lowry.

It was time to forget Samantha Jefferies. Forget about how she made him feel. About how something warm and clean grew in his chest when she laughed; how her breath hitched when he kissed the side of her neck—the expression in her eyes after a panic attack. As if she were ashamed of showing her weaknesses.

He rubbed absently at the ache over his heart at the thought of not being around to talk her through an attack. She would face it alone because she hated anyone seeing her vulnerabilities—didn't want to admit that she had any. Men like Blake Lowry would never understand her and never care enough to try.

Dammit, he thought when the ache grew into an actual physical pain. When had she burrowed so far under his skin that the thought of her unhappiness made him want—*need*—to wrap her in his arms, protect her from the world? Slay her dragons?

But she didn't want him to slay her dragons, and after the incident at the art gallery, it was very clear that she didn't want anything from him at all. Hell, she hadn't even been able to look at him.

It wouldn't be easy, he thought as the sign for Juniper Falls was briefly caught in his headlights. Hopefully, by the time he returned to San José, his damn heart accepted that it could never have what it craved.

He rounded the next bend and was forced to slam on the brakes as he came up behind two truckloads of firefighters. Cursing softly, he reminded himself to pay attention or he'd be needing the medical care he was supposed to be giving.

He followed the trucks through town until he was forced to pull to the side of the road as they turned into the hospital parking. Even as he killed the engine, a loud *whop-whop-whop* filled the night air. He looked up as a helo flew overhead, gaining altitude as it banked over the valley and rose up the steep sides of the mountain to disappear over Chapman's Ridge, its searchlights picking up the growing smoke-cloud being pushed north by the wind.

Frowning, he killed the engine and slid from the Jeep. Was the fire closer than he'd thought or had something happened at the hospital, he wondered, as he took off through the trees. Was that the reason for the truckloads of firefighters?

The instant he broke through the trees, he saw that the hospital parking lot had been turned into a fire-and-rescue Incident Command Center, which explained the firefighters. A mobile operations vehicle was parked off to one side of a large marquee and with the area lit up like a carnival, he could make out a volunteer wildfire-services vehicle along with forestry-and-park-services trucks that had begun to disgorge their cargo.

Several firefighters were helped through the doors of the hospital's small emergency room while others headed toward the long military tent used for rescue operations. A sheriff's department vehicle—blue lights flashing and doors open as though it had just arrived—was parked off to one side. In the open doorway, a uniformed deputy stood talking into a handheld radio, the bursts of static reaching Adam across the distance.

Intending to get information, Adam started toward him just as a figure emerged from the tent and headed straight for the cop. Adam only saw the person from behind but something about the way they walked seemed familiar. So familiar his gut clenched when the cop's eyes took a leisurely journey over the woman, a smile of appreciation lighting his half-illuminated features.

Blinking his gritty eyes, Adam ground his back teeth together, wondering if his mind was playing tricks on him because for one moment there, the woman had reminded him of—

Then she turned her head, the external light spilling across one side of her face. Adam froze in his tracks, his breath backing up as husky laughter drifted lightly in the night air.

What the hell? Samantha?

Even as he watched, the cop accepted something from her, threw back his head and with a laugh, toasted her with what looked like a disposable cup before lifting it to his smiling mouth.

An indefinable host of emotions stormed though Adam, tightening his chest. Disbelief, shock, anger and a whole bunch of others he couldn't seem to get a handle on. The overriding one was the impulse to storm over there and snatch her away from the other man.

What the hell was wrong with him?

And what the hell was she doing here? It was as if thinking about her had conjured her out of thin air. But this Samantha was unlike any he'd ever seen. Dressed in form-fitting jeans and a loose plaid shirt, rolled up to her forearms, her hair carelessly pulled into a messy topknot, she appeared casual and more relaxed than he'd ever seen her in public.

Before he could attempt to sort out his roiling emotions, or march over there and demand to know what the hell she thought she was doing, someone appeared in the hospital entrance to beckon her, interrupting her cozy little chat. The cop straightened at the interruption, an expression of impatience crossing his face, but Samantha was already moving away.

Suddenly, Adam was no longer exhausted. Furious energy surged through him. Eyes locked on her disappearing back, he followed, determined to find out exactly what she thought she was doing. He'd left her safely in San José. What the hell did she—?

A large hand slapped against his chest, bringing him up short. "S'cuse me, bud. Unless you're injured, you can't go in there."

Adam was so intent on following Samantha, he hadn't seen the deputy until he was almost on him. Instead of replying, he looked down at the hand on his chest and for just an instant was tempted to vent all the emotions that had been tearing him up inside for days.

He controlled it—barely—reminding himself that he wouldn't be able to help anyone from lockup.

"I'm a doctor," he said, voice chilly and flat when he had no right to be angry with Samantha or the cop. He'd given up that right the night of the gallery function.

The guy looked him up and down, his expression derisive. Adam knew exactly what he saw. He hadn't slept in nearly three days and it showed. His clothes were rumpled, stained and he couldn't remember the last time he'd eaten.

"Yeah," the deputy snorted, hands on his equipment belt. "And I'm Yosemite Sam, so you can just—"

"Dr. Knight?" A voice gasped behind him, drawing their attention. "Oh, my God, it is you." Adam immediately recognized the nurse hurrying up behind them.

"What is it, Hannah?"

"You couldn't have come at a better time," the nurse said with a relieved wobble. "I was looking for one of the volunteer medics but you're a godsend."

"What happened?"

"Frank Pearson was just brought in with chest pains and breathing difficulties." She hurried ahead to push open the swing doors. "They've been clearing lines up near Widow's Bend and we're worried it's a coronary."

Instantly forgetting about the deputy, Adam followed the nurse, concern for Frank momentarily replacing his driving need to find Samantha. He blinked gritty eyes as the bright lights and sounds of an active ER assaulted him. It was the busiest he'd ever seen it. Summers could get pretty busy with the tourist season but the place was filled with people. After the past three hours of dark and quiet, it was almost too much for his tired mind to take in.

"He's in the last cubicle," Hannah said when someone called her name, leaving Adam to push past firefighters in full gear to get to the cubicle. Leah was holding the oxygen mask over the clearly distressed man's nose and mouth, attempting to calm him.

Adam barely recognized Frank Pearson. The volunteer was covered in soot, his eyes red-rimmed, looking like any number of the wildfire victims Adam had treated closer to the family ranch. His eyes were squeezed shut and he was struggling to breathe, his features twisted into a grimace as he pressed a balled-up fist to his chest. Beneath the soot, and the oxygen mask, his skin was gray and sweaty.

Adam acknowledged Leah's relieved smile of greeting and casually placed his fingers on the man's left wrist to check his radial pulse. "You don't look so good, Frank," he said, his attention fixed on the man's face. His pulse was ragged and elevated but still strong.

Frank gave a hoarse laugh that morphed into a wheezing cough, his body arching helplessly as he fought for breath. He finally collapsed back against the bed and lifted a shaky hand to pull away the mask. He was sweating profusely. "You're not looking so good yourself, Doc," he wheezed with a chuckle through blueish lips. "City life not treating you so good?"

"Better than you, my friend," Adam smiled, attempting to lighten the tension as he guided the oxygen mask back in place. He turned to Leah. "See if you can find me a spare stethoscope," he said quietly. "And I'd appreciate someone hunting down a clean pair of scrubs. My clothes have been through a lot today."

She nodded and hurried off.

He gently pressed down on Frank's bottom eyelids to check for soot and burns, noting that his lashes and brows were slightly singed. "Keep breathing into that mask, Frank," he murmured calmly. "And just relax. We'll have you feeling better in no time."

"Lorena," Frank gasped, grabbing Adam's wrist. "And...the kids. They...need...me."

Adam gently but firmly replaced the mask. "Yes, they do but you have to breathe, Frank, or Lorena will have both our hides."

"Hurts like I've been kicked in the chest, Doc. Promise you won't let me die."

"You're not gonna die, Frank," one of the other firefighters burst out angrily when Leah reappeared to thrust a stethoscope at Adam. "Dammit, Doc. Tell him."

"Guys," Leah said firmly, taking charge. "He's not going to let Frank die but you need to give him room to work. Why don't you get something to eat and drink? There's plenty in the tent outside. We'll take care of Frank." She waited until they stepped out of the cubicle before asking, "Adam, what do you need?"

"How's the lab situation?" he asked, fitting the stethoscope earpieces into his ears. He was fairly certain Frank was suffering nothing more than smoke inhalation but a few blood tests would confirm his suspicions. The student doctor gave a small headshake. "Sonar?"

"Dr. Kendal's using it for a pregnant patient that was brought in a short while ago," she explained. "We've been taking in patients for a few days and those brought in a few hours ago are ahead on the list."

"X-rays?"

"We've got a queue there too, Adam, and the tech has been working overtime. Everyone is urgent so we can't push him in."

Adam removed the scope from his ears and pressed the thumb and forefinger of one hand to his eyes. "All right. Put him on the list for a sonar. I want a full chest, concentrating on the area around the heart." He handed the chart to Leah before turning to the volunteer firefighter. "Frank, the sonar is just a precautionary measure, so don't start reading too much into it." He grabbed a tongue depressor and a penlight and gestured for Frank to open his mouth. Once he was done checking the airways, he replaced the mask. "Any headaches, numbness or tingling in your extremities?"

Frank nodded jerkily. "Feels like pricks under my skin and my head's killing me."

Adam gently probed the back of Frank's neck up into the base of his skull to check for injuries he might be unaware of. "Nausea, double vision?"

"Some," Frank rasped. "Eyes a bit blurry and I've had a couple dizzy spells."

Adam reached for the pressure cuff on the wall behind the bed. "Leah will set up a drip with antibiotics and put you on a nebulizer while we wait for sonar. I don't think we have anything to worry about, Frank. Your heart sounds fine but your lungs don't. In the meantime, I'm going to treat you for smoke inhalation, so I need you to relax and concentrate on that breathing."

"Need...to get...out there, Doc," the man rasped, looking alarmed. He struggled upright, his breathing even more labored as he panicked. "Can't stay. The fire... It's bad. Lorena...the kids... Mrs. Kershaw?"

"The deputies can handle that," Adam said firmly and quietly, expertly fitting the cuff around Frank's arm. "I promise. What I can also promise is that you're in no condition to go haring off to check on them. Let the deputies do their job." He looked at a couple firefighters hovering outside the cubicle as he inflated the cuff. "And the rest of the team can handle things without you for a while. Right, guys?"

There was a chorus of consent. "They're bringing in more guys from Portland and Seattle," one grimy man said. "We'll be okay, Frank. Just listen to the doc."

At their words, Frank blinked rapidly, briefly looking away as though overcome with emotion. He waited until

Adam finished taking his blood pressure before rasping, "My…chest…hurts real bad, Doc."

"Your BP is elevated but that's a normal response to smoke inhalation," Adam assured him. "The chest pain is most likely related but we'll check to be sure. Try to give your vocal cords a break. They've been scorched." He turned to go and indicated with a slight head incline for Leah to follow. Once outside, he dropped his voice. "Give him two milligrams of midazolam and watch his breathing. If he gets too agitated, we might have to intubate him. Any luck on finding me some scrubs?"

"We sent one of the volunteers. Where should we bring it?"

Adam scrubbed his hands over his face and gave it a moment's thought. "Any shower available?" He badly needed a shower, sleep and food. Oh, yeah, and there were a few things he wanted to say to Ms. Jefferies that were burning on his tongue.

Leah immediately led him away from ER, down a passage toward the back of the hospital. "The Incident Command Center brought their own ablutions, so I'm sure no one will mind if you use the employee locker room."

"I know where that is," Adam said, reaching out to touch her arm. "You go back to Frank. He needs those meds." He was about to turn away when he thought of something. "Is it possible the volunteer can find me coffee? I'm going to need it black and strong. Really strong."

"I'll get right on it," she said, her gaze searching his face. "But Frank's right. You look tired. When last did you eat or sleep?"

He thrust a hand through his hair and gave her a grim smile. "It's been a while. Wilbur Pass is—God, there's nothing left," he muttered, referring to the area around his cousin's farm. "A lot of the folks up there have lost everything."

Her face paled. "Ben?" she asked quickly, her hand going to her mouth in distress. "Is Ben okay?"

"A couple of minor injuries," he told her, turning away. He didn't think he'd be able to talk about the devastation he'd lived through the past few days. "We managed to save the horses and most of the house but a lot of others weren't so lucky, Leah. Now would be a good time to pray for rain."

She swallowed and gave a short nod as Adam placed a hand on the door, but before he could push it open, she said quietly, "She's here."

Knowing instantly whom she was talking about, Adam tried to pretend ignorance as he gave her a confused look across his shoulder. "Who's here?"

Leah rolled her eyes and huffed out an annoyed breath. "Ms. Jefferies. But then you knew that, didn't you?"

"No, I didn't, but thank you for the heads-up." He shifted his weight and stepped into the doorway, Leah's quietly spoken words again stopping him in his tracks.

"What happened, Adam?"

After a couple of beats, he sighed and shoved impatient fingers through his hair. The previous burst of energy had drained away, leaving him exhausted. The last thing he wanted was to discuss Samantha—or his feelings—with anyone. "What do you mean?"

"She's hurting, although she tries hard to pretend nothing's wrong," she said, tilting her head to one side as she studied him with sympathetic eyes. "Sam looks as bad as you do and I can see she's heartsick and miserable. When she heard we hadn't seen or heard from you, she looked—terrified." Her eyes searched his. "I thought—"

"What?" he interrupted, suddenly furious at the shame that swamped him. Furious with Samantha for putting herself in harm's way and ashamed because her confusion and misery was his fault. "What *did* you think, Leah?" he demanded. "That a beautiful, sophisticated woman like Samantha would give up her pampered, privileged lifestyle for a half-breed, hick doctor from a small back-woods town like Juniper Falls? A man who doesn't have the time to give her what she deserves?" He exhaled in disgust, more at himself than at her. "Grow up," he snapped. "This isn't some inverted modern version of Cinderella."

For an instant, he saw hurt flash in her eyes only to be replaced by anger. "You know what?" she snapped, scowling at him. "I never thought I would say this, Adam, but you're a snob. You're the only one who sees yourself like that. And if you didn't have a chip on your shoulder, you'd notice that Samantha isn't the least bit pampered like all those spoiled, rich debutantes you like to date. She's warm and sweet and funny and the most unspoiled person I know, as well as the most generous." She paused to take a deep breath. "Not only did she donate a ton of medical supplies to the hospital and pushed the governor to establish Incident Control here in Juniper Falls, she organized water pumps and generators in case of a power failure and the tents out there for the firefighters and people who've been forced out of their homes. And no, she didn't tell me about everything she's done. I overheard the mayor and the sheriff talking. And aside from seeing that everyone out there has food, beverages and a place to rest, she's been helping out with the ward patients and comforting the children affected by the fires." She turned away from him and started down the passage, throwing,

"Which one of your vain society princesses would do all that?" over her shoulder in a furious challenge.

Muttering a string of curses, Adam scrubbed his hands over his face. He didn't need to explain himself to anyone. He and Samantha were a disaster waiting to happen. Just look at his parents. They should never have met.

"Look, Leah," he said wearily to her departing back. "I don't expect you to understand but—"

She spun around. "I understand perfectly, Adam. The fact that you don't deserve her has nothing to do with who you are or where you're from. It's because you're punishing her for coming from the same world as your mother. And just in case you haven't figured it out. Samantha is *nothing* like the woman who handed you over to a man more interested in his broken dreams and the contents of a bottle than the innocent infant in his care." She didn't wait for a reply, her stiff back and stinging words leaving him with the sick feeling that she was right.

"Don't tell her I'm here," he called out gruffly.

Leah didn't reply but he thought he heard her mutter something uncomplimentary. Something that sounded like, "You're an ass."

CHAPTER THIRTEEN

MAYBE HE WAS an ass, Adam told himself as he stripped out of his soiled clothes and stepped into the shower, but that didn't discount the fact that he didn't want Sam anywhere near Juniper Falls. Not near him—where she would remind him of everything he would never have—and definitely not near the approaching fire.

By the time he left the locker room, dressed in clean scrubs, he was feeling a little more clearheaded. At midnight, this section of the hospital was quiet, so he quickly headed to ER and stuck his head through the door. When he saw that things seemed to have calmed, he went in search of food and coffee. No sense expecting anyone to wait on him.

Since he'd seen Samantha exit the tent with coffee for the deputy, he headed in that direction himself only to come up short when he saw her, laughing and chatting away with a group of dirty, sweaty firefighters like she was hosting a high society banquet.

The sight of her never failed to affect him in the most physical way. His heart began pounding, his gut clenched and he was sweating. When he realized he'd lifted a hand to rub at the ache beside his heart, he lost his legendary cool.

"What the hell are you doing here, Samantha?" he demanded when he was within earshot, the suppressed anger in his tone surprising not just her and the men surrounding her but himself, as well.

She gasped and spun around so fast, the man closest to her made a grab for her before she lost her footing. The sight of another man's hand on her, as well as the relieved joy filling her expression an instant before she masked her emotions, was like a blow to his chest. She hadn't however masked them quickly enough to hide the stunned hurt his words and tone caused.

The sight of that hurt, knowing he'd caused it— again—just made him angrier. And because he was angry at them both, he turned to the man wearing the vest identifying him as Incident Commander.

"Commander, I want her on the next helo out of here." He kept his voice low but she heard him, and her shocked gasp snapped his eyes back to her pale face and huge dark eyes.

She took a step backward and almost immediately, a couple of firefighters and a uniformed ranger surrounded her as though to protect her from his hostility. She ignored them, wide eyes on his as though she couldn't look away from the disaster unfolding around her.

He couldn't look away either. The instant they'd locked eyes, every emotion he'd struggled to deny came storming through him until he couldn't breathe.

From him, dammit. They were trying to protect her from him, and he hated that he'd been reduced to a jealous, insecure lover.

"Stop it," she hissed, finally pushing past the protective barrier of guys. "You're causing a scene. Go away and let me do my job."

No way in hell was he going away. Not now and maybe not ever. "And what job is that?" he demanded, unable to stop himself from wrapping his fingers around her arm and pulling her toward him. On some level, he recognized the over-large shirt as his, but the instant he drew her unique fragrance into his lungs, his mind went blank.

Through the roaring in his head, he heard a voice demand, "Who are you again?"

Someone stepped forward and clapped him on the shoulder, breaking the tension. "This is Dr. Adam Knight," Grey Larson, the new forest services area chief said, subtly nudging Adam away from Samantha. He'd gone to school with Adam, left for the military and returned to join the forest services. "He's a surgeon from San José but he grew up in the area and provides regular specialist medical care for the county. He's been helping out at Wilbur Pass."

Ignoring Grey and the commander, Adam turned to Samantha and growled, "Dammit, Samantha, this is no place for you."

"Why?" she demanded. "Because I'm some vain, useless debutante?"

Recalling Leah's accusation, he shook his head. "I never said that, Samantha. I don't think that."

"Don't you?" Her voice hitched alarmingly, making his heart clench in his chest. *Damn.* He hadn't meant to make her cry. He just wanted her safe. Away from the inferno of that hungry beast heading in their direction. The thought of what those monstrous flames could do to her soft silky skin had bile rising into his throat, choking the life out of him.

When he didn't reply, she took a deep breath and

firmed her soft wide mouth. "You know what, Adam? Prejudice goes both ways."

He blinked away the horrifying images he'd seen over the past few days. "What the hell's that supposed to mean?"

Looking mad, she snapped, "I'm busy," and shoved past him. "You figure it out."

Stunned by that uncharacteristic show of aggression, Adam turned to stare after her departing figure, her back ramrod straight, her jeans-clad hips twitching and the air surrounding her practically snapping with fury.

Finally becoming aware of the silence behind him, Adam turned back to see a mix of curiosity, censure and amusement in the expressions of the men around him.

"What?" he snarled, exasperated and a little embarrassed to be caught eyeing Samantha's bottom in those skintight jeans when what he wanted was to bundle her up and put her on the first flight to safety. Okay, so maybe that wasn't *all* he wanted to do but having her safe and out of danger was suddenly an overriding drive.

"You are one dumb ass," Grey said sadly, shaking his head.

"Yeah," Adam sighed, scrubbing a hand down his face, wishing he could rub away the heavy feeling in his gut. "That's nothing new."

"So, Knight," the commander said, his eyes intent on Adam. "How're you at field trauma?"

Struggling against the urge to follow Samantha and demand to know what she'd meant, Adam tried to focus on the IC's words instead of the need to have her in his arms or kiss her until the anger and misery in her eyes turned soft and sleepy with desire. Until *his* anger and misery melted beneath the touch of her gentle hands and soft lips.

"I volunteered for the local search-and-rescue over the summer holidays while I was in med school. Why?"

"We have a situation," the commander, a middle-aged man with military bearing informed him. "One of the rangers was checking the fire lines near Coopers Canyon and fell about fifty feet into a gulley. We're fairly certain he's injured, just not how badly. We're short paramedics and no one trained in traumatic fall injuries." Even as he spoke, they could hear the sound of an approaching helo. "You okay to fly out, Doc?"

Adam wasn't okay but assisting on a rescue would be the perfect distraction. His emotions were out of control and he had no idea how to fix things with Samantha so she would leave. Glancing back over his shoulder, he caught the flash of long legs disappearing through the front entrance. He couldn't blame her because he'd been irrational when he was always the cool voice of reason.

There was nothing cool or reasonable about his feelings for Samantha and maybe it was time to settle things between them. He couldn't live like this anymore. Wanting her desperately and hurting them both because she was too good for him.

He sighed and accepted a cup of black coffee from Grey. There was always time after they'd brought in the ranger.

"Yeah," he said, taking a healthy slug of the strong, sweet brew, "I'm fine."

"Good," the commander said briskly. "I want you on that team."

The instant Samantha found herself in a quiet dimly lit hallway, she sank back against the wall and squeezed her eyes closed against the wild emotions swamping her—

anger, hurt, love and joy all mixed up inside her, making her feel a little crazy.

And then because she needed to hide the furious tears slipping through her tight lids, she slapped a hand over her eyes and bit back a sob.

Dammit, dammit, *dammit!* Why on earth was she crying? What the heck was wrong with her that the mere sight of Adam—tall, darkly handsome and very much alive—had sent such joy and relief swamping her that her knees had almost buckled. Okay, so she'd nearly flung herself at him, but one glimpse of his furious expression had frozen her, the hurt slicing deep enough to wound.

Deep enough that she might never recover. God, she thought, rubbing her palms over her face to eradicate every evidence of tears. What the hell was she doing here? The past few days had been hell not knowing where he was or if he was okay. When she'd seen him stalking toward her, looking all rumpled and tired, his mouth pressed into a tight line of fatigue, she'd felt such a rush of relief that for a moment she'd been dizzy. But he'd been furious, yelling at her and demanding that she be put on the next flight out.

As if she were an errant child caught playing hooky.

Biting her lip, she fought the hurt and confusion pressing in on her. And even as she gently banged her head against the wall in frustration, anger began to build too because having people leave wasn't something new. Her parents, her siblings, her grandfather, Lawrence and now Adam. She didn't know what was wrong with her that caused them to leave, but that didn't mean she had to continually watch them do it.

Coming to an abrupt decision, Samantha spun around, mouth firm and shoulders straight. It would be okay, she told herself. She was strong and she was fine on her own. She certainly didn't need a man to make her feel complete.

Determined to ignore her crazy seesawing emotions, she headed to the tiny children's ward. There was always a little one needing a hug and a quiet story to banish their fears and heartache.

She just wished she could banish hers as easily.

Adam double-checked the injured ranger for shock and froze when the aircraft lurched sideways and then dropped before the pilot managed to wrestle the craft upright again. The wind was getting worse and he sent a wary look out the window and wondered if the red glow in the sky was a little brighter than before.

Powerful gusts of wind buffeted the aircraft, the air supercharged with dry crackling heat that seared his eyeballs and sent his hair lifting off the back of his neck. Whether from the static in the air or a foreboding, he didn't know. But he suddenly wished he'd insisted that Samantha leave Juniper Falls, maybe even bargained with the commander—his help in exchange for flying Samantha out. But even as he thought it, he knew he could never withhold his help even to save someone he loved.

Adam abruptly stilled. There was a sudden roaring in his head as though the universe were demanding his attention. Demanding he finally acknowledge what had been there all along.

Love. He loved Samantha with everything in him. And the thought of her in the path of those greedy flames terrified him. She was his. His heart—his only. And getting back to her was suddenly more important than his pride.

More important than his life because he knew that without Samantha he had nothing.

He straightened, his eyes whipping to Grey's in the awful knowledge the instant before he felt it—felt the helo shudder. There was a terrible grinding noise as the craft was thrown sideways, tilting at an impossible angle as they plummeted into the darkness below.

Through the blood thundering in his head, he heard the pilot yelling, "Brace yourselves," and all Adam could think was that he'd been offered love—offered *everything*—and he'd walked away from it.

Sam carefully placed the sleeping toddler in the empty crib and after pulling the blanket over the little body, paused to brush the tangle of curls from the child's forehead. For just an instant, she mourned the fact that she would never have a child of her own, because the thought of having a baby with anyone but Adam seemed—abhorrent.

Maybe she should just get cats, she thought with a sad smile. Become the youngest cat lady in San José—

Abruptly, everything in her went on alert. Her head jerked up and she spun around to see Leah standing in the doorway. The med student's face was a mask of shock, her eyes huge and devastated in her pale face. Sam instinctively knew something terrible had happened to Adam.

An awful pressure built in her chest—her ears rang—and before she realized she'd moved, she was grasping Leah's arm and dragging her out of the children's ward. She stared at the younger woman, her throat tight with dread. She could barely voice the terrifying thoughts in her head.

"What happened?" she demanded, her heart seizing in her chest, her world narrowing down to this moment.

"It's Adam," Leah whispered, her throat working furiously. Her huge eyes swam with tears. "He went out with the rescue helicopter. It—" She broke off with a sob before continuing, her voice tight with fear. "It went down a half hour ago and—Sam, they have n-no idea if there are any s-survivors."

Sam's mind went blank. She heard the roar of white noise in her head, and the next minute, she realized she'd slid down the wall and Leah was shoving her head between her knees.

"Breathe, Sam," the younger woman ordered, her voice hitching with emotion. "B-breathe. Come on, in and out. Slowly. Don't give up on him. Just—*don't*." She said the words again and again, so softly it became a chant that filled Sam's head, surrounding her until she wondered if Leah said the words for Sam, herself or—or for Adam.

Oh, God. Adam.

An image of his broken body flashed into her mind, sending pain stabbing through her head. Her heart felt as though a giant fist were crushing that fragile organ and all she could think about was that she'd been a coward. She'd been so wrapped up in her own insecurities that she hadn't thought about how Adam felt. About *his* insecurities. He'd been rejected by his socialite mother and believed he wasn't good enough for Sam. But what he'd done with his life made her ashamed of herself, her fear of facing her feelings.

He'd blown hot and cold because she was always the one to pull back every time he got too close. She was afraid of the intensity of her feelings, afraid of risking her heart. Besides, what would such a strong, selfless man like Adam want with a woman who was too afraid to live, too afraid to love?

Because she *did*, she realized with blinding clarity. She loved him. With every breath in her body. With every beat of her bruised heart and she hadn't told him. Hadn't given him an inkling to how she felt because she was afraid of him walking away.

Now she might never get to tell him and the thought left her hollow. Empty.

And praying for a miracle.

Adam tucked his arm against his ribs and winced as he climbed one-handed down from the truck. He'd told their rescuers he was fine and had insisted on helping those in worse shape than himself, but he knew he had a cracked rib or two, a head wound that bled like a stuck pig and a laceration on his left bicep.

He would probably have a headache for a few days and he'd need a couple butterfly bandages.

The others hadn't been so lucky and Adam had done what he could, insisting the pilot, injured ranger and Grey be flown to Fresno. The pilot had sustained a serious head injury and Adam suspected Grey had a ruptured spleen and needed emergency surgery. The rest of the flight crew were like Adam—walking wounded—and could get medical care in Juniper Falls.

All he could think about, as he moved gingerly toward ER, was finding Sam and convincing her that she was his.

And then there she was, illuminated in the doorway. Adam froze, too afraid of what he might—or might not—see in the huge eyes locked onto his.

In the instant before he knew either of them had

moved, Adam saw more than he'd hoped for. Her eyes burned fever-bright, they almost glowed in the dim light. He saw terror at the blood and joy that he was alive. He saw relief and a love so huge he felt his throat close. Then Sam was flinging herself at him and he had to let go of his ribs to catch her.

Her body crashed against his and even as he winced against the pain radiating through his body, he was wrapping her in his arms as though he would never let her go. She buried her face in his sweaty, bloodied neck, and when he went to ease her away from him because she was everything that was sweet and fragrant, she gave an inarticulate protest and clung harder to him. For several long moments, he enjoyed the feel of her body against his.

He dipped his head to press a kiss to the top of her head and he felt her body shudder. And even before he heard the first sob, he felt the hot splash of her tears against his skin.

"Hey," he murmured, dipping his head to hers and burying his face in the wild tangle of soft hair. "I'm here," he murmured over and over, uncertain if he was reassuring her or himself that she was where he needed her.

Finally, the storm of weeping lessened and she loosened her hold. "I'm s-sorry," she hiccupped. "I d-didn't m-mean to c-cry, Adam, but you s-scared me."

"It's okay, baby," he crooned softly, rubbing his cheek in her tousled hair, grateful to be alive if only for this moment. "I scared me too. Especially when I thought I might never get to hold you again." He shifted and pressed a kiss to her forehead but she ducked her head.

"Don't l-look at me," she said quickly. "I scare everyone when I cry."

He chuckled softly and nudged her chin until he was

looking into eyes as damp as the early morning sky after a storm. "I don't scare easily, Samantha Jefferies. My ancestors were warriors."

"Oh, God," she sniffed, catching his wrist when he caught her tears with his thumb. "I must look awful."

Staring down into her familiar face, Adam felt his heart turn over in his chest. "You could never, Sam," he murmured, dipping his head to touch his lips gently to hers, tasting tears as well as home. "You're beautiful. Even when you cry."

Sam gave a watery laugh and let her lips cling to his. "You're a terrible liar, Adam Knight."

"Oh, baby," he rasped, love and relief crashing through him. "I wouldn't mind drying your tears for the next fifty years. You're beautiful. You'll always be beautiful to me."

Everything in her stilled. After a couple of beats, she lifted her head and pushed away a few inches so she could see his face.

Her eyes searched his. "What—what are you saying, Adam?"

"I'm such an idiot," he said roughly. "For trying to send you away when you belong right here. With me. I love you, Samantha Jefferies, and I'm not about to let you go."

Sam gasped, her eyes wide and a little shocked as she stared into his. The universe seemed to still. As though the very air was holding its breath. It was then that Adam realized they had a growing audience and they too seemed to be holding their breaths.

"You—you *love* me?" she gasped, looking stunned. As though she couldn't conceive that he might.

"Oh, yeah." He bent his head to crush her lips with his for a moment before sliding his mouth to her ear.

"You don't think I make an idiot of myself or declarations like this every day, do you? Especially in front of an audience."

Sam gasped and whipped her head around to see the entire ER as well as all the firefighters and rescue crews all gathered around, watching the drama unfold.

"*Omigod*," she yelped, jumping back, her hand flying up to cover her flaming cheek. "Why didn't you tell me everyone was looking?" she squeaked. Her retreat brought her bumping into Adam, her elbow catching him right where a huge bruise was forming on his side. Pain exploded through him and lights exploded inside his head. He heard a muttered oath and felt himself falling.

Sam cried out and tried to catch him but he was a big man, taking them both down. From a distance, he heard someone barking out instructions in a voice tight with worry, then he was being lifted and carried.

When he next surfaced, bright lights burned against his eyelids and for just an instant, he was confused. Then his memory returned in a rush and he groaned. He'd passed out like a little girl—right at Sam's feet.

Way to go with impressing his woman.

"Adam," an imperative feminine voice demanded, "Can you hear me? Open your eyes before I call Aunt Coco." He groaned again and turned, taking in Samantha's pale worried face through eyes narrowed against the bright light. Her eyes were filled with fear—for him.

Her fingers jerked against his and he realized she was gripping his hand fiercely. Her breath hitched as it did when she was having a panic attack, "Breathe, baby," he croaked. "Look at me and take a deep breath."

"Dammit, Adam," she rasped, her throat working convulsively. "I'm not having a panic attack, and why didn't you tell me you were injured?"

For long moments, he stared at her, wondering if he'd entered an alternate universe. "Why?" he croaked, licking his parched lips.

There was a quick wrinkling of her brow as she lifted an ice cube to his lips. "Why what?"

His forehead tightened as he stared up into her face, noticing for the first time that she didn't have that wild panicked look in her eyes and her skin wasn't sheened with the perspiration that usually accompanied an attack.

His hand gripped hers and although her fingers trembled in his, her skin was warm silk. He frowned. "Why aren't you having an attack?"

She stared at him for a couple of beats as though he were insane. "You're lying here bleeding from a head wound and possible internal injuries and all you can worry about is whether I'm having a panic attack?"

He nodded, then winced when pain lanced through his brain. "It's just a couple of cracked ribs," he explained. "Nothing serious."

She gave a watery snort and brushed the hair off his forehead. "You're crazy, you know that?" And when he continued to watch her, her face flushed the wild rose that never failed to entrance him. "All right," she burst out, looking embarrassed. "I—I did have one but only at the thought that I might never see you again." She sucked in a deep breath and looked like she was about to admit to something heinous. "I love you, Adam," she admitted in a rush, her flush deepening and her eyes looking just a little bit panicked. "A warrior needs a woman who won't fall apart at the first sign of trouble." Her breath rushed out. "So, no more panic attacks for me."

His smile started small, just tugging the corners of his mouth. "God, woman. You have no idea how much I love you," he declared, joy filling him until he laughed and pulled her down to his mouth. "I don't care about your panic attacks, only that I'm there to help you through them. You're everything I dreamed of having for myself, Samantha. You make me feel like I'm finally home. Be mine." And then he was kissing her, coaxing her lips, reveling in the softness of her mouth, adoring the way her lips clung to his and desperate for the taste of her heart spilling into his mouth.

When he finally came up for air, he kept her close, secretly pleased with her ragged breathing. "Come home with me Sam." He kissed the corner of her mouth. "Build a life with me." He brushed his lips across her eyelashes. "Make a life with me—for at least the next fifty years."

She sucked in a sharp breath and pulled away, eyes damp and luminous in her flushed face. "Oh, Adam."

"Forgive me for being a prejudiced idiot," he said fiercely, afraid that she would say she loved him but couldn't be with him. "I'm so in love with you I went a little crazy there for a while because all I could think about was that you were too good for someone like me. I panicked."

"Someone like you?" she asked gently, her face radiating love and joy as she cupped his face in her hand. "You mean a man who stole my heart despite my determination to remain heart-whole? A man who gives everything of himself to others because that's who he is? A man with more love, compassion and courage in his little finger than anyone I know?"

"Marry me, Sam," he coaxed softly, wondering for just an instant if he were dreaming. But her hand was warm and gentle on his face, her breath a brush of love. "I know I'm not much to look at and I don't have the pedigree of your Boston blue blood but I—"

Sam gently placed a finger against his lips, dipping down to replace it with her mouth. "You're everything, Adam," she murmured, her eyes shining with the force of her emotions. "And you're perfect for me."

A sound drew their attention, and they looked up to see the entire ER—and the rescue crews—had followed them into the ER to blatantly eavesdrop. A couple of nurses sniffed, looking teary-eyed and several men wore huge grins.

"Thank God for our audience," Adam chuckled, palming the hand still cupping his cheek. His eyes caught hers. "With all these witnesses, you have to say yes."

Sam gave a watery chuckle and hid her face in his neck. "Yes," she murmured against his throat. "With you, it'll always be yes."

Adam couldn't prevent the grin that split his face.

"She said yes," he told the impatient crowd, and with the roar of approval embracing them both, he took her mouth in a kiss that began their future.

A future destiny had gifted him.

* * * * *

FALLING FOR THE SECRET PRINCE
Alison Roberts

'Roberto Baresi is our father.'

Emilia actually shook her head. 'But your surname's Di Rossi, not Baresi.'

'I go by my mother's maiden name. I didn't want my background known when I came to study and work in America. I didn't want special treatment or media attention. I wanted to be like everyone else. Like you, Emmy... Being able to work hard and achieve my dream of becoming a doctor.'

Emilia's head was spinning. 'Wait...you're telling me that you're the son of a king? That would make you a...a prince?'

He was holding her gaze again and she could see the absolute honesty in his eyes. 'Yes.'

A single word but one that suddenly opened a gulf between them that was wider than an ocean. He was nothing like her. They were suddenly so far apart that they could have come from different planets. He was a prince. Part of a royal family that could be traced back for centuries and she was a girl who hadn't even known who her father was and had to be taken away from her mother's damaging lifestyle. He was a man who'd always had a privileged lifestyle and a future to look forward to, whereas she was a girl who'd been labelled wild enough to get shunted from foster home to foster home, becoming more and more lost until someone—that amazing teacher she'd had in the eleventh grade—finally believed in her enough to let her dream of a different future.

So she'd been bang on the mark in thinking she didn't know very much about Dom, hadn't she? It was, in fact, so much of an understatement that it should have laughable. But it wasn't. This wasn't remotely funny. Emilia couldn't quite identify the swirl of emotion that she could feel building inside her head—and her heart—but it wasn't pleasant. And it was powerful enough to be preventing any speech right now. Having opened her mouth and then closed it again, she had to give in and wait for the initial shock, or whatever it was that was paralysing her, to wear off.

Continue reading
FALLING FOR THE SECRET PRINCE
Alison Roberts

Available next month
www.millsandboon.co.uk

COMING SOON!

We really hope you enjoyed reading this book.
If you're looking for more romance, be sure to
head to the shops when new books are
available on

Thursday 29th October

To see which titles are coming soon, please visit
millsandboon.co.uk/nextmonth

WE'RE LOOKING FOR NEW AUTHORS FOR THE MILLS & BOON MEDICAL SERIES!

Whether you're a published author or an aspiring one, our editors would love to read your story.

You can submit the synopsis and first three chapters of your novel online, and find out more about the series, at **harlequin.submittable.com/submit**

We read all submissions and you do not need to have an agent to submit.

IF YOU'RE INTERESTED, WHY NOT HAVE A GO?

Submit your story at:
harlequin.submittable.com/submit

MILLS & BOON

LET'S TALK

Romance

For exclusive extracts, competitions
and special offers, find us online:

📘 facebook.com/millsandboon

🐦 @MillsandBoon

📷 @MillsandBoonUK

Get in touch on 01413 063232